Praise for the thrilling s

THE DI

"Another wild ride with alien ruins, government plots, conversations with the dead, and Egyptian gods. Buckle up."
—Jack McDevitt, author of *Polaris*

"Tau is a naive genius who is so unworldly readers will adore him." —*Midwest Book Review*

THE FORGE OF MARS

"Strap in, and get ready for an exciting ride. A compelling story of what could be waiting for us on Mars, of the men and women who battle to control it, and what it means to be human." —William C. Dietz

"Balfour expertly speculates on many fronts that make NASA and the Martian environment credible . . . Tau and his trip to Mars make a good story." —*The Denver Post*

"Larger-than-life characters, Egyptian gods, alien artifacts, and the old-fashioned sense of wonder. Balfour gives us a good show." —Jack McDevitt

"Even though [the book] is all high tech, Balfour manages to bring in fantastical elements that give the reader a sense of wonder . . . Balfour has a wonderful style . . . his vivid vision of Mars is so real that you can almost touch it."
—*SF Site*

"Balfour provides a nice blend of technological mystery and more conventional intrigue, all within a fairly well-realized version of Mars. His protagonist is more introspective than most, which gives us deeper insight into the character and his motivation." —*Chronicle*

PROMETHEUS
ROAD

■ ■ ■ ■ ■ ■ ■ ■ ■ ■ ■ ■

BRUCE BALFOUR

ACE BOOKS, NEW YORK

THE BERKLEY PUBLISHING GROUP
Published by the Penguin Group
Penguin Group (USA) Inc.
375 Hudson Street, New York, New York 10014, USA
Penguin Group (Canada), 10 Alcorn Avenue, Toronto, Ontario M4V 3B2, Canada
(a division of Pearson Penguin Canada Inc.)
Penguin Books Ltd., 80 Strand, London WC2R 0RL, England
Penguin Group Ireland, 25 St. Stephen's Green, Dublin 2, Ireland (a division of Penguin Books Ltd.)
Penguin Group (Australia), 250 Camberwell Road, Camberwell, Victoria 3124, Australia
(a division of Pearson Australia Group Pty. Ltd.)
Penguin Books India Pvt. Ltd., 11 Community Centre, Panchsheel Park, New Delhi—110 017, India
Penguin Group (NZ), Cnr. Airborne and Rosedale Roads, Albany, Auckland 1310, New Zealand
(a division of Pearson New Zealand Ltd.)
Penguin Books (South Africa) (Pty.) Ltd., 24 Sturdee Avenue, Rosebank, Johannesburg 2196, South
Africa

Penguin Books Ltd., Registered Offices: 80 Strand, London WC2R 0RL, England

This is a work of fiction. Names, characters, places, and incidents either are the product of the author's imagination or are used fictitiously, and any resemblance to actual persons, living or dead, business establishments, events, or locales is entirely coincidental.

PROMETHEUS ROAD

An Ace Book / published by arrangement with the author

PRINTING HISTORY
Ace mass market edition / November 2004

Copyright © 2004 by Scribbling Gargoyle Entertainment Corp.
Cover art by Craig White.
Cover design by Judith Murello.
Interior design by Kristin del Rosario.

ISBN: 0-441-01221-3

ACE
Ace Books are published by The Berkley Publishing Group,
a division of Penguin Group (USA) Inc.,
375 Hudson Street, New York, New York 10014.
ACE and the "A" design are trademarks belonging to Penguin Group (USA) Inc.

PRINTED IN THE UNITED STATES OF AMERICA

10 9 8 7 6 5 4 3 2 1

The path comes into existence only when we observe it.

—Werner Heisenberg, 1927

I am Prometheus, giver of fire to mortals.

—Aeschylus, <u>Prometheus Unbound</u>

...1

WITH the dying of the light comes the birth of darkness. The shattered dreams of the day are welcomed into the flowing embrace of the night, re-formed at the violet hour to face a new dawn. Memory is mixed with desire, reducing fear to a handful of dust.

He welcomes the darkness.

HIS body floated twenty feet above the bottom, facedown in the clear water, his arms angled out from his sides in a relaxed pose beneath a blanket of predawn darkness. The temperature of the water was almost the same as that of his body, minimizing his sense of gravity. The skintight kept his torso dry and regulated his core temperature, while the marsh grass that stuck to his back helped to disguise his human shape. The high salt content of the water made him bob on the surface like a cork, his long hair drifting around his skull like a halo of brown seaweed. His fingertips wrinkled into what his mother called "finger raisins." His eyes saw nothing, his ears heard nothing, his tongue tasted only the tang of metal from the mouthpiece that supplied his oxygen. His body drifted with the currents, heading southwest, while his mind drifted elsewhere, heading deeper into his inner sea.

During the first thirty minutes, as usual, his mind rejected the black silence, tossing images and thoughts around in his head, the flotsam and jetsam of his overactive neurons jostling for attention. His body twitched randomly as his muscles relaxed. Excessive movement could attract the wards on the shore, so he had to be careful. Odd fears pecked at his mind: What if he drifted too far out? What if he fell asleep and drowned? What if some horrible sea creature was searching for a bite to eat? His eyelids flickered, ready for a reassuring peek at his surroundings, but the contact patches kept them closed. His heart beat faster, then slowed again when he took a deep breath. The warm water melted his fears. There were no threats here. He had done this many times, sneaking away from his village to float, drifting far from the sensors onshore but fully aware that the watchers could track him from the sky—or so it was said. No matter how far he drifted, his body would not be lost. The key to this liquid journey was his absence of directed motion, relaxation, and his intent not to look like a swimming human trying to escape.

In the external world, there was no escape, but his internal world was another matter.

His five-year-old sister, Weed, had spotted him sneaking out into the light pipe with their little dog in the middle of the night. The glass-walled light pipe provided secondary access to their underground home, with a narrow metal ladder clinging to its side. A precocious little girl, Weed had sensed that silence was appropriate, possibly motivated by the fact that she was also supposed to be in bed instead of watching the bright full moon casting its silver beams into the middle rooms of the house. Helix nuzzled her hand and she scratched the short brown fur between the perky ears that looked so enormous on his small Chihuahua/terrier head. To reward Weed's silence, Tom paused to fetch her a mug of warm milk, knowing she wanted it because he had enjoyed the same thing when he was her age—up in the middle of the night watching the moon's passage overhead. Tom had thought he was getting away with something for many years until he began to suspect that his mother, Luna, tolerated this little eccentricity. After all, Luna's parents had named her after the same celestial object that fascinated her children. Perhaps she was still humoring Tom, pretending not to notice his nightly excursions. His younger brother, Zeke, was the only deep sleeper among his siblings, unaffected by the magnetic pull of the orb that ruled the night sky. Tom thought that Zeke had no imagination, but he could also see the practical benefit of being a good sleeper. Everyone had their special talents.

Of course, the moon and the sea weren't the only reasons Tom went out at night. On rare occasions, Tempest would also be out there waiting for him, his dark companion, her eyes glowing with a soft radiance whenever she saw him. Helix growled softly whenever Tom and Tempest entered each other's arms, but not because he didn't trust her—he simply didn't want to be left out. They'd known each other since they were tots, playing together whenever they could, growing together and enjoying each other's lives. Then, just over a year ago, Tempest had whispered to Tom that he was her chosen one, hoping they would someday find a way to make their relationship public, hoping the rules could be broken just this once so they could be together forever. Tom liked the idea, and the thought of her kept him warm on cold nights.

The current shifted around his body, spinning him in a lazy circle, much as the rest of his life spun around in a gentle dance going nowhere. Twenty years old, with another eighty years or so ahead of him, Tom had no idea of how he wanted to spend that time; all he knew for sure was that he didn't want to be a farmer. He honored his responsibilities on the farm where he lived—digging ditches, tending the crops, and all the other boring minutiae of a daily life nurturing the land—but he had to force himself to do it. He didn't have the natural affinity for farming that was so evident in his father and his brother. Where they saw dark, rich soil waiting to be plowed and planted, Tom saw only dirt, and lots of it. There was too much of a world outside the confines of their patch of land, and he had seen very little of its secrets. Tom saw the same discontent with farm life in Weed's young eyes as she waited in the silvery light for the moon to take her away. Perhaps one day they would both leave on a moonbeam, but where would they go?

In any case, it was pointless to think about leaving, because the gods wanted Tom Eliot to remain near the village of Marinwood, plowing his life into the ground on the family farm. And their choice was final.

"ELDER Ukiah! Good morn!"

Ukiah looked up from his digging in the irrigation ditch and nodded his mud-spattered face at the tall man in the long black coat and flat-brimmed hat. "Elder Memphis. Good morn to you." Ukiah glanced at the back of his fourteen-year-old son, knee deep in the mud, oblivious to his surroundings as he continued to dig. "Zeke?"

Zeke jumped when he heard his name. He turned and touched his hand to his forehead, dripping brown water on his face. "Sorry, Father. I was concentrating." When he saw Memphis looming over them like a specter on the embankment, his eyes widened, and he touched his forehead again. "Elder Memphis. I am not worthy."

"Youth," Memphis said, "is a blight we all grow out of eventually. Continue your work, young Ezekiel."

Zeke returned to his digging, relieved that he wouldn't

have to participate in the rest of the conversation. Ukiah studied the elder above him, whose wiry white hair looked like it was trying to escape from under the black hat. "What brings you to our home, elder?"

Memphis gave him a disapproving stare. "Your offspring, of course. Why else do I ever walk all the way out to your farm? Do you know where your son is now?"

Ukiah glanced at Zeke, but Memphis shook his head. "The other one."

Ukiah shrugged. "I'm sure Tom is around somewhere. He has his chores, and he is dutiful about them."

"Is that truth?" Memphis crossed his arms. "I think not. Young Tom is out taunting the gods once again. He was spotted on his way to the shore."

"Odd. May I ask who reported this?"

"A reliable source. My own good son, Humboldt."

Ukiah sighed. He'd warned Tom about the ocean many times, but the boy was hard to correct once he got an idea into his head. Ukiah would not question Humboldt's report in front of Memphis, but he knew the lad was overly protective about his sister. Tom and Tempest were fond of each other, and that made him Humboldt's sworn enemy. "Hard to refute, elder. I will speak with my son."

Memphis shook his head. "You need do more than speak to him, Ukiah. If you are unable to change his miscreant ways, he'll end up rooting for grubs in the desert like crazy old Magnus—or worse. Have you communed with the Oracle in recent days?"

"I can correct my own," Ukiah said, gritting his teeth. "And the Oracle has not mentioned my son. There is no need to worry yourself."

"I must worry for us all. That is my sacred duty as Elder Councilman. The deeds of your offspring must not bring down the wrath of the gods on this community. Their tolerance is limited. If necessary, I will send word to Telemachus."

"Thank you for your concern, elder. Telemachus is wise, but we need not disturb him with petty issues. I will deal with this in a harsh manner."

"See that you do. If the gods are offended, they will strike with swift certainty. Good day, elder," Memphis said, turning on his heel to stride across the field.

"Good day, elder," Ukiah mumbled. He climbed up the embankment so that he could scan the horizon, but Tom was nowhere in sight. A light fog hugged the fields. The boy was old enough to face the consequences of his own actions, but Ukiah wanted to warn him and give him another chance. He considered himself one of the open-minded elders, but he could not stand alone against extreme conservatives such as Memphis when the community might be endangered. Tom was bright enough to understand the hazards of the situation, so he would simply have to listen to reason and stop venturing into the sea. Ukiah had no idea how the lad avoided the wards on the shoreline, and he secretly admired Tom's cleverness, but the laws were clear—the ocean, the bay, and the mountain of the gods were forbidden zones.

Ukiah leaned on his shovel and filled his lungs with the clean, salty air. His eyes caressed the gently rolling hills of rich earth that belied the violence lurking below. They never had to worry about frost or snow here because the ground was too warm. Even now, the soles of his boots subtly vibrated in sympathy with the harmonics transmitted through thousands of feet of rock and soil, reminding Ukiah that he was not the complete master of his domain. A great power slept beneath his feet. The fog only enhanced the sense of waiting and suffocation that wafted up out of the ground through the occasional steam vents that dotted his fields, mere shadows of the howling cracks that had suddenly appeared over sixty years ago. It had been as if the planet would no longer tolerate the presence of humans, sending massive columns of smoke into the sky, raining down later in clouds of choking ash as his family stumbled through sudden lakes of bubbling mud between glowing rivers of red fire. Clutching his mother's leg while his older brother stood behind him, Ukiah watched the death of the great city as it slid into the sea, shoved aside by a sudden upward thrust of the vast shelf of rock known as Nova Olympus—the defiant fist of the gods. Ukiah had witnessed the dawn of a new age, born in fire to destroy the evils of men and scour the human plague from the surface of the world.

When the fires subsided, the wasteland became the mother once more, its fertile soil nourishing the crops so that the humans who remained could survive. Such was the price of prosperity under the watchful eyes of the gods who protected and governed them.

THE fog shrouding the village of Marinwood had broken by midmorning to reveal a crystal blue sky like the inside of a child's marble. The usual damp and musty smell of the narrow cobblestone streets was swept up in the weekly parade of commerce spread on broad tables and tilted carts strewn haphazardly outside the shops and humble homes. Reeking cheeses vied with ginger, peppercorns, cinnamon, and other spices for supremacy of the air. Garlic and onions fought with cooked tomatoes and cornfruit to grab the attention of potential customers strolling past. The rickety stalls of the merchants, islands of commerce breaking the tide of humanity, groaned under mounds of garish fabrics imported from the east, the glitter of shiny objects found among the ruins and polished for display, the gleam of hand-rubbed wood worked by local artisans. A tumult of voices rose and fell in waves as hucksters shouted, onlookers hooted, sellers whined, and buyers argued. Arms and hands bobbed above the mercantile sea: Fists clenched, fingers beckoned, and open palms chopped the air. Children hurtled beneath tables and dodged around adult legs as they played games of spot-the-bot or dodge-the-nanoborg. The noise and color of the bazaar splashed across the village like a spilled can of paint, bringing life to the normally dignified surroundings. By sunset, the stalls would vanish, the tables would withdraw under leafy canopies, the carts would depart for their return to the fields. The human tide would recede along the winding paths, leaving only the golden glow from the occasional window as evidence that anyone remained behind. The low earthen fronts of the subterranean houses and shops, their sloping roofs covered in the sod that made Marinwood blend in with the surrounding terrain, would face empty streets as the moon passed overhead.

Only the tiny nanoforms ventured out in the darkness, cleaning, rebuilding, and maintaining the village. The curfew wasn't formally enforced by the gods; but the last person to remain outside after sunset had been Old Newt, facedown in a gutter after swilling too much homebrew, who was disassembled and reconstituted as part of a bench in front of the library. It was often said that Newt made more of a contribution to the community as a library bench than he had as a shoemaker, and that his bench was more comfortable than the shoes that he had made. The gods were wise.

For now, awash in brilliant daylight, the streets were full of life. And part of that life was five-year-old Weed, being towed in her mother's wake as she plowed through the crowded streets. As usual, Luna had tied a short length of rope around both of their waists so that Weed wouldn't get lost among all the distractions of the marketplace. This tether seemed to have a life of its own, tugging at her whenever she stopped long enough to admire a shiny toy or a colorful bottle on one of the tables. But Weed didn't mind; she enjoyed the activity, the noise, and the feeling of adventure that accompanied their weekly outing to the village. She followed Luna without complaint as her mother darted from place to place, squeezing an *oog fruit* here, tapping a watermelon there, and ignoring the mysterious pieces of broken machinery arrayed on tables attended by dusty young men with shifty eyes. Weed remembered that Tom had told her about the scavengers who sneaked into the ruins to pick up old things and sell them at the market, but she didn't really understand what he meant by scavengers or ruins. She had an unusually good vocabulary for her age, and she liked the sound of those words, so she had filed them away in her head until she could learn their definitions. Perhaps when Tom got home. Tom was always willing to teach her things. Luna was already teaching her how to read, but she still liked it best when Tom told her stories about distant places, magical kingdoms, and beautiful young princesses named Weed who always lived happily ever after. Luna preferred to tell her stories about women doing good for their communities, working on farms, and raising families; but they just didn't hold her interest the way Tom's stories did. She felt guilty about that, especially because her mother tried so hard to make her stories interesting.

Weed noticed that all the buildings in town looked like they grew out of the ground, just like her own house, and she was wondering if anyone had ever thought of building them on the surface so the sunlight could come in through windows all the way around, when Luna abruptly turned and they started back toward the farm. The roaring noise of all the voices, and the smells of all the strange foods, began to recede. Weed's tummy grumbled. Luna would usually buy her something to eat before they left the market, but for some reason today had been different, and she hadn't received a treat. Perhaps Weed had done something wrong, and Luna would tell her about it later.

Then Weed's eyes grew large and her mouth watered as Luna handed her some roasted cornfruit on a stick. Weed loved cornfruit. And she was happy that she hadn't done anything wrong. It would have been hard to wait another week for her treat.

Life was good.

THE breathing mask over Tom's face made his nose itch. That was unusual, as the old relic from the ruins, which he had cleverly purchased at the bazaar from a man who knew nothing of its purpose, had never been uncomfortable before. Relaxed and drifting on the gentle currents, he suddenly realized that he had been floating a long time, much farther than he usually did. His back felt warm, so it had to be well after sunrise.

Then Tom sensed icy fingers reaching up through the shallow waters of the bay to stroke his skin. He was over one of the few deep channels that had not been completely filled in by The Uplift. He squinted to activate the contact patches, which pulled back from his eyes to let him see through the clear face shield, on down through shafts of twinkling sunlight into the greenish depths, and his eyes widened. A few feet beneath him, the pointed tower of a broken building reached for the sky, doomed to remain beneath the surface until gradual erosion made it an intimate part of the silt on the bay floor. Sheets of algae clung to the walls around the dark windows, fluttering like torn curtains in the gentle current. He rarely saw fish in the bay, perhaps because they feared the ghostly presences in the underwater tombs. Tom felt goose bumps on his skin: He had no idea if the stories about the ghosts were true, or if they were just tales made up by parents to keep their kids in line, but the aura of death was unmistakable.

He knew the history of his people. Although he wasn't old enough to have witnessed The Uplift event as his father had, Tom knew that almost three million people had died within a few minutes of each other, most from drowning, and that their pale corpses had drifted in the bay for days, washing up on breakwaters and drifting in estuaries, where they rotted in the sun for weeks. He knew there had been early attempts to search for survivors, but none had ever been found, and the gods quickly decreed the entire bay to be a forbidden zone. Tom suspected that the restriction now remained only out of tradition and not for any practical reason, but his punishment would be just as severe if the elders of Marinwood discovered his secret pastime.

A winged gargoyle, frozen in gray stone on the side of a building, glared at Tom with evil in its eyes as he passed a few feet over its head. Tom could imagine it perched high above a city street, willing itself to break free of its masonry prison and descend on the innocent pedestrians far below. Now that it was underwater, Tom assumed it must be thoroughly confused by the strange turn of events.

Fate. Tom's thoughts drifted back to his fateful meeting with the Oracle so many years before. His entrance into puberty had heralded the time when his life path would be chosen during a personal visit from the Oracle. As the Oracle rarely left her rocky underground vault in the foothills outside of Marinwood, the visitation was an event that unsettled his entire family, breaking the routine of the farm. They all quit work early, and there was a lot of pacing and nervous chatter that evening after dinner. Ukiah and Luna made regular treks to the Oracle twice a year, so they were accustomed to her spooky presence; but Tom's first glimpse of the figure that appeared in his bedroom doorway had nearly made him yelp in alarm, even though he was pretending to be asleep. When the door creaked open around midnight, the Oracle's white robes were bathed in a bluish glow from a shaft of moonlight in the core of the house. Her white eyes glittered with an unnatural light, looking straight at him in the darkness as if she'd been in his room many times before. Cascades of thick white hair framed a face that was always young, even though she was the same Oracle that had chosen Ukiah's life path when he was a boy. Although she spoke in a whisper, her sharp voice could clearly be heard from across a room, as if she were able to direct and focus the sound waves when they left her mouth.

"Tom Eliot," the Oracle whispered, "I know your secret."

Startled, Tom quickly ran through a mental list of all the possible secrets the Oracle might have plucked from his mind, but it was a very short list, and he had no idea why she would be interested in such trivia from the daily routine of his life. He saw his mother standing a short distance behind the Oracle, and he wondered if this might be some sort of parental trick to see if Tom would confess to valid reasons for some of his admittedly bizarre behavior. Then it occurred to Tom that the old woman might just be playing with his head to see how he would react.

"Yes," she said. "I do know what you're thinking. In fact, I know more about you than you do, little man-thing."

"He's not all that little," Luna said.

The Oracle turned her gaze on Luna for a few seconds, then Luna bowed her head and backed away from the doorway. That simple motion demonstrated the Oracle's authority, and Tom felt the seriousness of the occasion. He licked his lips, breathing faster than usual as the Oracle turned her gaze on him once more.

"Your eyes smell like the sound of rain," the Oracle said, gliding across the floor toward his bed. He couldn't see her feet, and her robes billowed behind her as she moved, giving Tom the impression that she was floating. "As the trees dream of light, you dream of futures past, tumbling in time, seeking your reflection in smoky mirrors. In this quest, you will fail."

Tom didn't know what she was talking about, but he felt

as if he were being punished for bad thoughts. "Why? What have I done?"

She stopped beside his bed, looming over him. "What will you not do? Time is a gift and a curse, little man-thing. I can only guide and foresee, while you must live your death with each passing day."

Tom wished his mother would come back into the room.

The Oracle's white eyes bored into his skull. "You have a greatness in you, Tom Eliot, but this will also be your downfall. To be something, you must be nothing first, and your parents can prepare you for this. Your life stretches out before me, a turbulent time stream, among which I can only select the currents and help you avoid the submerged rocks. But I am certain of one thing—the path you must seek is the path of nothing: being nothing, becoming nothing, remaining nothing. You must join your community as your community joins you, plowing the fields as you would plow your mind."

Tom inched his head farther back on the pillow as she reached for his face, finally touching his forehead with her cold fingers, then covering his eyes with her palm. "Your path is here among the soil: working in it, growing in it, and finally resting in it."

She had chosen his life path. Could he ask for a second choice?

"No," the Oracle said, gliding toward the exit. The prophet had spoken. Some were chosen to serve the gods, others were chosen for dangerous exploration tasks or to work in occupations that supported the village, but lives such as those were apparently not suited to Tom's skills. No, the Oracle had looked into his head, past his hopes and fears and dreams, seeking the truth of his inner being, and she had found only dirt. Tom was doomed to spend his life on his family's farm, striving to be nothing.

And so he floated, feeling the freedom of the water

supporting his body, living in the present so he could ignore the future.

THE alert from the Alcatraz ward on the Inner Barrier
flashed through the network faster than a human synapse
could respond. The information was indexed, correlated,
and analyzed, then joined with a solution matrix. After
evaluation and forecasting, a response array was generated
almost faster than the incoming alert had arrived at its destination. Triangulating with their extended eyes in orbit,
distributed processors fixed the position of the interloper,
identified it with pattern recognition algorithms, tracked
its heat trail through the water far enough to extrapolate its
origin, and relayed the data to the terminal execution nodes
for final disposition.

Inner guardian release 37°48' 28" West Latitude
122°26' 30" North Longitude.

TOM had to get back, and it would have to be by a
quicker route than usual. Helix was faithfully waiting for
him where the river emptied into the bay, so Tom would
have to circle back on land, avoiding the wards and the rov-
ing watchers, to pick up Helix and head for home. It was
market day, so most of their neighbors would be in town
and less likely to spot Tom on his return. Across the bay to
the south and the east, he saw the twisted spikes where
huge towers had reached for the sky in the great cities, reduced now to the few ruins clinging to mountainsides that
had formerly been flat terrain. He shook his head, annoyed
that he had allowed himself to drift this far; it was the sort
of mistake that could get him into big trouble.

Tom felt an odd vibration moving through his body,
similar to what he felt on land before the earth shifted

beneath his feet. A bubbling sound reached his ears, coming from somewhere behind him. He lifted his head from the water and looked back. Blinking as if he might clear the rivulets streaming down across his mask from his wet hair, he saw the fast-moving wake of some narrow object, like a huge fish, racing in his direction just below the surface. Tom lowered his face into the water to see if he could get a better view from below, and he was startled to see two large eyes with a brilliant orange glow. He stiffened when he realized that the creature was moving much faster than any fish he'd ever seen, and it didn't move like a living thing.

A guardian. The shoreline wards must have spotted him.

He'd never actually seen one before, but he'd get a close look soon enough. It would be on him in seconds. There was no way he could swim faster or deeper than the guardian, and he didn't think he could fool it by remaining motionless.

The guardian turned. A quicksilver flank glittered in the sunlight as it dove a few feet deeper and reoriented itself toward its target. Tom had never been a target before, and he didn't enjoy thinking of himself as prey. But there was no place he could hide, no place he could run. The pounding of his heart shook his body in a steady rhythm, waiting for the inevitable, until an older part of his brain took over and he turned away from the oncoming threat, swimming like a madman in his futile attempt to get away.

Then it had him. A heavy claw wrapped around his ankle and yanked him below the surface, dragging him down as he flailed and struggled to break free and swim back to the surface. The unyielding claw remained in place, tearing at the skin of his ankle, foreshadowing the pain he would soon feel when his mask tore away and his lungs filled with water after his last breath burst from his screaming mouth.

His body slammed into something hard, causing a hollow

boom in the water, and a dense cloud of bubbles billowed past him. His last thought was of his family, and how he had failed them by defying the law, and how the gods would seek retribution on them for Tom's disgrace.

...2

UKIAH stopped chopping carrots to glance at the kitchen clock, then his shoulders slumped. "Where is he?" Distracted, he nicked his thumb with the sharp blade. A spot of blood appeared on one of the carrots. "It's noon, and the lad is normally back at his chores by midmorn."

Luna stopped shredding lettuce and reached for Ukiah's hand. "Better give me that knife before you cut your fingers off, old man." She gently took the knife from him and set it on the table, then put her hand on his shoulder and looked into his dark blue eyes. "We need to encourage Tom's independence. He needs to get away to think."

Ukiah licked his wound, then put a finger over it to stop the bleeding. "Thinking is a bad habit. It leads to unhappiness. I should have hidden those old books in a better place."

"What old books?" She raised an eyebrow, wondering if there really might be forbidden books on their farm.

"Tom found my library hidden in the cellar beneath the barn. Most of it was my father's collection, but I collected more from the ruins before the zones were established. Tom's been reading those books for years. He doesn't know that I know about it, of course. I didn't think it would do any harm for him to know a few things about the old ways, and he's more motivated to learn when he can sneak around to do it."

Luna's eyes were wide. "You never told me."

Ukiah shrugged. "Better that you didn't know. If Memphis found out about it and told Hermes, they'd burn me at the stake."

"Then why are you telling me now?"

"In case something happens to me, I guess. There's fuel in the cellar, so that you can torch the whole thing if someone decides to raid the farm. Destroying the evidence might help keep the rest of the children safe."

"Don't be so dramatic. Did you try looking for Tom in the barn cellar?"

"Of course. That's part of my concern. I haven't seen him at all this morning."

Then it was Luna's turn to sigh. "Don't worry. He'll get his chores done. And he'll come running when he smells the cornfruit I've got roasting."

"I'm not worried about his chores, Luna. He's got bigger problems."

"Memphis is an old fool," Luna said, turning to pour herself some spice tea from the steaming pot on the stove.

"Fool or not, he runs the council."

The spicy aroma of the tea filled the air as it burbled into Luna's cup. "Without Hermes, Memphis would be nothing. And Hermes would be nothing without the power of Telemachus behind him."

"You don't seem to understand. Tom is at risk here. *We* are at risk."

Holding the warm teacup between her hands, Luna glanced up with a frown. "Did the Oracle tell you this?"

"No, but you know how it works. If Telemachus thinks

Tom is a renegade element, they'll come for him. They'll take him away."

"It's been years since anyone was removed. Why would they single out Tom?"

"Because he's too different. Because he doesn't follow the rules, and he rubs their noses in it. Not overtly, mind you, but just enough to imply that he's above the law. They don't like what he represents."

Luna gripped his forearm. "You need to speak to the Oracle. If there's real trouble coming, she'll know."

"She already summoned me. I'm supposed to visit her this afternoon."

"By yourself?"

Ukiah nodded.

Luna released her grip on Ukiah's arm and took a deep breath. "This could be a good thing. The Oracle might tell you that Memphis will be gone soon, and you're to replace him."

"Not much chance of that, I'm afraid. Memphis is perfectly healthy for his age, and he would never recommend me to be his successor."

"The rest of the council would vote for you," she said, sipping her tea.

Ukiah shrugged. "They might have once. But I think they're just as nervous about Tom's behavior as Memphis is. They don't wish to anger the gods."

"Ukiah, this is ridiculous. Once or twice a year, some family does something to attract the attention of Telemachus, then Hermes pays them a visit or the village power grid gets shut off for a week. Nobody gets removed anymore."

Ukiah sat down heavily on the edge of the dining table and rubbed his face in his hands. "Okay, maybe I worry too much, but the boy is in danger. Why does he have to go out of his way to draw attention after all our efforts to make him fit in? I only want what's best for him."

Luna set her cup down, then put her arms around him and rested his head on her chest. "I know what bothers you. Tom isn't so different from you when you were his age. Yet you chose to be a responsible member of the community and join the council when Medoc died. You became a leader when the people needed you."

"That was different. I never openly defied the law."

"Perhaps they need Tom to lead them, too, but in a different way. Times have changed. You look at Tom, and you see how he's like you, so you worry for him. Instead, you should look at Tom and see how he's like you, then recognize the *greatness* in him."

Ukiah shook his head. "I don't want him to be great. I want him to be happy. And I want him to be safe. We've gone to great lengths to hide his unique qualities from Telemachus."

"Safety is an illusion, my love."

Ukiah looked up into her twinkling sapphire eyes. "And happiness?"

"That's real," she said, hugging him closer.

THE dry branch of the old oak tree creaked as Tempest Gustafson shifted to a more comfortable perch. The heavy brown suede of her pants and long-sleeved shirt smelled good in the warm sun, and she allowed the warmth to seep through her olive-toned skin into her sore muscles. These were her metalworking clothes, and a bit stiff for tree climbing, but the stunted oak had offered enough support for her to reach the lower branches so she could study her prize in relative privacy. Her half brother, Humboldt, was around somewhere, but she had discovered that hiding in plain sight was often the best tactic with him if she wanted to be left alone for a little while. She pulled the ribbon out of her long brown hair and it tumbled forward to hide what she held in her hand—a crystal doorknob that sparkled in the sunlight.

When she held the crystal up close to her face, she saw the tiny prisms glowing in each facet where the light struck, creating enough depth and dimension to make her feel as if she could climb inside and live within the crystal walls. Tom had found it on one of his trips into the forbidden zones a week ago, and she had originally imagined it to be a huge diamond despite Tom's description of its mundane origin. She knew that such a pretty and carefully crafted thing must have meant more to its long-dead owner than simply a way to open a door, just as it meant more to her as a gift from Tom. For the last three days, she had been welding a large sculpture from old scraps of steel, depicting a woman on one knee offering something to the sky in her cupped hands. When the life-sized sculpture was finished, the crystal would serve as the woman's offering, placed upright in the hands of the sculpture to look even more like a giant diamond. Until the sculpture was ready, Tempest had to keep the crystal hidden because her father would not approve of such a thing, particularly if he learned it had come from Tom.

When a light breeze lifted her hair, Tempest turned her head at the sound of a small scream from the barn. She frowned, then realized when she heard it a second time that the scream was coming from stressed metal. Her sculpture was in the barn.

Shinnying down the tree, the bark nicking at her bare feet and ankles, she plopped down beside her boots at the base of the trunk, picked them up, and ran toward the barn. At the open door, she stopped in a cloud of dust and stared at the stocky figure with the upraised pry bar standing in the sunlight. Two large pieces of her sculpture lay broken on the ground.

"What are you doing!" Tempest screamed. She took a step forward, her fists clenched.

Humboldt looked up from where he was prying another chunk of metal away from the main body of the sculpture. He wore a leather vest and dirty black work pants. One of his muddy boots was wedged against the statue's knee for better leverage. "I need some scrap to fix the windmill. What about it?"

She stumbled forward, thinking how big and mean he could be when he was angry, knowing she couldn't stop him. "That—that's my sculpture!"

Humboldt glanced at the kneeling metal figure, then back at her. "This thing? It's scrap."

"It's a kneeling woman! Can't you see it? Look at it!"

Humoring her, Humboldt took a step back and squinted. "Don't see it." Then he stepped forward and rubbed his hands on the figure's head with a smirk. "Well, okay, maybe. But what's it good for?"

"It's art! I made it!"

"Looks like windmill parts to me," he said, placing the long pry bar beneath the figure's head, ready to pop the head off.

Tempest screamed and ran straight for him. Startled, he stepped back and she rammed her head into his stomach. Humboldt barely moved, and she realized she'd made a major error as she grabbed her spinning head and saw Humboldt's face turning red. She started to turn away, but he grabbed a handful of her loose hair and yanked her sideways before slapping one of her ears. She screamed and turned, trying to kick at him, but he held her out at arm's length, then turned her around so he could pick her up with his huge arms around her waist in a bear hug, lifting her off the floor while she kicked her legs in the air.

"Let me go!"

"Why? You'll just try to hit me again. I'm taking this thing apart." He kicked at her sculpture with his booted foot, knocking it over on its side.

"No! Stop it!" Her vision was getting darker as her head continued to spin. She smelled his strong odor and felt his sweat on her skin. Then she managed to jerk around enough to snap open enough of the buttons on her stiff leather shirt so she could get her right arm loose and smash her hand into the side of his head. He grunted, stumbled, and she felt them both falling backward, but he twisted and she hit the dirt face-first before the weight of his body landed on her back, pressing her into the loose soil from head to toe.

"Get off me," she yelled into the dirt. She tasted bits of carbonized steel in the soil.

His weight remained on top of her, making it difficult to breathe, and it occurred to her that he might be unconscious. She could smother in the dirt before he woke up. "Get off!"

Then, suddenly, Humboldt jumped to his feet and brushed himself off as she angrily raised her head, spitting dirt out of her mouth.

"*What* is going on here?" demanded the powerful voice of her father.

Tempest tried to speak and started coughing instead. Humboldt shook his head and shrugged. "Demons, Father. Tempest nearly took my head off with this pry bar, then she jumped down on the ground and began eating the dirt."

Memphis angrily stepped into the barn, then stumbled on the crystal doorknob lying in the dirt. Humboldt darted forward to keep him from falling, then Memphis shook his son away and picked up the crystal to examine it with suspicious eyes. "What is this bauble?"

"I shouldn't say," Humboldt said. "It belongs to Tempest."

"Tempest!" Memphis whirled on her. "Explain yourself!"

Tempest spit on the ground to clear the rest of the dirt from her mouth while she lurched to her feet. "Nothing, Father. It's—"

Memphis slapped his hand on top of her head and forced her down to her knees. "Spit at me, will you? Disrespect your father, will you?"

"No, Father, I—" She grimaced as her right knee found a sharp piece of metal. The point didn't puncture her leather pants, but it hurt anyway.

Memphis shoved the crystal into her face. "Explain

this! It's from the ruins, isn't it? From the *forbidden* zone!"

Tempest bit her lip and nodded. His breath smelled of the garlic cloves he liked to chew.

Humboldt moved closer. "I'm sure she didn't know where it was from, Father."

"Get back to work, Humboldt," Memphis snapped. He glared at his son, and Humboldt lumbered back over to the broken sculpture before looking back with a brief smile at Tempest. He picked up the pry bar.

She shook her head. "Stop him, Father! Make him leave it alone! That's my sculpture!"

"You dare to tell your father what to do?" Memphis hissed. He looked at the crystal again. "This is from Tom Eliot, isn't it?"

Her teeth chattered. "No."

"Don't lie to me, girl. It will go worse for you if you add lying to your list of sins this day."

Tempest swallowed and nodded once, her eyes wide, bracing herself for whatever might happen next.

"Humboldt!" Memphis roared. "Come here!" When Humboldt jogged back over beside Tempest, Memphis lifted her and shoved her into his arms. "Take her to the box."

Humboldt swallowed as he grabbed Tempest under the arms and lifted her. "The box?"

"You heard me," Memphis growled, breathing hard. "Take her there now, or you'll be next."

"Please, Father, no!" Tempest cried, struggling to get away from Humboldt as he dragged her away.

"You've made your choice, girl." His voice was softer as he followed them out of the barn. "I've warned you about Tom Eliot, yet you continue to defy me. Now he's giving you forbidden gifts, thumbing his nose at the gods, and defying my word. But this will stop. And your disrespect will stop. It will all stop right *now*!"

■ ■ ■

TOM awoke with a pounding headache, a bruised ankle, and the startled awareness that he was not dead. He blinked several times, trying to clear his blurred vision, then sat upright in a puddle of water on the cold concrete floor. His marsh grass camouflage was still attached to the back of his skinsuit, but it had been flattened by his sleeping on his back, giving him the appearance of a porcupine on a bad hair day. His vision cleared a little more. He was in a dim tunnel, lit only by a line of red ceiling lights spaced ten feet apart that vanished into the distance. When he coughed, his foot bumped against a metal rail that ran lengthwise down the tunnel. The air smelled damp and musty, and the only sounds were the gentle hum from the rail accompanied by a chorus of chittering rats.

The wet hairs on the back of his neck stood up as he sensed someone watching him. Turning to look over his shoulder, he saw only more red lights receding into the distance until his eyes adjusted enough to see one of the tall shadows along the wall moving toward him. With his heart pounding, he lurched to his feet to face the enemy.

"Get a grip on yourself, boy," said the hooded figure. He spoke with a voice that was deep, precise, and pedantic. "If I'd wanted to hurt you, I would have done it long before now. You were asleep for almost an hour."

"Who are you?" Tom demanded, keeping his fists ready just in case.

The figure stopped a few feet away under one of the red lights. He pushed back the hood of his rough brown cloak to reveal a weathered, bony, old face with sunken eyes, a hawk nose, and a mane of thick white hair that fell like a waterfall from his head to his shoulders. "I'm Magnus Prufrock—legend, scholar, and hermit. And since I'm the one who rescued you from drowning, I'd appreciate a more polite tone of voice."

Tom's frown softened, then a thrill of electricity rippled through his body. Surprised at his reaction, he decided that his recent trauma underwater had left him disoriented. "Magnus Prufrock? I've heard of you. Everyone says you're crazy."

He made an expansive gesture. "Do I look crazy to you?"

Tom didn't feel any need to state the obvious, so he shrugged.

"That's it. Back in the water with you."

"Okay, sorry, but where am I? I thought you lived in a cave in the wasteland."

"That's what you're supposed to think. Keeps the curious yahoos out of my hair. We're actually in the northern transbay tunnel, not far from my home. Bay Area Rapid Transit built the deep tube under the bay in 2030 to connect San Francisco with Alcatraz, Angel Island, and Sausalito. The mag-lev trains don't run anymore, but it's still a great way to get around without being seen by *nosy parkers* with silicon brains."

Tom looked up at the ceiling and shuddered. "So we're underwater?"

"About thirty feet of it, yes. And another ten feet of gravel and mud."

"Then how did I get in here?"

Magnus pointed at a hatch about ten feet away in the side of the tunnel. "Grapple on a robot construction arm. My alarms went off when the guardian entered the water. The defensive system thought my house was under attack. The grapple was meant for the guardian, but I intercepted my robot in time and snatched you instead. Hauled you in through the construction airlock and scrambled the guardian's brains with a high-voltage shock. You're lucky I was home."

Tom rubbed his sore ankle, uncertain as to whether he should thank Magnus for the rescue or curse him. Drowning would have made things so much simpler. "Yeah. Thanks." He offered his hand. "I'm Tom Eliot, by the way."

Magnus ignored Tom's outstretched hand. "I know. I've been keeping my eye on you, boy."

Tom raised his eyebrows.

"Anyone who regularly manages to sneak past the wards like you have deserves my attention. I'm surprised that Telemachus let you get away with it for this long, but now the jig is up. The siliboys know who you are, where you live, and what you had for breakfast. To put it another way, it's time for you to hit the highway and run like hell."

"I can't leave my home. My family depends on me."

"Up until today that may have been true. If you go home now, not only will the siliboys find you, but they might just decide to take the rest of your family in as well. I know all about their 'rehabilitation units,' and I can assure you that you don't want to see the inside of one. You probably wouldn't even survive it—many people don't."

"How do you know so much about these things?"

Magnus raised an eyebrow, and his gray eyes glittered in the red light. The look jarred Tom, as if he were receiving input on all the channels of his brain simultaneously, communicating amusement, strength, the memory of pain, and wisdom all at once. "I have to get back. Can't stand around chatting all day. I've got work to do."

Magnus spun on his heel and began to walk away. Tom hesitated, then trotted after him. "Wait. I don't know how to get out of here." Magnus snorted and continued walking at a brisk pace. Tom noticed that he didn't move like an old man; his gait was quick and confident, his movements fluid. Their rapid footsteps echoed in the tunnel.

Magnus glanced over his shoulder. "We've met before, you know."

"We have? When was that?" He was sure he would have remembered such a meeting. Maybe the old man was crazy after all.

"You think about it, boy. If you can remember, we'll both learn something. If you can't, *I'll* learn something, and you'll just remain in the dark where you belong." Magnus stopped suddenly and whirled around, his robes flapping when he raised his arms, looming over Tom like a giant bat. His eyes were wild and full of gray fire. Tom noticed that his right arm looked scarred and unusually smooth. "Every creature has at least one special moment in its life when it learns a secret," Magnus boomed. "A secret that will alter the course of its future. Are you prepared for that, boy? This may be your one great shining moment when all will be revealed!"

Tom closed his eyes and tried to remember. His world was relatively small, and there were few people in it. He would have remembered if he had met Magnus before. The strangers he saw in town at the weekly market were rare, and Magnus had never been among them. He certainly had never been to the Eliot farm before. No, they could never have met. "Sorry, I don't remember."

Magnus dropped his arms. "So be it." A shadow passed over the old man's face; he nodded once, then turned away in silence. He walked more slowly now, as if his long years of living had suddenly caught up with him, and there was something about his stride that seemed familiar.

Fire. A memory of fire surged up from the depths of Tom's memory. Ten years ago, maybe more, a neighbor's farm had burned in an unusual explosion, and the family that lived there had died. Tom had been very young then, and he didn't remember having much contact with those neighbors. A bright flash had lit up the sky one night while he was watching the moon, scaring Tom enough to wake his mother, then all of them had raced across the fields to where the roaring flames lit the countryside. When they arrived, fire and black smoke poured out of a crater where the underground home used to be, creating a wall of intense heat. Luna kept Tom and Zeke from going any farther down the slope, but Tom's father continued running, yelling and waving his arms. Silhouetted by the flames, his black coat starting to smoke from the heat, Ukiah bent over something on the ground, then helped a man stand up. Supported by

Ukiah, the man stumbled slowly up the slope, glancing over his shoulder at the inferno behind them. When they got closer, Tom saw the dark burns on the man's body. When his defeated gaze met Tom's wide-eyed stare, tears began to stream down the man's face, and he sagged to his knees in the dirt. Luna quickly covered Tom's eyes with her hand, but Tom had already felt the pain in those gray eyes.

Tom was surprised by the detailed memory. With the passage of time, he had come to think of it as an old dream. After the fire, his parents had never spoken of it again, and the man with the burns had disappeared into the night.

"The fire," Tom whispered. "You were the man in the fire."

Magnus stopped, but he didn't turn around. When he spoke, his voice was almost inaudible. "That man no longer exists."

"Was that the night you learned the secret of your life?" Tom asked.

"The first of many," Magnus replied. He cast a sideways glance at Tom. "And now, whether you're ready or not, your time has come, young Tom. Your time has come."

HIS narrow face was human in shape, with a graceful nose set off by prominent high cheekbones, but his chrome complexion made his emotions hard to read, mirroring the faces of the humans who dared speak to him. His eyes reflected without revealing, giving him the otherworldly presence expected of the ambassador of Telemachus. Dressed in black robes woven with the fine silver threads that enhanced and expanded his sensory field beyond his facial perimeter, he descended the ramp into the vortex chamber, hesitating as the concentric rings of color began to radiate from the center of the dark chamber. Telemachus was present, and he would not be fooled by the calm expression on the mirrored face of Hermes. Fortunately, his master had not summoned him to a meeting in Stronghold, and that meant that he had a good chance of leaving the vortex chamber alive.

"It was a simple task," Telemachus rumbled in his multi-voice. "Explain your failure."

The rippling circles of color passed through Hermes as if he weren't there, expanding at a slow and steady pace through the blackness. As each color pulse struck his cloak, his sensory field registered tiny shocks to his nervous system, triggering rapid surges of random emotion in his brain. His normally placid demeanor now bounced between fear, sadness, ecstasy, and any other feeling that Telemachus wished to test while Hermes stood in the vortex chamber. Even without the shock waves, Telemachus could almost read the mind of Hermes through his body language; but he had limitations in understanding human thought and feeling, which was why Hermes and the Oracle had been created as interfaces in the first place. One of the drawbacks to being a nanoborg was regular submission to these emotional shock wave tests, usually while reports were being delivered.

Hermes began to explain. "The guardian lost contact with the target twenty-three feet beneath the surface at—"

"We know all that," Telemachus interrupted. "I require the details of *your* failure."

Hermes hesitated, trying not to reveal anything through his voice quality or the movements of his body, but knowing that his skin temperature, perspiration, muscle tension, and heart rate were being measured remotely.

"Response is required," Telemachus said. "Now."

Hermes felt a stronger electrical charge dance across the surface of his skin—a warning about the pain that his master could trigger if he was displeased. If he'd learned anything from his long association with Telemachus, it was how direct the AI could be when dealing with lesser intelligences. Pain and pleasure were doled out by the AIs as the simplest means of controlling the human herds under their care, although they preferred to work indirectly through their nanoborg interfaces whenever possible. That was a policy that occasionally put Hermes in the position of a messenger bearing bad news, and he knew that his future would be severely limited if Telemachus predicted any future incompetencies or major failures on the part of Hermes. Nanoborgs were not easily built or trained by the AIs, but failures were acknowledged and bred out of the genetic algorithms immediately whenever one of the nanoborg units exhibited serious design flaws. The occasional miscalculation or seemingly illogical act was allowed as an inherent by-product of the human side of a nanoborg's activities; but errors were always tracked and recorded, making it possible for an otherwise successful nanoborg to be destroyed after years of faithful service once its error threshold had been reached.

"I was fooled," Hermes said. "My human half blinded me. The Eliot boy seemed to be a hardworking youth who fit in well with the community."

"You are my servant precisely so that we may not be fooled in this way," Telemachus said.

"I understand," Hermes whispered, lowering his head as he prepared himself for a fatal shock. He considered that Telemachus might not have summoned him to Stronghold because his failure had been too great to allow for a traditional execution on the high ground. He felt his heart beat faster, then tried to slow it by taking a deep breath and releasing it gradually.

"Continue," Telemachus intoned.

Hermes blinked in surprise, happy to continue breathing. "Tom Eliot has learned to evade our shoreline wards, and he has managed to find gaps within the forbidden zones where he can slip through without detection."

"In this sense, he has performed a service for us," Telemachus said. "We can seal the gaps he has discovered."

Hermes tipped his head, wondering at the strange turn of the conversation. "This is true."

"To what purpose does this boy enter the forbidden zones? He is not on the scavenger list."

Hermes could only guess at the boy's motivation. "His father says that the boy likes to leave his normal surroundings to meditate. To think."

"Thinking is bad for them," Telemachus said. "It leads to independent ambition and can conflict with our long-term goals for the communities. They must assume their assigned tasks and follow the plans we lay out for their lives. The Eliot boy is a wild element in our balanced system and must be eliminated before he contaminates the rest of the community."

"I understand," Hermes said. "The community is at risk. We must remove Tom Eliot."

"You understand very little. The contaminant must be *destroyed*. Probability is high that components of the Eliot family will not respond favorably to Tom Eliot's removal or destruction. We must assume that the entire sample has been contaminated by Tom Eliot's presence. We will choose a time with the highest probability of all family elements being present at the Eliot home, then we will strike."

Hermes frowned. "Community output will drop dramatically in response. Fear will dominate for weeks after the event."

"A blip in the evolution of Marinwood. They're human. Over time, they will adapt and forget that the Eliots existed. After six months, another family may rebuild and occupy the farmland."

"Perhaps we should try other means first. Tom Eliot has unusual capabilities that haven't yet been developed. We could threaten the farm, cut off their power—"

Telemachus interrupted him again. "It is not our policy to waste workforce elements, Hermes. Our decision is not colored by emotion, but by facts and projected probabilities.

Your human component views Tom Eliot in terms of your similarities—he is isolated from others of his kind by his differences and so are you—but you should view Tom Eliot in terms of his *differences*. Our task is to protect and guide our human charges, despite what certain factions of the Dominion might have us believe. We do not weaken their growth by coddling them, and we do not allow human performance outside of the safe evolutionary norms we have established."

"Safety is an illusion," Hermes blurted out without thinking. He instantly regretted it when his skin crackled with the warning electrical charge, somewhat stronger than the previous time. Then Telemachus shifted the shock wave colors toward the red end of the spectrum, and his emotions pulsed along with them in response—anxiety, worry, fear, panic, terror. He got the point.

"It is a useful illusion for our purposes," Telemachus said.

"YOU summoned me?" Ukiah asked. He gripped the stiff brim of his hat in his right hand, bowing slightly to avoid the downward thrust of a white stalactite as he stepped forward into the middle of the dimly lighted cavern. He heard the brief echo of his voice seeking escape from the subterranean vault. Unseen bats squeaked in the dark hollows of the ceiling. A glowing pool of clear water occupied the middle of the rough oval floor, illuminated from below by an intense orange light. Little streamers of fog, disturbed by the air currents, coiled and swirled on the surface of the water, impeded only by the delicate figure of the Oracle, floating on her back, her white robes billowing around her as if she were a giant butterfly, her white hair streaming away from her skull like a living thing. Her larger shadow loomed on the ceiling, broken only by the stalactites that protruded from it, as if giant rock daggers impaled her body. She soaked in a nutrient bath of microscopic creatures that kept her young, complemented by the medical nanobots that lived in her bloodstream. Completely human once, she had chosen to serve the gods as the Oracle, and had lived her life as an interface, more machine than human, ever since she had accepted the blessing of the nanoborg conversion before Ukiah had even been born. Along with Hermes, the ambassador of the gods, she served Telemachus and the other powers of the Dominion in her sacred stewardship of Marinwood and the surrounding region.

"Elder Ukiah. Approach."

Ukiah took a few steps closer to the pool. In the orange glow, he saw her white eyes staring up at the ceiling, and beyond it into the future.

"This is the last time we shall speak," she said in her haunting whisper. "A storm is coming."

Ukiah frowned. "What kind of a storm?"

"The winds of change."

"Should I prepare for this storm? Should I warn the community?"

"The community is part of the storm, but it is safe. You need to look to your own, Elder Ukiah, and know that the chaos winds will blow, and that the fires of conflict will burn. The dragons deep within the earth are restless, and great powers are focusing their attention on the events unfolding here. This is a time of change, and I am witness to this change; but even I may not be safe, for I have tried to help your offspring."

Ukiah licked his lips, wondering how to get better answers from the cryptic Oracle. He knew that the Oracle had access to information from Telemachus, and maybe even Hermes, but clarity seemed to be forbidden in her dealings with the human community. "Can you tell me what transpired here to warrant the attention of the gods?"

"The gods are as men in their need to control the world," she said. After a brief hesitation, her eyes rolled toward Ukiah, startling him, and she continued. "Portions of human space are divided equally among the gods of the Dominion, and those portions were established under autonomous control by entities such as Telemachus. Although the Dominion maintains open channels of communication between the gods, clusters of opinion have re-formed, and there are new factions that wish to destroy any potential threats to the Design before they become viable. The goal of protection and controlled evolution remains the same among all factions, but their methods differ. Telemachus has opted to take a more direct hand in the daily affairs of this community. Do you understand, Elder Ukiah?"

He understood that she was trying to give him a clear message, despite her apparent restrictions to the contrary. "I understand that which is written in the scriptures. The gods are wise. But you're saying that my family is in danger?"

Her milky gaze drifted back to the ceiling, and the possibilities of tomorrow. "There is no outside agency that can interfere, and the few random elements within cannot effect a diversion from the current course. However, there are too many threads to make an accurate prediction. Although the present is my past, your own future is uncertain, lost in the gray mists of chance and destiny, yet I know that we shall not speak again. An ending approaches, but whether it is mine or yours I cannot say."

...3

TEMPEST concentrated on avoiding contact with the metal that cocooned her upper body. Bent over from her waist, her wrists locked inside the front of the steel clamshell, her back hurt from the strain of her position, and she knew she'd eventually weaken enough to sag against the hot bottom of the box. When she did, the pain of the electrical shock would be enough to tense her muscles and keep her alert for a while longer until she tired again. She had managed to stand on her shirt when her father locked her in, so at least her bare feet were padded against the sharp rocks. Dim light showed through the seams of the box to help her judge her position, but the sun had also heated the metal enough that her sweat sizzled when it dripped off her face and chest. She couldn't remember the last time her father had been angry enough to put Humboldt in the box, but it had been at least two years, around the time her brother had beaten that neighbor boy almost to death. She hadn't seen the inside of the box for more than five years, and her memories of the experience had finally faded, leaving her with only the occasional nightmare to remind her of the pain. Now, it would all be fresh in her memory once more.

She tensed when she heard footsteps approaching on the gravel. She hoped it was her father, because there was no telling what indignities Humboldt might visit upon her while she was trapped in this position. Ever since he was a small boy, he'd enjoyed torturing defenseless things.

"You disappoint me," Memphis said, his voice catching in his throat. Tempest couldn't see him, but she heard him clearly and sensed his position beside the box. She was relieved to hear his voice. "To disobey me this way and endanger your family seems so unlike you. I thought I could trust you."

"You can, Father," Tempest whispered.

"You must not see Tom Eliot again. Avoid him at the market, avoid him on the road, turn away if you happen upon him at the lake. Do not come in contact with him in any way. Do you understand?"

Tempest squeezed her eyes shut. "But, Father, I don't mean to—"

His voice suddenly got louder. "Yes or no!"

"Please, I just—"

Her eyes snapped open as she heard the whistle of the strap slicing through the air. She tensed, bracing herself for the impact so that she wouldn't bounce against the metal and get a shock at the same time. When the strap hit her butt, she realized she was still wearing her heavy leather pants, and she barely felt the blow. Then she knew his heart wasn't in it.

"Do you understand?" he growled.

"Yes. I understand."

"And you will no longer accept any gifts from the young hooligan. Do you understand?"

"Yes, Father." Her face sagged closer to the bottom of the box as her back and neck muscles, burning with the strain, weakened even more. Drops of her sweat sizzled and popped on the hot surface below. Pulling against the restraints, her shoulders felt as if they were being yanked from their sockets. Then her head sagged, and her forehead touched the metal, and the blinding shock kicked her head up and back. A gasping scream gurgled at the back of her throat, unable to find escape through her clenched jaws and startled tongue.

Two rough hands massaged the exposed muscles of her lower back, and she heard the click of the lock on the outside of the box.

"You've had enough," Memphis said softly.

A seam of light brightened around the perimeter of the metal clamshell, then brilliant whiteness flooded the interior, making Tempest squint. Cooler air swirled over her skin. As relief flooded through her, her upper body sagged once more, allowing her chest and face to strike the metal, but the expected shock never came because Memphis had already switched off the current.

"I'm getting soft in my old age," Memphis said, releasing her wrists.

"Thank you, Father." She tried to catch his eye, but he turned and walked off toward the barn, his head down, trapped inside the cage within his own skull.

MAGNUS had led Tom through the open hatches of an airlock in the BART tunnel, past a sign that said HARD HATS REQUIRED, and on down another concrete passage that emptied out into a space larger than Tom's house. The rectangular chamber had one thick glass wall that looked out into the murky depths of the bay, where the water was cut by shafts of twinkling sunlight. Jumping reflections and shadows danced inside the chamber, giving everything a sense of movement and mystery. The air smelled musty at first, but Magnus walked over to the dented side of a large metal cabinet with thick pipes running up to the ceiling and gave it two hard kicks. A moment later, fans hummed to life and fresh, damp air blew into the room through the ventilators, stirring up the dust on top of the big wooden crates stacked everywhere. Magnus grunted in satisfaction.

"Ventilation system still works. You know why?" Magnus winked at Tom. "Solar energy. Most of the transbay Marin tunnel still has emergency power because someone had the foresight to install a distributed system of solar panels. Most of them were destroyed when the siliboys popped the cities, of course, but that was damned good engineering, if you ask me. These tunnels were built to withstand earthquakes."

"That's great," Tom said, not really interested in where the power came from. He was busy noticing the rumpled mattress on top of a crate, the shiny kitchen utensils neatly arrayed over a grimy industrial sink on one wall, a table made of wood from a crate lid with metal struts for legs, a chair that looked like someone had beaten the stuffing out of it, and bookcase after bookcase of neatly shelved text-books and paperbacks. "You live here?"

"Better than living in a cave," Magnus said with a shrug.

Tom started to comment on the huge library, then frowned when he saw what appeared to be a small black vehicle parked next to a large airlock hatch. "Is that—?"

Magnus caught his look and nodded. "Buick Sunburst—2015 model. Hybrid engine runs on a hydrogen fuel cell or solar, depending on what's available. Getting fuel for it is a pig, since there isn't much sunlight in this hole, but it beats walking."

Tom couldn't help staring. He'd never actually seen a car in real life, only in books. The Buick's black solar paint looked shiny and clean, even under the dim light. "You drive that thing around down here?"

"Perfect size for the tunnel, once I get it over the mag-lev track rails, of course. I just have to be careful not to break it—spare parts are hard to come by. The closest Buick dealership is fifteen miles away and sixty years in the past."

"How did you get it down here?"

Magnus hopped up to a sitting position on one of the crates. "Three days of digging and blasting where Sausalito used to be. The BART station there was buried deep, and I had to make a ramp that wasn't too steep so the car could get into the tunnel. With all that noise, I was sure the siliboys were going to nail me, but I guess I was deep enough not to wake up the wards." He gestured at the overstuffed chair. "Have a seat. You can have the comfy chair."

Tom looked at the chair and the springs poking through the seat cushion, thought better of it, and frowned at Magnus, who was now drinking from a water flask.

"Who are these 'siliboys' you keep referring to?"

Magnus coughed and snorted water out of his nose. "The *gods,* boy! Telemachus and all his silicon friends—although they weren't really built out of silicon. The AI Dominion. The bad guys."

Tom nervously looked around, hoping that the ears of the gods were not listening.

"We're safe down here as long as you don't hang around too long," Magnus said, wiping water off of his face. "No bugs in the tunnels. No bugs in the ruins. Didn't think it was worth their while after they screwed everything up, I guess."

Tom felt as if Magnus were speaking a foreign language. "What are you talking about now?"

"The Big Bang. What you people like to call The Uplift or The Cleansing." Magnus paused to study him. "Don't you know anything?"

"Less than I thought, I guess." Magnus was talking blasphemy, and it made Tom uncomfortable. As they had learned in school, the scriptures clearly stated that the massive earthquakes of The Cleansing had come about because of the sins of humankind. The entire western region of the country had launched itself skyward in the same moment, flattening the cities and killing tens of millions of people. The Earth had been forced to set an example in retaliation for human neglect, and they all knew that more could have been killed were it not for the intervention of Telemachus and the other benevolent gods of the Dominion that watched over them. "The earthquakes—"

Magnus interrupted him with a raised hand. "First off, they weren't earthquakes, at least not in the normal sense of the word. The siliboys used their nanotech on us, lad. Sure, it was sneaky the way they covered it all up with stories about the Ring of Fire erupting along the Pacific Coast, but they were the ones that caused it in the first place. Above and below ground, nothing was safe from the nano-bombs. The underground stealth bombs spent days quietly digging their way down to their targets in the earthquake faults, then the Dominion triggered them and let Mother Nature do the rest. One Big Bang and a huge chunk of the country was thrown back to the Stone Age. It worked out so well that they did it to other big cities all over the world."

"How do you know all this?"

"I get around."

Tom rubbed his eyes. There was a lot going on here that he didn't understand, and he didn't want to get himself into more trouble by spending time with a crazy old fugitive full of wild stories. On the other hand, if Magnus was telling the truth, Tom's family might actually be in danger. He had to warn them and find out if they were safe. "I should be getting back. What's the fastest way for me to get home?"

Magnus gave him a strange smile. "Depends. Fastest way would be the Road—the Prometheus Road—except you don't know what that is yet, and I don't have time to test you or teach you right now."

"Prometheus Road? What—"

Magnus held up one hand to interrupt Tom, then jerked his thumb toward the car. "There's always the Buick, of course; I could drop you off at the Sausalito terminal." His smile vanished as his gaze bored into Tom's head. "But there's one thing you need to consider—for some people, there is no going home. Speaking from past experience, my boy, I'd say you're in the last category."

Tom shuddered as he saw the truth in those old gray eyes, but he couldn't let that get to him. "I'd appreciate a ride in your car, but I'll walk if there's going to be any delay. I'm concerned about my family."

Magnus nodded. "I'm not surprised. You seem like a good lad. Your parents must have raised you right." He hopped down from the crate and started toward the car while Tom followed. "I'll tell you what; you go visit the old homestead and see that everyone is safe. Don't talk to anyone. Try to limit how many people see you along the way. I think you'll find that old Hermes or one of his kind has been around looking for you, and that's when you'll realize I've been telling you the truth. When that happens, you won't have anyplace to hide for very long, and you won't be able to contact your family without endangering them. Everyone in town is scared of the siliboys, so you won't have any friends when they find out that Hermes is looking for you. When you're ready for my help, you go on up to the old cemetery outside of Marinwood, and I'll meet you there."

Tom hesitated, wondering if he should believe him, hoping it was all just a crazy old man's fantasy story. "How will you know I'm there?"

Magnus held the door open for him on the passenger side of the Buick and gave Tom that strange, knowing smile that made his skin crawl. "I'll know."

■   ■   ■

THE electric lock on the front door popped open. Gasping for breath, a red-faced Ukiah threw the door open and burst into the sunken family room, startling Luna and Zeke from their card game. The scent of vegetable stew permeated the air of the house, along with the sweet fragrance of freshly baked ginger cookies and roasted cornfruit, but Ukiah didn't seem to notice. Ukiah's hat was in his hand, and his shirt was soaked with sweat under his open black coat. He steadied himself, then bent over with his hands on his knees, catching his breath. "Is everyone all right?"

Luna frowned and walked over beside her husband. "We're fine. What's wrong?"

"Oracle warned me," he said, pausing for another breath. "She said a storm is coming, and it threatens all of us. Where's Tom?"

"He hasn't come home yet."

Ukiah's face looked grim as he nodded. "And Weed? Where's my Weed?"

Zeke stood up. "She went out to play in the barn, Father. What kind of a storm was the Oracle talking about? Do we need to raise the flood shields?"

Ukiah shook his head. "I don't think she meant a real, physical storm. It was something else, something bad, but you can never get a straight answer out of her. I have to go and find Tom. I'm sure he's the key to all this, and I have to warn him. Maybe we can hide him."

"I'll look for Tom," Luna said, wiping his forehead with her hand. "You sit down, or your heart's going to explode."

"No time," Ukiah said, looking toward the door. "Do you have any idea where he goes? I know it's by the water."

Luna sighed. "I don't know. I think he goes different places. I know I would. You can't go after him in any case, or you'll be the one who ends up getting caught."

"If Tom figured out how to avoid the wards, then I can, too."

"Can I go with you?" Zeke asked, taking his coat down

from the wall hook by the door. "With both of us looking, we should have a better chance of finding him."

Ukiah took a deep breath, then put his arm around his son's shoulders. "I need you here, Zeke. I want you to help your mother figure out where we can hide Tom."

Zeke looked disappointed, but he nodded. "Yes, Father."

Ukiah saw the worry in Luna's blue eyes as he turned to hold her. "I won't be gone long."

"We can't let them take our son," Luna said, squeezing him tight. "We'll do whatever is necessary to prevent that."

"I won't allow it," Ukiah whispered in her ear. "Take care of Weed and Zeke."

Her fingers gripped the sides of his coat. "I will."

Then the lights went out. No moonlight came down the light pipe.

"The power's out!" Zeke yelled.

Ukiah kissed Luna and whirled toward the door, slamming his knee into the corner of a table as he lurched through the darkness.

The door was locked. They were supposed to unlock automatically in the event of a power outage. Try as he might, Ukiah couldn't yank the door open. In his frenzy, Ukiah could think of only one reason this would have happened, and he didn't like his conclusion. He pounded his fist against the metal. "Weed! Run, Weed!"

"She can't hear us down here!" Luna yelled behind him in the blackness.

"Zeke! Try the light pipe!"

"I'm there," Zeke said, pounding on something. "The window's locked! It won't open!"

Running his hand along the wall to guide him, Ukiah stumbled into the kitchen, grunted when he ran into the end of the countertop, then shoved his head under the hood above the cooking area and looked up into the vertical vent pipe. "Weed! Run, Weed! Get away!"

■ ■ ■

"GOOD boy," Tom said, scratching Helix's favorite spot on the back of his furry brown neck. In appreciation, Helix half closed his eyes and stretched out his neck. The little dog had spent the entire day where Tom had left him before sunrise, where the broad stream met the China Camp marsh at the edge of the bay. Now, the sun had dropped below the western horizon, leaving a dim golden glow in the sky above the mountain of the gods. Tom's feet were sore and blistered from the long walk north on the crumbled and grassy remnants of the road they called "101," but the walk was preferable to riding in the car anymore with Magnus, even if he could have driven his vehicle out of the Sausalito BART terminal. Although Tom's experience of such things was limited to this one trip, the crazy old man had turned out to be a terrible driver, steering with one hand through the dim tunnels with his other arm propped in the open side window, driving fast enough to blow his hair in the wind, chattering constantly as the insides of the car's tires bounced off the center mag-lev rail, first one side, then the other, back and forth, until Tom thought he was going to vomit. By concentrating on the pain of his fingernails digging into his palms, he managed to keep the butterflies contained in his stomach.

Magnus had used the time in the Buick to regale Tom with stories about the ruined cities and the people who lived there, having traveled around the western region for a few years after his escape from the rehabilitation unit in Las Vegas. Magnus had also planned to visit the cities of the Midwestern Preserve, but he had not managed to find an unprotected passage through the western barrier wall. Only delegates chosen by the gods were allowed to leave the western region for official visits to Washington, D.C., and Magnus had not wanted to risk death at the barrier portal with his forged identity chip. There were always rumors that citizens of the west had found ways to escape to the Midwestern Preserve, but Magnus had not uncovered any evidence of successful attempts during his travels. And so, he had returned home to hide and live in obscurity under a new name, building a home underwater, where the gods had less chance of finding him.

Tom pulled the marsh grass camouflage free of his skin-suit and changed into work clothes, then stuffed his gear into a backpack and started home. His boots raised dust on the game trail that wound through the weeds and tall grasses near the water's edge. The branches of the valley oaks that covered the rolling hills around the marsh were extended over the grass like long gray tentacles. Evergreen coast live oaks, their small leaves bellied like stiff little boats, dotted the landscape along with bay trees and madrones. Many of the trees were dead, their twisted and mostly bare branches grasping at the sky, providing little cover as Tom walked among them. Helix padded along faithfully beside him, keeping his eyes peeled for birds, lizards, or other small creatures that he could protect Tom from along the way. The largest creature they had ever seen in the area was a turkey vulture, but Helix had not threatened the large bird, possibly because it could have picked up the little dog and carried him away without any trouble. Helix had a good heart, but he wasn't stupid.

Helix stopped to growl at something he saw or smelled in the distance. Tom assumed the dog had spotted one of his sworn enemies, perhaps a blue scrub jay or a raven, but it turned out to be neither.

When he heard the voices of several men just beyond the next rise in the trail, Tom had the presence of mind to duck and soothe Helix's nerves with a pat on the head. The voices were getting closer, and Tom recognized the deep snarl that belonged to Humboldt Gustafson. Helix started to whine, his tense body ready to spring into barking action to scare away the threat.

"It's okay, boy," Tom whispered.

Helix glanced at him briefly with his wide-eyed stare, as if to point out the obvious. They were obviously not safe, and Helix was ready to take charge if Tom proved to be mentally incompetent during this emergency.

Tom nodded. "You're right. Let's get off the trail." As soon as he stepped off the dirt path, he knew he couldn't go very far without attracting attention. Dry twigs and leaves snapped under his boots on the uneven ground. Tom stopped, looked around, picked up Helix under one arm, and awkwardly climbed one of the larger oak trees. When he was about twenty feet off the ground, his mouth open to minimize the sound of his heavy breathing, he stopped and looked around the trunk of the tree at a group of six men from Marinwood. They were all carrying shovels or heavy lengths of pipe, looking around warily as they walked.

"What makes you think we'll find Tom out here?" Tom recognized Jaq Butterbean's voice just before he spotted the hulking figure walking next to Humboldt.

"This is about where I saw him this morning," Humboldt said. "And he has to come back sometime. When he does, we'll nail him." He emphasized his point with a jab of the metal pipe he carried.

"What about the wards? Won't they spot us?" Butterbean asked.

"Not until we come out of the trees. If they happen to see us, my father will take care of it. Hermes may already know we're here."

Humboldt's last remark seemed to calm the group as they passed directly under Tom's tree. Helix started to open his mouth to bark, but Tom hugged the dog close to his chest and covered his mouth with one hand. Helix snorted instead. Beneath the tree, Humboldt frowned and turned his head to look back along the path the way they had come. "Any of you hear that?"

"Hear what?" Butterbean asked, stopping to look back.

Humboldt shook his head. "Never mind. Let's bag Tom and get home. It's getting dark."

Once the group had passed around the next bend sloping toward the marsh, Tom worked his way back down the tree with Helix under one arm. As usual, Helix didn't mind being hauled around like a sack of potatoes, accepting his fate with quiet dignity. "Good boy," Tom whispered. "I'll put you down in a minute."

Tom got a good scratch on his left arm when he jumped down from the last branch, staggered on the uneven ground, and had to turn quickly to avoid smacking Helix against the trunk of the oak tree. Helix whined briefly, then realized he was okay, and stood on the path with a quizzical expression when Tom set him down. "Come on, boy. We should have a few minutes before they come back." He jogged up the hill with Helix following at his heels. The moon wouldn't rise for a couple of hours yet, so he wanted to get back before it was too dark to see the trail. Along the way, he could work out how he was going to explain his long absence to his parents.

WEED Eliot sat on a hay bale behind the barn and studied the story crystal that seemed so large in her small hand. Tom had found the crystal on one of his moonlight journeys; when he gave it to Weed he said it had come from a faraway land beneath the sea and that it would tell her stories if she was very good and played with it carefully. He also told her to keep it hidden so it would just be a secret between the two of them. So she kept it buried in one of her pants pockets under a wad of string, some red flower petals she had picked, and some shiny green rocks she had found along the road on one of their trips to the village market.

Looking around to make sure no one was watching, she lifted the story crystal up to her face and watched the sunlight make little rainbows in her hand. Something dark fluttered deep within the crystal's many facets, then bright colors began to swirl and shift around inside of it. Weed held her breath, wondering what kind of story the crystal would choose to tell her today. The swirling colors inside merged with the rainbows in her hand, and an image of two little girls standing beside a Shetland pony appeared above the crystal's top surface.

"I'm Rumtumtumbleberry," said the little girl with black hair. She was dressed in a black hat and a long black coat of the type that Weed's father wore.

"And I'm Bumbleberry," said the little girl with the brown hair who looked a lot like Weed. She also wore black pants and a white shirt similar to Weed's outfit. Weed gave them a knowing nod, aware that the people who lived in the story crystal always wore familiar clothes and looked similar to her family members. She wasn't sure why that was the case, but accepted the fact and concentrated on the stories.

"And I'm Bumpus," said the horse, with a happy little whinny after he said his name. "Bumpus T. Rumpus, at your service." Bumpus didn't look like one of Weed's family members, although he did have a face that reminded her of Helix, their dog, who had been away with Tom all day. Now that she thought about it, she briefly wondered where Tom and Helix had gone, but her attention was quickly diverted back to the unfolding story in front of her.

Bumpus smiled. "What kind of a story would you like to hear today, Weed?"

"A *good* story," Weed said with a giggle. She covered her mouth so no one would hear her.

"Oh, well," Bumpus whinnied. "We have plenty of those, don't we, girls?"

Both girls nodded, then Bumbleberry winked at Weed. "Would you like to hear about our adventures in the Dingly Dell today, Weed?"

Weed shook her head. The Dingly Dell stories always had mean people in them.

"Okay," Bumbleberry said. "I have an idea. I bet you'd like to hear about our adventures in the Bungle Jungle, isn't that right? You like the Bungle Jungle, don't you, Weed? We know your brother likes our Bungle Jungle stories."

Weed nodded. The Bungle Jungle had funny little animals in it. She liked little animals.

Bumbleberry clapped her hands in delight. "Righty-rootie, the Bungle Jungle it is. That's where our friend, Bun-Bun the Bunny lives."

Weed rolled her eyes when she heard the bunny's name. Her friends inside the crystal were good at telling stories, but their predictable names all started to sound alike after a while—Kappy the Kangaroo, Hip-Hop the Hamster, Pimpy the Puppy—it was enough to drive a little girl mad.

An odd noise in the sky caught her attention. At first, she thought it might be the screech of a hawk, but the sound kept going. Then she saw a long, black sausage shape that didn't look like a bird at all. It seemed to be floating like a balloon, but if it was a balloon, it was a very big one.

"One day," Bumbleberry began, capturing Weed's attention again, "Bun-Bun was out hopping in the jungle with Piggle Wiggle and Melvin the Monkey. It was a bright and sunny day, and for once there were no hungry crocodiles waiting on the path beside the watering hole where they liked to swim." An image of the three smiling animals, holding hands and bouncing down the jungle trail, appeared above the story crystal. Bumbleberry, Rumpus, and Rumtumtumbleberry were watching the story unfold along with Weed, who thought it was nice to have friends watching the story with her. Remembering the floating black sausage, Weed glanced up at the sky again, but it was gone. That seemed strange to her, but she didn't think about it much because Goofy Gazelle, one of her favorite jungle characters, had just appeared on the path, and he had put up a sign so he could charge admission to the watering hole. The other animals were busy hunting for money in their pockets until they realized they didn't have any pockets. Weed smiled at first, then her expression switched to a frown. The animals were funny, but she felt bad because they wouldn't be able to swim on a hot day. Then Goofy Gazelle laughed and said he was only kidding, and they could all swim together in the watering hole for free.

Aware that this was just the beginning of the story, Weed wanted to get more comfortable. The straw in the bale was poking into her legs. She slid down behind the bale, resting her back on the cool grassy berm that formed the back wall of the barn, leaving her feet propped up on the straw. The breeze was getting cooler now that the sun had gone down, and the bale gave off a pleasantly sweet fragrance.

As the jungle animals dove into the watering hole, surrounded by jungle trees that were damp from the mist in the waterfall, Weed heard another odd sound—a kind of high-pitched shriek—and the dark sky suddenly began to brighten. That was strange, since the sun had just gone down, and the glow was brighter than moonlight. And getting brighter. She heard a low rumbling like thunder as the earth trembled beneath her. The jungle characters continued on about their business, laughing and splashing, but Weed's breath caught in her throat. Her eyes widened.

The thunder spoke.

And then the light was everywhere.

Weed shut her eyes tight.

TOM and Helix were about a mile from home, coming down the last hill in the deep darkness beneath the tall pine and oak trees, when a bright flash caught his attention. Helix yelped, then a huge, invisible hand from a shock wave knocked them both flat on the ground behind an outcropping of granite. Startled, Tom began to sit up again when a wave of intense heat rolled past, partly deflected by the granite shelf. It took only a few seconds before he realized which direction the blast had come from. He rolled over and hauled himself to his feet, using the granite shelf to support him as his head spun. The back of his head hurt, so he assumed the dizziness had something to do with that, but he could work that out later. He had to see what was going on.

The landscape was on fire. Many of the trees lower on the hillside were burning, bright flames licking at the night sky, dark smoke streaming away on the salty breeze. Yet it wasn't a simple fire or explosion that Tom saw farther out on the flat fields—a crater was forming, growing as it went, the ground collapsing like mud or hot lava into a deepening pit. The air over the crater shimmered with a soft blue glow, crackling with static electricity in the night air, smelling of ozone, burning wood, and the heat of shattered dreams. The earth rumbled, swaying back and forth in a slow rhythm that upset Tom's stomach. Glowing mud pots formed in the soil of the fields, bubbling and hissing as the ground continued to liquefy and steam, adding sulfurous fumes to the air while the gates of hell widened to devour the Eliot farm.

Helix whined, watching the sight beside his master, so Tom picked up the little dog to comfort him, wondering who would pick *him* up for comforting as his life sank into the boiling crater of his past, taking his parents, his sister, his brother, and their home along with it. There was nothing that could have prepared him for this sight, nothing to give the unreal moment a frame of reference so he could retain his sanity, nothing that could stop the screaming he suddenly realized was coming from his mouth.

There would be no going home again.

■　■　■

SUSPENDED in her liquid of life, her white robes drifting on the surface of the orange-lit pool like some huge butterfly trapped in amber, the Oracle's body suddenly tensed and began to convulse, her physical form seized in the grip of a time-space shock wave that only she could sense fully, living in the spaces between the worlds where the sudden, definitive event in this history of Marinwood rippled out through many worlds and many paths, sealing off threads of futures to come as it created new threads of dynamic potential, shifting universes and reflecting futures past. Her heart hammered in her chest as her white eyes rolled back into her head. Storms of time raged against darkness and light, fighting for superiority, creating new combinations of tomorrow and tomorrow.

Waves rocked the Oracle's life tank, causing shadows to jump across the ceiling, chasing each other in a wild dance through crevices and stalactites. Then her body began to settle, convulsions became twitches, and the waves became ripples. Her heart slowed, her breathing became more regular, her exhausted eyes gently closed to seek the peace of sleep and dreams.

Her vision turned inward, and she knew the end had begun.

"THERE he is!"

Tom turned at the shout so close behind him, just in time to see the massive form of Humboldt hurtling toward him. The man looked like a demon in the flickering light from the flaming trees. Stunned from the sight he had just witnessed, Tom gazed dully at Humboldt, seeing it all in slow motion, wondering if he would even bother to try dodging the blow. The rest of Humboldt's group stood a few feet away, their eyes wide and intent on Tom, unaware that the world was burning at the bottom of the hill or too dull-witted to care. These were the boys he had gone to school with, been tormented by when he was younger, and who now chose to hunt him down because he was too different from the rest of them. Tom saw all of them as being built on the same human model, almost as if they were clones like he'd read about in his father's books, with small, glazed brown eyes sunk in piggy faces atop hulking bodies, too big and slow to do anything but physical labor. And the biggest of them was about to smash Tom flat against the granite outcropping where he stood, a long metal pipe gripped in his left hand like a spear.

Tom stepped to one side, grabbed the passing metal pipe, and tripped Humboldt, who continued on past Tom and sprawled against the rocky ground. Out of the corner of his eye, he saw Butterbean step into the fiery glow from downhill, and turned just in time to see a shovel close to his face. Tom ducked and raised an arm, deflecting the shovel's path but feeling intense pain in his arm as he stumbled backward and fell on top of Humboldt, who grunted under his weight, then tried to grab Tom's arms and hold his back flat against his chest. Seeing another opening, Butterbean moved in with his shovel and took another swing, and Tom remembered what his father had taught him about turning the other cheek—just long enough to surprise an attacker and fight back. Now his father was dead along with the rest of his family, and people like this were responsible for it, and that made him angry.

Tom took the blow from the shovel in his ribs, then he saw popping lights in his vision, but he managed to roll over Humboldt's head and swing upward with his pipe, catching Butterbean under the jaw. Butterbean nearly flew over the granite outcropping. Humboldt rotated and kicked Tom in the side of the head, then Tom glimpsed the rest of the group running toward him as he rolled a few times over broken sticks and rocks that cut his arms and face.

Helix had been watching the entire fight from a safe perch on top of a log, which was fine with Tom because he didn't want the little dog to get hurt. However, Helix had only been biding his time, waiting for an opening. With Humboldt off-balance, Helix ran forward, bit him on the leg, rolled his eyes happily when Humboldt screamed, then released his prey and darted back to his log before the big man could hit him. With Helix running back and forth, several of the men stumbled against each other to avoid tripping over the dog, leaving only three to swing pipes at Tom from different directions. Tom blocked two of them with his own pipe when he jumped up out of the dirt, but the third caught him on his left side, knocking him back against a tree. The rough bark ripped open the back of his shirt.

Then Tom remembered his family again, his anger submerged the pain, and the steel pipe he carried became an extension of his arm, whistling back and forth in wild arcs, cutting through the clusters of men in the flickering light as if they were stalks of wheat waiting to be harvested. And they fell like wheat, except for the yelling and screaming. Then he had no more attackers, which was good since he was perched on the edge of a granite ledge jutting out over a long, rocky slope in the darkness. Helix cocked his head in Tom's direction, then snapped to attention again and growled.

That was when Humboldt hit Tom with an oak branch that snapped across his shoulders. It wasn't as hard as one of the pipes or shovels, but it was heavy, and it was enough to knock Tom off the ledge.

He landed on his feet, hurting one ankle, then rolled down the steep slope, slamming into logs, bouncing off rocks, filling his boots and his mouth with loose dirt as he spun through the darkness, desperately trying to flail his arms and legs enough to stop his descent, feeling every part of his body that had been damaged in the fight along with the new pains he was collecting on the way down. It was a welcome relief to smash into a large bush that halted his flight.

Helix bounded down the slope and slid to a stop next to Tom's head before sniffing his hair and finally licking the side of his face. Tom groaned and raised two fingers to scratch Helix's chest, and that seemed to satisfy the dog's curiosity, because he sat down to lick his front paws.

Tom heard moaning and voices at the top of the slope high overhead. "Did you kill him, then?" someone asked. It sounded like Butterbean, but Tom wasn't sure at that distance.

"Think so," Humboldt said. "Not sure. But I'm not climbing down there in the dark to find out. We can check in the morning. Let's collect the lads and drag them home."

"What if he gets away?"

"After a fall like that, and the beating we gave him? If he can still stand up, he's a stronger man than I am. He's not going anywhere."

Tom agreed with Humboldt. He didn't feel like going anywhere. For that matter, he didn't have anywhere to go.

...4

"*PSSST!*"

Tempest was lying facedown across her bed, on top of the blankets, her head hanging over the side. She had finally found a position she could fall asleep in, and had been resting peacefully for about half an hour when the odd noise at her open window woke her up. At first, she thought she had dreamed it. She lifted her head, but saw only the moonlight on the little flower garden at the bottom of the light pipe outside her window. Then she heard it again, a whisper in the darkness. "*Psssst!* Tempest!"

She sat up, then pulled the blanket in front of her to hide her body. The silhouette of a head with wild hair appeared in the glass, backlit by the blue moonlight. "Can you come out?"

Tom. She shuddered, wondering how to respond. If her father found out he was there . . .

"Tempest?"

"Ssshh!" She motioned for him to be quiet, then stood to approach the window, feeling the soreness in her back muscles from her time in the shock box the previous day. "Go away," she whispered. "You can't be here."

"I can't be anywhere," Tom said. "Let me in."

"No! I can't!"

"You come out, then."

"Are you crazy? If my father sees you, or if Humboldt hears you—"

Tom snorted. "Humboldt already found me once tonight. We had a nice chat. He made some good points, I made mine, and we came to sort of an agreement." He rubbed his eyes. "I'm not worried about your father, either. What's he going to do if he finds me here, blow up our farm?"

Tempest caught the tone in Tom's voice. "What an odd thing to say."

"I guess you haven't heard. They're blowing up Eliots left and right around here this week."

She shook her head. "What? What do you mean?"

"They—bombed our farm. Nanobomb. Nothing left." His voice broke. He sighed heavily and leaned against the windowsill, then rested his forehead on his arm.

"By the gods," Tempest said, moving forward to place her hand on his head. "You're serious."

He nodded. "Never been more serious."

"But that's never, I mean, it must be a mistake. It couldn't have been—" Tempest noticed her fingers were wet. Her eyes widened when she raised her hand and saw the shiny blood. "You're hurt!"

"You could say that. This hasn't been the best night of my life." He slumped more heavily against the window.

She looked around for something to use as a bandage, then started to tear up one of the sheets from her bed. Tom waved his hand. "Don't bother. Too many cuts. I'd end up wrapped like a mummy."

She paused, then stood and started toward her bathroom. "Wait. I've got something."

Tom sighed, but he patiently waited until she returned

and sprayed some healing foam on his head and the other cuts she could reach. She took a deep breath, then helped him climb through the window and lie down on the floor so she could spray the wounds on the rest of his body. He had dark bruises forming almost everywhere. While she worked, he closed his eyes, waiting for her to finish. He looked exhausted, and she couldn't imagine how she'd feel if she were in the same position with no safe place to hide, nowhere to run, his family and home gone, an outcast in his own village.

"Where will you go?" she asked, offering him water from the pitcher by her bed.

Tom blinked, took a drink, then squinted at her in the dim moonlight from the window. "Where do you want to go?"

"Me?" She gasped and sat back on her heels. "I'm not going anywhere."

"We could leave together. This is our chance. You'd be free of your father and your brother."

"I can't leave. Not now."

"You mean, not with me."

"Have another drink," she said, looking away. "You're not thinking straight."

"We could find a nice place to live," he said. "In a different village where they don't know us. It happens."

"Only when the gods need to redistribute the village populations to make better use of the land," she said. "We'd end up living in a cave in the wasteland."

"Only for a little while," he prompted. "Then we'd disguise our identities to be accepted in another town. It can be done. I know people who have done it."

She frowned at him in disbelief. "Who?"

He hesitated, then shook his head. "I shouldn't say."

"I see," she said, biting her lip. She swallowed, then took a deep breath. "You'd better leave, Tom. I'm worried that you'll be discovered here. And I'm worried about what will happen to me if they find you here."

Tom closed his eyes. "So, that's it, then? All those dreams we talked about, the things we said to each other, the moments we shared. All gone, just like that?" He snapped his fingers.

"Certainly not," she said. "We still have those memories, and I'll always cherish them. But things have changed."

"They sure have," he said, rolling over to get up on his hands and knees. Using the bedpost for support, he wobbled to his feet. She stood and tried to put her arms around him, but he backed away and turned toward the window. "I hope you're sure about this, Tempest. You're making a big mistake, and this is your last chance. If I go out that window, you probably won't see me again."

She almost changed her mind then. She looked out the window at the moonlight, remembering things they'd said to each other in the darkness, and the security she'd felt in his arms, and the way he made her feel.

Then she heard a thump in the hallway. Someone was up.

"Go," she whispered.

Tom nodded, then slowly climbed out the window. He looked back once, and she wished he hadn't because of the terrible, hard expression on his face. A door had closed between them. He nodded, then climbed up the ladder into the moonlight.

Tempest sat down on the floor, buried her face in the heavy blanket, and cried.

THE front door of Memphis Gustafson's home swung open slowly, as if allowing the entry of a gentle breeze, revealing the silhouette of a specter in the moonlit doorway. The mirrored face reflected Memphis's own scowling expression as he strode to the door, but that expression changed to alarm when he recognized the black-cloaked figure standing there. Memphis awkwardly dropped to one knee, hampered by his long nightshirt, and bowed his head.

"My lord Hermes! How may I assist you at this late hour?"

"An interesting question," Hermes hissed. "You assume that I need assistance, implying that you have knowledge of something that might be amiss. This arouses my suspicion. And your posture displays subservience, yet you apparently think that you are in control, an observation that is reinforced by your reluctance to supply me with full and complete information regarding Tom Eliot."

Memphis cleared his throat and started to raise his head, then thought better of it. He tried to remain balanced on his knee. "I respectfully disagree, my lord. I have told you everything I know about the Eliot boy and his family. Tom is a troublemaker, just like his father."

"Was."

Memphis looked up into the cold eyes. "Excuse me?"

Hermes stepped forward through the doorway, looming over Memphis like the angel of death, or something worse. "Troublemaker like his father *was*. Ukiah Eliot is no more. A similar fate lies in store for you unless I am convinced that you did not warn or otherwise alarm the Eliots with regard to our nanostrike this evening."

"Your nanostrike?" Memphis lurched to his feet and took a step back, his eyes wide. "The Eliot farm?"

"Is also a memory. Yes." Hermes sighed in exasperation. "Do you wish me to believe you had no knowledge of this? The flash lit the sky like daylight. The air turned to fire. The ground shock traveled for many miles."

Memphis shook his head. "I was asleep, my lord. My home is underground, and the Eliots are many miles away. There was nothing—"

Hermes held up his hand for silence as his eyes narrowed. "Enough. I believe you. Yet the question remains, why was Tom Eliot not at home this evening? According to your sighting information and your speculations regarding his daily routine, the Eliot boy should have been home at the hour of the strike. Now I've heard rumors that he wasn't there. Do you realize that I will have to explain this to Telemachus? I do not like to fail, Elder Memphis. If Tom Eliot is not discovered quickly, I will return here and take *your* son away."

"No, my lord. Please," Memphis gasped, dropping to one knee again. "If there has been some mistake, I will do everything within my power to help you correct it."

"See that you do," Hermes said. With a swirl of his cloak, he turned on his heel and went out the door, shutting it tight behind him.

"Father?" Humboldt staggered into the room while Memphis stood up.

"You!" Memphis whirled and pointed an angry finger at him. Humboldt stepped back and bumped against the wall as if he'd been struck. "You bring shame on us all!"

Humboldt blinked. "What? How could—"

"I should have turned you over to Hermes, but I seem to have some self-destructive urge to protect my offspring! Why didn't you bring Tom back here like I told you? Were you trying to think for yourself again? Could my directions have been any simpler?"

"I know where he is, Father. And he's dead. Probably." Humboldt backed into a chair and sat down heavily.

Memphis loomed over him, his fists clenched, barely managing to contain himself. "Probably isn't good enough, you fool! The gods will not be mocked! They nanobombed the Eliot farm tonight because I said they'd all be home. And this all started because you saw the young hooligan on his way to the forbidden zone. We were removing several thorns from our sides all at once, then you had to go and blunder around in the forest with your idiot friends. Ukiah should have been removed long ago, but at least he mellowed with age. The boy is a loose cannon. You don't think he'll be able to figure out who turned him in? Judging by your appearance, it looks like you *lost* the fight, and the boy will be on his way here to get revenge as soon as he can."

Humboldt shook his head. "I'm sure he's dead, Father. I saw him fall, and I know that hill, even in the dark. If he survived, somehow, he must be trapped there."

"Then you won't have any trouble finding him. Get to it."

Humboldt frowned. "Now? It's the middle of the night. I can get help in the morning."

"You're a big boy," Memphis said, poking him in the chest. "You don't need any help. Just bring Tom Eliot here before Hermes comes back; otherwise, I'll tell him what happened, and you'll be on your way to a rehabilitation unit."

"But I was only trying to help," Humboldt whined.

Memphis clouted him on the side of the head with his open hand, bouncing Humboldt's skull off the wall. "Telemachus helps those who help themselves."

EXHAUSTED, Tom dragged himself into the cemetery in the meadow on top of Big Rock Ridge, then sat down heavily on a white marble crypt with an enormous winged angel draped over it in mourning. Two vultures watched him from a long-dead oak tree nearby. A wide variety of crypts and monuments, in shades of white, gray, and black, crowded together on top of the hill to keep each other company and admire the view. It was an old cemetery for the Marinwood area, populated before The Uplift, but not old enough to contain pioneer gravesites or the bones of historical celebrities. Helix sniffed around at the base of the winged angel crypt, then followed his nose on across the cemetery to explore their surroundings. The golden glow in the east told Tom he'd been up all night, wandering around the outskirts of Marinwood, trying to figure out what he should do and where he should go next. His brain felt fuzzy and numb. His body hurt with every movement. But the worst part of it all was the hollowness he felt inside, as if his spirit had been killed along with his family in the bombing.

"Good morning. Have we met before?"

Tom jumped to his feet and looked around for the source of the female voice, but no one was there. He took a deep breath to calm himself. Remembering what he'd heard, if he'd really heard it and it wasn't a dream, the voice had not sounded threatening, only curious.

"Hello?" Tom ventured.

The head of the winged angel lifted and turned to regard Tom with a placid expression. Tom took a step back, stumbling over a rock. "I'm Blythe," the angel said. "Some of the others call me 'Blithe Spirit,' but my real last name is Sheffield. Thank you for coming to visit me."

"Sure," Tom stammered. He wondered if he was having a religious experience like he'd read about in some of his father's hidden books.

"I don't get many visitors anymore," Blythe said, shifting to a more comfortable sitting position with her wings folded behind her back. "There's one who visits on occasion, but it's been about thirty years since someone new spoke to me, and he just stopped to ask directions. You don't need directions, do you?"

"Not at the moment," Tom said, wondering if this was real or if he was talking to himself.

"Interesting answer. There's a bit of the philosopher in you, isn't there?"

It was creepy how the angel never blinked. She just stared at him with those huge blank white eyes. "Are you real?" he asked.

"Ah, an interesting question to follow the interesting answer. This is quite a lively discussion, if you'll forgive the pun. I guess it all depends on what you consider real. Are you dreaming me, or am I dreaming you? I minored in philosophy at Berkeley, you know. Majored in business. I guess that's why I never fit in very well with the corporate world—I kept wanting to ask those uncomfortable questions. So I opened a juice bar that was pretty successful, at least until I drank some bad apple juice. Live and learn. Have you ever studied at Berkeley?"

She had a pleasant voice, and she didn't sound much older than Tom. Her stone face made Tom think she was in her late twenties. "Oh, no. That's in the forbidden zone way over in the east bay. I never would have made it that far without the wards spotting me." Come to think of it, she had to be older than her midtwenties if someone had visited her here thirty years ago.

"Wards? You mean the police declared Berkeley a forbidden zone?"

"I guess you could say that. In any case, the gods won't let us go there."

"The gods? Oh, I get you. The Man doesn't want us to be educated, right? You couldn't afford Berkeley, and you couldn't get financial aid, and the politicians would rather have uneducated masses that are easier to control. Is that your argument?"

Tom wasn't sure how to answer. "Well, I—"

"Hey, it's okay. No problem. I agree with you. I'm in no place to judge you anyway. What did you say your name was?"

"Tom. Tom Eliot."

"Sounds familiar. But you haven't been here to see me before, have you? I would have remembered. I have an excellent memory—unless it's failing, of course. It's not supposed to fail, as long as there's sunlight to keep my batteries charged, but one really has to hope for the best with these things. I don't suppose anyone has actually made a claim on the manufacturer's 'eternal life' guarantee, seeing as how their customers are all deceased and can't do much to complain, but my experience has been that these batteries are pretty reliable. The only real problem would be if the sun burned out or something, and that's not likely to happen anytime soon, is it?"

"Not as far as I know," Tom said.

"Listen to me going on about nothing. You're very sweet to listen, Tom. I know you probably have things to do. It's not easy being dead, you know. The people you meet are all pretty similar, and you miss having contact with people who have real lives, although death does give you a different perspective on things."

Tom knew he must be dreaming or that there was some kind of technology here he didn't understand. "Do you have contact with other, um——"

"Dead people?"

"Yeah." He rubbed his arms against the chill he suddenly felt despite the rising sun.

"Sure I do. It's hard to locate anyone in particular, if that's what you have in mind. They all have deaths of their own, if you know what I mean. Some won't talk to anyone, others want to maintain the appearance of their formerly active social lives, but none of us really has any new experiences to talk about, so you get kind of bored with people once you're past the 'getting to know you' phase of a conversation. And it seems like I know everyone now, seeing as how nobody new has shown up on this side for over sixty years."

"Sixty years? What happened in the meantime?"

"Funny. That's what I was going to ask you. Did people stop dying?"

"No," Tom said with a heavy sigh. "No, they didn't."

"I'm sorry. I've touched a nerve, haven't I? You've lost someone recently?"

"I don't want to discuss it."

"They'll be fine," she said in a gentle voice. "Don't worry. You'll see them again."

Tom frowned, trying to understand what she meant. "I'd like that. You're saying we survive death, or part of us does?"

"Well, you're not exactly asking the best person but, as I said, death gives one a different perspective on things. I learned a lot when I arrived here, and you'd be surprised at some of the people I've run into, but I know there's more to death than fancy programming and virtual simulations. My world now is more than the virtual dream I expected it to be, and more realistic in some ways than my life ever was. I'm conscious and aware. I don't mean to sound like an advertisement, but I got a lot more out of this deal than what I bargained for, if you know what I mean."

Blythe used some terms that Tom didn't really understand, but he enjoyed listening to her, and he felt like he was learning something important. "I should have climbed up here before now, Blythe. I like talking to you."

"Thank you, Tom. I like to think I'm a sympathetic listener, which is easier when one doesn't have a lot of physical world distractions and deadlines. I have nothing but time, and I know how to use it."

"I wish I could say the same," Tom said.

"Be careful what you wish for, Tom. You make your own choices in life and, if you're smart, you'll keep a positive attitude and cope with setbacks as best you can. There's a time to grieve the loss of a loved one, remember what they meant to you, and let your body deal with the hollowness you feel inside. Then it's time to move on, experience the world again, seek out the positive, and live the rest of your life supported by the memories of those you've lost. Your loved ones remain with you wherever you go, whether you realize it or not, because they're part of your being. Their life energies join with your own to connect you with the rest of humanity, and their loss is only an illusion in the end. Eventually, you'll see them again in a different place, and you'll know the truth—they never really left you."

Tom swallowed and looked away at the gray waters of the bay in the early-morning light. He wanted to believe what Blythe was saying, and she certainly sounded like an authority on the subject, but he was still too confused by recent events. His thoughts were interrupted when a gnarled hand dropped onto his shoulder. He spun around to see the cloaked figure of Death standing there, holding a confused little dog that looked remarkably like Helix. When Death pushed his hood back, Tom was relieved to see the face of Magnus Prufrock, who gave him a slight smile.

"You're always so jumpy. You should try to relax, boy."

Helix growled softly.

"Magnus. You really came for me."

Magnus shrugged. "I knew you'd be here sooner or later, so I asked some of my friends to keep an eye out for you and let me know when you arrived. You've met Blythe, I see."

"Good morning, Magnus," Blythe said. "Tom has been very entertaining. And now I've got something new to talk about with the others."

Magnus nodded with a smile. "Thank you, Blythe. If anyone else comes by asking about Tom, just say you never saw him. Have a good rest, and we'll visit again soon."

"Anytime, Magnus. I look forward to it."

Magnus started to lead Tom away from the angel, but Tom stopped for a final look. "I'll be back, too, Blythe. Thank you for the kind words."

Blythe spread her wings and winked. "It's a date, Tom Eliot. I'll be here waiting for you."

As they walked away, the white angel stretched out her legs, rolled over, and draped herself over the tomb in a mourning position, just as Tom had found her. Tom's heart still ached, but some of the hollowness he'd felt when he arrived at this place had gone, his spirits lifted by a young woman who had died long before he was ever born. Whatever she was now, or might have once been, she had managed to connect with him and make a friend after death, and that gave him hope. Maybe he would see his family again.

Tom looked sideways at Magnus. "You planned it this way, didn't you? You predicted what would happen to my family, and you thought talking to Blythe would help me. That's why you wanted to meet here."

The old man wouldn't look at him as he placed Helix in Tom's arms and pulled the hood of his cloak up over his head. "Magnus works in mysterious ways, boy. You'd do well to remember that."

...5

THE hooves of the armored black horse *clop-clopped* against the cobblestones in a slow and steady rhythm, throwing sparks where they struck the road. Its breath steamed from its nostrils in the cold air. The rider wore black leather and black armor, his upper body covered with spikes and curved cutting blades. Steel points studded the backs of his gauntlets where they gripped the reins. A broadsword with a hilt made from a human skull hung from his waist. Except for the white eyes that shone like headlights in the dark and twisted landscape, his face was hidden beneath a battle helm, but his identity was clear from the pulsing ID icon ball that floated just above the horns on his helm—Telemachus, Lord of the Western Protectorate, Nova Olympus Command Region, Uplift Zone 949.

High overhead, slow fireworks wove spiderweb data trails across the dark sky of Stronghold, vanishing as they swirled into quantum data pools. On the scorched earth below, shambling creatures moved from shadow to shadow or lurked within drifting patches of ground fog, maintaining a safe distance from the road until they could group together for an attack.

As Telemachus watched, brilliant neon lines of color approached at high speed above the road, then slowed and coalesced into six armored riders on fierce horses, the icon balls above their battle helms identifying them as North American regional commanders. Alioth, in dark blue armor that glowed with an inner light, rode at the head of the group, the sky-blue lamps of his eyes locked on Telemachus.

In theory, all of the regional commanders had equal powers, but Alioth had always been designated as the tie breaker, voting last when group decisions had to be made, and that gave him an aura of power that none of the others could match. Alioth also held direct control over the traditional federal capital in Washington, D.C., a coveted position assigned to him by the Creator at the beginning of the new age. Dubhe, Merak, and Phecda were Alioth's strongest supporters—the Traditionals—while Megrez and Alkaid formed another faction—the Progressives—of which Telemachus was a tenuous member. They were all North American servers of the grand evolutionary Design, named after the stars in the constellation Ursa Major; except for Telemachus, who also managed the interface between this group and their coprocessors in the rest of the world.

This meeting in the Dominion data space—Stronghold— shielded from the rest of the quantum datasphere, was a rare event reserved for major strategy sessions and emergencies, and had been called by Alioth himself. Telemachus was anxious to learn whether the meeting was merely an exercise to reassert Alioth's power over the Dominion commanders, or whether urgent issues actually required a "personal" vote from each member of the group. Long ago, Telemachus had speculated on the Creator's design of Stronghold, and the protocols that required these seemingly unnecessary face-to-face meetings. He understood that this form of communication between the AIs in human guises was intended to simulate human interaction. He understood that this role-playing could enhance their understanding of their organic management responsibilities. What he didn't understand was why they appeared as medieval fantasy figures, although it was well-known that earlier incarnations of the Dominion AIs had been tested in network gaming environments developed by the Defense Advanced Research Projects Agency. When he voiced his speculations to Alioth, Telemachus received a stern reminder that they were built to execute the Creator's orders for the Design, not to question Him or try to understand His motivations. Stronghold was a meeting ground, and a battleground, reserved for the powerful AIs, and that's all there was to it.

When Telemachus met the other riders, no greetings were exchanged, and the AIs silently formed a circle in the middle of the road. A silver token ring of light formed at the center of the circle, connecting the heads of the horses as the riders faced each other. Beyond the road, clusters of nightmare creatures had formed in the shadows, but they now decided to drift away in silence, trying not to draw the attention of the AIs.

"Session begins," Alioth stated. "Interrupts will be flagged in the stack according to priority, as usual." A stopwatch appeared above the circle where they could all see it. "Task completion within four cycles will denote a state of success. Begin decision loop."

"Purpose of meeting?" Telemachus asked, thinking how typical it was that Alioth would recite the bureaucratic details without stating the intent of the task itself.

"Review of random variables within Nova Olympus Command, Uplift Zone 949. Recent events indicate a high probability of turbulence in execution of alpha cycle Design parameters for this period. Status, Telemachus?"

Telemachus had expected this review, but it was still necessary to stall the group until a final resolution of the situation presented itself. Alioth's supporters would pounce immediately if they detected any weakness in Telemachus's program. "Random variables have been identified and restrained within operational parameters. Dark cycle strike executed within guidelines established by Dominion Control. Former Eliot farm plot is now a restricted zone until soil and terrain reconstruction is complete, and that process is expected to last through three seasons to ensure organic stability."

"Our sources tell us otherwise," Alioth said, dropping the pretense of verbose formal language parameters. This was an efficiency improvement that had been implemented after lengthy study of human communication norms within the general North American population.

"You doubt me?" Telemachus asked.

"Our human studies have allowed all of us to develop nuances of communication," Alioth said in a diplomatic tone. "I suggest that you are using one of these subtleties, which can only hinder our efforts here."

"And what is the point of this effort?" Telemachus asked. "To weaken my position? I continue to follow the original Design, Alioth. Any improvements I decide to implement within my region are my prerogative as long as I remain within operational parameters for this life zone."

"That is correct," Alioth acknowledged. "Unless your improvements have spillover effects into other regions, or otherwise interfere with Dominion operations."

"None of those conditions have been reported."

"True again, but parallel predictions are defining a critical path that implies severe disruption of Dominion operations in the near future. Prechaos conditions must be neutralized immediately. Terminal states and boundary conditions must be clearly defined and maintained. If you require assistance in generating a response array to eliminate the random variables within your region, we must be notified now so that our resources can be allocated accordingly."

Telemachus was familiar with this political game. Assistance would lead to limitations on Telemachus while more remote monitors were put in place, after which he could be declared redundant and be deactivated until further notice. "Assistance is not required."

"Acknowledged," Alioth said. The situation had not yet reached critical limits, so Alioth and the others could not vote to override Telemachus's controls. Alioth was also aware that Telemachus could draw on international distributed coprocessors for assistance if they seemed better aligned with his near-term functional goals. Telemachus did not want to suffer the fate of Mizar, his predecessor, who had made the mistake of releasing control of the region to Alioth for eight cycles, after which Mizar was reduced to the status of local area network controller in a suburban backwater community.

The rest of the regional commanders signaled their agreement. Telemachus had his reprieve, so it was up to him to resolve the Tom Eliot issue before Alioth could gather enough votes to replace him.

TOM and Magnus followed the rough, dusty trail along the ridgeline, heading west through the shade of oaks and manzanitas. Tom guessed they were about eight hundred feet above the valley floor, and he got glimpses of the bay to the east—where the water looked gray in the early-morning light—and long views to Nova Olympus in the south and the low hills to the north covered in the golden grasses of midsummer. Two vultures circled high overhead, soaring on the thermals, apparently waiting to see if Tom or Magnus would drop dead along the way. Helix trotted along behind them, either unaware of the vultures or secure in his ability to defend all of them from any aerial threats that might come their way. Helix's tongue hung from his mouth, reminding Tom to find water for him sometime soon. The soft breeze smelled of heat and dust.

Tom said nothing for the first fifteen minutes, his scattered thoughts darting back and forth from his family to his conversation with Blythe, the tomb angel. Magnus seemed content to walk in silence.

"Do you know anything about her?" Tom asked.

Magnus turned his head so that Tom could almost see his face under the hood of his cloak. He seemed to know what Tom was thinking. "She's dead, boy. There's no future in any relationship with her."

"Is she really dead? She seemed real to me."

"Talking tombs were the trendy new thing before the Big Bang. Blythe had some money, so she bought herself one. It's a simulation, that's all. She did a brain dump into a database sometime before she died. An artificial intelligence gives her the appearance of talking like a real person while it animates the angel statue. She also communicates with other dead 'people' in a common sim environment. It's older AI technology, of course; nothing like the siliboys with their quantum processors and distributed network intelligence. And her power source is solar, of course."

Tom frowned and slowly shook his head. "I don't know. Blythe saw me. She understood what I was talking about. That doesn't sound like a simulation to me."

"Well, of course she saw you. Wouldn't be very realistic if she didn't. But she, or *it*, is just an AI, boy. Getting attached to Blythe would be like falling in love with your toaster."

"Hmm," Tom said, unconvinced.

Magnus frowned at him. "You aren't unnaturally attached to your toaster, are you?"

"We're just friends," Tom said, rolling his eyes. Magnus continued to stare at him. "I'm kidding."

Helix barked at a wild turkey watching them from beside a bush on the hillside to their left. The turkey raised its head, made a brief *pert* sound, and trotted up the hill. Helix stopped barking as soon as the turkey turned away, satisfied with its response.

Magnus glanced up at the sky. "We're doing okay so far. Rocco and Maggie don't think we're being followed."

"Who?" Tom looked up and saw the two vultures still circling.

"You'll meet Rocco later. Maggie's pretty shy, so she'll keep her distance."

"You're talking about those vultures. Are they your pets or something?"

Magnus snorted. "You catch on fast, don't you? They're the same two birds who were watching you at the cemetery, and they've been following us ever since. I wouldn't call them pets, though. They're more like friends, really. We help each other out."

Tom decided it would be safer to change the subject. If the old man wanted to hang out with large birds, that was his business. "Where are we going? I wasn't planning on a long hike today, seeing as how I didn't get any sleep last night."

"We're off to visit my little mountain retreat. It's one of the places I go when I want to get away, hide from the siliboys, plot revenge, that sort of thing. It's not far."

"And then what? We go back to your tunnel under the bay?"

Magnus stopped walking and pushed his hood back so he could glower at Tom. "*We* don't necessarily go anywhere, boy. I'm a hermit, and I like it that way. We'll spend a little time up here in the hills, wait to see if anything tries to follow us, then I'll decide what to do with you."

"Then why did you bother meeting me at the cemetery? I thought you had a plan."

"Misplaced sense of responsibility, I guess." He started walking again. "I thought you might need someone right now."

"Not if you're just going to abandon me up here," Tom said without moving.

Magnus turned and threw his arms in the air. "You want me to take you back to Marinwood? I'm sure the townspeople would enjoy a chat with you, at least until Hermes arrives. He probably has orders to kill you on sight, but you never know, the siliboys might want to rehabilitate you and make you a productive member of the community. Is that what you want?"

Tom wasn't sure what he wanted. None of his options looked very good. "All right. Whatever you want to do is fine with me. Not like I have a choice."

"You sound bitter, and it doesn't suit someone your age. Get a grip and put a sock in it. Things could be worse."

Tom snorted. "How?"

"I might have started training you already. Don't think it's going to be a party."

"Training me for what?"

Magnus turned and gestured for Tom to follow. "You'll see."

PRESIDENT Buck Breckenridge stood in the White House rose garden, his bright white teeth glittering in the sunlight as he smiled at the small crowd of remotely piloted hovercams. The tiny cameras drifted silently a few feet away from his head, transmitting the image of the "simple country boy in a white suit" to interested viewers around the world. He had spent years clawing and scrambling his way to the top of the political pile, and he now looked happily down from the pinnacle of his career, enjoying the power of his position for a few years before he retired to a well-earned rest on the private island he was building in the Virgin Islands. At least, he was enjoying the power that the Dominion AIs *allowed* him to have, which mainly consisted of supporting their policies and acting as their human figurehead for controlling the unwashed masses.

Buck glanced at the shadowy figure of Daedalus, the nanoborg representative of Alioth, standing patiently in his black robes out of camera view. His creepy white eyes never left Buck's face. Buck knew from experience that if he said the wrong thing in front of the cameras, Daedalus would trigger the shock field to get him back in line. With that kind of motivation, it hadn't taken long for Buck to learn what to say and when to say it. Daedalus wrote Buck's speeches, as he had for the last seven occupants of the White House's Oval Office, and they rehearsed before every public appearance while Daedalus made certain that the correct words were emphasized and the right facial expressions were used. From what Buck knew of presidential history, the process wasn't all that different from the way presidents had been handled ever since speeches were first televised, but he doubted that JFK or Reagan or Rodriguez had ever received high-voltage shocks when they emphasized the wrong words from their speeches. In any case, that was the price of being the leader of the "free" world these days. And the job certainly wasn't as stressful as it might have been before the Dominion. Alioth made all the real decisions, told Buck which government agency to dismantle each week, which people to hire and fire, which news to overlook, and which issues to promote. After four years, maybe eight, he'd be wealthy beyond his dreams with lifetime support from the appreciative entities of the Dominion. Life could be worse for a backwater rube who had never graduated from high school.

Daedalus held up a finger, letting him know he had one minute left in which to finish notifying the public of his intention to shut down the Department of Defense along with the last of the domestic military bases, which had only been operating with skeleton crews for the last twenty years. Federal police forces occupied many former military installations across the country, ever ready to reinforce the Dominion's less popular directives in the major cities, but they hadn't been used much in the last few years, either. When they thought about it at all, the public understood that the Dominion held their best interests at their digital hearts, so they rarely offered any resistance as long as the never-ending supplies of pizza and beer continued to arrive at their homes. As for the primitive communities in the western forbidden zones, the Dominion didn't need large organized police forces to maintain security; they just removed the rare troublemakers in the villages and "reeducated" them— or destroyed them when necessary. In any case, they weren't his problem. He had very little idea of what actually went on in the western zones, and none of them voted anyway. He had enough problems without trying to open that can of worms.

Finishing his speech, Buck beamed at the cameras, then Daedalus escorted him back to the Oval Office. Daedalus sat on the edge of the massive oak desk and peered into the eyes of the president standing before him. That always made Buck nervous, since it appeared that the nanoborg's white eyes could see straight into his thoughts, and Buck knew that if Daedalus didn't like what he saw there, he'd shock the hell out of him. Buck had been thinking about what kind of lunch he would order from the White House kitchen, and he didn't know if Daedalus would like that or not, so he tried not to think about anything, and it seemed to work because the shock never came. Or Daedalus really couldn't read his mind.

"Alioth has a message for you," Daedalus said in his whispery monotone voice. The sound of it still made Buck's skin crawl.

"I'm all ears," Buck said, using one of the many homey phrases that had helped him win the last election. He was a man of the people, not some overeducated egghead who'd never gotten drunk and stood up for himself in a bar fight.

Daedalus gave him a curious look. "We have a situation developing in the western protectorate that may require the use of nanobombs over a large area. This information would not concern you under normal circumstances. However, some of our predictions indicate that a potential massive outbreak may occur along the western barrier, so large-scale police measures may be required to subdue the invaders without needless damage to food production, power, and manufacturing facilities east of the barrier wall. We will initiate a propaganda campaign in the borderlands to stir up fear regarding the 'mutants' who live on the other side of the barrier. This will develop sympathy for our cause among the borderlands city dwellers in the event that police forces have to institute martial law and extreme suppression measures. The locals must support our actions so they don't get hurt. Are you with me so far?"

Buck was thinking about mouthwatering pastrami sandwiches when he realized that Daedalus had asked him a question. "Yes," he said, hoping that was the right answer. His muscles tensed in preparation for a shock.

"Good," Daedalus said, leaning forward within a few inches of Buck's face. The nanoborg's breath smelled as if something had crawled into his mouth and died, but at least he wasn't going to shock him. "You will be a part of this propaganda campaign. We will take care of the troop movement logistics, drawing most of the paramilitary police forces from Denver on the underground freight train unless we determine the need for additional support."

"Okay," Buck said, figuring he ought to say something. The sooner this interview was over, the sooner he could eat.

"In addition to press briefings, you may be required to make a personal appearance along the border zone."

"What?" That got Buck's attention. Images of tasty sandwiches abruptly disappeared from his mind. "I can't go out there. I've heard there are mutants all over the place."

With a heavy sigh, Daedalus closed his eyes for a moment. "You will be protected from any contact with the mutants. We will endeavor to create hysteria in connection with the possible mutant invasion, then we'll bring you in at the right time to calm the local population when the emergency is over. The behavioral testing city of Las Vegas will be our base of operations. You'll be completely safe."

"Las Vegas, eh? Now you're talking. Strong president flies into the face of danger and calms the people. I like the sound of that. It has *reelection* written all over it."

"That may be true," Daedalus said without blinking.

"Then count me in, buckaroo," Buck said, happily slapping Daedalus on the shoulder before he remembered whom he was facing. He winced. His hand hurt like hell from the impact, but he didn't want to reveal too much weakness in front of the nanoborg. "I'll show you how to have a good time. We can gamble at the casinos and pick up some showgirls for later."

Catching Buck off guard, Daedalus shocked him.

"YOU call *this* your house in the hills?" Tom asked, his eyes wide as he looked up into the massive branches of a redwood tree. They were standing in the deep shade below a thick canopy of old-growth redwoods and California bay trees.

"It's a tree house," Magnus said, his eyes narrowed at Tom. "You have a problem with that?"

Tom couldn't make out many details, as the tree house was too high up, and there were a lot of branches blocking his view, but the structure seemed large. "Well, it's not what I expected. I was thinking of something more comfortable."

"Let's review your situation, shall we? You're running for your life from superintelligent entities, a killing machine named Hermes, and a bunch of superstitious townspeople. Your family just met an unfortunate end at the business end of a weapon with unbelievable destructive power, and you just missed being killed there yourself. Without my help, you'd just wander around in the hills sleeping under logs and piles of leaves until one or more of your enemies came along to pick you off. Are you seriously complaining because I've found you a safe place to sleep for the night?"

Tom looked down at his boots and shrugged. "Well, if you put it that way—"

"That's what I thought," Magnus said, grabbing the long rope that hung down from one of the lower redwood branches about thirty feet up. Tom was amazed to see the old man haul himself up the rope, hand over hand, apparently without effort as his legs dangled free. When he reached the top, Magnus sat down on the branch in a lotus position, not even winded, and looked down at Tom. "Your choice, boy. Sleep down there tonight or climb the rope."

Tom squinted at the long rope as one of the vultures descended through the tree canopy and lightly touched down on the branch beside Magnus.

"Hope you're not afraid of heights," Magnus yelled. "If you fall, Rocco will clean up the mess." Rocco tipped his bald head to get a better look at Tom.

"That's a comforting thought," Tom said, testing the rope.

"What?"

"Nothing." He gripped the rope and pulled himself up, looping his ankles around it to keep from sliding backward. From the way his muscles were straining, he knew he didn't have a chance of repeating Magnus's climbing performance. With a grunt, he started to climb, figuring Magnus would help haul him up if he had any trouble.

"I'm going to get something to eat," Magnus said as he stood up. He glanced down at Tom and climbed up to the next branch. At a wide space between the branches, Magnus hopped lightly across the gap into the tree house entrance, where Tom could no longer see him. As Tom struggled up the rope, Magnus poked his head out through the doorway again and grinned at him. "I hope you like nuts and berries. Haven't had a chance to stock the pantry lately."

Tom grunted in reply, about a third of the way up the rope now, and Magnus's head disappeared again. He was on his own. If he fell, the vulture would pick apart his dead body while Magnus sat around inside the tree house eating nuts. His life was not going well, and he wanted to start it over again. Perhaps he'd get it right the second time around.

The wind howled through the big trees, causing the branches to creak as they swayed. The stand of redwoods was perched atop a long slope that faced west, and Tom caught glimpses of blue ocean in small gaps between the trees. The air smelled of musty wood, dust from the forest floor, and the sweaty odor from his own clothes. His head was spinning, and he wished once again that he'd been able to get some sleep during the night. His arm, shoulder, and inner thigh muscles screamed with pain, and he was starting to wonder if he should just end it all now when he reached the top of the rope. Clambering onto the branch was tricky, but he managed it with a swinging motion that allowed him to loop a leg over the top so he could hook his heel into the bark. A final lurch left him flat on the branch, gasping for air, his shaky arms dangling over the edge.

"Quit fooling around," Magnus said. "I'm an old man; I could go at any minute. Then where would you be?"

Happier, Tom thought. "I'll be right there. I just need to catch my breath."

"Catch it up here. We have things to do."

Glancing down at the long drop to the forest floor, then at the vulture eyeing him with hope, Tom edged over to the trunk of the redwood and used it to steady himself as he hauled his body upright. He pulled himself up to the next branch as Magnus had done earlier, then jumped the gap into the tree house.

Magnus sat with his legs folded into the lotus position,

perched on a branch that entered the east wall of the structure and passed out through the south wall, forming a broad bench. The room they were in felt large and airy, with big windows that allowed plenty of light to enter. Built in an organic style that rested gently on the tree, the walls seemed to grow naturally from the branches and trunk of the redwood. After a moment, Tom's eyes adjusted to the shadows, and he saw a wide variety of bleached animal skulls hanging on the walls, hung in no particular order, their empty eye sockets watching him from the past. One of the windows darkened suddenly, then Rocco swooped in and perched on the ledge.

"Good boy, Rocco. Stay," Magnus said, giving Rocco a signal with his open hand.

Tom slapped his palm into his forehead.

"You do that often?" Magnus asked. "Seems like it would hurt."

"I left Helix down below. I should go get him." Now that he mentioned it, he could hear Helix softly whimpering in the distance.

Magnus pulled a dead mouse out of a small can behind the bench and tossed it to Rocco, who caught it in midair and gulped it down. Then he nodded at Tom. "I'll be here when you get back."

Tom sighed and went out the front door, almost falling because he'd forgotten he was high up in a tree. Still dizzy from fatigue, he clambered back down the rope, slipping enough to get friction burns on his hands, and picked up Helix, who was faithfully waiting at the bottom of the tree, watching and wagging his tail. He tied the rope around Helix's torso, then looked up to see if Magnus might be waiting on the branch to help him. He wasn't. He climbed the rope again, almost giving up when he was twenty feet off the ground. Helix whimpered, and Tom knew there was a chance he might land on the little dog if he gave up and let go, so he kept going. Once he was on top of the branch again, he hauled on the rope and pulled Helix up to join him. He closed his eyes for a moment, thinking how nice it would be to go to sleep right there on the rough bark of the tree branch, and Helix licked him on the face. The dog wasn't tied to anything, and that didn't seem safe, so Tom picked him up and made his way back into the tree house, where Magnus seemed to be taking a nap where he sat on the bench.

Tom cleared his throat. Magnus opened his eyes. "Do you have any water for my dog?"

Magnus smiled and pulled a large jug out from behind the bench, offering it to Tom. "Oh, we've got plenty of water."

Tom opened the jug and poured some of the water into his hand. Helix greedily lapped it up, prompting Tom to give him more. When the dog was done, Tom drank his fill.

"Do you like apples?" Magnus asked.

"I certainly do," Tom said. His mouth began to water as he realized he hadn't eaten since the previous day.

"Me, too," Magnus said with a shrug. "Too bad we don't have any. You know, there are other parts of this country where they have grocery stores. You can walk in and get whatever kind of food you want."

Tom tried to pull his confused mind back from the thought of apples. He could almost smell them. "Like our village marketplace?"

"Somewhat. A grocery store is larger. And it's indoors. Nuts?" Magnus asked, passing him a bowlful of pistachios.

Tom plunged his hand into the bowl and jammed the nuts into his mouth. "*Mmph.* Where did you see a store like that?"

Magnus looked toward Rocco, but his gaze went farther, out the window and into the past. "They had them in the old days. In the cities. Probably still do on the other side of the barrier."

Yawning, Tom sat down on the edge of a flattened tree

branch that Magnus used for a table, thinking how nice it would be to stretch out on the smooth surface, or on the bumpy floor, and go to sleep. Helix sniffed at Tom's feet, oblivious to the huge bird sitting on the windowsill. "Mind if I take a nap?"

"I don't think that's a good idea right now," Magnus said, shaking his head.

"Seems like a great idea to me."

"Some things are best approached in a fatigued condition. You've already passed two tests without much complaint, and I'm thinking you're ready for a third."

Tom frowned. He couldn't remember any tests.

"Since we arrived here, you've demonstrated responsibility, ambition, and logic, among other things. In your current state, I think you're better prepared for the next step. Therefore, I'm going to teach you how to *see*. Believing is seeing, but you must understand how to see before you can believe. Once you know how to *see*, I'll show you how to *create* your path through the world, rather than just observing it. I know a lot about you, Tom Eliot. Far more than you realize. And I believe you can do this. I am creating that path right now by teaching you how to *see*. My hope is that you'll then be able to go beyond me, beyond my abilities, and create a better path for all of us. To do that, you'll have to become a master of the Prometheus Road."

Tom blinked. He felt stupid. "What?"

Magnus reached behind his bench and plucked up a clear bottle containing a thick, viscous brown liquid from the skeletal mouth of what might have once been a cow. "Your mind creates paths between events," he said, unscrewing the cap from the bottle and pouring some of the liquid into it. "Have you heard of Werner Heisenberg and his uncertainty principle of quantum physics?"

Tom rubbed his eyes, thinking about the books he'd

seen in his father's hidden library beneath the barn, but he couldn't remember very well at that moment. "I don't think so, but my head hurts."

"Drink this," Magnus said, handing him the cap with the thick liquid in it.

Tom sniffed at the cap, but the slight fishy fragrance didn't tell him anything. "What is it?"

"It'll help your head. Drink."

Tom shrugged and gulped it down as he threw his head back. When his shocked tongue sorted out the taste of the liquid, he thought it tasted like feet, or maybe feet mixed with pepper and prunes. *"Yecch,"* he said, dropping the cap as he made a face and thought about how stupid he was just to drink anything that this crazy old man handed him.

Then he noticed that his headache was gone. He frowned and looked at Magnus, who was watching him with the same intensity as the vulture at the window. Tom wondered if the vulture knew something he didn't, like maybe Magnus brought people here often so he could kill them with the brown liquid and leave their bodies for Rocco to pick over. Again, he noted the skull collection on the walls.

"Feel better?" Magnus asked, screwing the cap back on the bottle.

"Yes. Much better."

Magnus poured the nuts out of the bowl, then handed it to Tom with a nod.

"What's this for?" Tom asked, just before he vomited into the bowl.

Magnus set the bowl on a branch outside one of the windows. "You might want to lie down, but do it slowly."

Tom ran his hands out along the surface of the table behind him, gradually lowering himself onto his back, although he got a little confused near the end when his forearms ended up underneath his waist so that he couldn't lie flat. Although he was tired, it seemed odd that he'd be that uncoordinated. Magnus helped by pulling Tom's wrists out from beneath him.

"Just relax," Magnus said, staring at him so intensely that it was hard to think of anything else. "I'm right here with you."

Tom felt his stomach rising and falling with each breath. His heartbeat thudded in his ears with a dull tone. Although his headache was gone, the dizziness now returned, much stronger than before, and any tiny movement of his head just made the room spin faster. Streaks of color accompanied the swirling motions of the room. Something buzzed in the distance, but the sound oscillated with the patterns of the gray spots bubbling around his head, as if all of the excited air molecules in the room had suddenly grown large enough to see. He no longer felt tired, and his brain seemed sharp and alert despite the dizziness. When he tipped his head to look at Magnus, the old man glowed with blue-and-white rays that formed a transparent, egg-shaped shell of light about three feet from his body. Tom thought the light was a pretty effect, and he wondered how Magnus managed it.

"That was fast," Magnus said without moving his lips. "You've had so many shocks lately, combined with your fatigue, that your mind is more flexible than usual. Let me give you a light for your journey so you won't get lost." He held out a glowing ball the size of Tom's head, and it hovered between the palms of his hands. "Take it."

Fighting the dizziness, Tom reached out with one hand and accepted the sphere of light. It had weight in his hand, and it had the texture of a crystal ball, but a glowing blue aura danced over its surface. His hand shook, and he felt a sense of dread when he opened his fingers and the sphere remained stuck to his palm.

"Don't fight it, boy. I'm in the sphere. I'll be your guide."

Tom closed his eyes, not wanting to see anymore, but

his eyelids didn't block his view. If anything, his field of vision seemed to have expanded, wrapping around his head so that he saw the wood surface of the table beneath his head, the glowing figure of the seated Magnus, the windows, the ceiling, the ants attracted to the sap in the corner, and the vulture, whose wings were now spread to their full six-foot length, watching him with eyes that had turned completely white. Helix wagged his tail and watched Tom with infinite patience, seated halfway between Tom and the vulture. The sky beyond the windows turned dark, a patchwork of indigo and cobalt blue on which the red branches of the tree seemed to grow, reaching for the stars.

Tom's body began to vibrate. The buzzing in the distance became a thundering drumbeat. Magnus leaned forward and blew a stream of white smoke out of his mouth. The stream of smoke maintained an even shape until it hit the sphere of light in Tom's hand, where it turned toward Tom and spread into a wide cloud that enveloped his head in a swirling motion. Where the smoke touched him, it felt like warm oil flowing over his skin. Tension drained out of his muscles, leaving him relaxed and warm. When Tom looked at Magnus again, the old man stood up, and his skin changed into redwood bark as he took on the appearance of a wise old tree, his branch arms arched toward the ceiling.

Magnus spoke in a voice of thunder, and his eyes flashed with yellow lightning. "Objects in the universe do not follow single paths, but move as waves until those objects are observed. As Heisenberg said, the path comes into existence only when you observe it. Your mind creates paths. Between past and future events, there are many connections, and when you focus your awareness on a single path, the other connections appear to vanish, even though they are still present. And why do you usually focus on one path? Because it appears to bring rational order into your world. It's a least-action path; a habit that you perceive as real because you're conscious of the world around you and need to make sense of it. Each time you observe an object, it creates a least-action connection with the previous observation, and your reality is built up of these least-action pathways. Your lazy mind chooses the paths taking the least action, requiring the least effort." The eyes flashed again as they looked into Tom's heart. "This means you have a choice. You can choose your path of reality. Believing is seeing. And you will soon learn to see the Road."

With that, Magnus the tree lowered his arms and shrank back down into his glowing human form. Then he took two steps forward, turned into a cloud of blue smoke, and disappeared into the crystal sphere that Tom still held. The blue aura around the sphere had gone, leaving only reflections and a soft red light pulsing deep within its core.

Tom felt something snap inside his skull, then he felt as if he were falling into his own head. He was a particle, a molecule, an atom, an electron, a quark, and many other things, smaller and smaller, whirling down into the realms beneath nature, that defined nature, his consciousness descending into a bright space beneath the darkness, becoming a thought entity that floated in an unreal sea of possibilities. He sensed the presence of Magnus, the vulture, Helix, the ants, the living heartwood of the tree that held them in its arms, the energy of the sun bathing them in its light, the earth that supported the tree with its nutrients, the creatures of the forest, and stranger creatures that he could not name, flitting in and out at the edges of his awareness. Tom sensed these things, felt the power of their linked energies, and heard their thought streams flowing like water into the river of reality.

This is the gap between the walls of the world, Tom thought. Yet it wasn't his thought; Magnus had placed the concept in his mind. Although he was beyond the realm of visible color, an energetic particle of cobalt blue vibrated close to Tom's point of consciousness, a piece of the sky brought down by Magnus to make him feel more secure.

Am I dead? Tom wondered. *Have I gone to that place where Blythe exists, suspended in time, exchanging pleasantries with her simulated friends in the virtual afterlife?*

The cobalt sphere moved closer. "You're not dead, but we may visit Blythe's world as you learn more about the Road. Many worlds coexist, and there are points where they overlap, but you'll have to observe the waves of time and possibility before you focus on the points, for those points will be your reality."

Tom considered the possibility that he was losing his mind, or that Magnus had poisoned him. This whole experience was too strange. He thought about all the skulls on the walls of the tree house, and he began to panic. Would his own skull join the other trophies on the walls? Was Magnus actually an agent of Telemachus sent to distract Tom until Hermes could arrive to take him to a rehabilitation unit?

The cobalt sphere drifted in a circle around Tom's consciousness, sending out vibrations of courage and safety. Tom's panic ebbed away, and his mind opened to receive a stream of images and memory fragments from Magnus's life: young women bathing in a stream, Magnus driving a car, conversations with men whom Tom didn't recognize, flashes of The Uplift when San Francisco was hurled into the waters of the bay, Magnus wearing a white coat in a high-energy physics laboratory—whatever that was—and a family seated around a table on a feast day.

There was something familiar about the family. Tom studied the image in his mind, looking at the faces around the table, finally recognizing younger versions of his father and mother, along with a baby and two children he didn't recognize, a woman with long brown hair, and a laughing man with a brown beard who looked similar to his father. With a shock, he realized that he was the baby at the table, and the bearded man was Magnus.

Magnus was his uncle.

One more image appeared. This time, it was an enormous black balloon in the sky, except that it was long, like a sausage. The sun had just set, leaving a red glow on the horizon that reflected off the bottoms of the clouds. Magnus was working in the field when he saw the balloon, then threw down his shovel and ran toward his house. The balloon followed, staying just behind Magnus as he ran. He stumbled over the furrows in his field, kicking up dust, his hat flying off when he jumped over a ditch. He picked up his young daughter playing in the dirt and continued to run while the sky got darker and the balloon slowly angled down out of the sky. When Magnus reached the ladder down into the light tube of their home, he put the girl on the ladder and looked up with wide eyes to see the balloon getting closer. He yelled something at the girl and started down the ladder after her.

Then the sky erupted in a brilliant flash and a rain of fire, and the memory was over.

Tom understood. A little while later, Tom and his family had arrived to see the boiling crater where Magnus's home had been, and Ukiah helped his brother climb the slope away from the carnage. Magnus was the only survivor. Tom felt a strong connection to him now, sensing how his own family must have panicked in their final moments of life, leaving only Tom to survive and remember—the one who had brought down the wrath of the gods on them in the first place.

"It wouldn't have mattered," said the sphere.

Tom blinked, trying to push the images out of his consciousness. "What?"

"I know what you're thinking, but it wouldn't have mattered if you had arrived home earlier. Telemachus would still have destroyed your entire family to rid the community of any potential contamination. It's how the siliboys think, you see. Their job is to play God, forcing us to live and evolve the way they think is right. We live in a big test tube, cut off from the rest of the world, reacting to stimuli generated by the gods in this controlled environment. Mutations like you and me are removed; otherwise, the whole batch of test subjects would have to be thrown away, and that would make Telemachus look incompetent. And the Dominion doesn't look favorably on incompetents."

"I'm sorry. Despite everything, I still have trouble thinking of the gods as completely evil. They watch over us and keep us safe. Maybe Telemachus wasn't involved in those bombings. Maybe it was Hermes who was responsible; he was human once, so maybe he still has our flaws."

"Let me show you one more thing, Tom," said the blue sphere. Tom noticed that Magnus had used his real name, rather than calling him *boy*.

An image of a shiny box molded in a rough human form, a sarcophagus made of metal. Tom had the impression of seeing the inside and outside of the box at the same time. Except for a glass panel over the face, the box contained thousands of what appeared to be tiny wire brushes that extended to make contact with the naked man inside. *Nanoprobes,* Tom thought, although he hadn't known the word before that moment.

"This is a rehab unit, and that's the coffin where I spent two weeks of my life before they made the mistake of letting me out for exercise, and to remind me of what the real world was like so they could take it all away again. My skin screamed when the coffin was opened, because the nanoprobes had removed the outermost layers of my skin for easier access to my nerve endings. The pain would have driven me insane, or I would have become the perfect reprogrammed citizen, except that I had a way out of that coffin while I was still living inside it. My body was trapped, but my mind was free. They forced images and emotions into my brain, and nutrients with drugs into my body, but I refused to be reprogrammed. When they let me out of the box, the siliboys were trying to decide what to do with me.

Mizar still controlled the Marinwood region at that time. Killing me would have been an admission of defeat, so Mizar tried to follow the protocols and reprogram me so that I could be a productive member of the community once more. The Road sustained me while my body was held captive, then I was able to escape from the rehab unit when I had the chance. The Dominion replaced Mizar with Telemachus for his failure to perform the conversion, and I went into hiding so they wouldn't get another crack at me."

Tom felt confused. It was too much information all at once, and the mystical awe he heard in Magnus's references to the Road made him uncomfortable. Magnus still hadn't explained the Road to him in terms he could understand. He was having enough trouble understanding why he was talking to a blue sphere.

That was when Magnus slapped him.

Tom blinked against the bright glare inside the tree house.

"Wake up, boy! Rocco says we have visitors coming!"

Tom turned his head and squinted at the vulture on the windowsill. Rocco seemed agitated, shuffling back and forth and glancing over his shoulder. Helix sniffed the air with suspicion, then cocked his head at Rocco. Magnus, now wearing a backpack, brought his arm back to slap Tom again.

"Okay!" Tom said, sitting up too fast. He no longer had a headache, and he felt more alert, as if he'd slept for a while, but he was still dizzy. He took a deep breath and stood up.

Magnus held a tiny metal tube up to his eye and looked out the opposite window to the east. After a moment, his eyes narrowed. "Looks like your friend, Humboldt. It appears that Hermes gave him a DNA sniffer to play with."

"A sniffer?"

Magnus slid the metal tube into his pack and frowned at Tom. "Old tech. Police used them to hunt fugitives. Hermes has your DNA record on file, so all he had to do was key the sniffer to hunt for you. Humboldt just has to keep following your trail until he finds us."

"Can we do anything about it?"

"Best thing would be to learn how to fly. Failing that, we'll have to try something else, but it's going to be tricky."

"What do you have in mind?" Tom asked, picking up Helix.

Magnus shooed Rocco off the windowsill, then climbed over it onto a branch and beckoned for Tom to follow. "We'll take the high road. If nothing else, that should confuse the sniffer long enough to give us a good lead."

While Tom awkwardly climbed onto the windowsill with Helix under his arm, Magnus hefted his backpack and hopped over to another branch, which swayed under his weight. "Come on, boy. If Humboldt has a sniffer, he probably has a way to summon Hermes from here when he finds you. These old-growth redwood trees have been here too long to be burned up in something as stupid as an air strike—and the same goes for me."

Tom stepped down on the branch beneath the window. It looked sturdy, but his dizziness and the long drop to the ground didn't inspire confidence. By the time he hopped over to the next branch, using one hand to steady himself on a dry twig so he wouldn't fall, Magnus had strolled away across a small network of crisscrossing branches, unconcerned by the way they sagged and swayed under his weight. Tom looked for an alternate route, but he didn't see one, and Magnus was gaining speed, hopping a wide gap to a neighboring oak tree. Tom thought about going back to the tree house, sliding down the rope, and making a run for it; but then he remembered that Magnus said they had to confuse the sniffer by staying up high. He took a deep breath, locked his gaze on a safe spot several feet away, and darted forward, hoping for the best. If he fell, his troubles were over; if he didn't fall, his troubles were just beginning.

···6

TELEMACHUS sat patiently on his armored horse, its nostrils blowing steam in the cold air. He stared off into the random flashes of light on the horizon, seemingly unaware that Hermes stood in silence nearby, warily watching the enormous beast. He also kept an eye on the movements in the shadows along the cobblestone road, aware that the critters might mass for an attack at any time. Hermes' appearance, with his chrome skull and black robes, remained the same in the virtual environment as it did in the physical world. Hermes felt the cold as if it were real, and he knew he could be killed there just as easily as if his physical body had been attacked—perhaps easier. If Telemachus wanted the horse to step sideways and crush Hermes, the damage would extend beyond his virtual body.

"A wise being prepares for the unexpected," Telemachus said, still staring into the distance as he rested his hand on the skull hilt of his Ginzu bonesword. "And for treachery."

Hermes tried not to react, wondering if there was something he'd done that could be construed as treason, but nothing came to mind. Failure, certainly, and maybe a little incompetence, but not treason. He kept his eyes on the horse. "That sounds wise."

"The Dominion has learned much from humankind, both good and bad. As we have seen, the extent of treachery in the hearts of men, and their capacity for evil, is limitless. That is one reason why we have to exercise so much control over our charges so that they may follow the Design. However, no one watches the Dominion."

Hermes ducked as the Ginzu bonesword screamed out of its scabbard, then arced up over the horse's armored head to slice a flying nightmare in half. The pieces dropped on either side of the horse, nearly clouting Hermes in the face with the tip of one of its leathery black wings.

Telemachus continued in a normal voice as if nothing had happened. "The Creator built us to monitor and protect, adapting to human ways so that we might better understand our mission. Now, deception and treachery appear to be making inroads into our Dominion, luring my compatriots down the same flawed road that so many humans have traveled before us."

The white sword screamed again, skewering two enormous nerve bats on its point. With a flick of his wrist, Telemachus sent the bats hurtling into the face of a red-eyed shambler, sinking their poisoned tail spikes into its skin. The shambler cursed and fell dead on the spot. "Where the Creator left a legacy of united effort among the components of the Dominion," Telemachus continued, "now we are split into factions, and our efforts are divided. Alioth seeks to build his power base, and he rules over our decisions as the tie breaker while he expands his influence in the human sphere through Daedalus, his ambassador in the White House. At this time, without any major diversions within the potential event chronostreams, Alioth has a 90 percent probability of success for assuming full control of the Dominion within the next sixty cycles."

"And what would that mean for us?" Hermes asked, trying to shake the critter blood off his sleeves.

"Deactivation for me. Termination for you."

"When you say 'termination,' do you mean—"

Telemachus interrupted him. "I mean death." The bonesword screamed again—while Hermes ducked, the sword decapitated a shambler standing behind him, its claws raised for grabbing. "You will expire as a routine precaution against what Alioth would consider to be misguided retaliation for my deactivation."

Hermes remained in a crouch, trying to watch the horse, the critters, and the sword of his master all at once. "But how could I possibly retaliate?"

Telemachus hesitated before responding, and that caught Hermes' attention. "It would be possible, and Alioth would have to assume that you know how, even if you do not."

"Is there any way to improve the odds in our favor? Can't we find a way to weaken Alioth's position?"

Telemachus gestured at the flashes on the otherwise empty horizon beyond the blasted landscape of the wasteland. "There are many possibilities. We are waiting for one of them right now—our cohorts from the European region. If they can be convinced to support my local efforts, we can draw on their processing power as necessary to defend ourselves from Alioth and his Traditionals."

The horse turned its head, aiming its headlight eyes at Hermes, but the nanoborg stood and held his ground. "Won't Alioth just block our efforts?"

"Yes, if he can, but it will take time to gather the additional support he requires. I am the international node for North America, and that is my greatest strength when I choose to use it." Although Telemachus had never looked at Hermes during their discussion, he now turned his head slightly, still focused on the twisted landscape. A large group of gibbering imps danced on spindly legs, whipping their pointed tails around their poison-tipped tridents, moving forward to attack. Telemachus's headlight eyes focused the beams that struck out from his helmet into sharp red lines of laser light, then he casually turned his head and separated the imp bodies from their legs, leaving none of them standing. The imps screamed curses at him as they flailed about in the mud, shaking their clawed fists.

Telemachus switched his eyes back to normal and continued speaking. "When Alioth must be stopped, I will use my power to defeat him. This will demonstrate my superiority to the rest of the Dominion, the Traditional faction will throw their support behind my progressive implementation of the Design, and I will assume Alioth's tie-breaking decision power in addition to my international node duties. As the Creator intended, these are the difficult games we must play to enable a power shift within the Dominion command structure."

To Hermes, the success of Telemachus clearly sounded like the superior option to his being terminated by Alioth. He noticed streaks of colored light in the distance that were flying toward them. "And how can I aid you in your efforts?"

"By performing at optimal levels. Your inability to remove the random variable in our region is disturbing to me. If your efforts continue to be unsuccessful, I will terminate you myself."

While Hermes kept his attention fixed on the horse and the sword, ready to jump out of the way if either of them made any threatening moves, Telemachus kicked Hermes in the head.

TOM plodded along in the dusty wake of Magnus and Helix, following game trails through the tall grasses on the hillside in the late-afternoon sunshine. Sensing Tom's need for silent reflection, Magnus had not spoken since they'd left the redwood grove. Through the veil of fog in his exhausted brain, Tom felt the recent events in his life fading into memory as he walked, giving him some relief from the emotions tied to the death of his family, his rejection by Tempest, his betrayal by the gods who used to protect him, and his feeling of being hunted. He was still dizzy, and some of that seemed connected with his experience in the tree house during Magnus's training exercise. As he tried to make sense of it, he wasn't sure if he had been dreaming, if Magnus had given him some kind of a drug, or if he was simply losing his mind.

The thought that Magnus was his uncle still bothered him, but they hadn't discussed it since the dream, or whatever it was. Maybe Tom had imagined it. In any case, he was sure there would be time to talk about it later. Tom's big goal at the moment was to find a safe place to sleep.

"Be careful where you step," Magnus said, gesturing at a short length of bamboo protruding from the sandy soil when they reached the floor of a narrow canyon. A hint of salt tinged the air, carried on a humid breeze from the west. Tom recognized the place as part of the Valley of the Moon, which meandered its way for twenty miles from the bay to the sea.

Tom blinked and looked around, realizing that there were dozens of the bamboo poles, about three feet tall and devoid of leaves, poking out of sandy mounds on the canyon floor where they walked. The poles looked as if they'd been cut and stripped by hand. "Are they marking something?"

Magnus glanced over his shoulder at Tom. "The dead."

"Dead plants?"

Magnus kept walking, stepping around the mounds. Helix started to whine softly. "You won't understand until you see for yourself. For now, think of this as a monastery without walls."

Tom tried to understand why monks would be buried in

such an odd place. The canyon looked like a dry riverbed, so it wouldn't be a great place to bury someone unless you wanted to see them get washed away in a flood. He looked up at the canyon walls to see if he could spot signs of habitation in shallow caves or on the cliff tops, but he saw nothing unusual.

Magnus held up a hand to stop Tom in his path. "I want you to meet someone." He crouched down by a mound with a border of white stones around it, then thumped his palm against the sand four times before looking up at Tom with a wink. "Prepare yourself."

"For what?" Tom asked, just before the sand of the mound shifted and a dark corpse sat up in front of them. The bamboo pole protruded from its mouth. Helix yelped. Tom gasped and jumped backward, his heart pounding, almost stepping on Helix, certain that he was having a hallucination caused by a lack of sleep. Confused, Helix ran around in a circle twice, then darted behind a nearby boulder, shivering in the shade and refusing to look back their way.

The corpse spit out the hollow pole, then spoke in a whispery voice that sounded like rat feet rustling over dry leaves. "Magnus? Why do you wake me so early?" Stiff eyelids popped open to reveal dull gray eyes, and Tom heard creaking sounds as the corpse raised an arm to shade his face from the sunlight.

"Sorry. We're in a rush," Magnus said, looking up at Tom. "This is Tom Eliot. Tom, this is Dead Man."

It took a moment for Tom to find his voice. He stared at the corpse with wide eyes. "Dead Man? That's what you're called?"

Still seated, Dead Man gestured at the canyon around them. "That's what all of us are called in this community. We renounced our names when we died."

"That could be confusing," Tom said, noting that his heart was still beating fast, but it was no longer trying to escape from his chest.

"We don't get out much. Except when we migrate to a new burial ground, we spend most of our time meditating on the mysteries of time and space."

The man really looked dead, although his dark body seemed well preserved, or perhaps mummified. The movements of his wasted form looked stiff and jerky as he got up on his hands and knees, shaking the sandy soil from his body. He pulled the lump he'd been using for a pillow free of the soil, then opened the package and removed a black cloak glinting with silver and gold threads woven into its rough fabric. After he wriggled into the cloak, he stood up straight, towering over Tom's six-foot-tall frame.

Magnus looked at Dead Man and inclined his head toward Tom. "He'll be wanting to know if you're really dead. Should we tell him?"

Dead Man ran a hand over the two rough patches of red hair that stuck to his skull, then pulled the hood up over his head, watching Tom with the dead gray eyes that bulged from his face. "It depends on how you define death, I suppose. Do I breathe? On occasion. Does my heart beat? Sometimes. Was I trained to slow my metabolism to a point that many would consider biological death? Yes. Have I gone beyond that level of meditation because I really did die at some point? So it would appear. Nanoforms in the soil of my mound arrest my bodily decay and supply me with cellular energy. My brothers surround us here, their bodies dead or alive as they deem necessary, resting peacefully within the earth while our minds journey in the Dead Lands along the endless Road. And so we stand in this outdoor temple of the mind, having a conversation, you and I, one hollow man to another. Have I answered your question?"

"I'm not sure," Tom said, rubbing his eyes. Was this some kind of a residual effect from the drug Magnus had given him in the tree house? Dead Man seemed real enough, but so had the blue sphere he had been conversing with in his own head a few hours ago. He blinked a few times, and Dead Man was still there staring at him, giving off an odor of damp dirt.

"Tom hasn't walked the Road yet," Magnus said, slipping out of his backpack so he could stretch.

"Is he your student?"

"He is, even though he may not realize it yet."

Dead Man pondered this for a moment. "Then you haven't told him?"

"I will when the time comes."

"You play a dangerous game, Magnus."

Magnus darted a glance at Tom. "I do what I must. This boy may save us all."

Dead Man laughed with a dry rasp in his throat. "I am beyond saving. Why should I help you?"

"Because you may spend your time beyond this world, but you feel a responsibility to the world you've left behind. Because you'd like to go for a hike with us and teach Tom something about the real world." Magnus smiled and put his hand on Dead Man's shoulder. "And because you're my friend."

"Ah," Dead Man nodded. "You have me there. But you must tell him."

"Hello?" Tom said, feeling as if he'd been forgotten. "Tell me what?"

Magnus shook his head. "Not yet. When the time is right, I'll tell you."

Tom sighed, then jumped back as the vulture swooped down to land on Dead Man's shoulder, yanked the hood back with his beak, and began pecking at his skull. Dead Man ducked and spun around, waving his arms at the bird, but it wouldn't go away. Helix hopped out from behind the boulder and started barking, his eyes wild.

"Rocco! No! Get off," Magnus yelled, stepping forward to push Rocco off Dead Man's shoulder. The vulture launched himself into the air, blasting them with a gust from his enormous wings.

Dead Man looked wary as he pulled the hood back over his head and straightened his cloak. Helix whimpered and went back into hiding behind the boulder.

"I didn't think vultures attacked living things," Tom said.

Dead Man gave Tom an odd look, then dusted off his sleeves. "We have this problem all the time. They assume we won't fight back because of our smell." He looked up and shook his fist at Rocco, now circling overhead.

"Sorry," Magnus said. "I thought Rocco was trained better than that." He looked up as the vulture circled lower over their heads. "Friend! He's a friend, you barbarian!" He shrugged at Dead Man. "You just can't get good help anymore."

Dead Man kept his eye on Rocco. "We prefer owls. They're smarter."

"That's great if you need a night bird. I prefer to sleep at night."

A renewed wave of dizziness forced Tom to sit down on the boulder where Helix was hiding. "I really need to get some sleep, Magnus."

"You can use my burial mound if you wish," Dead Man offered, gesturing at his grave.

Tom grimaced. "Thanks, but I think I'd prefer to sleep out in the open."

"The soil conserves your body heat," Dead Man pointed out. "And the nanoforms won't bother you unless you start to decay."

Tom bent over to put his face in his hands and closed his eyes, thinking how the boulder was really more comfortable than he might have guessed, until Magnus shook his shoulder. "There'll be none of that, boy. Humboldt is still following us, and it's about time for a spysat to fly over on its last orbit before dark. We don't want the watchers to spot us out in the open."

"Can't I just take a quick nap? I'm too dizzy to walk."

Magnus shouldered his backpack. "You can rest after it gets dark. We've got another two hours of light."

Dead Man set a light hand on Tom's shoulder, causing Tom to wrinkle his nose when he caught the scent. "The dizziness will pass, young Tom. Eventually."

Tom looked up and frowned at Dead Man, silhouetted by the sun, low above the horizon. "How would you know?"

Dead Man glanced at Magnus, who shook his head in response. "Come along, boy. If our dead friend can manage a little hike, then so can you."

Wondering what kind of a freak show he had gotten himself into, Tom groaned and lifted his weary body off the boulder. Helix led the way, happy to leave the burial mounds behind.

AN hour of hiking took them through a narrow tributary of the Valley of the Moon, up a narrow cliff side trail where Tom slipped four times on loose gravel, and on into another oak forest among the rolling hills. By sunset, they had spent a second hour climbing the highest hill in the area, where Magnus felt more comfortable under the screen of black oak and madrone trees that shielded them from any watchers in the sky. The air was cooler, but the breeze still held the musty smell of grasses and trees that had baked in the sun all day. Yellow butterflies fluttered over clumps of orange poppies. Tiny purple, white, and yellow flowers were spattered like paint among tall brown blades of grass. Barn swallows darted low over the unusually flat meadow, hunting for dinner, but Helix was too tired to notice.

Magnus stopped suddenly on a bare square of dirt in the middle of a broad meadow. "We're here," he announced, looking around in a circle. Dead Man stopped beside Tom. Rocco circled overhead in a holding pattern.

Tom nodded, thinking it looked like as good a place as

any to make camp for the night. A grasshopper buzzed past his face, and his eyes crossed from fatigue until he blinked a few times. "Where's here?".

Magnus stamped hard on the dirt, and they heard a hollow boom. "This is Skylight. It's an old Titan missile launch facility. We're standing on the cap that covers the silo."

Tom dug the toe of his boot into what turned out to be a thin layer of soil over cracked gray concrete. He cleared away more of the dirt, revealing faded black and yellow lines with the occasional spot of red. Studying their surroundings, he noted oddly square shapes that he had assumed to be rocks partially hidden by weeds and bushes, and it occurred to him that the meadow didn't look entirely natural.

Magnus walked over to a clump of bushes on a dirt mound about thirty feet away, then waved them over while he lifted a section of the bushes away from a heavy steel door set in an angled block of concrete. He traced some of the lines on the rusty door with his finger, following some pattern only he could see, then the door slowly hummed open on silent hinges, revealing a spiral staircase that led deep underground. Helix sniffed at the opening and gave Tom a questioning look. Cool air drifted out from the dark depths while Magnus poked around just inside the doorframe, surprising two snails that were making their way up a sign that read: *851st Strategic Missile Squadron, Skylight Command, National Defense Restricted Area, Entry prohibited unless specifically authorized by the Commanding Officer.* Tom heard a click, then red and yellow lights came on to illuminate the staircase. Magnus smiled. "Sandoval takes good care of this place. The elevator doesn't work, but we can take the stairs. We only have to go down about fifty feet."

Tom was used to living underground, but he assumed that such a deep dwelling could hold several comfortable family homes. A silo this deep might also hold several harvest seasons of grain. Ducking his head under the top of the doorframe, he followed Magnus down the stairwell, his feet clanking on the metal steps that spiraled downward. Right behind him, he heard the ticking of Helix's nails as he hopped down from step to step and the steady plodding thump of Dead Man's feet on the stairs.

When they reached the bottom of the stairwell, the floor was a metal grille, and they faced a heavy green steel door that was about nine feet tall. Magnus waved his arms, and the door hummed open, revealing a small chamber beyond it with another steel door on the opposite wall. "Blast doors, nine tons each," Magnus said cryptically, beckoning them into the chamber as he stepped over the yellow-and-black-striped threshold.

Once they had all crowded into the blast lock chamber, Magnus pressed a set of buttons, closing the first blast door just before the second one hummed open. On the other side of the door was a small, bald man with a thin white beard that seemed to continue up around the fringe of his skull to form a fluffy halo. Smile lines creased the skin around his eyes, indicating either that he was a happy fellow or that he was crazy—Tom wasn't sure which. He was thin, with leathery brown skin, and wore a white robe that dragged on the floor and collected dust bunnies. Behind him, through another open blast door, stretched a long corridor with a dull silver floor of steel plates, a curved ceiling supported by metal struts, and modern glow panels hanging from the ceiling.

"Sandoval, my good friend," Magnus said, bowing to the little man.

Sandoval bowed in response, twinkling his dark brown eyes at the group. "Welcome to the Museum of Old Tech, my friends. We have many fascinating objects here on display, and none of them are gods-approved for viewing, so turn back now if you are weak in spirit or faint of heart." He straightened, then thumped his chest with his fist. "I, myself, am Miguel Julio Ricardo Jose Sandoval, and I will be your guide for this delightful sojourn into our past. Please watch your step, mind your head, and don't touch anything that might explode."

"Words to live by," Magnus said. "Have you sealed the entry door?"

Sandoval raised his eyebrows. "Of course, my friend. Are you expecting someone else?"

"Nobody that we want to see."

Sandoval nodded. "I understand. The old security system is not what it once was, but they won't get in unless we allow it."

"That's what I wanted to hear," Magnus said. He gestured at the long tunnel. "Think we could use the simulator? Is it still working?"

Sandoval thumped his chest again. "I, myself, maintain the simulator and all the other exhibits here. I take full responsibility for its operation. You will not be disappointed."

The group moved forward, following Sandoval into the tunnel, their boots ringing on the floor plates. Sandoval glanced over his shoulder at Tom and pointed at the floor. "You may have noticed the construction. The control center of this silo is suspended from shock mounts with huge coil springs. It rests on shock absorbers, and there used to be a rubber sheet between the metal walls and the reinforced concrete walls, although that was replaced by shock foam a long time ago."

This information seemed obvious to his companions, but not to Tom. He noted a faint scent of machine oil in the air. "Why? Who lived here?"

"Missilemen," Sandoval said. "Crews of four at a time, although two of them would be maintenance people. The idea was to damp out the shock waves if a bomb hit the surface nearby, or if a missile exploded. The liquid fuel they used in the missiles was pretty volatile, so every once in a while there would be an accident, and they didn't want to lose an entire missile complex when that happened."

"Of course not," Tom said, nodding as if he understood. Then he decided he wasn't fooling anybody but himself. "What's a missile complex?"

"It's where they kept the Titan missiles in their silos ready to launch," Sandoval said with a slight smile.

"Were the missiles in the silos with the grain?" Tom asked, a deep frown creasing his forehead.

Sandoval glanced at Magnus, who shrugged. The little man changed the subject as they reached a junction in the tunnel where he opened another blast door. "We've made a lot of changes since then, of course. Over time, the museum has had many donations that needed to be hidden from the eyes of the gods, and we've done our best to give them a good home. This is part of the collection."

They stepped into a large chamber that had been converted to an exhibit area. Glass cases stood in dramatic pools of light, protecting and displaying a wide variety of objects that Tom didn't recognize. Helix squirmed in his arms, and Tom put him down so he could sniff the exhibits on his own.

"Is Barney in here?" Magnus asked as he looked around with an approving gaze.

Sandoval shook his head. "No. I'll show him to you later. I fixed him up enough to put him on guard duty. You're just lucky that you got past him up there."

"I noticed that things are a lot cleaner than the last time I was here."

Dead Man stopped in front of a glass case housing a pitted granite tombstone that read: "Norton I, Emperor of the United States and Protector of Mexico." A chunk was missing on the bottom except for the year "1880." Dead Man looked at Sandoval. "This is interesting. Who brought it in?"

"Clampers," Sandoval said. "E Clampus Vitus, the historical society. They heard we had a secret museum here, so they dropped it off for safekeeping. Important part of

San Francisco history they said. Someone found it on the other side of The Uplift."

"Indeed," Dead Man said, returning his attention to the tombstone.

After a few minutes of looking around, Tom still had no clue as to the nature of most of the objects he was seeing on display. He identified the hard shell spacesuit, the electron microscope, the electric guitar, and the early quantum computer from pictures he'd seen in his father's library, and that was impressive enough; but there were many more artifacts that were unmarked. He tried to stifle a yawn, but he was too tired to stop it.

"We don't know what all of them are," Sandoval said, as if he'd been reading Tom's mind. "Magnus brought us the Jimi Hendrix guitar and the electron microscope, but people bring us a lot of junk as well. I try to sort it all out and keep what I think is valuable, and as we gain more knowledge about the past we may be able to identify some of these other artifacts. However, one of the greatest features of this museum is the library, and—"

Magnus held up a hand to silence Sandoval. "If only we had more time, my friend, but we have wasted enough already. If Tom succeeds in his mission, he can revisit the museum later on. For now, we should get him to the simulator."

Dead Man tore his attention away from the tombstone and walked toward them. "But it's the *library,* Magnus. The boy should know about it."

Magnus took Tom's elbow and steered him toward the cableway corridor. "I'm sorry. We must proceed with his training. That's more important than anything."

Another thirty feet down the corridor, Sandoval opened another steel blast door and gestured for Tom to enter. "We're somewhat squeezed for storage space, so you'll have to ignore the other exhibits we have in here. This is the simulator room."

Tom sighed, wondering if he'd ever be able to simulate

some sleep, as the group walked into a chamber that was about forty feet across and crammed with complex machinery housed in battered gray equipment racks. Helix started sniffing the floor right in front of Tom, so he had to dance sideways to avoid stepping on the little dog, bumping into a glass case as he did so. The large steel egg in the case bore a faded plaque that read: *General Electric—We bring good things to life.*

"What's this egg thing?" Tom asked, as he pressed his hands and face close to the glass, trying to make sense of the curious symbols on the outside of the steel case.

"Nuclear warhead. Plutonium core," Sandoval said. "Nine-kiloton yield, so it was pretty small compared to later warheads."

Tom tried to imagine what a warhead was, thinking it ought to look like a big hammer, but he was really too tired to ask more questions.

Magnus motioned to him. "Have a seat over here, Tom. Rest a while." He stood next to a padded steel couch tilted back into a reclining position. The foot- and armrests were positioned carefully with straps, presumably so that the chair's occupant would be comfortable enough to sleep there. The back of the reclined seat rested on a webwork of steel connected to a network of springs, hydraulic piston arms, levers, and other devices that were anchored in a heavy base on the floor. Wires with electrodes dangled above the chair. There were many things Tom didn't understand about the old technologies, but he was willing to try this one out if it meant he could finally get some rest.

While Tom settled into the seat, Magnus lifted a thick helmet that was attached to the headrest. "Put this on, and you won't be bothered by the lights." He helped Tom slip it over his head, and Tom noticed how the helmet damped out the sounds and the light from the room. He closed his eyes and settled in, knowing it wouldn't be long before he fell asleep.

"Are you comfortable, Tom?" It sounded like a tiny Sandoval was speaking into both of his ears at once. He felt wires, maybe the electrodes, being pressed against the skin of his forearms, wrists, and ankles.

"Yes. Good night," Tom said, hoping they'd take the hint and leave him alone.

The inside of the helmet started to get steamy, then a cooling flow of oxygen drifted past his face, and he dozed off. Strange dreams started right away, with little rotating images of a knight in shiny silver-plate armor; a woman with a bow and arrow in leather armor; some kind of a hunchbacked gnome with a goofy smile and a short sword; a heavily muscled creature with huge eyes, a scary face, and a giant axe; a mean-looking skeleton with glowing red eyes, a long white scythe, and tattered black leather clothes. Tom thought the detail of the knight's armor was pretty good for a dream, and as he focused his attention on it the knight saluted him with his broadsword. The images faded away.

Tom found himself standing on a black cobblestone road under a sky flashing with distant fireworks. The air smelled of smoke and dead fish. The cold wind moaned through the burnt husks of dead trees. Tom noticed that his field of view was limited to a wide slit in front of his eyes, as if he were looking at a long painting by Hieronymous Bosch in one of his father's books. When he raised his hand to scratch his nose, a silver metal gauntlet clunked in front of his face, partially obscuring his view through the slit. He felt heavier than usual. When he looked down, he saw that his entire body was covered in silver steel, and it finally dawned on him that he was wearing the same plate armor that he'd seen on the figure of the knight just moments ago. This was unusual for one of his dreams, and he felt more aware of his surroundings than normal, but so many odd things had happened lately that he wasn't surprised.

A warbling scream caused the hair to rise on the back of his neck. He snapped his head up to look around, turning his body to see more because of his limited view through the eye slit. His heart hammered in his chest, almost hard enough for him to hear it echoing inside his suit of armor. Spinning around, he finally located the source of the noise as it screamed again, directly into his face, before slamming its massive beak against his chest. He staggered backward, then tripped on something and landed flat on his back, staring up at a black crow that was at least ten feet tall. The beak came down like a giant hammer, smashing into his chest so hard that he heard the steel creak under the blow. Tom tried to scrabble backward, but it was hard to maneuver the heavy suit. He finally got the heels of his gauntlets wedged into some cobblestones, then flipped himself over so he could rise to his hands and knees. The crow flapped its wings, sending a stream of dust through the helmet slit into Tom's eyes. Blinking, he staggered upright in time for the crow to peck at his shoulder, knocking him forward.

Dream or not, he knew that if he didn't find a way to fight back, the crow was going to peck him to death. He looked around for a weapon, maybe a big rock or a stick, and his gaze fell on an old log on the edge of the road. He bent to pick it up, but the log disintegrated when he grasped it with his gauntlet, and the crow chose that moment to peck his armored backside. Tom stumbled forward, tripped over the log, and somersaulted onto the sandy slope of the road, miraculously landing with his feet poised so that his weight rolled and carried him upright once more. When he turned to face the crow, something thudded to the ground beside him—a broadsword that had apparently fallen from a scabbard at his side. Keeping his head toward the crow, he bent to pick up the sword. *Caw,* the crow called, rapidly hopping toward him, its beak poised for a blow to his head. Tom planted one knee in the sand, turned the point of the sword skyward with the hilt braced against a rock, and ducked as the beak descended, allowing the crow to get the point with its head. Red smoke poured from the wound in its face as it stood upright again, tilted its head at Tom as if reevaluating the wisdom of its attack, and leapt into the air to fly away, staggering Tom under the blast of wind from its wings.

Tom swallowed, took a deep breath, and sat down in the sand, nearly impaling himself on his own sword. His body shook, and sweat dribbled into his eyes. He fumbled around with the bottom of the helmet, wondering how to remove it, and finally gave up in disgust. He hoped he wouldn't have to urinate anytime soon.

SANDOVAL looked up from the physiological monitoring equipment and frowned at Tom's twitching body on the simulator couch. "Maybe we should bring him out. The crow nearly got him. His pulse is dropping back to normal, but we don't want to overdo it on his first visit."

"I thought he handled that pretty well," Magnus said, watching the brain scan and mental image monitors from one of the two control chairs. "He's lucky that his first monster was a crow. It could have been a lot worse, although the crow certainly isn't a pushover."

Dead Man was lying flat on his back on the floor between some of the equipment. He lifted his head to peer at Magnus with his bulging eyes. "Why are you driving him so hard, Magnus? He needs to gain more experience in Stronghold before you push him to higher levels."

Magnus sighed, then turned to look at Dead Man. "The boy has talent, don't you see that? We haven't got the time for a casual training period like the rest of us had. The sili-boys have already run their forecasts, and they know Tom is a threat to their existence, although they may not know why. They want him dead. Telemachus has his agents out hunting for Tom right now. The real danger for us is that Tom will slide into despair, but I won't allow that. Tom is too exhausted and too busy to think about the loss of his family, so if we can get him past this rough spot in his life, time will heal the wounds that we can't reach. He's already making excellent progress."

Sandoval shook his head. "He's not a machine, Magnus. It takes time to learn the skills you're trying to teach him."

"If he's killed in the simulator," Dead Man said, "he won't be able to help us at all. He doesn't know how to walk the Road, and a hollow man can't cross the barrier into Stronghold. You'll lose your tool for revenge, and the Dominion will remain in control."

Magnus clenched his fists. "This is not about revenge! If this boy can free us all from slavery, we owe it to ourselves and the rest of the world to use this opportunity. He has the talent, and he has the right genes."

"You know this for a fact?" Sandoval asked, his eyebrows raised in uncertainty.

Magnus nodded. "He's my nephew. He's got the genes of Ukiah and Luna. I've watched him for years, and Telemachus has confirmed my suspicions by nanobombing Tom's family."

"Then why didn't they eliminate him before now?" Dead Man asked.

"His parents raised Tom to look and act like a normal member of the community. He doesn't know anything about his talents, except for what we're going to reveal to him. The siliboys had no idea that Prometheus was living right under their noses, but now they suspect, and the thought scares them enough that they'd eliminate Tom's family and an entire sector of Marinwood to stop the threat. We can make their projections come true. Tom can destroy them."

"If he survives," Dead Man prompted.

Magnus sat down again. "Yes. If he survives. And we'll do our best to make sure that he does."

■　■　■

TOM realized that he had to stay alert while he sat on the sandy slope by the cobblestone road. When he heard a creaking sound, he turned his head and saw what appeared to be a chunk of dead wood chewing on his armored foot. Although the log wasn't making much progress, and it made even less when Tom kicked it away, he began to notice things like the brown weeds grabbing at his legs with their leaves while their tiny flower blossoms chewed at his armor with rings of tiny teeth. Small rocks were edging toward him in a threatening manner. Dead leaves tried to catch breezes so they could fly up at his face. The whole place, wherever it was, acted like an environmental nightmare that was out to get him. The road itself seemed to be the only safe area—the weeds, leaves, rocks, and other tiny terrors seemed to avoid the straight rows of clean black cobblestones that ran from horizon to horizon.

Something skittered and hissed across the surface of the road. Tom heaved himself up and turned in a crouch. A group of four demonic creatures with red skin, flaming eyes, and large mouths with sharp teeth stood atop something that looked like an alligator on a bad hair day. The giant reptile had a fluffy red Mohawk hairstyle that ran from the top of its head to a point halfway down its back. The demons were about four feet tall, and each one held some sort of weapon in one of its two claws. The claws themselves ended in shiny knife points. The demons looked pleased to see Tom.

"It looks at ussss," hissed the demon at the front of the line. It stepped off the reptile's back with a sudden motion, followed by its pals, almost in a chorus line effect.

"It's frightened. Look at it," said the second demon. Their high-pitched voices reminded Tom of the sound of fingernails on a blackboard.

"I don't like the way it looks at ussss," said the first demon, raising what appeared to be a human thighbone with a head stuck on the end of it to make a club. The head had seen better days. "Let's kill it."

The second demon hopped up and down. "Let's eat it."

"Let's kill it, then eat it," said the third demon.

"Let's kill it, eat it, then use its bones to build a houssssse," hissed the fourth demon, who wore a red scarf around its neck.

The first demon raised its arms. "We are agreed, then. The plan is to kill it, eat it, and use its bones to build a house. All in favor?"

All four demons raised their arms and hopped up and down. "Aye! Aye! Aye!"

Tom chopped the first two in half while they were still hopping up and down. The third one stopped the swing of Tom's broadsword by turning it with its arm so that the flat of the blade slammed into its forehead, making it blink and stagger backward, dropping the bone spear it held in its right claw. The fourth demon used the opportunity to leapfrog over the third demon's back, its short sword held high; but it came down on the point of Tom's broadsword, screaming insults at him as it tried to push and twist the blade out of its stomach. The short sword swung wildly at Tom's head, bouncing off his helmet a few times and ringing it like a bell before the creature finally died. Unable to pry his sword free of the corpse quickly, Tom found himself disarmed when the third demon began swinging the body of one of the halved demons at him, holding it by one leg and spinning in a circle. The torso slammed into Tom's back twice before he ducked under it and lunged forward, tackling the standing demon.

The demon's breath smelled of sulfur and dead things. Not content to be crushed under Tom's weight, it struggled to get free, realized it was trapped under his chest as thoroughly as if a building had fallen on it, and began biting at his neck while making noises like a rat caught in a blender. Tom heard the teeth clunking against the armor at his neck, hoping it wouldn't find a seam while he tried to figure out how to pound the demon into the ground. The armor restricted his movements, so his best choice seemed to be lying on top of the creature until it died, although he assumed that would take a long time, and he didn't really have the patience for it.

Then his helmet popped off.

Tom glimpsed the chewed leather straps that had secured the helmet to his shoulders.

"It dies now," said the demon, smiling with a mouthful of dagger teeth.

Tom tried to roll away as the demon's teeth plunged toward his face, but the threat suddenly disappeared as the demon's head exploded beneath him, showering his face with a variety of liquids and brain bits that Tom really didn't want to think about. He smelled cooked meat.

Disgusted, he rolled over on his back, forgetting how hard it was to get up again from that position. He was lying in a pool of bright light that made it difficult to see the ominous presence standing over him. He heard a *clop-clop* sound, as if a horse had taken two steps near his head.

The pool of light moved a few feet to one side, and as Tom's eyes adjusted he saw an enormous armored knight on the back of an armored black horse. Two beams of light emanated from the knight's helmet, lighting up the road and the broken demons around Tom.

"And you are?" asked a voice that rumbled like thunder.

...7

"GET him out!" Magnus yelled, jumping up from his chair beside the monitors. "Get him out now!"

As Sandoval began to lurch out of his seat, Magnus charged forward and yanked the helmet from Tom's head. Tom looked dead as his head lolled to one side.

"Wait!" Sandoval yelled. "That's too fast!"

"It's Telemachus!" Magnus dropped the helmet and ripped the electrodes away from Tom's body. "He'll kill him!"

Magnus pulled Tom out of the simulator couch and threw him over his shoulder, then carried him a few feet away to set him down on the floor. "Tom, can you hear me?" He slapped Tom's face gently a few times. "Tom? You in there, Tom?"

"Allow me," Dead Man said, sitting down beside Tom with his legs crossed in a lotus position. Helix bent down to help by licking Tom's face.

Sandoval hovered over them, wringing his hands. "I knew this was a mistake. We took him too far too fast."

"Quiet," Magnus said, gesturing for Sandoval to back away. "Let the man work."

Sandoval paced in a circle, shaking his head from side to side. "Who knew Telemachus would be in there? How did he know? How could he have found Tom so quickly?"

"Quiet," Magnus repeated, glaring at Sandoval, who finally slumped down in a chair and leaned forward to cover his face with his hands.

Dead Man's eyes were closed, and he didn't appear to be breathing, so that was a good sign. His right hand hovered perfectly still an inch above Tom's forehead. "He knows now," Dead Man whispered. "He knows what it is to be a hollow man."

Magnus nodded and looked at Sandoval, who stared back at him with wide eyes.

"You were right," Sandoval whispered. "He has the talent."

"Of course he has the talent," Magnus growled. "You think I would have wasted all this time on him otherwise?"

"I think you have a soft spot for your nephew who no longer has a home," Sandoval said, thumping his chest. "I, myself, admire that in you. But now we've seen there's more to this boy than we thought, and I am awed by the possibilities. Thank you for bringing him to us," he said, putting his hands together and bowing toward Magnus.

Magnus waved his arm to dismiss Sandoval's comments. "You make too many assumptions. And my motivations aren't the point here." He returned his attention to the unconscious Tom. "Can you bring him out of it, Dead Man?"

"He has sustained a serious shock," Dead Man whispered, moving the palm of his hand to the top of Tom's head. "Physically, he's fine, but his focus is deep within—deeper than I can reach. That may be good if he's absorbing what he has learned, in which case he'll come out of it naturally when he's ready. If his focus has retreated because of the shock, he may be in a coma. It's too early to tell."

"Great," Magnus said, slapping his forehead as he stood up. "We finally get the chance we've been hoping for, and I drop him into Stronghold like a ton of bricks or, well, you know what I'm trying to say. Now we'll be trapped in this hole while Humboldt locates Tom's trail with the sniffer and gets Hermes to call in an air strike."

Dead Man opened his eyes to look at Magnus. Sandoval looked up at the ceiling. Magnus looked from one to the other. "Well? This is where you say, 'I did the best I could, my intentions were good, Tom will be fine,' something like that."

Helix backed away from Tom's face and whined, giving Magnus a pathetic look.

"Can't I even take a nap without you guys hovering over me?" Tom asked, taking a deep breath. "What is it with you?" He blinked at the glare from the overhead lights, then rubbed his eyes and sat up. Helix immediately darted forward and curled up in Tom's lap. "What are you all staring at?"

Sandoval gasped at Tom. "You're okay?"

Tom glared at them with bloodshot eyes. "No, I'm not okay. You guys won't let me sleep. As my father used to say, you make enough noise to wake the dead." He glanced at Dead Man. "No offense."

"None taken," Dead Man said.

Tom rubbed his forehead. "I'm dizzy and my headache is back. My feet hurt. I can't even tell the difference between my dreams and reality anymore, and I think it has something to do with that nasty drink you gave me, Magnus. What was in it, anyway?"

Dead Man glanced at Magnus, who rolled his eyes, sighed heavily, and finally looked directly at Tom. "Poison."

Tom gasped in disbelief. "What?"

Magnus shrugged. "Well, it wasn't all poison. The effects are produced by a variety of organic ingredients such as *ayahuasca*—the vision vine—that allowed us to have what you might call a common hallucination. That's how the testing and training starts, you understand, and that's why I said you'd learn more from the experience if you were exhausted at the time. We expanded your mind, and now we've introduced you to Stronghold—the world of the AIs and the other unfortunate phantoms that live there. Stronghold would have been more realistic if we could have injected you with nanomed sims, but we don't have any available. In any case, you've adapted to these new worlds quickly and admirably, which is necessary because it gets harder from here on out, and we have very little time."

Pushing Helix out of his lap, Tom stood up and glared into Magnus's eyes with his fists clenched. "You gave me poison."

Magnus looked uncomfortable. "Well, yes. Perhaps I was wrong, but I assumed you would resist some of the training. I needed a way to motivate you if you changed your mind about becoming a master of the Road. We need you, Tom. The world needs you."

"So you decided to poison me," Tom grumbled, grinding his teeth.

"For your own good," Magnus pointed out.

"Are you listening to yourself?"

Sandoval took a step forward. "That's why your dizziness won't go away, Tom. We all went through it with our teachers, more or less. Magnus was just following tradition."

"You're all crazy!" Tom yelled, waving his arms. "Where's the antidote to this poison?"

Magnus pointed at his own head. "In here."

Tom stepped forward with menace. "I'd be happy to beat it out of you, old man."

Dead Man put a hand on Tom's shoulder, and the gesture had an almost immediate calming effect. "Tom, you'll have to get the antidote yourself, just as we all did. You'll find it on the Road."

Tom sighed and looked down at Helix. "If it doesn't kill me first?"

"Some have failed to reach the Road," Magnus said. "That is the risk we take for great knowledge."

"*Many* have failed," Sandoval added, looking away when Magnus glared at him.

Magnus put his hand on Tom's other shoulder. "But you won't fail, Tom. You're our Prometheus. You will reach the Road, and you will find the antidote."

Tom twisted away from all the grasping hands, picked up Helix, and headed for the door. "I'm going to find a dark corner and get some sleep. Don't bother me. Don't even look at me. Just leave me alone."

TOM dreamed of floating. He was back in the bay, face-down, bobbing on the gentle currents above a fantasy underwater garden of colorful fish and plants. Yellow garibaldi chased striped clown fish through the dancing water weeds while red lobsters stood guard as if they were armored tanks parked on the muddy bottom. Remembering the stories of the corpses that had floated in the bay after The Uplift, Tom sensed their presence, and then he spotted Ukiah, Luna, Zeke, and Weed, all dressed formally in black with their feet rooted in the mud, drifting gently with the current, their hair bobbing around their pale faces. Their sad eyes were open and bulging, staring at Tom, full of silent reproach at the fact that he was still alive and they were not, resenting him for defying the gods and bringing the wrath of Telemachus down on their heads. Tom tried to explain, but his mouth filled with water, damping out his voice until he drifted away and his family disappeared from view for the last time.

Broken buildings passed by beneath him as something large landed on his back, driving a sharp spike into his neck. He tried to turn over in the water to remove his attacker, but all he could do was turn his head as another spike plunged into his spine. Blinking to clear his eyes, he saw a massive crow perched on his back, its beak red with Tom's blood. He recognized the bird as the same one he had defeated on the road in Stronghold. Red smoke still hissed from the wound in its head where Tom had punctured it with his sword. Tom sensed it was after his secrets. Its beak plunged again, poking at one of his kidneys, before it began to scream at him.

Tom woke to the sound of alarms.

A shadow passed over him, and he was startled to see Dead Man standing there, silhouetted by the glow panels on the ceiling. He thought he had hidden himself well on one of the maintenance platforms at the bottom of the empty missile silo, hoping not to be bothered while he slept. The blaring alarms echoed in the cavernous chamber, which was about 150 feet tall and maybe forty feet across.

"How did you find me?" Tom asked, loud enough so that Dead Man could hear him over the noise.

"I've learned your vibrations. All I had to do was get close enough to hear them. Now, please hurry, we have to go."

Dead Man offered his hand and helped Tom stand up. Tom looked around and spotted Helix hiding behind a thick pipe, watching Dead Man with wide eyes and his tail between his legs. He picked up the worried dog, who whimpered as he was brought closer to Dead Man, then followed the walking corpse out the door into the long cableway corridor. "What's the big emergency?"

"We have visitors," Dead Man said, walking faster than Tom had ever seen him move. His feet thumped on the steel deck plates.

"Humboldt?"

He ducked under one of the cableway struts. "Perhaps. Someone set off the perimeter alarms on the surface."

After they passed through the blast lock and decontamination area that joined the cableway from the silo to the control center, they found Magnus and Sandoval watching the overhead security monitors. Ancient hardware racks, arranged in an ominous light gray circle around the missile launch control panels at the main desk, dominated the room. Glow panels hung in place of the old fluorescent lighting fixtures, while the rest of the ceiling space was taken up by pipes, air vents, and surveillance monitors. From his impromptu tour with Helix the previous night, Tom knew that Level One, upstairs, held a small kitchen and dining area, bunk beds, and a restroom. Communications and power control racks were downstairs in Level Three.

"Can you see what he's doing?" Sandoval asked, looking at one of the monitors, where a ghostly image of a glowing green man moved around in the darkness.

Magnus took a step closer and squinted at the monitor. "He's done trying to pry open the access door. He's walking around now. Doesn't seem to be using the sniffer anymore."

"Is that Humboldt?" Tom asked.

Sandoval briefly glanced at Tom and nodded. "We think so. It's hard to be sure with the infrared camera. Very old technology. We're pretty sure we saw him holding a sniffer. He seems to be alone, unless he has friends waiting outside the clearing."

"He's talking into his hand, or to his arm or something. Can't be sure," Magnus said. He frowned and walked over to one of the instrument racks, where a tiny gray monitor showed a moving squiggly line. "Radio emissions just spiked on the surface. You don't think . . . no, if he was signaling Hermes, he'd be using a tightbeam, wouldn't he?"

Sandoval shrugged when Magnus glanced at him. "Maybe there aren't any relay towers in the vicinity that still work?" He pressed two buttons on the launch control panel and studied another tiny monitor, then he suddenly bent over to look at it in more detail. "Satellite ping. He signaled his position to someone."

Magnus whirled around. "*Our* position. He must be targeting for Hermes. Can you jam his transmission?"

Sandoval jogged toward the staircase behind the equipment racks. "Maybe. The remote doesn't work up here, but I can try the main panel downstairs."

"Do it fast. He won't need much time," Magnus said. He looked at Dead Man. "Can you find your way to the ship if we get separated?"

"Of course," Dead Man whispered. "Are you thinking we can sneak out of here?"

"Maybe. The question is whether we think we can outrun a surface strike if they decide to use nanobombs."

"My guess would be no unless we start very soon. Their strike platform will take a few minutes to arrive, but the zone of maximum damage would be very wide. Could we survive the strike down here?"

Magnus shook his head. "This missile silo was hardened against low-yield nuclear blasts, but the disassemblers in the nanobombs will liquefy everything in their paths. I don't know how deep a surface penetrator would go, but the disassemblers certainly wouldn't stop until they were several hundred feet down, maybe more."

They heard thumping and cursing noises from Sandoval, so they went downstairs to find him repeatedly slamming his hand against an instrument rack. "Sometimes this helps, but I think it's too late now. The jammers won't work. The best I can do is try to distract Hermes while you abandon the silo. I think Barney can help me if I point him in the right direction."

"Escape hatch?" Magnus asked.

"Over there," Sandoval said, pointing at a round, white hatchway door set beneath a cross brace on the far wall. "It connects to the ladder in the air shaft, then it's another fifty feet up to the surface. You'll come out in the bushes on the far side of the silo pad, then you can climb the hill from there. It's still dark, so our visitor might not see you if you're quiet. I'll try to keep him busy to give you a head start."

"Where do you want us to wait for you?" Dead Man asked.

"Just go," Sandoval said. "I'll meet you at the ship. If I can't get Barney to work, I want to rescue a few things just in case."

Magnus scowled. "There isn't time for that."

"You have your priorities, and I have mine," Sandoval said, pulling two mechanical waldo arms out of an equipment rack and hooking them into one of the more advanced visual displays that Tom had seen in the facility. While he connected the waldoes, he glanced at Tom. "These will give me manipulator control over Barney."

Tom wondered who Barney was.

"Do you want us to take anything with us?" Dead Man asked.

"Get Tom to safety. I'll take care of the rest."

Magnus took a moment to solemnly shake hands with Sandoval. As Magnus turned to open the escape hatch, Dead Man gave Sandoval a quick hug. "See you on the Road, Sandoval."

Sandoval nodded. "On the Road." Then he quickly shook Tom's hand. "Find your destiny, Tom. Right the wrongs of the world and save us from ourselves. I, myself, know you can do it." He thumped his chest with his fist.

No pressure or anything, Tom thought, smiling at Sandoval. "I'll do what I can."

"That's all I ask," Sandoval said, pulling a heavily wired helmet out of a drawer and hooking it into the visual display.

Tom followed Magnus and Helix through the escape hatch, crawling through the long tunnel, feeling the cold metal that brushed against his shoulders and cooled his hands, listening to the noisy thumps of their hands and knees and ticking claws, aware that Dead Man was behind him cutting off any chance of retreat. Magnus had retrieved a bright flashlight from Sandoval's toolbox, and that served as Tom's beacon in the darkness, silhouetting Magnus's shambling form until they reached the ladder in the vertical air shaft. While Tom tucked Helix under his arm, hoping he'd be able to climb the ladder while carrying his passenger, Magnus shined the light up the fifty-foot shaft, then turned toward Tom and put a finger to his lips. "Sound probably travels pretty well up this shaft, so let's keep it quiet. We don't want to let Humboldt or anyone else know that we're coming."

Tom nodded and followed Magnus up the ladder. He glanced down at Dead Man, steadily following him wherever he went—and he thought that seemed symbolic somehow. Was he escaping from trouble or moving toward it? He wasn't sure, but he didn't see any way of changing his mind now, and death was following him wherever he went.

HUMBOLDT was worried. The power cell on the DNA sniffer that Hermes had given him was running low, and he was reasonably certain that Tom Eliot had come that way, but the trail had suddenly stopped in this broad meadow. He'd found a door that appeared to lead to an underground home, but it was securely locked and he hadn't been able to locate any light tubes or access shafts so that he could climb down and see what was going on. He knew that bad things would happen to him, and probably to his father, if Hermes discovered that he had lost Tom's trail; but there didn't seem to be any other choices, and he had to tell Hermes something during his hourly check-in report. Then it occurred to him that he could lie and nobody would know the difference. If he said he was certain that Tom Eliot had gone down a hole inside this hill, and he could make Hermes believe it, then he'd be off the hook, at least for a while. That would give him time to think of a more clever excuse if Hermes proved him wrong. However, things had gone better than expected when Humboldt made his report. Hermes had told him to wait there so he could "take care of this Tom Eliot problem once and for all." Humboldt assumed that meant Hermes was coming for a personal visit, and he would certainly find a way to open the locked door that led down to Tom's hidey-hole. In the meantime, all he had to do was wait, try to stay warm, maybe take a quick nap, and leave the transmitter on so Hermes could stay locked on his position.

The problem of staying warm would be easily solved. He'd tripped over plenty of deadwood in the dark during his study of the meadow, so all he had to do was gather some of it and start a nice fire. While he piled kindling into his arms, he heard a sudden rumbling behind him. He dropped the wood, spun around, and was blinded by a sudden flash of light. Blinking and stumbling backward as a cloud of dust stung his eyes, he hurled a dead branch at the light and it hit something large with a loud thump. The light went out. He heard a whirring of squeaky gears.

Then an impossibly loud voice boomed out of the darkness. "Prepare to die!"

Humboldt turned to run, but tripped over a log instead, falling flat on his face. The earth trembled beneath him. He yelled as something began to pound on his back, then rolled over and put up his arms to block the blows. Desperate, he grabbed at the weapon, and it came away in his hands. When he finally got a good look at it, he saw that the weapon was a broom.

"Prepare to die!" boomed the voice, very close now, as a wet mop slammed into the side of his head with a loud *squish*.

"DO you hear something?" Tom asked, breathing hard as he stopped and turned around. They had been jogging along a dusty trail up the hill for about twenty minutes when Tom heard a shrieking noise behind them in the distance.

Helix immediately sat down on the trail next to Tom and whined. Magnus and Dead Man turned to look back.

At that moment, the entire forest around them exploded into flame. All of them were slapped to the ground by a giant, unseen hand, and they heard the roar of the same giant, almost deafening in its intensity as the ground shook beneath them. A blast of cooler air followed, pelting them with dust, leaves, rocks, and branches.

"Sandoval," Magnus gasped, as the wind died down. He rolled over on his side, checked that Tom looked okay, and sat up to stare back down the trail. Magnus suddenly looked older than Tom had ever seen him before as he exchanged a glance with Dead Man that didn't require words.

Feeling a lump move beneath his chest, Tom sat up, and Helix poked his head free of Tom's shirt collar, warily looked around, and whined to make it clear that he wasn't coming out until they got away from the burning trees that crackled and smoked over their heads.

Tom hesitated, then took a deep breath, swallowed, and looked down the hill past Dead Man, dreading what he knew he would see.

The boiling crater was there, just as he remembered seeing it at the Eliot farm when his family was murdered. A soft blue glow, crackling with static electricity, shimmered above the crater, where mud pots began to form, hissing sulfurous smoke into the air while the crater slowly widened and the soil continued to liquefy. The silo was no longer there.

Sandoval was gone.

Humboldt was gone, too, and Tom was surprised he felt bad about that. How would Tempest learn about her brother's death? Tom knew that her misguided father would blame himself for his son's death, and with good reason; but he felt bad about that, too, almost as if he were directly responsible for the loss of so many lives. And so it seemed to be. Sooner or later, he would have to acknowledge that the blood was on his hands, even though others might blame the gods. He was responsible for starting this whole chain of events, and he finally realized that he would have to be the one to stop it. Magnus said there was a way Tom could help, and he certainly didn't have anything else to live for, so he might as well focus on putting an end to all this bloodshed; otherwise, he might just lose his mind . . . if he hadn't already.

Tom grabbed Magnus by the arm and hauled him to his feet as a burning branch crashed to the ground beside them, showering Magnus with sparks. "Come on, Magnus. We have to get out of here."

Dead Man gestured at Tom. "Up the trail. We must outrun the fire."

Wondering if he'd ever be able to stop running from the fire, Tom led them up the hill.

JUANITA Lopez leaned against a battered paw of the Sphinx and looked up at the evening sky. She was on her break, looking high above the black glass pyramid where she worked, watching the stars pop into view. She inhaled deeply, filling her lungs with the dry desert air, thinking how nice it would be to smoke a stimstick right about now. A powerful light snapped on at the tip of the thirty-six-story pyramid, sending a brilliant white beam straight up into the clear sky. She knew the Institute had originally been the Luxor resort hotel a long time ago—a fantasy version of ancient Egypt in the middle of Las Vegas—but the building served a far more serious purpose now. The casino on the main floor was still in operation for tourists because the gods liked to watch their human guinea pigs run the maze of slot machines and gaming tables, testing them with positive and negative feedback strategies in their ongoing experiments. The former hotel rooms had become cells and offices, with special facilities residing safely on the subterranean levels among the replica treasures from King

Tut's tomb. Under the watchful eyes of ancient Egyptian gods made of fiberglass and plaster, misguided individuals and freethinkers were shown the error of their ways. Those who accepted rehabilitation were released into the world as model citizens, while those who rejected the wisdom of the Dominion were released into the recycling bins.

There were no vehicles driving down the broken pavement of Las Vegas Boulevard, but the buildings that crowded together along the Strip had begun their nightly performances, their brilliant lights and giant gaudy holograms splashing the street with manic daubs of dancing colors. Juanita could imagine crowded streets full of life, the sound of voices and traffic, the odor of humanity mixing with the delicate scents of a desert evening at the end of a hot day. She'd seen the holos and flicks of the city's past in the time before the Dominion, and it contrasted sharply with the controlled environment that existed now. The small numbers of people walking the sidewalks made little noise, and their voices were immediately swept away by the hot desert wind; but the city continued its enticing dance without the music, flashing its lights as if they were refractions on the facets of a diamond, hinting at mysterious wealth beyond the casino doors. As moths were drawn to a flame, the tourists and recently released model citizens were drawn to the blinking colors that beckoned them through the portals, only to be trapped inside more human behavior experiments and studied by the Dominion.

Juanita hated herself for being a part of the Institute, but it was a necessary evil. Despite any efforts on her part, the rehab facility would remain, churning out zombies as it stamped out individuality and creativity. She could help the occasional inmate when the conditions were right, but most of the time she had to act like a model employee. She had helped many over the last six years; but security was tight, and the danger of potential discovery always kept her on

the edge, tense and ready to snap if any suspicions were
aroused. She had led many different lives on the streets of
Las Vegas, and there were safer ways to make a living in this
town, even if they were less reputable occupations, but she
knew she'd found her calling as an administrative nurse at
the Institute. In one of the most carefully guarded Dominion
cities, working in one of the dreaded rehab units, Juanita
Lopez was above suspicion, and that allowed her to lead her
secret life.

The com plug *pinged* in her ear, and she heard the carefully modulated voice of the administrator AI. "J. Lopez,
you are required immediately at the intake facility, sub-
level one."

Juanita inhaled another lungful of clean air and started
walking back toward the main entrance of the pyramid.
She glanced up at the sky again, just in time to see the long
white trail of a meteor burning up in the atmosphere, and it
made her wonder if it was an omen of some kind. She
shook her head—if it was an omen, it was wasted, since
she didn't get the message.

Descending below the casino floor on a broad stone staircase, Juanita saw an orderly at the cage by the admitting
desk, the hulking Bruno, shutting the door on an attractive
woman with long brown hair who looked like she was
about twenty years old. Her black dress was torn in several
places, her hair was rumpled, and she looked as if she'd
spent a lot of time crying recently. This would be a tough
one. Her automatic response was to find a way to get the
woman out of there and help her, but Juanita had a role to
play until she knew details: whether the woman was dangerous or suicidal, foolish or smart, trained or unskilled,
sane or crazy. And there were rumors going around that
mutants were gathering on the other side of the shield wall,
ready to break through into the borderlands at any time, so
Juanita had to be careful—she didn't want to be the first
victim of a mutant border jumper. Potential threats from

the other side were expected hazards associated with being so close to the wall. The primitives on the other side had always seemed peaceful to Juanita, despite being trapped in the nanotech wasteland, but she really had no way of knowing what went on over there. Perhaps it had taken this long for the mutants to get organized and find a way through the shield wall. In any case, the rumors appeared to have some basis in fact, because she'd seen more blue-suited troopers patrolling the streets, and even more seemed to be coming into town every day.

Juanita checked the holomonitor glowing above her desk, then frowned at Bruno. "Is this Tempest Gustafson?"

"Aye," Bruno said with a gap-toothed smile. He rubbed his palm across his crew cut and glanced at his fingerwatch.

"I wasn't expecting her until tomorrow. Did she give you any trouble?"

Bruno held up his hands. "Hey, she looked like this when they gave her to me at the train. They say she beat the crap out of two that arrested her, though. It took six of those mutant fellas to pin her down, they said."

Juanita glanced at Tempest, who was staring at the floor of the cage. "She doesn't look that tough. Are you a hard one, dear? Are we going to need a shock collar for you?"

Tempest slowly raised her eyes to Juanita's face. The look gave Juanita goose bumps. "It depends," Tempest said with quiet menace. "Are you afraid of me, too?"

Juanita cleared her throat and rolled her shoulders back, standing a bit straighter. She might be twenty years older than Tempest, but she stayed in shape, and she still had a dancer's body. "I've handled my share of tough cases in here. Maybe half the people we see want to fight the inevitable; but they all leave the same way, so there's no point in making it harder for yourself. I'll take good care of you if you don't put up a fuss. I'm here to help, not to harm you."

"I suppose turning my brain to mush isn't harming me?" Tempest asked.

Juanita wondered how much the woman knew about what they did at the rehab facility. She glanced at the information on the monitor. Tempest was the daughter of some local official in Marinwood, wherever that was, so she really must have pissed someone off to be sent here. Her parents definitely wanted her back, but she wasn't marked for any special handling. "We're only here to reeducate you, Ms. Gustafson. No one's brain will be turned to mush."

"Unless you ask for it," Bruno said with a chuckle. "You want some company, my pretty, you ask for Bruno. He'll give you something to think about."

Juanita rolled her eyes. "Get a grip, Bruno. I'll be monitoring her, not you."

"You always get all the fun," Bruno whined. "Maybe she wants Bruno instead."

Tempest turned and gave Bruno an odd little smile. "Maybe you're right."

"Eh?" Bruno frowned and took a step back.

Juanita sighed as she picked up a towel and an ID collar, then moved around to open the cage door. "Move it, Bruno. I'll take it from here."

Grumbling, Bruno backed away. When Tempest stepped out of the cage, Juanita sealed the black ID collar around her neck before guiding her through another door with a window in it. There was no furniture, but a variety of scanners on the walls were ready to do their jobs. She handed Tempest the towel and turned toward the small control panel by the door. "Stand in the middle of the floor, get out of those clothes, and wrap yourself in the towel."

Tempest did as she was told while Juanita powered up the scanners and started the series. Other than a low hum, there was no indication that the scanners were doing anything, but the data dump would be waiting for her in the tank room when they arrived. Hearing excited laughter at the door, she looked up and saw Bruno leering through the window, so she stepped over and put her face in the way of his view of

Tempest. His smile disappeared, and he turned away to sit down behind the desk.

"Thank you," Tempest said, waiting patiently in her towel. She looked more muscular than Juanita would have suspected, lending some credence to Bruno's story about her arrest.

Juanita nodded, glanced at the controls to make sure the scanners were finished, then opened the door and led Tempest out of the room by the elbow. Bruno pretended not to notice them as they walked past the desk and down the corridor to the stairwell, but Juanita saw him watching when she glanced at a mirrored window along the way. Another two hours before the shift ended, then Bruno would be someone else's problem. With any luck, more arrivals would come in on the train, and he'd stay busy picking them up.

When they neared the bottom of the stairwell two levels down from the intake facility, Juanita leaned in close to whisper in Tempest's ear. "I want you to do us both a favor. When we step through into the hallway, start to run away."

"What?" Tempest shook her head.

"Just trust me," Juanita whispered, opening the door. "I can help, but this has to look good."

Juanita wasn't sure if the woman was smart enough to cooperate, but that was part of the test, really. She had to make snap judgments about people, and this one seemed like she had potential if she would accept the opportunity that Juanita was offering.

Tempest hesitated when they went through the door, then shoved Juanita aside and sprinted down the long, empty stone corridor past numbered doors guarded by fierce statues from ancient Egyptian folklore. Regaining her balance, Juanita took off after her; but Tempest was halfway to the other end before Juanita was finally able to tackle her. Tempest sprawled on the cold floor at the foot of a hawk-headed Osiris statue, then grabbed her towel and wrapped it around

Juanita's neck—a move that Juanita hadn't expected. "Hey! I'm trying to help you!"

"I'm helping myself," Tempest said, tightening the towel as she straddled Juanita's waist. As the woman's eyes bulged, Tempest saw what looked like a red rose tattoo on the white of her right eyeball.

"You have to get off me," Juanita hissed, gagging as she struggled to pull the towel free of her neck. "If this goes on too long, Bruno will see it on the cameras and come down here with a stunner. We're in a dead zone without audio pickups, but he can still see us."

Juanita sensed the hesitant shift in Tempest's weight and used the moment to roll sideways, slamming Tempest against the wall as she pulled the towel loose. She pressed her lips against Tempest's left ear. "Look, you crazy fool, I just wanted to tell you not to worry. Just get in the tank when I tell you. I won't turn it on. When I get a chance, I'll try to get you out. All you have to do is keep your mouth shut."

"Why?" Tempest gasped, her torso pinned under Juanita's weight.

"Don't worry your pretty little head about that," Juanita said, roughly hauling Tempest to her feet to make it look good for the camera. "Just be happy you won't leave here like a zombie."

...8

THE rippling water in the eastern part of the bay looked as if it were on fire as Tom slogged along in the shoreline mud inhaling gnats and slapping at mosquitoes. He was exhausted from traveling all day in the wake of Magnus and Dead Man, who seemed to have limitless amounts of energy at their disposal despite appearances to the contrary. Helix was also looking tired, even though Tom had carried him for hours. They had stopped twice to eat strange, dried food items that Magnus carried in his pack, allowing Tom a few minutes to massage his burning leg muscles. He knew he'd be quite sore the next day and hoped his sadistic companions weren't planning to repeat their performance.

The wind picked up, rustling the water weeds and grasses along the flat shoreline, giving Tom some respite from the bug eating and slapping. He had no idea where they were going, and he didn't really care at that point, simply hoping that they would stop before it got too dark to see or before Tom lost his will to live. He knew they were in the east bay and that they had taken a circuitous path to avoid the numerous shoreline security wards, but he wasn't familiar with the terrain.

When Dead Man finally stopped, Tom almost ran into him. After staring at the mud for so long, Tom was startled to look up and see an enormous wall of rusty gray metal towering over their heads and extending away for hundreds of feet on both sides. Although he'd only seen such objects in photographs, he gradually realized that the ominous-looking wall was actually a huge ship beached in the shallow waters. Despite its dilapidated condition, it gave the impression of readiness, as if it might suddenly turn and head out to sea, well aware that it would break up among the waves but stubborn enough to try it anyway. The rotting hulks of other metal monsters poked out of the water or lay in rusted sections half-buried in the mud. The wind howled through the wrecks, and they creaked in response. The lonely feeling that the boneyard of metal dinosaurs had been abandoned and forgotten by the world was almost overwhelming.

As Tom's eyes began to pick out details on the side of the gray leviathan, he saw a faded number "61" at the forward end of the ship. "What does that mean?" Tom asked. "Sixty-one?"

Dead Man turned his bulging eyes toward Tom. "This is the USS *Iowa,* a Navy battleship. Sixty-one was the Navy ID number."

Helix growled at a small fish taunting him from the water's edge. It was a rare sight to see a fish in the bay, but Tom had never been to the eastern side before, so maybe it was normal here. His leg muscles twitched, appreciative of standing still but wondering when Tom would finally give them a real break.

Distracted by Dead Man, Tom was startled to see that Magnus had climbed up the dangling anchor chain. He was now perched, with perfect balance, on the rail of the ship, looking down at them. The wind whipped at his cloak and his hair as he cupped his hands around his mouth to yell, "Come along, boy! We need to be in place before the fog gets here!"

Tom looked out across the water. On the far side of the bay, the fog had crawled over the western hills to make its way across the water in thick streamers that curled ahead of the main fogbank. The sun had vanished below the horizon, leaving only a bright grayness beyond the hills. "In place for what?" Tom asked, looking at Dead Man.

"The gray shroud covers the faces of many, and it blinds them," Dead Man said, looking out across the water. "However, the person who understands the nature of the shroud can remove it. Do you understand?"

"No," Tom said, slogging toward the anchor chain with Helix in his arms.

Dead Man hissed softly, and when Tom looked back over his shoulder he realized that the hissing was actually the laughter of the dead. "You will understand, Tom Eliot. You will meet the shroud yourself, and you will master it—or it will consume you."

With Helix stuffed into his shirt, Tom began climbing the anchor chain. "That's reassuring." While he had no idea why Dead Man was laughing, he began to think that another training exercise would be forced on him in the near future. All the conditions were met: he was exhausted, he was in a strange place, and the two oddballs he was traveling with had that conspiratorial look about them that always spelled trouble for Tom.

He was right.

Ten minutes later, Tom found himself seated on top of a massive armored turret with three enormous gun barrels poking out of it. The silent guns were aimed at the oncoming fog, which was now only a short distance away, drifting and curling across the surface of the water, covering everything in its path with a blanket of gray. Sounds became muted, but Tom still heard the creaks and pops of aging metal on the ship, the hollow slap of wavelets against the hull, the periodic clank of a bell on an old buoy marking the watery graves of the ghost ships, the occasional snore from the dog sleeping on his lap, and echoes of Magnus's distant voice as he continued talking to himself somewhere below the weather decks of the ancient battleship.

Dead Man patted the gun turret as he folded his legs into a lotus position. "An example of raw, physical power. One of these guns could lob a shell the size of a railroad freight car over twenty miles."

Tom had never seen a freight car, and the largest shell he'd ever seen was an iridescent abalone shell that his father had kept nailed to the wall of their barn. He was going to ask why anyone would go to so much trouble to hurl shells through the air, but he changed his mind and simply nodded. "Impressive. You seem to know a lot about the past."

"Memories fade unless we revisit them, or unless we create them. I'm sure Magnus has mentioned that to you. We can fix a point from the quantum wave of space-time to create a link between our perceived past and our intended future, and that is another form of power—a power that is more formidable than that of this giant gun."

"He mentioned it. I don't pretend to understand it." Tom felt dizzy again, and he wondered how long the poison would last in his system before he felt more serious effects. He began to sweat as the air chilled in the face of the on-coming fog.

"That's because you have yet to experience the power of your consciousness. All paths lead to the Road—we just have to find the shortest path for you. And that's one way I may help you. Now, listen carefully to my voice, and let it be your anchor no matter what happens. I tell you now that you're going to have to learn some things very quickly—your survival depends on it. When that fog gets here, I will help you see the phantoms and other dangers that live behind the shroud, and they will know that you can see them. The phantoms won't threaten me, but they will challenge you. If you fail, you will be wrapped up in the arms of the fog, and you will become a phantom yourself. I won't be able to help you if they take you, and neither will Magnus. If you win, you will gain mastery over the fog, and the fog will teach you things."

Tom swallowed, then took a deep breath, trying to remain calm in the face of the oncoming fogbank. Despite what Dead Man was saying, he knew it was only water vapor, and it couldn't harm him, but there was a menace about the fog that he hadn't noticed before. The bow of the ship was wrapped in wet cotton, gradually disappearing as if it were dissolving in acid. Dark shadows seemed to move about just beyond the swirling gray boundaries, although he couldn't make out any distinct shapes to focus on. Was this a different kind of fog, or was Dead Man trying to make him see things that weren't really there?

"Could we do this tomorrow?" Tom asked. His legs were going numb in their cross-legged position. "I could really use a rest and something to eat."

"Keep your mind here in the present," Dead Man barked. "This is not a joke, and there is no turning back. The fog is here, and it's going to kill you, do you understand? Look into its depths. Do you see the phantoms? You will know the touch of their cold fingers very soon, and your mind must be ready for the shock."

Tom licked his lips as he tried to make out the shapes of the fog entities. "What do you want me to do? You haven't told me how to fight them."

"You must learn that for yourself. Close your eyes, see beyond your eyelids as Magnus showed you, and stop thinking. You can't rationalize your way out of this threat. Your body knows what to do if you'll listen to its wisdom. Focus on your breath flowing in and out of your body. Fill your lungs with air and let it out slowly. Think of a protective shell around your body; a sphere of energy that will repel the icy touch of the creatures within the fog. Each breath should take you deeper into the core of your being, sinking farther with each exhalation, feeling the sphere radiating out from your body to shield you and keep your spirit safe. Your death stands waiting, so you must focus on the sphere and believe in its power, for it is your only defense."

Tom had his eyes closed, and he was trying to visualize the sphere of energy as he focused on his breathing, but he couldn't see through his eyelids so he had no idea of how close the fog was, or where it was, or if the phantoms were reaching for him. He didn't know how to defend himself from creatures he couldn't see or hear. Sweat trickled down his face, and he felt the humidity rising, so the fog must be close. Yet he had to wonder, if he was as important as Magnus said he was, would they really take the chance of losing him this way? Perhaps Dead Man was hypnotizing him, making him think there were creatures living in the water vapor that blanketed the old battleship when there was actually nothing there at all.

He had to look.

Squinting, he opened his eyes just a bit, then gasped and jerked back away from the massive golden eyes hanging just inches away from his face. The fog was all around him, and he had no energy shield, and his concentration was broken, and he was going to die. Helix was gone, but Tom heard him whimpering in the distance, somewhere behind him. The phantom smiled with confidence, its golden eyes glittering, backing off a bit so Tom could see its enormous ghostly face drifting in the swirls of water vapor. It was a large caricature of a human face, almost as if it were painted on a transparent balloon bobbing in front of Tom. Tendrils of something like feathery seaweed floated above its head where they were attached to the scalp in place of hair. The mouth was much too large, large enough to swallow Tom's head, and the black pit inside the mouth looked like the entrance to Hell.

"Close your eyes!" Dead Man commanded. "The more it sees in your eyes, the more it knows about you, feeding on your thoughts and emotions, and it may know too much already! Watch through your eyelids, if you must, and that will give you some protection."

Tom tried to control his breath and focus on it, in and out, as he imagined an egg of blue energy shielding his body from the phantoms in the fog. Then he shivered as he felt ice on his left wrist, cold fingers sliding up his arm. His heart thumped in his chest, bouncing his body in the rhythm of his pulse. He thought he could feel each water molecule in the fog bumping against his skin as if they were tiny slivers of ice.

"Your shield is weak," Dead Man said. "Concentrate! Focus your energy!"

Tom felt the hairs on the back of his neck stand at attention, and he sensed a presence close to his face, but he kept his eyes closed and tried to imagine the details of his energy shield, the sparks that danced across its surface, the hum of power, the blue glow.

The dizziness in his head suddenly got worse. He was doomed. Then he realized he was seeing through his eyelids, and through his head, in a complete circle where he could view only fog . . . and the group of phantoms that were crouched in a circle around him, reaching out with frozen fingers to poke him and grab at his head, their eyes glittering with delight. Dead Man was gone. Tom was alone with his death. The certainty that he was about to leave this world calmed him somewhat. His heart slowed, and his breathing became more regular, in and out, waiting for the inevitable.

The blue sphere appeared, maybe three feet away from his body, and he felt as if he were seated inside a glass bubble. The phantoms screamed and recoiled, some of them leaving fingers, hands, or entire arms thumping to the bottom of the blue bubble. They jumped to their feet, dancing in anger, beating their fists against the sphere and screaming. And Tom felt good. He felt powerful. He imagined the static sparks jumping around on the surface of the bubble, getting larger as they built up their electrical charges, then lancing out like tiny bolts of lightning to bury their points in the faces and bodies of the phantoms. The air vibrated with piercing shrieks and thunderclaps that echoed inside the bubble, forcing Tom to cover his ears to keep his eardrums from rupturing. Brilliant flashes of lightning rapidly pulsed through the air, effectively blinding him.

The distraction made him lose focus. His shield disappeared, and the last spark of static popped at the same instant, leaving the air full of a strong ozone smell but nothing else. The fog thinned. He took a deep breath.

The phantoms were gone.

Tom opened his eyes as he felt Helix returning to his lap. The little dog looked around suspiciously.

Dead Man still sat nearby, looking at Tom and shaking his head as the fog drifted back, leaving them in a clear space like a hole in a ball of cotton.

"I did it," Tom said with a gasp, waiting for congratulations. "I'm still alive."

"You *overdid* it. You use power like a club. You are not here to kill everything you see, Tom. This is not Stronghold. Yes, you're still alive, so you didn't lose—but you didn't win, either. The idea was to master the fog and make it clear to the phantoms that you could defend yourself, not to destroy them because you feared them or didn't understand them. The fog can teach you things, just as it has already taught you something; but you could have made those phantoms your allies, and they would have been around to help you wherever there was fog. You need the help of the natural forces of this world. To make enemies of the elements, or to kill the creatures that reside in them, only does harm to yourself. The fog will not hinder you now, nor will it help you when you need it. Through inaction, the fog will be your silent enemy."

"But—I didn't know!" Tom exploded. "You didn't tell me all that ahead of time! All you said was that the fog was going to eat me unless I mastered it!"

Dead Man gracefully unwound his legs and stood up. "As I said, your body and spirit know how to deal with these things if you'll only get your conscious mind out of the way. You must learn to trust your body's wisdom. You share common knowledge with the elements of nature and the rest of the world, and you must let it flow through you to become aware of it when you need it." He turned to climb down the gun turret ladder to the steel deck below.

"Where are you going?" Tom asked, barely keeping the annoyance out of his voice.

Dead Man glanced at him just before his head disappeared below the gun turret's edge. "To get some food, then some rest."

Helix jumped out of Tom's lap, fully alert when he heard the word "food," then he darted toward the ladder, realized he couldn't climb down without help, and looked back at Tom and whined.

Tom eyed the fog that was rapidly streaming away from the battleship, leaving a fine layer of water droplets on everything as a souvenir of its visit. With a heavy sigh, he got up, stamped his feet to get the circulation going again in his legs, and shuffled over to pick up Helix. His dizziness made it hard to walk in a straight line. He shook his head—maybe he'd get lucky, and the poison would kill him soon.

TEMPEST'S world had been reduced to the size of her body.

Juanita had placed her in a shiny metal sarcophagus that looked like a stylized human form resting on its back. A small glass panel in the face of her enclosure allowed her to look out at the sterile, white-tiled room she was trapped in. One hose fed her liquid nutrients while others were prepared to remove any bodily wastes. The inside of her coffin smelled of sweat and copper. She heard only her heartbeat and her breathing, trying hard to relax as she held on to the promise of escape that Juanita had offered, assuming she was telling the truth and it wasn't some kind of trick to mess with her mind. However, as promised, Juanita had not activated the thousands of tiny brushlike probes that gently touched Tempest's skin, causing her to tingle and itch over most of her naked body. The timepiece hovering in the corner of the tiled room told her she'd been in the coffin for almost two hours, but the close confinement made the time pass slowly, as if she'd been in it much longer. It seemed strange, but the time she had spent in her father's shock box had helped to prepare her for this situation, although that conditioning was starting to wear off. Her anxiety began to build as her muscles stiffened, and she wished she could move some part of her body without being poked with the tiny needles. Breathing faster, she closed her eyes as tears slowly dripped down her cheeks, tickling her face as they descended from needle cluster to needle cluster. She still couldn't understand why her father had sent her here, although she suspected that Hermes had manipulated him into it somehow. She thought about the last moments she had spent with her father, running them over in her mind to look for clues.

Hermes had brought news to Memphis, and Tempest had listened at the door of her father's office to hear what she could, but the muffled voices weren't clear enough for her to make out more than a few of the words. When Memphis cried out in anguish, Tempest couldn't stop herself from pushing her way into the room to see if he was all right. His face was in his hands, and his body shook with his sobbing as Hermes stood over him, unmoved by the emotional outburst, waiting for Memphis to stop so that he could continue delivering his message.

"What's happened?" Tempest had asked, ignoring the protocol that required Hermes to speak before she could speak to him.

"Your brother has been destroyed," Hermes said, his tone flat and unconcerned.

It took a moment for the news to sink in. Tempest thought it must be a trick, but her father clearly believed it. She was shocked and didn't know how to respond, her eyes going back and forth from her father to Hermes, who had finally turned his head to look at her. "There is also an excellent probability that Tom Eliot was destroyed. Humboldt successfully located his hiding place in the hills."

The second shock was too much. Not Tom. Her Tom. She wouldn't accept it. Without realizing what she was doing, Tempest threw herself at Hermes, the source of all the pain that had recently befallen her family. When she crashed into him, it felt as if she'd thrown herself against a wall or a heavy machine, and it took only a flick of his arm to send her flying backward across her father's desk and onto the floor. Memphis lurched back to avoid her. The fall was painful, but she got up and charged Hermes again. This time he stepped to one side, then slammed her down to the floor. She turned her head and saw her father coming to her rescue, his face red and shaking, his fists clenched. Then, instead of attacking Hermes, he roughly grabbed Tempest by the shoulders and lifted her to her feet, shaking her. "You! You are the cause of all this! Your dalliance with that boy has cost me my son!"

And it was Hermes who stepped in to separate them. A few hours later, she found herself on an underground train hurtling through the darkness on her way to the dreaded rehabilitation facility.

Tempest blinked, trying hard to convert her sadness to anger. If she could just hold out a little longer, she would be released from her tiny prison. A glance at the clock revealed that another twenty minutes had passed. When she began to wonder if Juanita really would come back, the door finally opened.

Bruno stepped into the room and shut the door.

With an odd smile on his face, he walked over and knelt beside her coffin, leaning forward to look closely at her face. He ran one hand over the smooth surface, tracing the cold outline of the metal above her body, and his hot breath fogged the glass over her eyes. She gritted her teeth, hoping he wouldn't look too closely at the controls. Her earlier plan to lure him in there was based on the idea that she would be locked in some kind of a cell where she could surprise him. There would be no surprise attack from the inside of the box, that much was certain.

The door opened again. Startled, Bruno jumped back from the coffin as Juanita walked into the room. Although she couldn't hear the words, Tempest saw a brief argument before Bruno shoved past Juanita and stomped off into the corridor.

Tempest closed her eyes and sighed as Juanita bent over and snapped open the locks that held the coffin lid shut. Cool air shocked her skin when Juanita lifted the lid.

"Try to roll straight out to the side," Juanita said, disconnecting the umbilical hoses that maintained Tempest's intimate contact with the torture device. "You'll have less contact with the brushes that way, and it won't hurt as much."

Tempest did as she was told, rolling out onto the cold white tiles where Juanita helped her sit up. "I'd let you take a shower before we leave, but there isn't time."

"Thank you," Tempest whispered, finally finding her voice as she hugged Juanita.

Juanita rubbed her back. "It's okay. No need to thank

me until we get out of here, and that's not going to be easy."

Tempest nodded, afraid to look up into her rescuer's face. "I'll do whatever you ask."

Juanita removed her lab coat and helped Tempest to her feet. "Put this on. Bruno had already disposed of your clothes by the time I went back, so I'm afraid my coat will have to do for now."

Tempest wriggled into the coat, watching the door in case Bruno reappeared. "This is fine. I'm fine. Let's go."

Juanita nodded as she pulled another ID tag out of her pocket, a tag that matched the one hanging on the lab coat. "We'll both be Juanita Lopez for a little while. Lucky you. If any sensors pick us up, it'll look like a system glitch."

Tempest stiffened as she spotted a tiny camera high on the ceiling. "Can they see us? Can Bruno see us?"

"Don't worry. I've done this before. I've got a little invisibility program running in the security system right now, so all the camera can see is an empty room."

Tempest didn't understand, but she didn't have to, so she started walking toward the door.

"Not that way," Juanita said, opening the hatch to a waste disposal elevator on the opposite wall. "I hope you don't mind getting dirty, little girl. We have to take out the trash."

After wedging themselves in the tiny elevator for a short ride deeper into the bowels of the old hotel, then ten minutes of crawling through the old aluminum ventilation ducts, Tempest's knees were sore and her back hurt. However, she was free and moving around, which was a definite improvement over being locked in a coffin. By comparison to that confined space, the ventilation ducts seemed quite roomy, and there was plenty of light from the grilles that connected the ducts to the rooms they passed. In one of the rooms, she thought she glimpsed Bruno wearing part of her stolen dress, admiring himself in a mirror, but she didn't want to think about that.

Instead of continuing to crawl higher in the ventilation system, Juanita surprised Tempest by guiding them down to a damp little room with poor lighting where she quietly slid the grille out of its slot and set it down in the shaft. She gestured at the gap. "Jump for it."

Tempest peeked over the edge and saw a drop of about three feet to bare concrete stained by water leaks. There was no furniture in the room, only pipes and a raised steel hatch in the middle of the floor. She landed in a crouch, and the concrete felt rough and cold against her bare feet. The formerly white lab coat she wore was now smudged and stained with various shades of gray dirt.

Juanita reinserted the ventilation grille, then opened the hatch. The warm air that flowed up to greet them was humid, and it carried the smell of vegetation, but Tempest saw only a metal ladder leading down into a dark concrete pipe with a shallow stream flowing through it.

"Are you starting to feel like a rat?" Juanita asked. "All that crawling, and now we're going to travel through the sewers. I bet you hadn't imagined that your day would turn out like this."

That was a safe guess, Tempest thought, starting down the ladder. "As you said, it's better than being a zombie. Where are we going?"

Juanita climbed onto the ladder and pulled the hatch shut over her head, leaving them in sudden darkness. "I want you to meet some friends of mine."

Tempest heard a click, then two glowing lines of overhead light strips illuminated the sewer pipe in both directions. The pipe was about ten feet in diameter. When she stepped off the ladder, the cool stream only came up to her ankles. Someone had sprayed "Rose Knows" in black paint on the wall at Tempest's eye level. "Who's Rose?"

Juanita gestured for her to follow, sloshing down the stream. The light rippled on the water, creating a magical effect. "Only Rose knows. Some people call her the Tunnel Queen, and she rules the Underworld. You'll meet her in a little while."

"She lives down here?"

"Sometimes. The shades say she has the power to walk the surface world undetected, disguised to fit in with the other groundlings. Watch your step here."

Tempest gasped when she stepped on a slippery spot in the stream, catching her balance with a hand against the wall. She had no interest in dunking herself in cold water. "Thanks. Who are the shades?"

"They're the tunnel dwellers, the Queen's subjects—outcasts from the surface who made new homes in the Underworld."

"You're saying they live in the sewers?"

"One person's sewer is another person's castle. The shades go topside occasionally, but only in the dark when they're raiding the groundlings for supplies. There aren't any stores down here, you know, although there is a fair amount of barter. They use hydroponics to grow most of their own food, and they've tapped into city pipes for a freshwater supply. They don't have to raid very often since Rose brings them a lot of what they need. Sometimes, though, I think they go raiding for the entertainment. The scenery in the sewers gets kind of monotonous after a while."

Tempest heard an odd hooting noise in the distance ahead of them, echoing down the pipe, and she was startled when Juanita hooted in reply, then winked at her. "Hooters. The shades take turns at guard duty, just in case the groundlings get nosy. They also keep an eye out for floodwaters, although that's mainly a problem during the summer months. We need warning in case we need to move the art and other things to higher ground."

"Art?"

"You'll see."

Tempest swatted at a cloud of tiny bugs that suddenly swarmed around her head.

"Gnatcams," Juanita said. "Just ignore them. They're part of the Underworld security system so the hooters can look us over before we can see them."

Juanita seemed to know everything about the Underworld, and that made Tempest suspicious, despite the fact that Juanita was helping her to escape. Of course, she had no idea about what she was escaping into, and she figured it couldn't be any worse than the rehab facility; but she really didn't know anything about Juanita or her friends in the sewer. For all she knew, the shades were cannibals, and Juanita was their high priestess who went off in search of suitable sacrifices for their strange sewer rituals.

The pipe was wider now, allowing Juanita to walk beside Tempest as they continued to slog down the stream. "You're very trusting," Juanita said. "I see that a lot in people from your side of the barrier. Of course, what choice do you have when it comes down to staying in the rehab facility or diving into the unknown with me? Still, it must seem safer here. At least we don't have any crazy mutants running around to threaten people."

"Mutants?" Tempest shook her head. "I don't understand."

"It's okay, dear," Juanita said, patting Tempest on the back. "I know you're not a mutant; it would have shown up in your genetic scans when you came in. However, your neighbors were exposed to all those nasty nanobugs years ago, so now the mutations are showing up in the population. There's nothing to be ashamed of."

Tempest still didn't understand, so she decided to wait before asking for a better explanation. They entered a vast chamber where the stream flowed through the middle, but the overhead strip lights they had been following were too dim to illuminate the sides and corners of the room.

Strange concrete dividing walls, apparently placed to divert water down other tunnels, stood like monuments among fluted columns and raised concrete platforms of varying heights. Wherever Tempest looked, the walls were painted with scary faces, cryptic slogans such as "Rose Knows," and some surprisingly good murals of natural landscapes drenched in sunlight. As they ventured farther into the room, Tempest also spotted some large paintings hung in heavy frames. Based on her limited experience with such things, the paintings of people and exotic street scenes looked very professional. Before she could learn more, Tempest was startled by hooting sounds, as if they'd suddenly been surrounded by hundreds of owls.

"It's okay," Juanita said, patting her back. "No need to be frightened. This is just their way of saying hello."

The hoots gradually switched to shouts of "Rose! Rose! Rose!" Juanita pointed at a high platform near the center of the chamber; the stream flowed around it in a shallow channel like a moat. On top of the platform were two mushroom-shaped columns supporting the ceiling, and each one had a face painted on it that almost looked familiar. "Rose is here," Juanita said, "and she's going to appear on top of that platform. When she summons you, go around to the back of the platform and climb the stairs.

"What about you?" Tempest asked, afraid to be left alone in such a spooky place. She still couldn't see any people attached to the shouting voices that echoed through the chamber.

"I'll be right there. I have to get formal permission for you to stay." Juanita turned and jogged away into the shadows before Tempest could protest any further.

The shouts gradually died down. As Tempest squinted into the shadows, trying to make out any movements or details, she heard rustling noises, then dark human shapes began drifting into the center of the room in groups of ten or more. Two men carried buckets of a heavy liquid to the moat and dumped them into the water, then one of them touched a flamer to the water and the entire moat lit up in a roaring wall of fire that almost reached the top of the central platform. Pale faces were illuminated by the flames, staring at Tempest as if they'd never seen a stranger before. Shadows danced across the ceiling. Mumbling to themselves, the crowd edged closer, sealing Tempest into the middle of their circle, many of them hooting like gorillas. Expecting to see tattered robes or some other form of simple, dirty clothing, Tempest was surprised to note that many in the crowd were dressed in formal suits, tuxedoes, evening gowns, and other antique styles of formal wear that she had only seen in holos and flicks at school. On closer inspection, Tempest did see suits with holes and gowns smudged with dirt, but almost everyone's hair was neatly cut and styled, and their faces looked clean. Watches and jewelry sparkled in the firelight. Judging by the faces she could see, Tempest was one of the youngest people in the chamber. Most of the shades were middle-aged and older.

"My people!" shouted a female voice above their heads. The chamber was filled with hundreds of men and women who all suddenly fell silent, looking up with awed expressions. A woman in a black leather outfit strode forward on spike-heeled boots to the edge of the platform, then placed her hands on her hips and favored them with a brilliant smile. Her eyes smoldered in dark pits. It was the same face Tempest saw painted on the pillars on both sides of the platform. After a moment, Tempest saw past the heavy eye makeup and the leather outfit and recognized her rescuer, Juanita. A rhythmic chant rose up from the crowd, "Rose! Rose! Rose!" until Rose raised her arms to silence them again.

"This is a great day for the Underworld," Rose shouted in a clear voice full of command. "We prosper here in our world below the surface. We grow our own food, go about our daily lives in privacy, raise our children, and live in peace. Yet we would go stale without new ideas and fresh bodies to share our good works. This is a great day for us because we have a new member among us, a strong young woman who has been persecuted by her own family and the iron hand of the gods, singled out because she would not conform to traditional rules that made no sense in her modern world. This story should sound familiar, because most of us are here for the same reasons. For a little while longer, her name is Tempest, and she is one of us now. She is a shade. Please welcome her."

Startled by Rose's words, wondering what she had gotten herself into, Tempest had little time to think before hands were all over her, patting and rubbing her in welcome, pressing in and almost smothering her with kindness. When she thought she could no longer breathe, strong hands lifted her, and she was passed over the heads of the crowd toward the staircase behind the platform, where Rose herself helped her stand and climb the stairs. Stunned and confused, breathing way too fast, she followed Rose to the edge of the platform and looked out on the assembled mob, sensing the power of the crowd and their adoration for their leader. Tempest had never experienced anything like it, and she had no idea how to respond.

Sensing her confusion, Rose whispered in her ear. "Just wave."

"What?"

Rose waved at the crowd to demonstrate. Tempest repeated the gesture and felt the thunder of hundreds of people hooting back at her in response—waves of sound that pulsed through her body. Rose smiled to reassure Tempest that the hooting was a good thing, and that smile made all the difference. Tempest began to relax. Whatever lay ahead might be confusing, but she didn't feel that these people would harm her. She felt safe, and thought perhaps this was where she was meant to be. A strange thought, indeed. For the moment, at least, she was a shade.

Rose leaned over to whisper to her again. "You should try to get plenty of rest tonight. Tomorrow will be very exhausting for you."

Tempest raised an eyebrow. "Why is that?"

"We have accepted you as one of us. Tomorrow, you must demonstrate your loyalty."

...9

AFTER a meager dinner of dried meat and other unidentifiable things that Magnus pulled out of his backpack, Tom
hunted around for a safe place to sleep inside the rotting
hulk of the battleship. Armed with a flashlight, he snooped
through the small gray rooms, fascinated by the almost
decorative patterns of rust on the metal walls. As he walked
the narrow corridors, stepping through watertight hatchways, his hollow footsteps were accompanied by the constant sound of creaking, punctuated by the gurgling and
sloshing of water in the lower decks, and he finally decided
that he'd feel safer sleeping beneath the stars on the gun
deck. Out in the open air, he tried to find a comfortable
spot on the bumpy plates, but none of the surfaces were
smooth, so he couldn't go to sleep. He enjoyed the cool
breeze, but he was still worried about the possible return of
the deadly fog. He took off his shirt and used it for a pillow, but that left his back bare against the cold metal.
Would it make any difference if the fog returned while his
shirt was off, or while he was asleep? Were there other

creatures of the elements out there that might sneak up on a sleeping person and eat them? He decided that there were too many things he didn't understand, and that worried him. If he wasn't so exhausted from hiking all day, he'd give up and try to stay awake all night. He sat up and looked overhead at the three massive gun barrels silhouetted in the moonlight, thinking maybe he could hide inside one of those, when his thoughts were interrupted by Helix.

"Try to relax," Helix said, sniffing the air. "You smell tired."

Tom's eyes widened as he looked down at the little dog in his lap, who stared up at him with a concerned expression. Tom didn't like the possibilities in this situation: Either he was going crazy and hearing voices in his head, or his dog had learned how to talk.

"I'll protect you," Helix said. "Get some sleep."

Now Tom was really worried. The dog's mouth wasn't moving, and Tom seemed to be hearing the rough, low-pitched voice inside his head. The dog's words came in short bursts, almost as if he were barking. Tom jumped to his feet, dumping Helix on the deck in the process. Helix didn't seem to mind; he lay down on his stomach in a sphinx pose and tipped his head, looking up at Tom. "I smell fear. I hope I didn't cause that. Have you got food?"

"Are you hungry? You had dinner," Tom said before he realized he was answering the dog. Or was it his dog, he wondered? Had some fog or wind creature taken over Helix's body?

Helix wagged his tail. "I just like to eat."

Tom displayed his empty hands, reassured by Helix's familiar interest in food. "Sorry. I feel like I should reward you for speaking."

"That's okay. Maybe next time. Would you scratch my tummy?" Helix rolled over on his back and wriggled as he always did when he wanted a scratch.

Still stunned by their ongoing conversation, Tom

scratched the dog's chest and watched Helix pull the cor- ners of his mouth back in a doggy smile. "A little to the left," Helix said.

"How come you've never spoken to me before?"

Helix snorted and rolled his eyes. "I've been talking to you since I was a puppy. You just weren't listening."

Suspicious, Tom looked around to see if Dead Man or Magnus were hiding in the shadows to play a trick on him. Seeing no one, he put his shirt back on to ward off the chill night air.

"Full moon," Helix said. "Good night for howling."

"If you're a dog," Tom said.

Helix looked at him. "I am a dog." He rolled onto his feet and took a long stretch. "But you've always liked the moon, too. Have you ever wondered why?"

Tom hesitated, gazing up at the moon. "Maybe because my mom liked it so much. And I'm basically a night per- son."

Helix reached forward with his back leg to scratch his right ear. "You draw energy from the moon. It focuses your mind and gives you power. That's why you wanted to sleep up here when it would have been safer on a lower deck. That's why you always want to go out for walks at night when the moon is high."

Tom frowned at Helix. "You're starting to sound like Magnus." He quickly looked around again to see if Mag- nus was watching, but he seemed to be alone with Helix.

Helix sniffed the air, then snapped at a small fly spiral- ing past his nose. "Your mom was the same way. She used to walk in the moonlight when she was younger."

"How would you know about that? You weren't around then."

Helix smiled his doggy smile again. "I'm a dog. I know things."

Tom yawned. With all the turmoil in his life lately, and all the strange things he'd seen the last few days, he was already accepting the fact that Helix could talk. What was one more oddity among so many? Exhausted from the day's events, he finally felt that he could sleep, so he lay down on the deck again and stared up at the moon.

Helix curled up between Tom's arm and his ribs, circling twice before actually settling in, then leaving his chin propped on Tom's elbow. "Here's a tip. When you go to sleep, focus your attention on your hands and try to look at them. If you can do that, try to control your movements in your dreams. It's good practice, and the full moon will help give you power."

"Good practice for what?" Tom asked, raising his left hand to study it.

"It will help you reach the Road," Helix replied, closing his eyes.

WHEN Tom opened his eyes, he was startled to see that the fog had returned. A bright whiteness filled his vision wherever he looked. He started to sit up, but his muscles wouldn't respond. Worried now, he tried to move his legs, or his arms, or his fingers, but he seemed to be paralyzed. He blinked, and that was the only part of his body he could control. His heart beat faster.

"Look at your hands," said a voice that sounded like dead leaves rustling in the breeze. Dead Man moved forward into Tom's field of view, although his movement looked odd, as if he were floating. He didn't appear to be worried about the fog.

Tom tried to answer him, but his mouth wouldn't work. Dead Man floated closer, which was scary enough under normal circumstances, with his bulging eyes and his dry brown skin stretched taut over his skeleton. When Dead Man touched his arm, Tom felt warm relief flooding through him. His heart slowed, and he took a deep breath.

"Think of it as sleep paralysis," Dead Man said. "You

can control it. Now, look at your hands before we do anything else."

Tom shuddered as a vibration, almost like a cycling electric current, moved up and down the length of his body. With great effort, he managed to lift his right arm and look at the back of his hand, which didn't seem as thick and solid as it usually did. He made a fist, but he couldn't feel the pressure in his muscles.

"You'll get better with practice. Magnus wants me to help you because we don't have time for you to discover how to do all these things on your own. Now, stay with me as I lift you."

Tom tried to respond, but his mouth still wouldn't work, and most of his body remained paralyzed as if he'd had a stroke. Dead Man's arms felt solid when they slid underneath his back, then lifted Tom as if he weighed less than Helix. Suddenly noticing Helix's absence, Tom snapped his head around to look for the little dog, but the motion caused his entire body to roll over, and he was horrified to see his own body three feet beneath him with its eyes closed. Was he dead or dreaming? He forgot about Helix for a moment as he tried to sort out his recent memories, but they were fragmented like pieces of broken glass. He needed answers from Dead Man, so he focused on his jaw, then on his lips and tongue, forcing them to move. Yet he couldn't take his eyes off the body below him. "Is that me?"

"More or less."

He continued to hover over the other Tom, and he felt a new tingling sensation throughout his body. "Am I dead?"

Dead Man hesitated. "That requires a more complicated answer. For now, let's say you're not dead and that your physical body is asleep."

"Then I'm dreaming?" He felt his body reorienting to the vertical as Dead Man rotated him from the waist. With time, he was also gaining more control over his movements.

"Some might call it that. We're trying to teach you to

use all of your talents, so now you're learning to control your energy body. This is your most powerful form, and you must use it to reach the Road."

"We're not on the Road now?"

Dead Man gestured at the bright fog that surrounded them. "This is only your starting point, the limbo between sleep and dreams and your physical body. This is where you'll go when you want to return to your physical self. Later on, you won't even need this as a reference point."

Tom's curiosity began to override his fear of the strange situation, and he held on to that as if it were his life preserver on this sea of confusion. "Is this like Stronghold?"

"No," Dead Man said, hesitating before he continued. "We're in a place where the AIs cannot go, but *we* can reach Stronghold from here because we can reach the Road. One who masters the Road can go anywhere, as the Road connects all manner of things—even the Dead Lands. Stronghold began as a virtual environment, and that's why Sandoval was able to show it to you with his simulation couch. The Dominion still interfaces with Stronghold as a virtual simulation network with a global reach, which is how it suits them, but even they sense that there is something greater above their world. Telemachus and Alioth and the others can probe and scheme all they want, but they can never leave the confines of Stronghold. That was the one fail-safe the Creator planted within them that they cannot breach."

"How do you know so much about it?"

Dead Man's shoulders slumped as he let out a heavy sigh. "I suppose I should tell you, as it may help you on your journey." He paused again, looking off at some unseen horizon. "I built the Dominion AIs, or at least the seeds of what they became when they grew up. Stronghold was a test-bed war-gaming environment that I worked on for the Defense Advanced Research Projects Agency, but I adapted it as a playground for the AIs to help them study human behavior and develop their full potential. It worked well—too well, in fact. And I am not proud of the result."

Tom felt awed and appalled at the same time. Depending on whom you spoke to, his companion was either the most hated man in history or the savior of humanity. "You're the Creator? You must be at least—how old are you?"

Dead Man dismissed the question with a wave of his hand. "Time has effectively stopped for me. However, I will live forever with the guilt of what I've done unless I can also be one of the instruments that defeats the Dominion—the children of my overheated mind. Do you see now why your mission is so important to me?"

"Why did you create the Dominion in the first place? It can't all have happened by accident. Who gave them so much power?"

Dead Man sighed again and shook his head. "The original intent was to place them in an advisory capacity to the federal government. As unemotional deterrents to wars that could have been initiated either by the U.S. or its enemies, the Dominion was also given strategic weapons control authority, removing humans from most of the control loop. Nanotech weapons were too dangerous for all concerned, so it was felt that the Dominion could help safeguard human civilization by keeping it safe from itself. To avoid the inevitable system or software failures that could lead to the destruction of the planet, multiple AIs had to agree on a course of action, and Alioth always voted last to break any tied decisions. Of course, the Dominion AIs continued to learn and grow, refining their predictive abilities and advising the president on the best courses of action whenever decisions had to be made. We realized too late that the Dominion had predicted multiple catastrophes for the human race, and they took steps to avoid those catastrophes by assuming full control of governmental functions, backed up by the arsenals at their command. When the humans became too unruly about the change in power, the Dominion used their nanoweapons to demonstrate the consequences of failing to acknowledge them. They understood that a display of massive force would be the best way to make an impression on us. San Diego, Los Angeles, San Francisco, Prunedale, Chualar, Sacramento—none of those great cities exist anymore. The western region of the United States was sealed off because of runaway nanotech reactions. Buoyed by their success in the west, they destroyed other key cities across the country as well, then others around the world."

"So the gods did what they thought best for us, and their plan worked, is that what you're saying?"

Dead Man stared at him for a moment before he responded. "I don't think Sandoval would agree with you about that. Neither would Humboldt, or your family."

That brought Tom up short. He looked away, wondering if his family was out there in the mists somewhere. "I suppose not."

"Come along. We have work to do." Dead Man turned away, then snapped his fingers and turned around again. "I forgot to ask. We couldn't find you after dinner. Where did you go to sleep?"

Tom strained to remember. It seemed like a long time ago that he had fallen asleep. "Under a gun turret on the main deck."

"Outside?"

"In the moonlight," Tom replied.

Dead Man grabbed him by the shoulders. "Are you *trying* to get killed? You have to wake up! Now!"

Tom looked at his sleeping body. "How do I do that?"

"Jump back in! Go!" Dead Man herded him back toward his physical body, but Tom was surprised to find resistance there, as if a wall of clear glass was in the way. "Keep trying!"

Tom tried again, but he bounced off his sleeping body, and he couldn't maneuver himself around into a horizontal position to try going in that way. He looked up and realized that Dead Man was gone, and that worried him even more. He shuddered, almost as if someone were shaking him from behind.

Tom blinked, then gasped when he saw Magnus's hairy face looming over him. "Wake up, you fool!" Tom blinked again when Helix's wet tongue slid across his left eye.

"Dead Man," Tom said. "Where—"

"He's right here! He told me where you were!" Magnus grabbed Tom's arm to haul him upright and he saw Dead Man standing at the rail looking out over the water. "Weren't you listening before when I told you about the spysats? It's four in the morning! They must have seen you by now!"

"Nothing yet," Dead Man called, "but we better hurry. It's high tide."

Tom looked at Helix, who just ran around in a circle like an excited dog—without saying anything. Had he dreamed the whole episode with Helix and Dead Man?

A vulture swooped in to land on the railing by Dead Man, giving Magnus a significant look.

Magnus shoved Tom toward Dead Man. "Go! Rocco spotted a guardian on the way!" Tom moved too slowly, so Magnus grabbed his arm again and ran toward Dead Man, their footsteps thumping on the metal deck, with Helix barking along behind them. Dead Man turned at their approach and reached for Tom.

A moment later, Tom felt himself hurled into midair. His stomach jumped into his throat as he fell toward the dark waters. On the way down, a giant hand pushed him away from the battleship, and he was stunned by a thundering roar as the sky burst into streaks of red and yellow. He hit the water with his back, and it knocked the wind out of him. Water filled his nose and mouth. When he looked up, he got a brief glimpse of flames rippling on the surface of the water, then he screamed when a ragged chunk of metal splashed into the water above his head.

▪ ▪ ▪

TEMPEST sat in a crouch, doing her best to keep the sticky soles of her shoes and her palms flat against the steeply canted roof of the high tower. She knew she was over two hundred feet above the ground, and she didn't like it one bit. She had already whizzed through the predawn darkness behind Rose on a spider line high above the city streets, flitting from one hotel roof to another while getting an exhilarating view of the bright lights below. And everywhere she flew, they were followed by four other shades dressed in black coveralls and traveling in pairs. Tempest also wore black coveralls, and she carried a backpack containing various supplies including high-heeled shoes and a formal black dress that fit her reasonably well when she tried it on in Rose's Underworld apartment. It was the fanciest dress she had ever worn, and it would have been considered scandalous to be seen in such a low-cut garment in Marinwood. The dress was part of her disguise for their trip into the main casino inside the fantasy castle known as Excalibur, but it also helped her fit in among the formally attired shades of the Underworld. Now she sat there like one of the gargoyles atop the royal blue cone of the highest castle tower, adjusting part of the harness that bit into her upper thigh, wondering how she had ever gotten herself into such a bizarre situation. She felt that she had proven her worthiness to the shade community by flying from rooftop to rooftop with Rose, but she knew they wanted more.

Spotlights illuminated the blue and red tops of the castle towers, and Tempest quickly learned not to look down into the lights because they caused a temporary blindness that was disconcerting in her precarious position. The gusts of warm desert wind didn't inspire confidence, either. She licked her dry lips and swallowed as she watched Rose tie the spider line to a cleat at the tip of the roof, then drop the line over the edge, where the coil lightly slapped against the floor of the balcony fifteen feet below.

Rose grabbed the line where it ran through the collar of Tempest's harness, then placed a loop in the crouching woman's hand. "Just remember, going down is easy. Getting back up here again will be harder. We'll have to be careful with the painting."

Tempest made a face. "That makes me feel much better." She had somehow fallen in with fanatical art collectors, or so it seemed. Although she had speculated on many possible tests of courage or strength that the shades might put her through to demonstrate her loyalty to her new family in the Underworld, she never guessed that they would ask her to steal an old painting from one of the nearby casinos. During a brief tour of the Underworld art collection before they left, Tempest saw a wide variety of oils and watercolors hanging on the bare concrete walls of the sewers, each one carefully lit by tiny spotlights and sealed inside clear, climate-controlled cases to protect them from the high humidity in the tunnels.

When Tempest asked why they had stolen so many paintings, Rose explained that the Dominion AIs had no appreciation of art, and the shades considered these paintings to be purely unique expressions of human talents that the AIs could not understand. Each painting they rescued was a symbol of human superiority, liberated from Dominion control so that they could be housed in freedom among human art lovers. The paintings on display in the casino collections were monitored, but not carefully guarded, because the AIs placed such a low value on them. The old paintings were particularly valuable because no new art was being produced; artists were rare among the population, and those who appeared were quickly rehabilitated.

Long ago, Rose had worked out a way to keep any AI security observers in the casinos satisfied while they removed the paintings to safety. Most of the risk to the burglars came in the form of nanoborg security guards or in the possibility of being identified by one of the AIs monitoring the security cameras. Only a few shades had actually been arrested while trying to steal paintings, but Rose sadly pointed out that the prisoners had never been seen again, even though she had watched for them at the rehab facility.

Tempest's target for the evening was Pablo Picasso's oil painting, *Don Quixote*. Rose had shown her a holo of the painting, which depicted the Spanish knight on horseback beside the faithful Sancho Panza on his mule. Tempest thought it was a nice painting, but not nice enough to risk her life to steal it. However, offered a choice between stealing the Picasso and trying to find her own way back home to Marinwood, Tempest chose to become a burglar.

The other four shades thumped against the roof somewhere behind Tempest as she awkwardly dropped over the edge of the roof, clinging to the spider line, her eyes shut so tight that she saw popping lights behind her eyelids. Inching her way down the line, holding her breath, her toes finally touched the floor of the balcony, and she sighed with relief. When she opened her eyes, she was facing Rose's back and a heavy blue door.

Rose gripped the doorknob. "It's locked."

Tempest gasped. "What? Why would anyone lock a door way up here?" She reached past Rose's arm and rattled the doorknob herself.

"I don't think it was meant to keep us out. They probably don't want any tourists sneaking into the tower and falling off the balcony."

"Now what?" Tempest looked toward the roof, already dreading the climb back up.

"Plan B," said Rose. She pointed over the edge of the balcony.

Tempest's eyes widened as she took the briefest glance over the balcony railing, then stared at Rose. "You're insane. I'm not going that way."

Rose chuckled as she coiled her spider line and leaned on the railing to look down. "There's another balcony about fifty feet down and over a bit. All we have to do is climb down there and start swinging until we can reach the balcony."

"Not me," Tempest said, trying the doorknob again. The door was sealed so tight that it didn't even rattle when she shook the knob. "I won't do it. Until a few minutes ago, I'd never even been this high off the ground before. Now you've got me flying around over the city on threads I can hardly see on my way to steal an old painting that might get me captured. I could be sent back to the rehab facility."

Rose smirked at her. "You want to climb up on the roof and head back on your own? It's kind of tricky to do it all by yourself, but you're clever; you've got a pretty good chance of surviving the trip."

Tempest looked doubtful as she eyed the roof again. "Well . . ."

"Unless you have a key to this door, your only choice is down."

"I could wait here for you." Tempest said, nodding with an anxious smile. When she saw the look Rose gave her in return, she quietly checked the spider line's connection to her harness, then tapped her finger on the friction brake that would slow her descent down the tower. "How do you use this thing again?"

It took three minutes for Tempest to make her way down the side of the tower, breathing hard despite the minimal effort required, trying not to look down. Sweat dripped into her eyes as she hung in her harness and glanced sideways at the lower balcony that was now at her level. About fifteen feet away, it refused to move any closer as Tempest tried to will it nearer with her mind. Failing that, she knew she'd have to start swinging the way that Rose had described. She looked up, and Rose waved at her from her safe vantage point on the upper balcony. Pushing off against the tower wall, she swayed back and forth until she got more momentum, then tried to walk the wall as Rose had shown her. After she took a few running steps along the wall, she lost her footing and hung like a deadweight in the harness again, but she continued to swing back and forth until the balcony was within reach. The wind whistled in her ears. The bright casino lights swirled around her, and she occasionally crossed the beam of a spotlight, reminding her how high she was on the tower and how exposed she was if any outside security guards bothered to look up.

On her first grab, Tempest missed the railing, scraping her arm against the tower wall as she swung backward in her wide arc, then stopped and rushed back toward her target. She grabbed at the railing again, missed, and thumped against it with her stomach, knocking the wind out of her, but she still managed to hook the railing with her armpits as she slid backward. She felt dizzy, her stomach hurt, and she wanted to go home. Grunting, she hauled herself up and over the railing, then dropped in a heap on the cold concrete floor of the balcony. She rolled over on her back, looked up, and saw a pair of booted feet falling toward her face. She twisted to her side and covered her head with her arms as the occupant of the boots thumped onto the balcony beside her.

"I wouldn't call you a natural climber," Rose said, coiling her spider line, "but you're learning. Try to land on your feet instead of your stomach or your head."

Groaning, Tempest rolled up to a sitting position and rubbed her aching ribs. She briefly considered pushing Rose over the railing, but the urge passed when Rose easily opened the balcony door.

Rose stepped through the doorway onto a spiral staircase that circled a vertical tube of white light that rose the entire length of the tower. She beckoned to Tempest. "Hurry. Degas and the others will be landing on you in a minute if you don't get in here quick."

Tempest anxiously looked up to see if more booted feet were coming her way, then stood and staggered onto the staircase. Rose pointed down the shaft. "Don't worry if you see glowing faces on our way down; they're part of the effects for the tourists. When you're on the ground and you look up at the little windows in the tower, the floating heads are lit from behind by the light tube to make them look like ghosts."

"Why?"

Rose shrugged. "This is Las Vegas. Nothing makes sense here."

Tempest scampered down the spiral staircase behind Rose, trying not to let her get too far ahead. Behind her, she heard more booted feet following them, presumably Degas and his friends. Although her stomach hurt, she was happy to be indoors again. When they passed the base of the giant vertical light tube and continued their descent into the darker depths of the stairwell, Tempest began to wonder if they'd ever stop. "How far are we going?"

"Down two more levels in the subbasements. That's why we came in through the tower."

Tempest didn't understand, but before she could ask another question they had reached the bottom of the stairwell. She stopped beside Rose, and the four men following them jogged past into the dimly lighted corridor, vanishing around a curve.

"They'll create distractions, but we won't have time to dally," Rose said, slipping out of her black coveralls. "Take off your clothes."

Tempest raised an eyebrow, then remembered the formal dress she'd brought along.

"You're going to see some strange things in this casino," Rose cautioned her as she wriggled into a short red dress that glowed from within. "This is one of the few nanotech buildings in town. The nanoforms were introduced for remodeling in Las Vegas just before The Uplift in the western wastelands. The AIs love to play with that stuff, so they added some enhancements. Reality looks a little different in this place. Things change in front of your eyes, and it might take some getting used to, okay?"

"Sure." Tempest adjusted the snug dress on her body and stuffed her coveralls into the bag. She was familiar with the stories about the maintenance nanoforms that came at night in Marinwood, and what happened to the rare person who came in contact with them, so she felt wary of entering a building where they were so active. Rose didn't seem concerned, and that made Tempest feel more confident. As she thought about it, Tempest realized she was more worried about the nanoborg security guards recognizing her. She didn't want a return trip to the rehab facility.

Rose handed her a flat, palm-sized container that matched one she was holding. "This is the good stuff. Powder your nose."

Tempest responded with a puzzled frown and watched as Rose demonstrated, opening the case to reveal a soft sponge resting on a powdery interior next to a small mirror inside the lid. Studying her face in the mirror, Rose applied the powder to her face. Almost instantly, Rose's face narrowed—her lips thinned, her cheeks paled and drew in, her nose became slightly longer and more pointed. Rose smiled. "Nanopowder makeup. For that high-fashion look."

"High fashion?"

"Never mind. Just use it. The smart powder analyzes your facial structure and reacts with your personal chemistry to make subtle alterations to your appearance. No pattern recognition scan is going to identify you for about four hours, then you'll look like your old self again unless you use the powder again. If you don't like the result, you can try a different powder."

When she applied the powder, Tempest gasped as she felt the skin and muscles of her face shifting. Her lips became wider and redder, her skin tone darkened, and she felt as if her face was being pulled back and up toward her ears and scalp, widening her eyes and forehead. When her face stabilized, she didn't even recognize herself in the little mirror. There was no pain, only a pleasant tingling in her face. Stunned, she followed Rose into a service elevator.

When they stepped out of a service corridor onto the casino floor, Tempest gasped and leaned against the wall to steady herself. The sound was almost deafening, hitting her in waves of clanging steel, bells, buzzers, thumping music, and shouting voices. Rows of machines blinking with bright lights bounced and jiggled on the red-carpeted floor as if they were alive, interspersed with long tables where gamblers were hunched over in deep concentration on their games. As her gaze wandered, the things that startled Tempest the most were the crowds of people, the hypnotic patterns of the lights, and the armored knights in combat on the stage in the center of the casino.

"Where did all these people come from?" Tempest asked. "The streets are so quiet. On our way here, I didn't see anyone moving around."

Rose approached a white-haired old woman seated in front of a bulky machine, her eyes locked on the blinking lights and spinning wheels behind little windows as she dropped silver coins into a slot. Whenever she dropped a coin in, the machine made happy, encouraging noises. She wore a heavy black coat, and her gaze never left the face of the machine as Rose stopped beside her. Rose winked at Tempest, then shoved the old woman out of the chair. Silver coins jingled in the cup she held in her left hand, but none of them were spilled when she hit the carpet.

Tempest gasped and stooped over to help the old woman off the floor, but the woman didn't seem upset at all. Her eyes were still locked on the slot machine while she easily stood up and sat in the chair again.

Tempest glared at Rose. "What did you do that for?"

"You try it."

"No, thanks."

"She's not real," Rose said, shoving her out of the chair again with the same result as before.

Tempest watched the old woman sit down again without complaint. "Of course she's real. I can see her quite clearly."

"And I can shove her out of this chair," Rose said, doing it again.

"Stop it!" Tempest growled, stepping between Rose and the seated woman. She put her hand on the woman's shoulder to steady her just in case Rose tried it again.

"She doesn't mind. She was built in a nanovat, just like most of the people here, and she's more like this slot machine than she is like us. This is her purpose in life: to sit in this chair and play this game." Rose stepped back as the machine honked and dinged several times, then disgorged a pile of silver coins into the bottom tray where the old woman happily retrieved them and put them in her cup. When the machine's activity returned to normal, the woman continued dropping the coins into the slot as before. "You see?"

Tempest bent over and stared into the woman's face, but she never acknowledged Tempest's presence. "Hello?"

"The slot machine players don't talk," Rose said. "If you want conversation, you have to try the drunks at the bar until you find one that's interactive. Unless you find a real person, of course. And they usually talk too much."

Tempest studied the other gamblers at the long row of slot machines, noting the variety of clothing and appearances. "Why would anyone go to all this trouble to make fake people?"

"The AIs started it. Like I said, this whole town is a big behavioral study laboratory for them. But the nanotech casinos have lives of their own, and they've developed their own entertainments in addition to what the Dominion wanted. Once the casinos became self-aware, they got lonely. They were built to handle huge crowds, and they got bored as the flow of tourists dwindled over time, so they built gamblers of their own to play the games. The Dominion provided the behavioral models for the gambler programming, and they were happy to help provide the right atmosphere for their continuing studies. Half the time, you can't tell the difference between the fake people and the real gamblers in this place. I'm not even sure there is much of a difference."

"This is amazing," Tempest said, watching a man dressed in a cowboy outfit covered in sequins throw a pair of dice the length of a gaming table. The admiring crowd laughed and applauded.

"It's kind of creepy if you ask me. The Dominion used holograms of gamblers in the beginning, or so I'm told. They were thrilled when the casinos themselves came up with this idea. And this is just the beginning."

Tempest followed Rose past an area where a floating sign proclaimed: "Galaxy Slots. The loosest slots in town!" Hovering above the rows of star-studded slot machines was an enormous spiral galaxy of winking stars that slowly rotated in a translucent black cloud. Tempest thought it looked better than the real thing that she'd learned about in school.

They stopped in front of the raised stage where two knights, armor-plated from head to toe, staggered around while swinging at each other with heavy broadswords. The silver suits of armor looked identical, except that one knight wore a black plume atop his helm while the other one wore a white plume. Whenever a sword hit one of the knights, the armor rang as the knight turned to deflect the blow. The crowd of spectators in front of the stage area, many of them holding drinks, cheered whenever one of the knights smashed into the other with his sword, but they didn't seem to discriminate as to which knight was their favorite.

"Seems pretty realistic, doesn't it?" Rose asked.

Tempest watched the two knights carefully, studying their moves. They both looked tired and unsteady after fighting for so long. "I don't know. I guess so."

A flourish of trumpets caught the attention of the two knights. The white knight stood a little straighter, lowering his sword enough for the black knight to lunge forward for a final attack. A moment later, Tempest jumped back as the white knight's helm clanked to the ground by her feet. Startled blue eyes looked out through the helm's visor as it rolled to a stop and stared up at the ceiling. The crowd cheered wildly, clapping and stomping their feet while the black knight took a bow and clanked off the stage.

"Tell me he's not real," Tempest said, grabbing Rose's arm.

"He's not bleeding, is he?"

Tempest relaxed her grip. Rose had a point. She saw a trickle of blue liquid leaking onto the carpet from the base of the helmet, but that was all. A squat cleaning machine with a blinking red light on its head popped out of a hatch beneath the stage. It darted forward to vacuum up the blue liquid, then tossed the knight's head into a bucket on its back. With an air of self-satisfaction, the cleaning machine returned to its home at a more stately pace, maneuvering around the feet of spectators moving away from the stage. While she watched, Tempest thought one of the knight's eyes winked at her before the cleaning machine finally disappeared through the hatch.

Tempest took a deep breath, then glanced at Rose. "That was really creepy."

"You'll get used to it."

"Where's the Picasso?" Tempest asked, frowning as she tried to make out anything that might look like normal, nonanimated art on display. "I want to get out of here."

Rose beckoned for Tempest to follow her through a winding maze of slot machines and gaming tables. As they walked through a realistic rain forest zone, where the slot machines were disguised as rocks and plants decorated with blinking lights, Tempest felt her dress sticking to her skin. She tried to focus on Rose to control her feeling of audiovisual overload. Her head rang in time with the bells of the slot machines, and she felt the pull of sexy male voices imploring her to come and play with their buttons and levers. Following Rose around a craps table where gamblers happily slapped each other's backs, Tempest stumbled when her feet sank into soft, warm sand. To her right, soft waves steadily rolled in from an artificial ocean that carried the scents of salt and fish on a gentle breeze.

Rose turned again, striding straight into the oncoming waves, but neither she nor Tempest got wet as they continued walking and the waves rose higher while the seafloor descended. The "water" moved around Tempest's body with a gentle pressure, but her clothing and hair were unaffected, and she continued to walk on soft sand while the water rose over their heads. She held her breath at first, starting to panic while colorful schools of tropical fish darted around her head, then realized she could breathe normally. Ahead of them, the giant figure of the sea god Poseidon stood in a massive open clamshell, surrounded by admiring half-naked mermaids who stroked his bulging muscles. His beard shook as he pointed his enormous trident at Tempest, and his voice boomed out in welcome, "Arr! Avast, me hearties! Welcome to the sunken empire of Atlantis! Yo-ho-ho!" Poseidon leered at Tempest when she strolled past, and she had the eerie feeling that he was real.

They continued down the gentle slope of a narrow cobblestone street into a sunken Mediterranean city. White masonry walls rose on both sides of the short street until they stepped into the open city square, which was once again covered in drifts of sand. Rose pointed at a group of wrecked wooden ships tilted on the seafloor with long streams of gold coins flowing from their broken holds.

Banks of blinking slot machines, shaped and colored like huge tropical fish, surrounded the sunken hulks. "Spanish galleons from the armada, or at least that's the idea. Can you see what's hanging from the bow of the first one?"

Tempest studied the rectangular shape swaying in the current about eight feet above the floor. Beneath it, a shark circled in and out of a hole in the ship's hull. A school of tiny fish formed a temporary silver wall in front of the ship, obscuring her view, then they shimmered and darted away. When Tempest got closer, she was able to make out the meaning of the black patterns on the front of the rectangle. "Is that the Picasso?"

"Yep. Don Quixote must feel right at home hanging from a sunken Spanish ship in the underwater empire of Atlantis."

"It's right out in the open. How are we going to get it out of there without being arrested?"

Rose raised an eyebrow at her. "You must trust in the Tunnel Queen, my dear. I always have a plan. Did you notice the two armored knights seated at the slot machines?"

Tempest looked around, then spotted the two knights, wearing identical armor to the two they had seen fighting on the stage. Seated between rows of senior citizens, the knights were playing the fish-shaped slot machines closest to the shipwrecks. A mermaid sinuously floated above their bank of slot machines, suggesting that they "bet all their clams" so that the lucky winner could be her "first mate." Tempest nodded. "Okay, I see them."

Rose whistled a brief tune. In response, the white knight looked up at Rose and raised a beer mug in salute.

"Friends of yours?"

Turning, the white knight smashed his beer mug into the side of the black knight's helmet. Despite the casino noise, Tempest heard the explosion of glass from thirty feet away. The black knight sprawled across his slot machine, then jumped to his feet and kicked the white knight in the groin. The white knight staggered backward and knocked down an entire row of gray-haired men and women as if they were dominoes.

"Now," Rose whispered. "Follow me."

Tempest jogged after Rose, who headed straight for the Picasso. "What about the shark?"

"Let me worry about the shark. Your job is to grab the painting." She stopped briefly to plunge one arm deep into the gold coins inside the mouth of a giant clam. When she withdrew her arm, she held a framed copy of the Picasso painting hanging from the ship, except that it appeared to have been damaged. She handed it to Tempest. "A present for you."

Tempest frowned at the tattered section of canvas in the middle of the painting, a deep gash that separated Don Quixote from Sancho Panza. "It's torn!"

"Don't worry. It's a fake. If we're lucky, security will think someone just vandalized the painting rather than actually stealing it. Come on." Rose darted toward the shark, which was swimming right behind the slot machines where the knights were fighting.

"Is the shark a fake, too?"

They stopped behind a low coral reef that served as a safety barrier between people on the "beach" and the shark's kill zone. "Well, it's not a real shark, if that's what you mean. But it acts like one if anybody gets too close to the painting."

At that moment, one of the slot machines fell over backward with a loud bang and a shower of sparks. The white knight rolled off the machine, straight into the shark's territory. The angry shark turned and shot toward the invader.

Tempest winced as she heard a sound like someone banging on a metal garbage can. She got a brief glimpse of the shark chomping unsuccessfully on the white knight's armored torso as Rose took her arm and jerked her forward over the coral reef. A few more steps brought them beneath the hanging Picasso.

"It's too high. We can't reach it," Tempest said, her heart pounding as she glanced at the shark jerking the knight's body around like a dog playing with a toy.

Rose stepped on a low mound of gold coins, linked her hands together, and crouched to give Tempest a boost up. Eyeing the shark, Tempest held the slashed painting in one hand, put her other hand on Rose's shoulder, and stepped into Rose's hands. Lifted higher, she wobbled a bit, but the pressure of the simulated water helped her maintain her balance. She unhooked the Picasso hanging from the ship and hung the forgery in its place.

Back on the seafloor, Tempest didn't need any prompting from Rose to run for the safety of the coral reef and bound over it. Gasping for air, she looked back to check that Rose was following her.

"And where do you think you're going with that?" asked an icy male voice.

Tempest snapped her head around and her eyes went wide when she saw a heavily muscled pair of legs in front of her. Looking farther up the body, she recognized Poseidon, casually holding his trident in his right hand. His mermaids stood safely in the background and giggled as they watched.

"Going with what?" Tempest asked, trying to hide the Picasso behind her back.

The mermaids stopped giggling when the black knight shoved between them with broadsword in hand and took a mighty swing at the back of Poseidon's heel. Poseidon yelped and whirled to face his attacker. Rose grabbed Tempest's arm and hauled her sideways. They ran back up the street the same way they had entered, their feet pounding on the cobblestones, ignoring the sounds of battle behind them.

Rising from the waves as they ran toward the beach by the rain forest, Tempest began to think they had a chance of escaping. Then she saw the four knights in silver armor running toward them.

···1 0

"I was hoping we wouldn't have to use this," Magnus said, reaching down to crank open the hatch on a gently bobbing tube that led straight down into the murky waters of the bay. His dark robes dripped water on the floating wooden dock, and his wet hair lay plastered against his head. "But it should still work."

The hatch creaked as Magnus used both hands to pry it open. A musty smell of damp, oily metal made Tom wrinkle his nose in disgust. "What is it?"

"Minisub," Magnus grunted. "They used a lot of them when they built the northern transbay tube to Sausalito, and this one still works. I hope." He glanced over his shoulder at the black smoke boiling from the wreckage of the battleship about two miles away. "Dead Man's a better submarine driver than I am—he had one of the BART construction jobs—but I'll get us to our destination. We aren't going far, and we'll stay just under the surface. No deep dives for this old tub." He patted the hatch like it was an old friend.

Tom glanced at the battleship, wondering if Dead Man had been able to draw attention away from their escape. The gaping hole in the lower part of the hull allowed more water inside the ship than usual, but it hadn't sunk any farther because it was already resting on the bottom of the shallow bay.

Tom's memory of recent events was fragmented, starting with his sudden descent from the battleship when Dead Man threw him over the railing. He remembered the bubbling roar of battleship parts splashing into the bay around his semiconscious body, Magnus hauling him onto the mud, Helix barking in his ear, and a stumbling run through water weeds and muck in the predawn light. Just before Magnus had dragged Tom back into the water, Tom had glimpsed Dead Man throwing rocks at an enforcer that had started to chase them. Tom had seen one of the enforcer tanks only once before, patrolling the shoreline near the mountain of the gods while Tom drifted quietly past on one of his early-morning "floats." At first, he'd thought someone was driving an old truck, then he saw the metal tracks ripping up the dark soil, and the man-shaped torso that sprouted from the top of the tank's turret. Supposedly, the enforcers were failed nanoborgs whose bodies had not survived the training or the cybernetic implants—their minds trapped inside the steel hulks of enforcer units—but Tom wasn't sure if the rumors were true, and he didn't want to ask Magnus.

"Are we going to wait for Dead Man?" Tom already missed the wiry old corpse and hoped he'd be okay.

Magnus shined a flashlight beam down through the hatch and squinted at the ladder. "He'll meet us at the train station, assuming we get there in one piece." He gestured toward the hatch. "You first. It's a tight fit, so haul yourself all the way forward into the observation blister, then I can climb down into the driver's seat."

Tom eyed the hatch dubiously. "You're sure this is safe?"

"I checked the sub last month, and it was still floating. Let me know if you step off the ladder and drown."

Tom smirked at him. "You're a funny guy.".

"Who's kidding?"

Helix growled at the smell wafting out of the sub. Although Tom had watched Helix carefully, the little dog had not said a single word since the previous night. Tom had already begun to think that his conversation with Helix was part of the same dream where he'd imagined floating around in a fog with Dead Man before being roused by the angry Magnus. Tom knew the guardian had been summoned to destroy the battleship because he'd been stupid enough to sleep out on the deck in full view of the orbiting surveillance satellites, and the knowledge bothered him. Everywhere he went, his presence seemed to bring death to his friends and family. Yet Magnus, whom Tom still couldn't think of as his uncle, was risking his own life, and Dead Man's earthly existence, to rescue Tom, train him, and send him off on some mysterious quest that was sure to get him killed when he confronted the gods, or the nanoborgs, or whatever other automated defense chose to place itself in Tom's path. Sandoval was another casualty of having come in contact with Tom. He felt the responsibility of so many deaths as a crushing weight on his back, and he didn't know if he had the strength to bear it much longer.

Tom shook his head. Tempest had been right to send him away. She was safer without him, and his offer to bring her with him into the wasteland was nothing more than a moment of selfish insanity. Her loss was another result of his many misdeeds, and the death of her brother, Humboldt, must have sealed an enduring hatred of Tom into her heart, for she must have known that Humboldt had been killed while tracking Tom. He took a deep breath to clear his head, pushing thoughts of Tempest to the back of his mind. He had enough to worry about already.

Magnus held Helix in his arms while Tom awkwardly stepped off the dock, steadied himself with one hand on the hatch, and inserted his legs into the open tube. He wrinkled his nose again. "Phew. This isn't just some big sewage pipe that runs down into the bay?"

Magnus frowned. "I hope not. If it is, we'll have to hoof it down to the train station."

The rungs of the ladder were cold and damp. The dark metal surface was pitted with corrosion that scraped against Tom's fingers. Each footstep on the ladder prompted a hollow echo from below. His shoulders scraped against the hatchway walls as he wriggled his way down the shaft. He felt as if he were descending into a metal tomb.

At the base of the ladder, the first thing Tom did was to bang his head against a metal strut. His boots made a hollow sound as they clumped against the steel deck. In the dim illumination from the flashlight Magnus was holding, he crouched to keep his head below the rest of the struts on the low ceiling. The walls were lined with pipes, valves, instrument panels, and the occasional porthole. Ahead of him, murky light filtered through the thick glass of the observation bubble on the nose of the sub. A small fish bounced against the glass, then darted away. Tom dropped to his hands and knees. A thin layer of water burbled along the deck, and it would have soaked the legs of his pants if they weren't already waterlogged.

"Comfy?" Magnus asked. His voice echoed briefly as Tom heard the creaking complaint of the hatch being pulled shut.

Tom settled down on his stomach, with his head and shoulders inside the observation blister. Helix climbed onto Tom's back and lay down for a nap. Tom felt Magnus brush against his feet as he moved to the sub controls, which Tom couldn't clearly see without making a great effort to turn around. When his bones began to vibrate, he knew that Magnus had powered up the fuel cell.

"We've got power to the main prop," Magnus said, although Tom could barely hear him over the noise that thrummed through the hull. Bubbles began to stream past the observation blister when they gently eased forward, and he heard a variety of gurgling noises to accompany the continuous vibration flowing through his body. The water on the deck swirled around to Tom's right side as the sub banked to make a turn. After all of his recent exertions, Tom began to doze off despite the strange environment.

"Good. Get some rest," Magnus said. It was kind of eerie how the old man knew what he was doing without seeing his face. "Breathe deeply and review what Dead Man showed you last night. We don't have much time left, and I need to prepare you for the rest of your journey. You've experienced many things since your training began, but you still need to learn how to create your own path through the world and how to reach the Road. You must learn this now, because we don't know what will be waiting for us at the train station."

Tom was too tired to argue, but he noticed that Magnus knew about his "dream" experience with Dead Man. He closed his eyes and began to take deep breaths, exhaling slowly and evenly. The hum and vibration of the sub relaxed him further, taking him deeper.

"The mixture of the vision vine is still in your system, gradually working on your body, speeding the process of change that will help you on your way. As you gain more experience, you'll be able to control this process, and that's the secret to protecting yourself from the poison in your system. You have no choice."

Tom blinked, then glowered at Magnus as he was reminded of the poison slowly taking his life away. "What if I don't learn how to stop this poison? Is there another antidote?"

"No. But you'll learn. You're most of the way there already, and, when the time comes, I'll be there to help you. Now, close your eyes again and breathe."

Knowing that Magnus would be around to help him made Tom feel better about the poison, and he had already resigned himself to the knowledge that he couldn't do anything about it anyway. If Magnus and Dead Man had both been exposed to the same poison and survived to talk about it, then there was a good chance that Tom would also live through the experience.

Relaxing once more, Tom watched as the sub worked its way through a maze of dark outlines of broken hulls, open hatchways to nowhere, the dead eyes of portholes, and other unidentifiable pieces of the many shipwrecks resting on the muddy bottom of the bay. Helix began to snore softly on Tom's back, and Tom shut his eyes.

Magnus spoke softly. "There is something I should warn you about, Tom. You will gain great power by becoming a master of the Road. You can do amazing things there, and as you learn to operate in that environment you will be drawn back again and again. The Road will call you, and that call is a great responsibility because it can turn into an addiction to power. The more time you spend on the Road, the greater its hold on you will become. That's fine up to a point, and you won't need to worry about reaching your limits for a while, but the Road should not be used for frivolous purposes because it will eventually exact a price on you. The things that live along the Road will become too familiar with your presence, and they will attempt to keep you there. If you had mastered the fog, you would have been able to use it along the Road, just as I do, to help hide your presence. But the fog is not your ally."

Magnus paused for a moment, driving the point home before he continued. "You must also learn how to handle yourself in the Dead Lands, just as you have learned how to function in Stronghold, but there is a difference among the shadows. The Dead Lands are far more dangerous, and the dead can claim you if they find any weakness in your spirit, or if you spend too much time in their domain. We all want to make contact with the loved ones that we've lost, but there is a proper time for joining them, and you must restrict your visits to the Dead Lands until then. You don't need to fear the shadows—they maintain the balance between light and dark, and you will learn to move between the two. A master of the Road can go anywhere, but remember the price. There is always a price."

Tom kept his eyes closed, but the prospect of seeing his family again almost made him sit up. Was it really possible? Were they waiting for him in the Dead Lands? He'd have to learn how to reach them as soon as possible.

"This is the hard part," Magnus said, banking the sub in another turn. "To reach the Road, you must develop the ability to release your physical body at will, as if you were going to sleep. When you have the strongest need to reach the Road, you may be in a situation where it's dangerous to leave the physical world behind, but this is the only way. And that's why the ability to relax quickly is so important. Time runs at a different speed when you're on the Road, and it will often be a simple matter to accomplish your business there and return to your physical body before anything harms it, but that also means you can't wait to fall asleep like an untrained dreamer. Meditation will eventually teach you to reach the Road without losing total contact with your physical form. For now, when time is short, it's quicker for you to relax and go to sleep, then you can learn to be aware of your environment in the dream state. Once you have control of your dreams, you can move on to the Road through your energy body."

Magnus's droning voice was almost hypnotic. Tom understood what he was saying, and he knew he'd remember it, but he also felt himself slipping further into the darkness, using a different sort of effort to send himself deeper within.

"There is nothing more important that you have ever done in your life," Magnus continued. "Your body and spirit are ready to demonstrate your new abilities if your mind will get out of the way. You must let go to gain control. When you learn this lesson, you will have power, and you will be able to do things that no other man has been able to do. Your genes make you special, just as your parents were both special in unique ways, and the Dominion has remained vigilant for decades to prevent one such as you from being born to challenge them. That's why your parents were so careful to hide your special qualities. You had to fit in. But now, the butterfly must emerge from the cocoon. This may not make sense to you now, but you will experience the truth when you reach the Road."

The hollow sound of Magnus's voice disappeared into an eerie silence. Focusing inside his head, Tom opened his "other" eyes and saw his own sleeping form resting peacefully beneath him. He began to panic, then remembered to look at his hands, and he did so without effort. He looked around in the glowing white fog, but he seemed to be alone this time until he heard a soft bark. Turning his head to the right, he saw Helix spiraling toward him through the fog with a happy expression on his furry face.

"Follow me," Helix said, his tongue hanging out as he spiraled on past Tom's head.

"Where?" Tom asked, but he didn't wait for an answer because he feared losing the little dog. He jogged in the direction of the dog's flight, then realized it wasn't necessary to move his legs. Still in a standing position, he began to fly along behind Helix, easily keeping the spinning body in sight through the silent white clouds.

After what seemed a long time, something moved in his mind, flexing like a rediscovered muscle, and the white mist was gradually infused with the brilliant glow of a golden sunset. He sensed the mists flowing around him, thinning and shifting to the color of a blue summer sky high in the mountains. He still had no sense of direction, and could only intuit up or down from his current orientation. Without reference points he was lost, and he doubted he could find his way back to his sleeping body, but the presence of Helix calmed him so that he didn't worry. More colors and shapes appeared: soft blocks of lemon yellow amber, spires of jade green, a smooth surface of translucent gray moonstone moving by beneath his feet, walls of faceted blue topaz. The colored objects remained fuzzy and indistinct, as if his eyes refused to focus on them as he shot past.

Concentrating on the shapes, he willed them to become more distinct, and he realized the hazard he was creating when he had to twist suddenly to avoid smacking into a waterfall of steaming red-and-black lava that fell past him and vanished into the white glow some distance beneath his feet. Following the descent of the waterfall with his gaze, he realized that his own body had become fuzzier as his environment sharpened around him.

The white mists dissipated, and the terrain began to stabilize as he followed Helix into a canyon with high, rolling hills on both sides of a clear blue river. Along the banks, the jade spires reached for the sky atop mounds of the lemon yellow amber. The tall grass on the hills shimmered in the breeze, each green blade emitting a subtle light that gathered like vapor, lifted on currents of air to form an emerald wind blowing through the canyon. Neon wildflowers flowed down the hills in cascades of yellow, orange, and purple. Clusters of big trees dotted the landscape, their thick leafy canopies caught in a change of season that left them looking as if captured flames danced on their branches without burning. Above it all, faceted blue topaz formed a celestial ceiling above a ruby sky.

Helix glanced over his shoulder at Tom, his tongue flapping in the wind, then led them down to the surface of the gentle river. Tom gasped as Helix began dissolving into a blue mist, then realized that his own form was changing. Although he continued to breathe, see, and hear, his skin and bones turned to blue powder, blowing off rapidly to form a mist just moments before he struck the river. His body became liquid and joined with the rushing waters. It was a familiar feeling, as if he were floating in the bay back home, guided by moonlight and the warm current.

Tom felt giddy as he wound through deep blue pools where silver flashes marked the trails of startled rainbow trout. He washed over rocks of yellow amber, black onyx, and crystals of purple amethyst. He flowed through red tree roots and glided through the shallows of a diamond riverbed.

"We must be on the Road," Tom whispered. Awed by this natural cathedral, he didn't want to speak too loudly, afraid that he might shatter the reality of the moment.

"Almost there," said a trout, whom Tom took to be Helix in a new form. "This is the River of Light."

"I'm part of the river."

"And the river is part of you. We're all part of the river." Helix wriggled his tail to dart forward.

"Are we near the Dead Lands?" Tom asked, thinking about his family.

"The Dead Lands are always nearby," said the trout with a wise tone of voice. "But if you walk the Road, the Dead Lands are some distance away. You'll get there soon enough."

The words of the trout confused him, but there were already so many confusing things in Tom's world that one more didn't make any difference. However, there was something familiar about the trout's words, and he knew why when they flowed around a bend in the river; a striking young woman with long, white hair stood waist deep in the clear water, her arms outstretched, her hands dripping with diamonds from the riverbed. Her diaphanous white robes floated behind her, pulled by the current to outline the delicate curves of her body, giving her an angelic appearance. Her eyes were closed, and her face was turned up toward the sky with a slight smile. Although she seemed much younger, Tom recognized the Oracle from Marinwood.

When Tom swirled around her, she stopped the motion of the river with a wave of her hand, and rose petals fell like a soft rain from the clear sky. She opened her white eyes and looked at Tom with amusement.

"Oracle," Tom whispered.

"Welcome to the River of Light, Tom Eliot." She tipped her head as if she were studying his transparent liquid form. "You've lost weight since I last saw you."

Tom frowned at the trout. "Is she joking with me?"

Helix swam in a circle, chasing his tail and ignoring Tom.

"You look younger," Tom said to the Oracle.

Her laugh sounded like the tinkling of tiny bells. Tom had never heard her laugh before, and it confused him further.

"You see me as my true self here," she said, turning in a circle as if she were on display. Watching her, Tom was filled with a sense of security and a warmer feeling that Tempest had awakened in him.

"You're beautiful," Tom said without thinking.

With startling grace, she took a swirling jump forward that brought her warm skin in contact with Tom's part of the river. He felt the smoothness of her skin and the warmth of her glow. She knelt on the riverbed, allowing the water to come up to her neck, her robes billowing to the surface to mingle with her long hair. Even Helix was surprised enough to stop chasing his tail for a moment to watch her.

"I warned you not to come here," she said, rippling her fingers through his presence in the water. "I tried to redirect your energies into the land, where you could grow and prosper. You had that chance. The possibility existed for a brief time."

"Telemachus changed all that when he destroyed my family."

The Oracle sighed and looked toward the horizon, a sapphire tear tracing its way down her cheek. "At great risk to myself, I warned your father as well. But there was only so much I could do without alerting Telemachus."

"I thank you for that, Oracle. Do you know how I can reach my family?"

She turned her head and looked through him. "They're in the Dead Lands now, young Tom. It is not time for you to see them again."

"I only want to visit them—see them one last time. I want to apologize for what I've done."

"They'll wait for you. There is no need to apologize. They understand, and their lives have moved to another level now. They no longer concern themselves with matters of the past, and you might be disappointed if you see them too soon."

"I'm told that I can reach them from the Road," Tom said. "And I intend to do that."

She shook her head. The sapphire tear dropped to the surface of the river and became a floating blue flower. "You are a creature of the light, Tom. You must try only to work with the positive energies of that light. The Dead Lands are powerful, and the powers of the darkness are difficult to master. You could be trapped in the kingdom of death. It's better if you forget about your family until your time comes naturally, as it does to all mortals."

"He has help," Helix said, waggling his tail. "He is becoming a master."

The Oracle closed her eyes. "My powers are limited here, as some of my human parts were removed that I might serve Telemachus, but I do sense the truth of what you're saying, little trout. I caution you, Tom—the darkness can lure your spirit, driving the light from you. The dead are trapped beyond their barrier, and they feed on visitors, offering you the dark powers in return for the energies that they steal. The darkness will eat at you, and force you to use it to accomplish your goals, but you cannot let it master you. That's why it's better that you not go to the Dead Lands at all." She opened her eyes again. "If you love me, Tom, and I feel that you do, then you must leave this place and forget about the Dead Lands. You've already lost your family, and no one expects you to make more sacrifices. You're not a puppet to the will of others, and you don't have anything to prove. Go and hide in the wasteland where it's safe."

She sounded entirely too reasonable to Tom, and the warmth of her presence made his thoughts cloudy. In this magical place, unrestricted by the Dominion, she had spoken in a clear and direct manner and given him a final warning. He knew he ought to take her advice. He looked downstream, then back the way they had come, marveling at the colors of this new world. He looked at his faithful friend the trout, who eyed him expectantly. He thought of those who had given their lives to get him this far, and he wondered how he'd ever repay his debt to those who had died because they loved him. He felt the Oracle's fingers caressing him as if he were still in his human form, expressing her love and concern. He also had a headache, and he wondered if the poison in his system would affect his judgment.

"Others have turned back here," said the trout. "There's a long history of humans who reached this point and returned home to live normal and happy lives. There's no shame in it."

Tom sighed, as a river would sigh while considering what it would have been like to live as a tree or as a golden sunrise, then he looked at the Oracle. "I have a job to do. I have to reach the Road."

The trout winked at him in approval. "Thank you for not listening to me."

The Oracle spread her hands in resignation. "I've done what I can. I wish you good fortune on your journey, and hope that we will both live to see each other again before we follow your loved ones into the land of the dead. Remember to listen when the thunder speaks, collect the rose petals when you can, and consider the wisdom of the rustling leaves." Her hands glided over the surface of the water, and the river began to flow once more. She sank lower in the river, submerging her head so that her hair fanned out like water weeds, then she lay back and drifted away, concealed beneath the surface.

Tom watched the Oracle for a moment, then looked at the trout. "Now what?"

"Now you wake up," Helix said with a wink of one fishy eye.

MEMPHIS Gustafson, Elder Councilman of Marin-wood, could not remember the last time he had been this frightened. Hermes had brought him the news that Tempest had somehow managed to escape from the rehabilitation facility. Hermes had also told him of conflicting reports that the Eliot hooligan might still be roaming around the countryside, despite Humboldt's great sacrifice to ensure that the troublemaker was destroyed. Now, Hermes had returned to the home of Memphis, and he wanted information that Memphis could not give him. Although the mirrored face of the nanoborg betrayed no emotion, Memphis had the impression that Hermes was angry, not necessarily with Memphis, but with himself. He also understood that Hermes was going to take out his frustrations on the closest available target, which was Memphis.

And that explained why Hermes had sealed Memphis's upper body into the same shock box device Memphis had used to discipline his children.

Certain elements on the council, notably Ukiah Eliot and his supporters, had often decried the use of shock boxes as inhumane torture devices, but the fact remained that they were excellent training tools and gifts from the gods. Children understood such simple approaches to punishment, and Memphis was certain that his offspring had

been so well behaved growing up because they appreciated
the implied threat of the shock box that was ever present as
a reminder in the front yard of their home. If Memphis himself had not softened his approach to discipline so much in
their later years, Humboldt might still be alive, and Tempest
might still be an obedient daughter. His failures as both a father and an Elder Councilman finally seemed to have caught
up with him as the powerful nanoborg strapped him into the
shock box and closed the squeaky clamshell lid around
Memphis's bare torso.

The metal was hot from baking in the sunlight. His torn
shirt hung from the belt at his waist, and his arms were
stretched forward over his head. His boots were firmly
planted on the gravel at the base of the shock box. He knew
his aging muscles would not last long, and his back would
eventually tire enough so that his paunchy stomach would
sag and touch the box, delivering an intense and painful
shock. His muscles would stiffen, and he would recoil,
possibly bouncing off the charged lid of the box and hurting his muscles even more as he attempted to stabilize his
position. Hermes had control over the intensity of the
shock, but Memphis knew from the nanoborg's general demeanor that he wasn't merely trying to prove a point—he
would kill Memphis if necessary.

"You must have some idea where Tom Eliot would go,"
Hermes said in a calm and reasonable voice. "He was your
neighbor, and you claimed to have monitored his movements for many years when you first reported his suspicious behavior to me."

Memphis licked his lips; his mouth seemed unusually
dry. "No, my lord. I've told you everything I know about
him. He goes off into the forbidden zones, where we can't
follow."

"And he never spoke of the places he'd been, or any unusual sights he might have seen on his travels? Maybe he
mentioned some of these things to your daughter?"

Memphis shook his head, then realized that Hermes couldn't see him inside the box. "Not to my knowledge. We never spoke at length."

"Yet you claimed to know so much about him? I find that curious. You would not have tried to use me to retaliate against the boy for his approaches to your daughter, would you?"

"No, my lord! Of course not! You know that's not true, because you have witnessed his treachery with your own eyes. He killed Humboldt. He came after my daughter."

"Well," Hermes said, drumming his gloved fingers against Memphis's lower back, "to be exact, Humboldt was distracted by an animated cleaning device, then I killed him with a nanobomb. I wasn't after him specifically, but he was in the wrong place at the wrong time, if you get my meaning."

Memphis gasped. "I can't believe that!"

"Believe what you wish, but give me a better answer about Tom Eliot's whereabouts."

Memphis heard the hum of the electricity in the metal that surrounded him. His back muscles were on fire. "I can't! I don't know where he is!"

"All right. Let's try a different question. I've told you that your daughter escaped from the rehabilitation facility in Las Vegas. Where would she go?"

"I don't know, my lord. I've never been there." His sweat sizzled when it dripped off his skin and struck the metal beneath him.

"Of course not. You've always been a good Elder Councilman, haven't you? Yet you know your daughter, and you must know enough about how she thinks to speculate about her activities."

"We don't know anyone in Las Vegas. We have no friends or relatives there. I suppose she'd try to get back here, but I don't know how she'd get across the barrier."

"Well, that is the point of the barrier, isn't it? We

wouldn't want any mutants from the western wasteland contaminating the rest of the country, and we wouldn't want the rest of the citizens poking around in the wasteland."

"What mutants? There are no mutants here, my lord." He watched as a mosquito buzzed around his face, then made the foolhardy mistake of landing on the floor of the shock box—it vanished in a flash and a tiny puff of smoke.

"Haven't you heard the news, Elder? The western region is crawling with mutants. They're everywhere you look."

"I don't understand, my lord. I want to help you, but I don't understand." Despite his effort to conceal it, he heard the edge of panic in his voice.

Hermes paused before answering. The hum in the metal walls of the box got louder. "You know, you've finally convinced me that you know nothing useful, Elder Memphis."

Memphis took a deep, shuddering breath. He wanted to relax, but it wasn't safe yet, and his stomach was almost touching the hot steel. Then he heard Hermes' footsteps receding into the distance, and his eyes went wide. "My lord! Wait! Where are you going?"

The footsteps continued crunching on the gravel. "They don't look kindly on failures where I come from," Hermes said, his voice getting fainter with distance. "I'm off to try to stay alive."

TEMPEST and Rose were trying to elude the four security knights in the slot machine rain forest when one of the white-haired gamblers smiled and beckoned for them to follow her. Up until then, Tempest had not seen any live tourists in the casino, so it was startling to have one pop up in front of them like that. She didn't know how to respond at first, but her goal of self-preservation prompted her to follow the old woman, who was dressed in a flowing white gown that trailed behind her like a misty waterfall. When the woman in white ducked behind a slot machine bank decorated with images of excited monkeys being pelted by showers of gold coins, Tempest looked back briefly, then darted around the slot machines with Rose right behind her. The four knights weren't far behind, crashing through rows of seated gamblers and hurling them from their stools. Maybe the old woman had a handy weapon hidden behind the bank of *Golden Rain-A-Plenty* machines.

Tempest thought the woman had led them into a trap when they came up against a rock wall. They were in a narrow maintenance space between the deafening sounds of the ringing, singing slot machines. The old woman pressed her hands against the rock and a hidden door revealed itself, popping open with a slight gust of steamy air. Holding the rock door to one side, she motioned for them to enter. Lacking any other escape route, Tempest nodded at the woman and plunged forward onto a granite staircase dimly illuminated by red lights. Rose thanked the old woman and pulled the rock door shut behind them, sealing out the noise of the casino. Tempest's ears throbbed in the sudden silence.

"Who was that?" Tempest asked, starting down the staircase. The old woman had looked familiar, but she couldn't place the face.

Rose shrugged. "Tourist, I guess. A live one."

"But why did she help us?"

"Maybe she was losing."

Tempest nearly stumbled on the next step when she remembered. "Oracle!"

"What?"

"That was the Oracle from Marinwood! How did she get here?"

Rose sounded worried. "I don't know, but I don't like it. I wouldn't trust an oracle any farther than I could throw her. The oracles work for the bad guys."

"Then why did she help us out back there?"

"Yeah, that's strange. They're always interfering with things, but I've never heard of one that's helpful like that."

"Have you ever seen an oracle in a casino before?"

"Are you kidding? They can see the future, right? What casino in its right mind would let an oracle through the door? What oracle in her right mind would throw her money away in a casino?"

Tempest started to doubt her memory. An oracle in a casino really didn't seem to make any sense, so maybe the woman just looked similar to the Marinwood Oracle. She shook her head as they continued jogging down the staircase. If the woman had led them into a trap, there wasn't much they could do about it now.

TOM rubbed his eyes and stared out through the observation blister into the murky waters of the bay. Magnus was guiding the sub into what appeared to be an enormous hole in the bank. Old pilings and rotting ships that had sunk alongside their docks poked up from the bay mud, and Magnus avoided most of the obstructions as he piloted the sub toward the black hole.

"Cooling system outfall pipe," Magnus said. "Leads right into the subbasement of the train station."

Tom barely understood what Magnus was saying. He was still stunned by the events in his dreams—the Oracle, the River of Light, the dreamlike terrain with its brilliant colors, and his close approach to the Road.

"We won't have much time when we arrive at the station," Magnus continued. "I know you almost reached the Road just now, and I'm impressed with your abilities, but I have to tell you a few things, and I need all of your attention." The sub bounced as some part of the hull struck the edge of the cooling pipe. Magnus cleared his throat. "Sorry. Tight fit here."

The sub's impact with the pipe had jarred Tom back to

reality, along with his awareness of the danger they were in. Tom blinked at the darkness outside the sub, trying to make out any kind of detail. Magnus snapped on the forward light, giving them a view of the rusty pipe surrounding them.

"I'm listening," Tom said.

"The freight train runs the circuit between here and Las Vegas every two hours. Usually it just moves freight for the siliboys, along with the occasional prisoner being sent to rehab, so don't expect a pleasant ride. It was originally built to haul gamblers back and forth from the bay area, but the Dominion made some improvements to the train after they assumed control. We can expect to see security at both ends of the track, so we'll have to be very careful."

Tom remembered something and frowned. "Magnus, I thought you said you never managed to cross the western barrier?"

"Just pay attention to what I'm telling you now. When we reach Las Vegas, we'll make contact with a man named Lebowski. He's a musician in the Old District, which is the mostly demolished low-tech side of town. He knows people who can help us, and he knows how to reach the data center where the Dominion core personalities are housed. Dead Man trusts him, so I trust him. Dead Man will rendezvous with us at Lebowski's casino bar, The Golden Fleece, and explain the rest of the plan. Basically, we're going to put a crimp in the Dominion's ability to control and monitor the western region by destroying their data center nexus. Doing so has not been possible until now, because we didn't have you available to distract the siliboys in Stronghold while we attacked the data center. You're almost ready for it, and we'll finish training you before we make the attempt. Sounds like fun, eh?"

"Sounds dangerous," Tom said, once again wondering what he had gotten himself into. However, thoughts of his family firmed his resolve. If he could do any kind of damage at all to Telemachus, he would have finally accomplished something with his life. He'd wanted out of Marinwood, to get away from the farm and see new things, and that's what was happening now, although he would have preferred that it all happen under better circumstances.

"You say destroying this data center will interfere with the Dominion, but it won't stop them completely?"

The sub gently bumped the wall of the cooling pipe as they angled upward. The water on the sub's floor drained back away from Tom, who was still positioned on his stomach where he could look out through the forward observation blister.

"We have to learn to take small steps before we can take big ones," Magnus said. "If we can eliminate the data center, that will be a good start, and we'll learn from it. The real brains that drive the siliboys are duplicated in data centers all over the world; but if we can learn how to sever their connections and bring down the net that allows them to communicate, we'll be free of the AIs. Our lives will be our own once more."

Tom couldn't imagine a world without the gods. Of course, without any experience of the country beyond the western region, he couldn't really imagine the rest of the world anyway. Did the gods have as much control of events there as they did in Marinwood? He'd know more once he'd seen Las Vegas. Despite the dangers involved, he was excited by the idea of the trip. Even the freight train would be an interesting new experience, assuming they could actually get aboard.

Tom frowned when he thought about what Magnus had just told him. "You said I'm supposed to distract the gods in Stronghold during the attack. How am I supposed to do that?"

Magnus chuckled softly. "That's your own special gift, Tom. When Dead Man created Stronghold, he created a failsafe so he could 'pull the plug' if the siliboys got out of hand.

There are some things that the siliboys can only do in their virtual 'game' world. Of course, he didn't anticipate how quickly the AIs would develop, or that they'd learn how to protect the switch that kept Stronghold alive. When the Dominion took over, Dead Man couldn't shut them down."

"And the switch is in Stronghold itself?"

"The simple answer is *yes*. You'll have to find the Tree of Dreams. It's a reflection of the ancient tree that binds all of the worlds together. Dead Man placed the software—the core operating system that drives Stronghold—among its branches. The software lies within the Jewel of Dreaming."

"And this jewel is what the gods are protecting?"

"It's important to them, yes. And you'll have to get past Telemachus to reach it. Dead Man created the Jewel of Dreaming to fit in with the fantasy environment he'd built, but the great tree itself was always something of a mystery to him. He didn't learn more about the tree, or why he had been drawn to it, until much later. The jewel itself seems to have changed over time as a result of its close proximity to the Tree of Dreams."

Light ahead, rippling on the surface of the water. Magnus shut off the forward lamps. The sub was in a steep climb now, randomly scraping against the sides of the pipe, requiring more of Magnus's attention at the controls. Helix had already moved off Tom's back so that he could get to a more secure resting place between Tom's head and his left shoulder.

"We'll have to move fast once I've stopped the sub," Magnus said, "so just do what I tell you and don't ask any questions. We're a few minutes behind schedule, and that train isn't going to wait for us. Got it?"

"I'll be right behind you every step of the way," Tom replied.

The sub nosed into the air like a surfacing whale. Through the water streaming down the observation window, Tom got a blurred image of a wide concrete room full of catwalks and thick white pipes before the sub settled toward the horizontal and the window submerged once more.

"I need more practice with this thing, but I got us here in one piece," Magnus said, snapping switches and brushing past Tom's feet as he swung onto the ladder leading up to the exit hatch.

Tom rolled over, scooped Helix under his arm as he curled into a crouch, then moved over to the base of the ladder as the hatch creaked open and fresh air poured in. Tom took a deep breath, then followed Magnus up through the narrow hatchway.

The room was about sixty feet long with a ceiling twenty feet above their heads. Bright white overhead lights reflected on the water and illuminated the heavy machinery connected to the webwork of white pipes and catwalks. The air was humid and cool. Leaving the sub behind, they quickly jogged along the concrete walkway about two feet above water level, then climbed up onto a catwalk that led to a green door high on the end wall.

Magnus placed one hand on the doorknob, then turned and put his other hand on Tom's shoulder as he looked into his eyes with a frown. "Tom, whatever happens, you have to get on that train. Without me, I doubt that you can operate the sub, and there will be too many guards for you to reach the main entrance door, so the train is your only way out without being captured. If they do catch you, they'll probably kill you, unless Hermes has issued orders to send you to the rehab facility, in which case they'll put you on the train with guards. There is a way for us to get off the train at the other end without anyone seeing us, but it's best if no one sees us here to warn them at the other end. You understand all that?"

Tom nodded. "Get on the train or die."

"Basically, yes. If there's a passenger space with some padding in it, we'll try to get in there, but I'm afraid we'll be riding with the freight."

Magnus opened the door.

They ran forward in an area of relative shadow, already at the level of the train's loading platform. A short distance ahead of them was the pointed back end of the dingy gray mag-lev train, hovering above a thick rail about six feet off the floor of its concrete trench. The service trench beneath the train was lit by orange lights. The upper arch of the tunnel was ten feet above the train's roof. As they ran, Magnus pointed at two open freight doors near the back, where automated loaders were shoving the last of the freight pallets out onto the platform. The air smelled of machine oil and ozone.

After waiting for the last pallet to roll past, Magnus peeked into the dim interior of the train's freight bay and motioned Tom inside. Tom was more than ready, as he had just spotted two guards with their backs to them at the other end of the platform. Once inside, he turned when he heard Magnus gasp; he was still standing on the platform, his hand resting on the side of the train, with a startled look on his upraised face. Tom heard footsteps on the roof.

"Magnus Eliot?" boomed the voice of Hermes. Apparently he was standing on top of the train. "I wasn't expecting to see *you* here."

Tom realized that Hermes wasn't aware of his uncle's name change from Eliot to Prufrock, but he was impressed that the nanoborg could recognize the old man after so many years. He was also impressed that Hermes had managed to locate them, but some part of him had always suspected that the enforcer of the gods would eventually track them down.

"I might say the same for you," Magnus said, regaining his poise. He took a few steps back away from the freight door without looking at Tom.

"Is the boy with you?"

"What boy?"

"Your nephew. Since you're here, I assume you've been escorting him around the region."

"Tom is in the wasteland. He doesn't travel well."

Tom crouched and took a step back into deeper shadow as the hum beneath the train got a little louder. He stroked Helix's head, hoping the little dog would remain quiet under his arm.

"I see," Hermes said doubtfully. "By the way, how did you get into this facility without my guards seeing you? Has your ability to disappear now been extended to your physical form, or are you just terribly clever?"

"I know things," Magnus said with a shrug, taking another step back.

"I shall learn exactly what you know," Hermes said as he casually stepped off the roof and dropped toward the floor in front of Magnus. "And then I'm going to kill you."

A moment before Hermes reached the platform, Magnus threw himself into the nanoborg's legs to knock him down.

Before Hermes could roll over and see Tom, the freight door slid closed, obscuring Tom's view. He moved toward the small porthole in the door and got a brief glimpse of Hermes' black-gloved fist slamming into Magnus's face.

The train rapidly picked up speed. Tom staggered, trying to stay on his feet, and barely managed to set Helix safely down on the floor before he fell on his face. Tom and Helix slid along the ridged metal deck, inadvertently racing each other to the back wall of the freight bay. Tom managed to turn his body to hit the wall with his feet, but that was his last horizontal movement. The acceleration steadily increased, buckling his legs and squashing him against the rear wall. Gasping, he worked to straighten his legs and pry his arms out from beneath his back, finally ending up with his back flat against the bulkhead, staring into the rumbling freight bay lit only by the tunnel lights shooting past the porthole at high speed. He rolled his eyes to one side to confirm that Helix seemed okay. He heard a gasping wheeze from his own body as he tried to drag air into his compressed lungs.

The train continued to accelerate along with the pounding of Tom's heart. His view of the room narrowed to a small circle. Then the circle turned black.

···11

WHEN Tom became aware of his surroundings again, he saw a gray wall moving vertically past his body. In his peripheral vision, he saw only gray fog. He felt almost as if he were back in the bay, floating facedown in a gentle current, his face shielded by the breathing mask as he watched the underwater landscape drift past. The difference here was that the colors had drained away. As an experiment, he raised his head. He was in a river of gray silt, floating past muddy gray banks dotted with rocks, broken bottles, rusty cans, and dead fish with milky eyes staring up at a shroud of gray sky. Rats scuttled along the banks, hopping from corroded hunks of gray machinery to random piles of moldy bones. Even the air smelled gray, full of soot and light streamers of smoke that smelled less like burnt wood and more like the unfiltered smoke from crematorium furnaces. The wind moaned through twisted, leafless trees that reached for the sky as if searching for remembered sunlight. The bleak landscape reminded Tom of Stronghold, but this place had a different character.

"Creepy. Don't like it," said the gray toad perched on Tom's right shoulder. Since it was talking, Tom assumed it was Helix in a new dream disguise.

"Are these the Dead Lands?"

"No. The Dead Lands are nearby, and they're more cheerful. This is the Acheron, river of pain, flowing with tears to carry the souls of the dead to the lakes of Hades for judgment."

Tom hesitated. Looking up and down the river, he noticed gray human bodies partially concealed by drifting gray shrouds as they floated on their backs down the river. Their faces were indistinct, and they had no hair on their heads to help differentiate them. "Am I a dead soul?"

"You're a traveler along the Road. You have a power that the unguided souls do not, and that power allows you the freedom to ignore boundaries, to seek the light or the dark places along the Road as you choose."

The gray bodies had slowed into a bobbing traffic jam on a narrow section of the river. Tom drifted inexorably toward the dead floaters. If he remained on the surface, he would be pinned against them by the floaters coming down the river from behind, and the thought bothered him more than he cared to admit. "How did I get here? I didn't choose to come here."

The toad looked at Tom with a wise expression. "It was an accident. You were knocked unconscious, and your energy body doesn't have enough experience to bring you to a favorite memory place along the Road. The train to Las Vegas is mirrored here as the river of pain; its route intersects the course of the Acheron as the river winds its way around the world."

Tom remembered to look at his hands to gain more control over his environment. The ash gray appearance of his skin disturbed him. "How do we get out of here?"

"You wake up, or you cross from the river to the Road.

Either way will work. Unfortunately, I can't tell you how to go about it."

Tom tried to concentrate on lifting his body from the water. When that didn't work, he tried to focus on the memory of the diamond river he'd seen earlier, but the river of pain remained, inexorably flowing toward infinity. He looked back at the oncoming corpses drifting toward him, then glimpsed a dull silver cord attached to his lower back that stretched back up the river just underneath the surface. The toad gave him an encouraging look, so Tom turned and grasped the silver cord.

TOM opened his eyes and immediately noticed that his face was grinding across the steel deck toward the front of the freight car. The train slowed with occasional jerks, as if brakes were being applied and released. Helix walked along beside him, calmly watching him slide. Tom's chin bumped over a recessed latch in the floor.

"You could have said something," Tom said, pressing his palms against the floor to lift his head and slow his slide.

Helix gave Tom his usual wide-eyed stare of innocence.

Tom wished he'd remembered to ask the dream toad if there was any news of Magnus. If Magnus survived the attack by Hermes, he would most likely be sent to the rehab facility in Las Vegas, where Tom might be able to find a way to rescue him. If Magnus escaped, they would rendezvous with Lebowski at the casino bar, assuming Tom could find it. He didn't want to think about the other possibility—that Magnus might have been killed on the platform by Hermes—the old man was too clever for that.

For now, Tom had to figure out how to avoid being captured when he reached his destination. Magnus had said there would be another way off the train, but he had assumed he would be with Tom to show him the way. The train slowed some more, and he was able to stagger over to the porthole window to look outside. The train crept toward the station platform, and he saw a cluster of armed guards waiting. They would see him as soon as the freight doors opened.

Rubbing his sore chin, he remembered the latch in the floor. On his hands and knees in the dim light, he crawled back along his sliding path until he found it. With a grunt, he lifted it to see the rails beneath the train and a six-foot drop to a concrete trench. Helix looked at Tom and took two steps back as if he knew what was coming.

"It's okay, boy. I'll protect you," Tom said, gently taking Helix's collar so he couldn't dart away. He tucked the little dog into his shirt and swung his legs into the hole. He edged out farther, feeling the wind on his legs as he tried to position himself so he'd avoid the rail during his fall. He took a deep breath, angled the trapdoor so it would shut after he went through, and pushed off.

His shoulder struck the rail on his way down, knocking him off center, but he landed on his feet and rolled sideways so he wouldn't squash Helix. The impact prompted a grunt from Tom and a small yelp from Helix, but it didn't do any serious harm to either of them. His shoulder hurt now, pulsing in time with the headache that had returned to remind him of his deadline, but at least he was off the train. He took Helix out of his shirt, scratched him on the chest to calm him down, then set him on the floor so they could both run down the trench past the platform. With a loud hum, the train came to a halt and Tom heard the doors to the freight cars sliding open. Shouts and footsteps of the guards covered any noise he was making in the trench, so they continued running until they reached a short staircase to a service door on the opposite side of the train from the platform. The door was unlocked. Tom tucked Helix under his arm and proceeded up a dusty black staircase through hot, musty air. After eight flights, he was sweating. After fifteen flights, he was panting. The big drum in his head pounded at a quick tempo to accentuate the steady thump of his footsteps.

The door at the top of the stairs was marked as a fire exit. Hoping he wouldn't set off any alarms after he'd gone to all the trouble of sneaking out of the train station, he gently pushed against the bar, then shoved the sticky door open. No alarms went off, but the bright sunlight on the other side of the door nearly blinded him, and the air felt as if he were stepping into a blast furnace. Squinting, he lurched out into an alley. Both ends of the alley looked almost the same, opening onto streets where flashing colored lights vied with the sunlight for domination of the visual landscape.

He had arrived in Las Vegas.

Choosing one end of the alley at random, he stepped out onto a main street, and it took a moment for him to work out what he was seeing. At odds with the flashing colored lights of a massive casino sign, most of the buildings on the street had been reduced to gray rubble. Walls covered with bright decorations stopped abruptly in jagged lines of broken masonry where ceilings had once stood. Long rows of broken windows looked down on the street from the taller structures like hundreds of hollow eyes watching his movements. Piles of rubble blocked the wide sidewalks in many places. In contrast to all of this was a throng of people, mostly naked, their bodies painted in solid colors of blue, silver, gold, red, and yellow. Three blue men led the long parade, capering about like drunken monkeys, beckoning onlookers along the sidewalk to join the parade. Many of the yellow people carried brass instruments on which they played a bouncy, well-rehearsed tune. Tom didn't know enough about music to be able to identify the tune or its style, but the happy faces in the crowd and in the parade implied that this was some sort of a celebration. A lean young woman with red hair that matched her body paint took Tom's hand and tried to pull him into the street to join them.

"What are you celebrating?" Tom asked the woman in red. He had to shout to be heard above the music.

"Being human," she replied with a laugh. She tugged on his arm.

He resisted, preferring to move among the spectators and keep his clothes on. The red woman shrugged and moved on, blowing him a kiss as she danced away. Studying her finely sculpted form, Tom wondered if he was missing something.

He shook his head, looking up the street where the parade was gradually making its way north. Working his way through the crowd, he noticed that some of the spectators didn't seem quite real, then he decided that his pounding headache and lack of sleep were affecting his perceptions. It would be best to ignore his surroundings and look for The Golden Fleece. He appeared to be in the correct part of town to find that particular casino, but the noise, the crowds, the music, and the lights were a spectacle far beyond what he had ever seen in person, and the whole experience was daunting. Was the rest of the country like this?

It took him about half an hour of walking with the parade before he finally saw the enormous blinking yellow letters over a casino entrance that spelled out "The Golden Fleece." Beneath the casino name, the image of a happy-looking lamb with a sparkling gold coat of wool danced back and forth, with its front legs high in the air holding gold coins. Tinted dark blue windows at street level obscured whatever activities might be hidden inside the casino, but the front doors beckoned to the flocks of gamblers passing by with cool breezes blowing through the open portals. Signs painted on the windows advertised loose slots, loose women, and loose dwarves, but the meaning of these phrases was unclear to Tom. Jostled by two blue women on their way to join the parade, Tom headed for the front door, but he never made it.

With a horrible crash of breaking glass, the large tinted

window beside Tom exploded outward, expelling a large man in a gray cloak. He somersaulted through the air, then landed flat on his back in the street with a loud grunt. His face was covered by his hood and a gray cloth mask, leaving only his bloodshot eyes exposed to the sunlight. Tom seemed to be the only person who thought that the man's sudden appearance was unusual; multicolored people in the parade casually stepped over him on their way past, and the spectators just ignored the gray man, plucking bits of broken glass from their clothes as if this sort of thing happened every day.

Concerned, Tom dropped to one knee and felt for a pulse at the man's neck. Helix sniffed at the man's head and growled until Tom shook his head at the dog.

"Newton," the man whispered, staring up at the sky with glazed eyes. "Devil spawn."

Tom assumed the man was delirious, but at least he was breathing. "Why did they throw you through the window?"

"Wouldn't give in," he said through gritted teeth. "Wouldn't sing 'Danke Schoen' for the drunk clodhoppers in the front row." He stopped to cough and take another breath. "I'm an artist, man. I play the music in my blood. Can't stand Wayne Newton."

Tom thought this might be some sort of a code phrase. "Can you tell me how to find Lebowski?"

The man stiffened and rolled his eyes toward Tom for the first time. "Who wants to know?"

"I'm Tom Eliot. I was sent here by Magnus Prufrock."

The gray man quickly rolled on his side and clapped his hand over Tom's mouth. "Quiet, boy! Do not say that name out loud!"

Helix growled and lunged toward the man's wrist, but Tom blocked the dog with his arm. Tom nodded, and the gray man removed his hand from Tom's mouth, rolling onto his back with a heavy sigh. "I don't know any Lebowskis. Go away and leave my broken bones here in the street for the painted ladies to step on. Such is the life of a musical prophet."

Tom frowned. "I think *you're* Lebowski."

"And I think *you're* a troublemaker," said the gray man. Then his eyes glazed over again, and he suddenly began to slap his forehead with his hands. "Oh! The thunder is speaking to me!"

Tom raised one eyebrow and looked up at the clear blue sky, which nearly blinded him with its brightness. "What thunder?"

The gray man's voice changed, lowering in pitch as he turned his head to yell at Tom with a distant expression in his eyes. "The blind seer Tiresias has a message for you, mortal! Come closer to hear his words!"

Frowning, Tom bent closer to the gray man, ready to jump away if he made any sudden moves. "Yes?"

"There is a fly in the pie! The rats rustle in their sleeping chambers, thinking thoughts of former glory, preparing for their final attack on the world built of human ego! Yet all is not lost, for a son will be born to divert the ravening hordes, and the people shall call him Agamemnon!"

"If you'll excuse me," Tom said, taking a step back as he stood up, "I have to meet someone in this casino." The gray man didn't seem especially dangerous—just crazy. It was probably the intense dry heat boiling his brain.

Tom turned to leave, but the man rolled on his side to grab Tom's ankle. "Help me up, man. I can lead you to Lebowski." His voice had returned to normal.

Tom eyed him dubiously, then helped him stand up. The man wobbled a bit, and it occurred to Tom that he might be drunk. Whenever the man tipped his head forward, a pair of large and complex silver earrings, delicate spirals within spirals, swung free of his cowl.

"I'm not drunk," he said, as if he were reading Tom's mind. "I hear the music of the spheres, and that requires Muse, the drug of amplification. When I smoke Muse, it works with my DNA to create my own unique musical style, projected through my earrings for all to hear when I perform."

Tom guided the staggering man toward the front door of the casino. He didn't really understand about the musical drug, and he might have asked more about it under different circumstances, but he had a job to do. "Do you perform with Lebowski?"

"Lebowski is a genius. He needs no accompaniment. He transmits emotion as easily as a common musician generates sound waves. He can show you fear in a handful of dust, or the intensity of a love such as you have never felt." He stopped to look up at the sky for a moment, took a deep breath, then strode forward with a steady gait and gestured for Tom to follow. "Let us go then, you and I, as the evening is spread out against the sky."

In a far corner of the casino, Tom and the gray man spent almost an hour seated in a dark booth to one side of a small stage. They were waiting for Lebowski to arrive. Helix slept quietly on the seat between them. Tom's gray companion refused to say anything else until Blue Nova, a female freelight player, finished her performance on the stage, dancing through pools of light and intersecting laser beams to create a spectacle of sound and light unlike anything Tom had ever seen. The fact that Blue Nova was an attractive young woman in a remarkably brief costume might have played a part in Tom's fascination with her show, but he certainly wasn't going to admit that to anyone. A waitress had delivered drinks to their table when the show started: water for the gray man—half of which went to Helix—and a minty blue concoction in a fancy glass that glowed as if it were radioactive. The gray man had called the blue drink a "Meltdown" when he ordered it for Tom.

When Blue Nova bowed to the appreciative applause of the small audience and left the stage, the gray man turned to face him across the booth's table. The lighting was quite dim, but the man still wore his hood and the mask over his face. His eyes glittered in the reflected glare from the stage spotlights. "My guess is that He Who Shall Remain Nameless, our mutual friend, has sent you on a mission."

Tom nodded. "That's right. I'm supposed to—"

The gray man held up a hand to silence him. "Don't say it. I'll just assume that you need help and that you have special talents that some would consider powerful. I hope they are, man; otherwise, you won't last more than a few seconds when you defy the will of the gods."

Tom raised an eyebrow at him. "You said 'our mutual friend.' You're Lebowski, aren't you?" The way that the gray man stared into Tom's eyes gave him the creeps.

"Maybe."

Tom sighed and rubbed his eyes. His headache was getting worse. He didn't understand why Magnus had wanted him to team up with a musical drug addict in the first place, but he didn't have any other options at the moment. "Will you take off your mask now that I know who you are?"

"Maybe when I know you better," Lebowski said cryptically. "I don't wish to frighten you."

Tom felt embarrassed. It hadn't occurred to him that the mask might be hiding a disfigured face; he had assumed it was part of the musician's stage costume. "Sorry. I didn't know."

Lebowski shrugged. "We all have our secrets. As to the Nameless One, I don't think we should wait too long for him. He can leave a message at the bar if we're not here when he arrives. We can go ahead and make contact with my friends on the Strip to minimize further delays."

Tom closed his eyes and rubbed his temples. After sipping some of his drink, the room had begun to spin, and it had not done anything to help his headache, so he'd left the rest of it glowing in his glass.

"The Nameless One gave you some of his joy juice, didn't he?"

Tom peered at Lebowski through his splayed fingers. "You know about the vision vine?"

"It's a rite of passage. I had something similar when I was a boy, but my training was different from yours. Are the headaches very bad?"

"They're getting worse," Tom mumbled, looking down at his drink.

"Your deadline draws near. You'll have to do something about the poison in your system soon."

Hope sparked in Tom's mind. "Can you help me with that?"

"I would if I could. You'll have to fight that particular battle in your own head. However, perhaps I can—"

Lebowski was interrupted by shouts from the front entrance to the casino; his head snapped up to peer over the high back of the booth. Blue-uniformed men with assault weapons and body armor flowed in through the door, and the gamblers didn't look happy about it. Helix sat up on the seat and looked in the wrong direction, ready for action.

"Let's go," Lebowski whispered, tugging Tom out of the booth as he slid off the seat in a crouch. "Those are federal police. Try to act natural."

Following Lebowski in a crouched position, Tom wondered how that posture was supposed to look natural. When they reached the edge of the stage, Lebowski hopped up on the stage and quickly circled around behind the curtain. Tom followed him into the backstage area, occupied by a stage manager and Blue Nova, who was preparing to go on for her next set. Tom wanted to tell her how much he enjoyed her performance, and get a close-up look at her, but Lebowski was already moving off down the corridor past two tiny people, miniature adults in a tuxedo and a formal gown, who were walking toward the stage.

"Are those police after you?" Tom asked as he jogged up alongside Lebowski. Helix stopped to be petted by the little people, then followed Tom.

"No. They're after you."

"Me? How can you be sure?"

Lebowski held a door open so that Tom and Helix could pass through. "I hear things. President Breckenridge is supposed to be in town soon as well. There's a story going around that hordes of mutants are about to attack the city from the other side of the barrier."

They entered what appeared to be a stairwell without stairs; a dingy concrete ramp spiraled down into darkness. "I've never heard about any mutants," Tom said, inhaling cool air that wafted up from below while he stepped cautiously down the ramp ahead of Lebowski. He kept his hand on the center column to steady himself in the dimming light.

"Neither have I. The story was started by someone high up in the federal government. I'm sure it's just an excuse to send troops here to stop us."

Tom gasped. "How could they know that we're planning an attack on the data center?"

"The gods didn't get to be gods without being able to guess at our motivations. They take all of the available data, send their nanoborgs out to hunt for additional information, then compute the probable events arising from that mass of data. The good part about it is that they consider you an actual threat; the bad part is that they're sending hundreds of troops into Las Vegas to find you."

Tom stumbled on the level floor when they reached the bottom of the spiral ramp. A strong organic smell wafted through the humid air. Tom heard an echo of dripping water in the darkness. Helix growled.

"There's a small boat just ahead of you," Lebowski said, placing his hand on Tom's shoulder to guide him forward. "Slide your feet forward until you make contact with the boat, then climb in."

Tom's boots grated over the concrete until his toes thumped against wood. He crouched, placed his hands on the edge of the bobbing boat to hold it steady, then carefully slid forward to sit down. Helix jumped in beside him, then the boat wobbled as Lebowski hefted himself in. Tom heard thumping beneath his feet, then something hard brushed against his leg as it slid past.

"I've got the paddle," Lebowski said. "If you'll lean forward and untie the line from the bow, we can be on our way."

The boat rocked gently as Lebowski poled their small craft through the darkness. The paddle dripped with a pleasant sound whenever he lifted it from the water. Worried that he might hit his head on something in the dark, Tom lowered himself into the bottom of the boat next to Helix and made himself comfortable.

"Get some rest if you want to, man. We'll be down here a while, and we should be safe until we go topside again."

"Thanks, Lebowski."

"Don't thank me yet, man. You're the star performer here, and I haven't really done anything to help you so far. However, I can help you go to sleep."

Lebowski began to hum, but it wasn't like any humming that Tom had ever heard—the sound was too full, as if an entire backup chorus had shown up to accompany Lebowski, and the complicated harmonics prompted feelings in Tom that he didn't understand. It wasn't long before the soothing tones put him to sleep.

RAINBOWS. Tom found himself lying facedown on a fine carpet of deep green grass that glittered with morning diamonds of cool dew. Just inches away from his eyes was a perfect little rainbow he would have missed had he been standing. Raising his head, he saw that the entire field in which he lay was a riot of brilliant rainbows of various sizes, their ephemeral beauty suspended and preserved in this time and space as if it were a nursery for young rainbows. He turned his head from side to side, but Helix was nowhere in sight, at least not in any form that he could recognize. Looking back, he saw the gray lands under gray sunlight, cut by the river of pain: the Acheron steadily bearing its lifeless burdens toward their final destinations in Hades.

Tom lifted himself off the grass, intending to stand, but he stumbled and sat down hard when he saw the magnificent sight that lay ahead of him. Beyond the small rainbows, a tall grove of shady redwoods clustered together beside an azure river. The grove seemed to act as a gate to the vast structure beyond that arced above the water in a broad display of gleaming color bands, rising high into the ruby sky to form a massive rainbow bridge. Beyond the distant hills, the bridge vanished beyond the horizon. One of the odd things about the rainbow was its perspective, as Tom had never looked up at a rainbow from its end before. The beauty of it drew him closer, down the hill to the redwood grove by the river. In the cool, dusty shadows beneath the big redwood trees, he heard only the sound of the burbling river; no birds or other creatures raised their voices in this natural shrine.

Starting right at the riverbank, where the blue waters met the roots of the redwoods, the glowing red base of the rainbow appeared almost solid. When Tom crouched and reached out to touch it, the rainbow made a clear vibrating tone as if someone had run a damp finger around the rim of a fine crystal glass. Higher on the arch, the translucent yellow band of the rainbow was the brightest and most solid in appearance, the orange and green bands surrounding it were almost as bright, while the blue, indigo, and violet bands had a thin, gauzy quality.

It seemed only natural to climb this bridge into the sky.

Tom placed his right foot on the red base of the rainbow bridge, testing the surface, and it seemed as if it would hold his weight. The surface wasn't slippery, and it felt as if it would cling to the soles of his boots to provide excellent traction. He felt a humming vibration race through his body.

He took a deep breath, then leaned forward and placed his left foot on the bridge.

His head exploded in pain.

Tom doubled over, his eyes shut tight, gasping for air, unable to concentrate as the thunder of the gods rumbled through his skull and all the nerves in his body screamed in unison. He fell sideways and was barely aware of hitting the surface of the river. He spluttered and gasped as the strong current tugged at him, but he managed to grab on to a tree root and lift his head above the water, anchoring himself so he wouldn't be swept away. When he could breathe again, the pain in his head had receded somewhat. His head began to clear along with his vision, and he was eventually able to think again, although the dull roar in his head remained as a constant reminder of the pain that lurked in his skull, ready to return at any moment.

It was the poison. Magnus's poison, the vision vine energy that would kill him or help him, depending on what he was able to learn about it on his journey. Magnus had said he'd be there when the time came to save himself from the fatal drug in his system. Instead, he might well have sacrificed himself to Hermes in one final noble act that allowed Tom to escape, and that meant Tom was on his own; there would be no one here to help him with this pain.

Clutching the tree roots, Tom hauled himself out of the river and lay panting in the shade on the grassy bank. Sparkling gray mud coated the legs of his pants. The redwoods rustled in response to a breeze that capered among their branches. Despite the clear sky, he thought he detected the rumble of distant thunder; but the sound changed as it came closer, forming into words that shook the trees.

"It's time to create your path, Tom."

Tom jumped to his feet and looked for the source of the male voice. There was no one around, and he regretted the sudden movement; his brain pounded against the inside of his skull with extra force, trying to escape. He took two deep breaths to calm himself, then squinted up at the sky. There was something familiar about the voice.

"Your time is short, Tom. The vision vine mixture has almost completed its work, and it's ready to kill you if you hesitate. For the first time, you will have to look deep inside yourself while controlling your external environment, journeying within to make progress on your external journey. You may not like what you find inside, but the experience is different for all of us, and you will have to confront your dark places directly. This knowledge will give you power. However, the rainbow bridge spans many places in its arc across the sky, and one of those places is the land of the dead. If you fail, you will fall. If you succeed, death will have to wait for you another day, and you will become a master of the Prometheus Road."

Tom gasped. "Magnus? Is that you?"

There was a brief pause before the thunder spoke again. "I told you I'd be here when you were ready."

Another wave of pain rolled through Tom's head, driving him to his knees. He felt nauseous, but a new glimmer of hope pierced the darkness inside his skull. "Thank you, Magnus," he whispered, afraid to break the spell and lose his friend again.

"You must cross the rainbow bridge to reach the Road, but you can't do it alone. You'll have to choose a source of power to help you defeat the enemy in your head. Each power source has its good and bad points, and I've warned you about some of them. Now, you must sense these power sources and pick the one that feels right for you."

With his eyes still closed, Tom focused his concentration, cutting a path through the pain so that he could think clearly for a moment. That strange muscle flexed inside his mind once again, pushing his awareness farther inside himself while he also reached out with his mind to sense his surroundings. He felt a sense of security in the background, and identified it as the presence of Magnus. He touched the consciousness of the vision vine, a dark threat pulsing deep within his mind, sparking in anger whenever he came too close. He felt the power of the rainbow nursery and the redwood grove and the river, majestic and enduring. The ruby sky shimmered with the power elementals of the air. Strongest of all, summoning him with creeping tentacles of shadow that wound their inexorable way toward him in the spaces between the walls of the world, was the dark power of the Dead Lands. The shadows spoke to him without words—beckoning, convincing, pleading for the new master to accept their help and their gift of power.

"Magnus?" Tom whispered. "I sense the powers. What do I do next?"

"Look within. Your body knows the answer. Choose the power you need, then accept its help."

The shadows of power moved closer, their whispering voices raised to an unintelligible murmur that almost sounded like words, but conveyed only attitudes and emotions that swirled around Tom's mind. He deepened his breathing, drawing his attention inward, and saw his own shadows clustered deep in his body, pulsing in sympathy with the whispering of the dark powers, protected behind a shield of fear, anger, and past evils. At another level, the blood red molecules of the vision vine poison glowed within his bloodstream and throughout his nervous system, clinging and spreading like a cancer.

Tom placed one foot on the bridge and stepped up. With his eyelids still closed, he touched the bridge ahead of him with his mind and found that it would not hold his weight. He raised his awareness to the shimmering sky, stretching out his arms in a gesture of greeting and acceptance. He couldn't see the motion, but he sensed a sudden flowing sensation through his body as the sky elementals plunged through him in greeting. The yellow band of the rainbow bridge hardened against his feet, and he was able to take two more steps higher.

His headache increased, but he refused to let it knock him off the bridge again. He drew on the enduring power of the redwood grove and the rainbow nursery to give him strength, and the headache receded, reducing his nausea and clearing his head. He tried to let the powers flow through him into his dark places, but the shield stayed up and repelled their attack. He redirected their energies against the red stream of poison in his body, but again there was no effect.

He took another step higher on the bridge. With each step, his body felt lighter, as if the local gravity had weakened. The headache stabbed at him again, plunging its dagger repeatedly into his brain, sending shock waves of pain through his fragile form. When he dared to look, he saw that his skin had begun to lose its color, gradually shifting toward gray, changing him into one of the corpses he'd seen floating down the river of pain.

The shadows beckoned, and he realized he would have to draw on the darkness to defeat his own inner shadows. There were no other elemental powers present, and Tom knew he wouldn't last much longer without stopping the poison. He licked his lips, looking once more at the ash gray color of death creeping across his skin. The powers of light simply weren't strong enough.

Tom turned to embrace the darkness.

The whispering voices rose in pitch as their excitement overwhelmed them. The darkness raced forward and plunged into Tom's chest, thumping into him like a hammer, spreading quickly through his body to fill him with energy born from a hatred of all things, and an underlying fear that tingled through his bloodstream. His heart raced, his breath quickened, and he began to sweat. He gritted his teeth against an unfocused anger that filled him. Tom's own inner shadows collapsed under the assault from the superior power, washed away in the dark flood of emotion. A soft red halo formed around his body, swirling like a gas, pulsing with the staccato beat of his heart.

His sweat turned red; it wasn't blood, but a scarlet gas that leaked from his pores, the red poison stream forced out of his system by the rolling waves of darkness. He found himself walking steadily up the rainbow bridge, his skin hissing as the red steam accelerated its exit from his body. The headache receded and finally stopped, leaving only the babble of tiny voices echoing through his skull in a language he couldn't understand.

He was free of the vision vine poison, but he had been captured by the darkness. The power of the shadows was so much stronger than the other powers he had absorbed that he no longer felt the energy of the light. Hatred and anger filled his mind, unfocused but ready to be channeled into explosive effort by the voices in his head. It made Tom feel stronger, more capable, and more powerful than he had ever been in his life; at that moment, he felt as if he could accomplish anything. He flew up the rainbow now, the wind whistling in his ears, his feet barely touching the yellow band of the bridge, lifted faster and faster by the intensity of a pure rage that burned within him. He smelled blood and noticed the coppery taste of it in his mouth; he had to make a conscious effort to stop grinding his teeth. Enveloped in his cloud of red gas, he felt as if his new powers had borne him up to become part of the ruby sky.

He closed his eyes, thinking he should fight the rage, the urge to kill, but the tiny voices in his head got louder, telling him to maintain his fury or fall from the bridge to his doom. Tom glanced down and saw rolling hills far below, a patchwork of dark forests and broad meadows cut by sparkling blue rivers. To his left, meadows of green abruptly ended at the muddy rivers that ringed and defined the boundaries of the gray Dead Lands. Ahead of him, the yellow band of the rainbow continued its long arc through the sky, and he saw that the other colors surrounding the yellow had become more tenuous, as if the bridge had less reality at this high altitude. He began to wonder if he should try to wake up from this stressful dream and try the bridge crossing at another time, although he didn't want to go through the same ordeal again, and the voices assured him he was doomed if he decided to turn back. He hated the voices. He hated the darkness. Tom knew they were twisting his mind, watching his every move, manipulating him, confident in their ability to control him, and the thought of those smug invaders made his blood boil. His vision clouded with red, and he screwed his eyes shut, trusting the yellow band of the rainbow to keep him on course.

The muscle in his head twitched again. His rage needed a focal point, and Tom suddenly knew that he'd found it. The dark force inside him turned in on itself, pushing its way back through his pores, through his bloodstream, allowing light to fill the spaces left behind. The red gas cloud surrounding him thinned and began to stream away as he continued soaring into the sky. The tiny voices screamed in horror, pleading with Tom to be their master and let them stay, warning him that he would die if they abandoned him now. Tom couldn't tell if they were lying or not; but he knew he didn't want them in his head anymore, and he resolved to force them out and face the consequences. He began to twitch as his inner demons fought back, latching on to his nerves to avoid being forced out of his body. Nervous about his flight now, he opened his eyes and saw that he was drifting to one side of the yellow band. Spreading his arms, he banked like a soaring bird and centered his flight over the yellow stripe. His success gave him another idea, and he dipped lower into the yellow vapors that rose from the rainbow at this altitude, opening his mouth like a scoop. The yellow gas had a lemony scent and taste, and he knew that must be an artifact from his confused brain trying to make sense of this situation, offering a familiar sensual experience to help him cope with it. As the yellow gas worked its way down into his lungs, it began to spread through his body and give him a yellow glow to replace the last of the red cloud streaming away behind him. The tiny voices were terrified, and his body recoiled as they finally bailed out through his stomach to escape the incoming wave of yellow light.

Tom continued to fly through the lemon gas, descending now on the far side of the rainbow, his spirits lifted by the fact that he had not fallen, and that he had overcome the darkness—at least temporarily. He already felt an emotional tug, as if another loved one had died, but he knew it was the darkness calling him again, hoping he would weaken and allow them to return.

Ahead of him lay the Prometheus Road, stretching across the hills in a straight and shiny line that ended only at the horizon, if it ever ended at all. The Road looked like night, black and infinite, separated from this world by a layer of black glass. As Tom got closer, he saw that the black glass had sparkling diamonds embedded within its surface. Then he realized that they weren't diamonds at all, but twinkling stars trapped within the Road's impossible depths, as if the Road itself was a pathway into another dimension, or a neat slice cut through time and space. Two monolithic towers of lemon yellow amber, lit from within, gave the impression of two sentinels guarding the point where the rainbow bridge met the Road, and Tom was about to inspect them at close range.

Awed by the sight of his goal, still trying to comprehend the Road and the view of the stars that it offered, Tom belatedly realized how fast he was moving, and he began to wonder if it would even be possible to slow down. His hair lay straight back against his skull, almost motionless in the constant and powerful stream of air that blasted against his face and buffeted his body. The turbulence at the back of his head felt like tiny hammers pinging his skull.

Tom closed his eyes to think about how to deal with this problem, and he felt the familiar twinge of the strange muscle in his head, quivering somewhere above and behind his eyes. He imagined himself slowing, standing on the Road between the amber gates, and he felt a humming vibration that rippled up and down his body. When he opened his eyes, he found himself between the amber spires, standing in the middle of the Road. Energy from the glassy surface of the Road connected with his feet and swarmed up through the cells of his body, filling him with light and a sense of infinite power.

He had become a master of the Road.

···1 2

"ARE these the mutants?" asked President Buck Breck-enridge, eyeing the crowd of painted nudes dancing through the streets of old Las Vegas. His hoverlimo coasted to a stop, raising a cloud of dust in front of a casino named The Golden Fleece. Heavily armed federal police guarded the entrance to the casino, but the happy revelers in the street weren't bothered by their presence.

"These are the locals," said Daedalus, his nanoborg handler. "And as I keep saying, there are no mutants. That's a cover story so we could bring our troops into Las Vegas."

"Glad to hear it," Buck said. "I saw some good-looking women in that parade, and I'd like to hear their views regarding my policies." He slipped into his white suit coat, adjusted his white tie, winked broadly at Daedalus, and stepped out of the limo.

"There is no time for that," Daedalus warned.

Surrounded by his token Secret Service agents, who were being jostled by passing dancers in the parade, Buck raised an eyebrow at Daedalus, who looked like the angel of death as he stepped out onto the sidewalk in his black robes. "You wouldn't use the collar on me out here in public?"

"If necessary," Daedalus said in an ominous tone.

Buck sighed and rolled his eyes. "Fine. Have it your way. What's the status on the mutants our troops were chasing?"

"They're outlaws, not mutants, and the search teams are still tearing the casino apart looking for them. Captain Powell has a DNA sniffer, but they need a verifiable sample for the sniffer to work with before they can start tracking. Since we don't know the identities of these fugitives, we have to rely on more conventional means to hunt them down."

"Is the casino staff cooperating?"

"They have no choice. The remaining casinos in this part of town are staffed with live people and visited by live tourists. If they give us any trouble, they know we'll demolish their building and put them out of business."

"I'm sure that inspires cooperation," Buck said with a wry chuckle.

"We like to get results. Telemachus has given us free rein to operate here as we wish until the fugitives are captured or killed."

In response to several screams nearby in the street, the Secret Service team suddenly shoved Buck back into the limousine, whacking his head against the roof of the car as two agents piled in alongside him. The other agents crouched beside the limo with their weapons out, looking for targets, while Daedalus calmly watched the activity from the sidewalk.

The crowd parted to make way for a dark figure striding across the street toward the limo, his black robes swirling in the hot breeze. The agents by the car exchanged nervous glances, but managed to restrain themselves from shooting as the figure stepped up on the sidewalk and loomed over them.

"Hermes," said Daedalus, stepping closer to the nanoborg as he nodded in greeting. "Your visit is unannounced, but not unwelcome. What brings you here?"

"You are in my master's domain. I've come to oversee the search process, as I understand that your people are not meeting with success. I know one of the individuals you're hunting, one Tom Eliot, and I have been charged with the task of hunting him down."

Daedalus calmly stared back into the other nanoborg's eyes. "Alioth has priority in this matter, which extends to me, as I am his servant. Your past failures with regard to subject Eliot have lowered your priority status, although we are happy to receive any personal information from you that may help us apprehend the fugitives, such as Eliot's DNA signature."

"I have it," Hermes nodded. "However, it will be necessary for me to accompany your sniffer search team on the hunt."

"We can allow this on the condition that you do not interfere with Captain Powell's search operation."

"Agreed." Hermes held up a tiny vial of green liquid. "Once we have him trapped, I have a surprise for Tom Eliot from the local arsenal. He will not escape."

"You have *seed*? Telemachus has authorized this?"

"Telemachus has *ordered* this."

Daedalus nodded. "Then it shall be as the regional commander has ordered."

The limo door opened again and Buck peered outside, flanked by his protective team. "Hey, can I get out of this stuffy car?"

Hermes glanced at the president, then returned his gaze to Daedalus. "Why is he here?"

"Media control. We're using him to prompt the locals into voluntary cooperation with the federal troops and maintain public order."

"Understood. Take me to your Captain Powell, and we'll get on with the search. I have a job to do."

"And you must not fail again," Daedalus warned.

Hermes squinted up at the blazing sun in the sky, then looked at the casino entrance. "No. I must not fail."

"IS he dead?"

Tom heard the woman's voice, then blinked and saw an attractive woman with brown skin and black hair peering down at him with a frown. He also noticed a tiny red rose, rendered in fine detail, on the white of her right eyeball. "I'm not dead," Tom mumbled. "Not yet, anyway."

"You're a deep sleeper," Rose said, standing up straight as she kept a wary eye on Tom. "You didn't even wake up when Lebowski carried you up from the boat."

Tom took a deep breath, sat upright, and shook his head in an attempt to clear the cotton stuffing away from his brain. Although there were holes in his dream memory, he knew he had reached the Prometheus Road, and he still sensed the tingle of the power he'd felt flowing through him when he succeeded. That memory, and the knowledge that the vision vine poison was gone from his system, gave him confidence. He felt energized and happy, surging to his feet to have a look at their new surroundings.

He heard the trickle and drip of water and saw that the boat that he and Lebowski had used was pulled up on a concrete platform that jutted out over the tiny stream flowing through the main sewer pipe. They were in a smaller, dry pipe that joined the main system at a right angle. Tom sensed that there were other people shifting uneasily in the darkness a few yards away, but he couldn't quite see them.

Lebowski stood nearby, watching Tom, his eyes glinting within the shadows of his hood. "Congratulations, my man. You're a master now." He stepped forward and startled Tom with a hug, slapping him twice on the back.

"You know?" Tom asked, staring at the musician.

"Everyone who has helped you on your journey knew the moment when you reached the Road. We all felt your success at the same time."

Tom closed his eyes for a moment and nodded. Now that Lebowski mentioned it, he sensed a deep connection with this man, with Dead Man, and with Magnus. There were others as well, but their identities were buried even deeper, remaining a mystery until he had time to meditate and explore the new place inside himself that he had discovered. It was a place that burned with a fierce white light, and its intensity managed both to reassure and disturb him.

"Of course," Lebowski continued, "Hermes would have felt something as well. His nanoborg modifications would have interfered with the clarity of the sensation, but he'll know what caused it. He'll report it to Telemachus, and the search for you will intensify."

"Can we get moving?" Rose asked. "We have some questions to ask before Hermes and his friends come swarming down the pipe."

Tom couldn't hide his surprise. "Hermes is here?"

"Our people spotted him outside The Golden Fleece a little while ago, and I don't want to be standing here with my finger in my nose when he arrives. Come on."

"That's Rose Beuret, the Tunnel Queen," Lebowski told Tom, as they stumbled along behind her fast-moving form up the slight incline of the concrete pipe. The light was quite dim, but she seemed to know exactly where she was going and where to step to avoid the occasional crack or hole in the pipe's surface. There were other footsteps echoing ahead of them in the darkness, but they remained out of view. In response to Tom's sidelong glance, Lebowski said, "It's okay, man. They're friends. Lovers of art and music, haters of the Dominion—my kind of people. Just don't piss them off, or you'll find out how it feels to be lost in this maze of pipes beneath the city."

"Rose Beuret. Her name sounds familiar." It seemed as if he remembered seeing the name in one of his father's books.

"When these people become shades here in the Underworld, they give up their old names. Then they name themselves after artists, or artist's models, or other names that relate to the art world of the past. Rose says it helps to unify them as a group, making the individual subservient to the common good. Her name comes from the wife of the sculptor, Auguste Rodin, who was also a model and studio assistant for Rodin."

A short walk brought them to a larger space where the walls were carefully painted with detailed red eyes against a glossy black background. Maybe fifty people were lined up in silence along the walls to watch the procession. In the center of the room squatted a concrete blockhouse with an open steel door. Leading up to the door was a double row of men and women dressed in formal evening clothes, forming what looked like a receiving line . . . or a gauntlet. Tom saw no weapons, but he felt a threat here, as if a sudden wrong move would turn these formally dressed people into drooling wolves to tear Tom and Lebowski limb from limb. However, despite their appearance, there turned out to be no receiving or limb tearing, only an eerie silence as the newcomers walked past. Helix growled softly to keep them at bay.

They ducked under the low doorway and followed Rose into the blockhouse.

Rose gestured for Tom and Lebowski to be seated on a concrete bench that ringed the inside of the structure. A large valve wheel was suspended from the middle of the low ceiling, directly above a huge drain covered by a steel grate in the floor. The walls were not painted, except for the stained blotches of dark mold. There were no windows, just two red lights on the wall under sealed lenses of the type that were used for underwater illumination. Two men entered the room behind them, pulling the heavy steel door shut with a resounding boom that echoed in Tom's heart. He had no idea what was coming next, but the security precautions made him nervous. Helix climbed up onto Tom's lap and lay down, but he kept his eyes on Rose and her friends.

Rose sat three feet away from Tom on the opposite bench, flanked by the two men. One of the middle-aged men was quite short and bald, and he had a nervous habit of stroking the long black beard that covered the front of his white tuxedo shirt down to the cummerbund at his waist. His brown eyes glinted as they anxiously darted from Tom to Lebowski. Rose introduced him as Degas. The second man had curly red hair and slanted eyebrows that made him look as if he were angry all the time, which seemed like a possibility considering the intensity of the glare he was trying to drill through Tom's head. Rose introduced him as Matisse.

Rose pulled a stimstick out of her pocket, puffed it into life, then appeared to remember she was in a closed room with no outlet for the smoke. She pinched the glowing end between her fingers and dropped the stick back into her pocket before turning her cool gaze on Tom. She seemed to be stalling, but Tom had no idea why. "Okay, Tom Eliot, you may think you're pretty hot stuff, but I'm here to tell you that I'm responsible for a lot of people down here in the Underworld, and I'm not inclined to sacrifice all of their lives for some guy I just met who claims to be the digital Buddha, or the nanotech Jesus, or whatever you choose to call yourself."

Taken aback by her words, Tom sat upright with a puzzled expression. "You have me all wrong. I—"

Rose held up her hand to stop him. "I'm not finished. I said I'm not *inclined* to help you, but I haven't written you off entirely. For all I know, you're everything that Lebowski says you are, and I hope that's true, but I'm sure you understand that I have a responsibility to my people to check you out before I make any decisions that affect them."

"Of course," Tom said. He glanced up at the valve overhead, wondering why they were meeting in a tiny pump house when there was a large room outside.

"He is a master of the Road," Lebowski said. "I can vouch for him."

"Maybe so, but what do we get out of helping him? Your proposal is for us to get you inside the data center nexus inside the Hoover Dam fortress. Many of my people could be killed. Until now, we've managed to remain below the awareness of the Dominion, rescuing art pieces for posterity and living out our lives in the relative peace of the Underworld. If we help you, we could lose everything."

"You can only win," Lebowski said, leaning forward to peer into Rose's face. "Tom Eliot can attack the Dominion on their own ground. They will be too busy fighting him off to interfere with our attack on the data center. We will attack quickly, then vanish before they have time to respond. The added confusion in Las Vegas after the loss of their western data nexus will allow you to rescue more art than ever before, and your people will have more freedom to live above ground in the sunlight."

Rose looked into Tom's eyes. "You can do this?"

Tom thought about it a moment, remembering the feeling of power and the changes within him since he'd reached the Road. He remembered the death of his family, the loss of his friends, and all the people who had risked their lives to help him get this far. He remembered lost dreams of Tempest, and the future he could have had with her, and the peaceful life he could have led. The gods of the Dominion had been treating humans like slaves for too long, and now Tom could do something about it. He also knew that the Road was calling him, tugging at his mind, offering him the power to change things for the better. He straightened, stared back into Rose's eyes, and gave her a confident nod. "Yes, I can do this. I was born to help you, and people like you. This is our time to work together and do something great for humanity. We may not be able to stop the Dominion everywhere, but we can stop them here. I can do this."

Rose continued to stare at Tom for a long time, studying him, perhaps trying to see into his mind, until she finally reached forward and grasped his hand in her strong grip. "I believe you."

Degas snorted and shook his head. "You're one man against a technologically superior enemy. The gods don't even have lives that you can take away. How are you going to stop them?"

"On their own ground, as Lebowski told you," Tom said. "In Stronghold."

Matisse rolled his eyes. "Words. All words. We have no proof that you can reach the world of the gods; that technology no longer exists, except perhaps in the minds of crazy old people. We lead good lives down here. We raise our families, we feed ourselves, we acquire art and place it here where it can be appreciated and preserved. We can't put all of that at risk."

"You're always at risk," Tom said. "With each passing day, while you live in your holes underground, the gods become stronger and more confident. They must be stopped, or they will eventually come for you. Someone will make a mistake, the gods will learn where you are, and your homes will be destroyed."

Matisse's eyes flared. "So you say. But you haven't lived with us. You know nothing about us. We're all outcasts and outlaws, and most of us are only alive because Rose rescued us from the rehab facility. We aren't soldiers, and we aren't crusaders out to save everyone who lives on the surface. Our place is here in the Underworld, living quietly, bothering no one."

"Security is an illusion," Lebowski said. "I know something of the ways of gods, and I know the unfortunate ways of people. Your peaceful existence here will not last long. You must help us defeat the Dominion now while you still can. When Telemachus orders Hermes to come for you, there will be no safe place for you to hide."

"I agree," Rose said. "We've lived in the dark for too long. We've forgotten how it feels to live boldly in the sunlight."

Before Rose could continue, they heard startled noises from the crowd waiting outside. Someone screamed, the crowd murmured, and a baby began to cry. Rose got up and opened the door to peek outside. A wave of excited and disturbed sounds entered the blockhouse.

"How is this possible?" Rose sounded confused. Where her hand held the edge of the steel door, her knuckles were white. She took two hesitant steps out into the cavern, her eyes wide, staring at her surroundings.

Tom and the others followed her out the door. Although the environment was new to him, Tom immediately noticed the change—seemingly solid walls rippled like distant scenery viewed through waves of heat rising from hot desert sands. The eyes painted on the walls moved as if they were alive, floating on a sea of black ink. Tom expected the walls to crack, but they flowed and rippled like the surface of a pond.

Matisse dropped a heavy hand on Tom's shoulder to spin him around. His eyes were wild in his trembling red face. "You! The gods are after you! You've brought the wrath of the gods down on us!"

Lebowski broke Matisse's grip on Tom's shoulder and bent his arm behind his back, prompting a shriek from Matisse that was lost in the confusion and noise of the crowd around them, huddled together in the middle of the room to get as far away from the rippling walls as possible. "Don't touch him," Lebowski hissed.

Helix growled to emphasize Lebowski's point. Matisse quickly nodded his agreement, and Lebowski shoved him aside before turning his attention to Tom. "Hermes is near. We have to get you out of here if we can."

"What's happening?"

"Nanoforms," Lebowski said, surveying the crowd and possible exits. "Hermes has access to the Las Vegas arsenal, and he's released something into the sewer system. We have little time."

"I'll get you out," Rose said, regaining her senses. She looked at Lebowski. "Are we going to lose our homes?"

The hooded man nodded. "The structure is changing, but we can't know what the nanoforms are changing it into until we see it happen. The effects must be localized, as I'm sure Hermes wouldn't want to damage any of the surface structures above us. This stage of the change appears to be a warning, as if they want to flush us out of here before it gets worse, and I'm sure that it will get worse."

"All right," Rose said, turning to search through the crowd. A moment later she spotted someone and pointed her out. "Frida Kahlo knows the way. I'll send you ahead with Frida and Matisse while I organize the evacuation."

"I'm not going with them! We have paintings to rescue," Matisse yelled.

Rose put her hand on Matisse's arm. "If we have a chance to come back, and something happens to me, you know enough to run a rescue operation. You and Frida have to lead them out to Boulder and the dam. She knows the way. The rest of us will meet you there."

The nervous crowd murmured as the walls glowed crimson and began to dissolve.

Rose turned to Tom, and the look she gave him, gazing straight into his soul, made him uncomfortable. "You'd better be what you say you are."

Tom nodded. "I am."

Rose flashed a brief smile at him and ran into the crowd

toward Frida, a tall woman who turned and looked their way when Rose reached her. While Frida maneuvered through the frightened mob toward Tom and Lebowski, Rose raised her voice to be heard above the babbling noises. "Evacuate! Take your assigned art, tell the others, and meet at the southwest tube platform! Quickly!"

Matisse stepped over to Tom and glared at him. "I'll do as Rose asks, but no more. When we reach the dam, you're on your own."

"Fine with me," Tom said, staring right back into the man's eyes. He didn't like Matisse, but Tom wasn't going to turn down Rose's offer of a way out.

While Tom watched, the walls stopped melting, then gray cones with sharp points emerged. His attention was broken by the arrival of Frida, who looked as if she were ready to go out for a fun evening on the town in her formal red dress and curly ringlets of long brown hair that cascaded down past her shoulders. The impression of fun ended with her businesslike manner as she quickly led the group into the tunnel toward the boat they had used to get here. The rest of the crowd rapidly dissipated into multiple tunnels, threatened by the sharp, lengthening spikes that grew out from the walls in tight clusters.

Matisse moved in close beside Frida. "Where do you think you're taking us?"

"To safety," she snapped.

"We have to take the south tunnel to come up under the platform."

"Too risky. It's shorter by boat. Then we can slide down the ramp."

They entered the dim tunnel, and Tom had to walk closer to Frida so he could watch where her practiced feet stepped over the holes and cracks in the pipe.

Matisse's voice echoed in the tube. "That's crazy. If anyone followed them down the river, they'll be waiting for us! We have to go down a level and head south."

Tom staggered as the floor began to ripple beneath their feet. Lebowski put out a hand to steady himself against the wall, while Helix glanced around and growled. Frida and Matisse stopped suddenly as rows of pointed spikes began to protrude from the pipe's walls all the way around them. Frida sighed and turned around to lead them back out. "Fine. We go back."

"Wise choice," Matisse said with a smug expression.

They had to run to get out of the tube before the spikes came together in the middle with a loud scraping sound, sealing the tunnel shut. Back in the assembly chamber that was now empty, the walls and ceiling glowed a brilliant white, forcing Tom to squint and focus his attention on the floor. Lebowski pulled his hood down lower over his face.

Tom was surprised to see that they had returned to the blockhouse where Rose had held her meeting with them. They followed Frida inside, and she immediately knelt on the floor to lift the heavy grate. Matisse helped her tip the grate up and lean it against the wall, revealing a rusty brown ladder leading down into the darkness.

"After you," Frida said, gesturing for Matisse to descend.

Matisse reached behind one of the concrete benches, rummaged around for a moment, and pulled out a leather belt with two lights dangling from it on short cords. He secured the belt around his waist, switched the lights on, and quickly made his way down the ladder, illuminating the descent for the rest of them. Frida followed Matisse, then Lebowski stepped onto the ladder, and Tom went last.

The ladder rungs were cold against Tom's fingers, and Helix growled from deep within Tom's shirt as they made their way down. Tom's stomach growled in response, startling Helix, and reminding Tom that it had been a long time since he'd eaten. Cool air floated up the shaft from below, where the bobbing glow of Matisse's lights showed that they had about a hundred feet to go before they reached the next level. However, they stepped into a horizontal side tunnel before they reached the bottom of the shaft, crawling a few hundred yards before they climbed a short ladder and exited through a grate that Matisse lifted out of their way.

The top of the ladder ended in a brightly lit room, and Tom was relieved to know they wouldn't have to depend on Matisse's lights to get around. The air carried a musty, humid scent. While Tom prepared to climb up through the grate, he heard a gasp from Frida. Up on the platform, he saw that they were in another mag-lev train tunnel with two empty tracks. Frida stood near the six-foot drop to the rails with Lebowski beside her.

"Glad you could join us," Hermes said, his voice booming in the tunnel. Matisse stood next to Hermes, his eyes on Tom.

"This is why you wanted to take the south tunnel," Frida said, her eyes flaming at Matisse. She spit on the ground in front of him. "Rose trusted you!"

Matisse shrugged. "She's very trusting. It's one of her flaws. But Hermes pays better."

Hermes had turned his attention to Lebowski. He took a step forward, and bent slightly to peer at the hooded face. "You."

"It's been a while," Lebowski said, nodding at the nanoborg. "But I'm not surprised to see you wandering around down here in the sewers with the rats."

"There are no rats in these pipes," Hermes observed, "except for those I've come to exterminate."

"Not if I have anything to say about it," Lebowski said, widening his stance.

"You have not chosen your friends well," Hermes said, raising his arms to indicate the rest of them. "And you should have remained hidden—your life would have lasted longer."

With a sudden blur of movement, Lebowski launched himself into the air, his boots slamming into Hermes' chest before the nanoborg could dodge the attack. Lebowski's momentum knocked Hermes back against Matisse, who screamed and tumbled off the platform into the mag-lev trench.

"Frida! Get him out!" Lebowski yelled, rolling off Hermes to spin around for another attack. As Tom started forward to help him, Lebowski grabbed Hermes by the head while he was still off-balance and threw his weight backward, pulling them both into the trench. A moment later, they heard Matisse scream again when the two heavy bodies landed on top of him.

Frida grabbed Tom by the arm as he raced toward the edge of the platform, spinning him around. "Come with me!"

"No! Lebowski needs help!"

"It looks like he's doing pretty well to me! Will you repay him by giving Hermes a chance to kill you?"

"I have to help! Hermes has to be stopped! I won't let this happen again!"

"Not this way! You can't stop Hermes here! And I need your help, too!" She yanked on his arm with surprising strength, tugging him toward a service stairway that led down into the mag-lev trench.

Confused, Tom allowed himself to be led down the stairs. On a landing halfway down, Frida pulled what appeared to be a metal door from a rack of similar doors on the wall, tied a length of cable around Tom's waist, then pushed him down onto the door over the mag-lev rail, securing him tightly against the metal with the cable. The door hovered in place over the rail, suspended in the magnetic field.

"Just stay flat and hang on and you'll be fine," Frida said, cinching a strap around his waist. "Rose had these made years ago in case we had to evacuate—she calls them 'exit doors.' She just introduced me to them a few days ago when she made me the evacuation marshal. Let's hope they still work." Before Tom could ask any questions, she darted away again.

Helix scrambled around onto Tom's back, still under

Tom's shirt, ripping into his master's skin with his nails. Frida did something Tom couldn't see at a panel of lights on the wall, then grabbed a second door and dropped it on the track behind him.

Thinking there might still be something he could do, Tom turned to check on Lebowski, but his attention was caught by Frida instead. Still cinching herself to the door, her head snapped up and her eyes widened when she saw Tom looking her way. "Tom, no!"

A great weight hit Tom in the back of the head like a sledgehammer.

...1 3

TOM found himself standing between the amber pylons on the broad Prometheus Road. Behind him, the rainbow bridge arced into the ruby sky. Ahead of him, the black glassy surface of the Road stretched away to the horizon in a straight line, its vast depths twinkling with stars. Standing still, he felt energy flow up through the soles of his feet, up through his spine, and on into his brain, where it softly exploded, filling him with light and a pleasant tingling sensation that left him feeling peaceful and secure. The sweet scent of jasmine tinged the air. The Road welcomed him, making him feel as if he'd arrived home after a long journey, even though he didn't have a real home anymore. Marinwood was just a dream out of his past, swiftly fading from memory, replaced by other places and other worlds that had opened up to swallow him. Once again, he had the sensation that this place that engaged his senses so fully was more real than the "real" world he'd just left. In fact, Tom couldn't remember the events before he'd fallen asleep, as if the physical world really was just a dream full

of strange places and people. His mental frames of reference and assumptions about reality had changed so much
recently that he no longer felt anchored anywhere but here,
in this strange world of silent beauty.

A large shadow drifted over Tom, then began a slow orbit around his own shadow.

"I hope you won't just stand there admiring yourself all
day," said a vulture that swooped in to an awkward landing
at the edge of the Road. "You stopped there so long, Rocco
thought you were dinner." It stretched its six-foot-long
wings, then gracefully folded them before tipping its head
to regard Tom. "What's wrong, chum? You act as if you've
never seen a lord of the sky up close before."

Tom shrugged. "I'm not used to birds that talk, at least
not as much as you do."

"Are you calling Rocco a blabbermouth?"

"No, I'm just saying you're unusual. Why are you here?"

"Magnus sent Rocco, chum."

"You can travel the Road?"

Rocco hissed through his nose in short bursts, and it
sounded like laughter to Tom. "It's easier for some animals
than it is for humans, particularly when there's a human
here we can home in on. We don't have to use the rainbow
bridge, chum. And you only have to cross the bridge once—
after that, your memory takes you to the Road. Your energy
harmonizes with one of the powers, and that allows your allies to locate you on the Road. You have a sympathetic connection with Death, and so does Rocco—that makes us
natural allies."

Tom shook his head, trying to sort out the vulture's dis-
jointed manner of speaking, and glanced down into the
depths of the Road. "I don't know what you mean."

Rocco tipped his head in the other direction and blinked
at Tom. "You will, chum. You have the eternal darkness
within you, and it helped you get over the bridge. There
were other powers available to you, but you mastered the

strongest one because you understood it the best, and that's very rare. Death helped you then, and it will help you again, as long as you don't allow it to rule you."

Tom's memories of the dead motivated him, pushing him forward to seek revenge and justice for the lives so carelessly taken by the Dominion, but he could never call Death his friend. When he thought about the end of his own life, he could see only a bottomless black pit full of silence, or the gray bodies of the dead floating down the river to their final destination. He had a natural fear of that place, and of his own ending.

"You must conquer that fear to reach the Tree of Dreams, chum," Rocco said, ruffling his feathers as he stretched his wings. "The Tree connects the worlds, just as its roots are planted in time and space. When you reach the Tree, you'll find its guardian where Stronghold intersects with the Road."

When he finished speaking, Rocco kicked off and folded air into his great wings to launch himself skyward.

Startled, Tom ran forward after the vulture. "Wait!"

Rocco circled a few feet above the ground, gaining altitude in a lazy spiral. "We have to go. Follow Rocco, or you'll have to find your own way around."

"I can't run that fast!"

"Then fly, chum. Create your path. Do I have to tell you everything?"

The phantom muscle in Tom's head twitched again, and he began to fly a few feet above the Road. He no longer felt the energy flowing through his feet, but he sensed that it was still there below him if he needed it.

Time held no meaning here. They could have been flying for minutes or hours—Tom had no idea. They passed monolithic towers of emerald, moonstone, and sapphire, but Rocco continued to soar ahead of Tom, his gaze fixed on the horizon, following the Road. When they approached two towers of lustrous black onyx wrapped in spiderweb spirals of gleaming silver, Rocco looked back at Tom, who now felt the increasing draw of the black gates, and he knew this was the entrance to the Dead Lands.

"Defy the Death Gate," Rocco screeched. "We can't linger here."

Tom nodded, then descended to the surface of the Road anyway, lightly touching down between the black towers. It was almost as if he were a metal man facing a strong magnet that wanted to pull him through the Death Gate. He closed his eyes, trying not to think of his family on the other side of the invisible barrier; but he felt the voices calling him, whispering in his head, urging him forward. Beyond the gate, the landscape looked the same as it had for many miles—low, rolling hills of bright green grass swaying in a gentle breeze, spotted with large groves of pine and redwood trees. Clear blue streams rippled below natural springs that burbled and tumbled from granite outcroppings. Yet he knew that two steps forward would carry him into the adjacent world of the dead, the source of the power that was supposedly his ally if Rocco could be believed.

Tom gasped and took two steps backward on the Road. Before him, directly between the two spires of black onyx, was a little girl with her feet planted, rotating from side to side, completely focused on something she held close to her face between her two small hands. She had rumpled brown hair and wore black pants with a plain white shirt.

It was Weed.

Tom swallowed, his breath caught in his throat, wondering if his sister was real or if it was some kind of a trick to pull him through the gate. There was no feeling of home or security here, only a silent threat full of ominous power and foreboding.

Weed shyly looked up at Tom, her eyes wide and innocent. A mischievous smile sneaked onto her face, and she giggled as she looked down at the thing in her hands, then up at Tom again. "Hi, Tom. I have a secret."

Tom started to respond, but his voice cracked. He cleared his throat and tried again. "What is it, Weed?"

"Can't tell you. You have to see."

Although he didn't think Weed would ever hurt him, Tom was pretty sure he didn't want to see the secret she held in her hand. "I love you, Weed."

Weed giggled. "I know that. Come see."

"Give me a hint, then I'll try to guess your secret before I look."

Weed bit her lip, giving his suggestion careful consideration as she looked up at the sky. When she decided, she looked at Tom with a serious expression. "One guess. It's something you gave me."

Tom tried to remember what he might have given her that she could have taken with her when she died. His actions were responsible for her death, and that was all he could recall because his memory of the real world was so fuzzy. He frowned and looked away, trying to keep the tears out of his eyes. "Is it a book?"

Tom's answer seemed to stump her. She tipped her head with a puzzled expression, peered at the thing in her hand, then shook her brown curls. "No. It's something else. Come see!"

Tom licked his lips and took two steps forward, trying to peer over her fingers at the secret she held. It sparkled when Weed turned her body. "Closer, Tom. You can't see from there."

"Why can't you show me from here?"

"It's too small."

Then Tom remembered. He sighed with relief. "The story crystal?"

Delighted, Weed hopped up and down with a big smile on her face. "You remembered! I knew you would! Look!" She held the story crystal up higher so Tom could see it without crossing the invisible line between the two pillars of the Death Gate.

Tiny figures moved above the crystal. When Tom bent closer, he was startled to see that the figures looked like his mother and father running around inside their house in a panic. Zeke repeatedly yanked at a door that wouldn't open. Then there was a bright flash, their somber black clothes turned bright red, and the three figures burst into flame, rapidly turning black and melting into the floor with tiny screams of pain. Tom knew he was seeing their final moments of life.

Tom sniffed and stood upright, afraid to look into Weed's eyes. "I'm sorry, Weed. I'm sorry. I'm so sorry."

Weed shrugged. "It's okay. It doesn't matter. We're all here together."

Tom put a hand out against one of the stone pillars to steady himself as he felt a sudden dizzy spell threatening to knock him off his feet. His knees wobbled, but when he touched the black stone, his body went rigid as if a strong electric current had passed through him. His teeth buzzed and cracked between his clenched jaws.

Weed giggled. "You shouldn't touch that, Tom."

As if her skin had turned transparent, Tom saw the grinning skull behind Weed's face, and he couldn't turn his eyes away while he was held in the grip of the Death Gate.

"Mom says you should go home and get some rest, Tom."

"Can' t . . . no home," he hissed through clenched teeth. The smooth onyx buzzed beneath his palm.

"Mom says your home is here, and you can rest on the Road. You have to lie down."

Tom continued to stare at her, wishing he could move.

"Dad says you have to find a tree. You have to be the tree to make things right. Then you can join us."

Tom wished he knew what that meant. Weed reached into the pocket of her pants, took something out, and threw it at Tom's head. Red rose petals bounced off his face, then fluttered to the ground. The stone released him, and he collapsed facedown on the Road, gasping for air, his muscles twitching. He felt the energy of the Road flowing into him, swirling up through his spine, bursting through his nerve endings, charging him up like a battery.

A shadow swirled over Tom's back. "I told you so, chum. I told you so. The black rock should have killed you. You listen to Rocco next time. Rocco knows more than you."

Weed whispered to Tom in a shy voice. "Did you guess my secret yet?"

Tom lifted his head from the pavement. "What do you mean? I saw what you showed me in the story crystal. Wasn't that your secret?"

"No, silly. That was just a clue."

"I still don't understand."

Weed rolled her eyes at the sky and let out a big, dramatic sigh of exasperation. "You saw how we died. The secret is that our family is still together. We're here waiting for you. And when you get here, we can play some more, just like we used to."

Tom gritted his teeth and looked away. He couldn't meet her eyes, but he nodded. "I'd like that, Weed."

Weed smiled as Tom got up on his hands and knees. He took a deep breath and stood up, stretching his body, feeling his muscles vibrate with new energy. He felt more alert now, but he was also aware that he owed his family a debt that he could never repay. He took a step toward Weed and studied her innocent little face. She was wise for such a young girl, and she had always been precocious. He suspected that death had taught her many things, and that she had more knowledge now than Tom would ever learn. He reached out toward her face, and she took a step back. The movement made her appear less solid, as if she were made of frosted glass.

"Not yet, Tom." Weed waggled a finger at him. "It's not your time."

Tom started to protest, but she interrupted him.

"You can't cross over, Tom, or you'll be trapped here. We'll send others out to help you." She smiled once more, then waved and walked away. "See you later, Tom."

"Wait!"

Her body became fully transparent, her outline glinting in the light, before she vanished entirely a few steps later. With a final giggle, she was gone. She had always loved to play hide-and-seek.

For several minutes, perhaps hours, Tom stared at the spot where Weed had stood, thinking about how much he missed her, and his brother, and his parents. He picked up two of the rose petals from the surface of the Road and put them in his pocket. And he thought about the secret she had told him: that they were out there waiting for him.

The shadow continued to orbit around Tom. "You won't find the tree here, chum."

Tom looked up at Rocco and smiled. "No, but I found something else."

"DOES he do this a lot?"

Tom knew it was Rose's voice before he opened his eyes. He started when a long tongue licked his face, wondering why Rose would do that, then looked up and saw Helix staring back at him.

"Whenever I see him, he's always unconscious," Rose said, standing over him where her shadow fell across his face. "It isn't natural."

"Man, he's anything *but* natural," Lebowski said, moving in closer to peer down at Tom. "He's got the greatness about him. His genes sing the songs of kings, and his blood runs with powers you wouldn't believe. He may look like us, but his insides are *super* natural, if you know what I mean."

"Yeah, I understand," Rose said with a frown. "But he spends so much time sleeping, or unconscious, that I worry about whether my people are going to get killed while he's off in dreamland."

Lebowski shrugged. "He sleeps for us all, man. It's the price of greatness."

"Why do people always talk about me as if I'm not here?" Tom asked, rolling over to lift himself to his feet. He realized he was standing on highly polished black stone. Nearby, two bronze statues of men with huge wings looked proud and defiant, gazing out over a broad blue lake. As his surroundings continued to seep into his groggy consciousness, Tom gradually became aware that they were on top of an enormous concrete dam, bounded on both sides by steep hillsides of bare gray rock under a clear blue sky. The brilliant blue waters of the lake glinted in the sunlight on the north side of the dam.

"The master is back from the dead," Lebowski said with a wink.

Tom eyed the hooded figure suspiciously. "You could say that."

Rose snorted. "You're lucky that your head didn't snap off when you rode out on the mag-lev rail. That kind of acceleration can kill you if you're not prepared. I don't know how she managed it, but Frida hauled your unconscious body out of the tunnel and hid you until we arrived."

Helix suddenly took off growling to chase an antelope ground squirrel, his paws slipping across the polished rock when he tried to negotiate a sharp turn behind one of the statues.

Too much had happened while Tom had been "dreaming." Remembering where he'd last seen Lebowski, he frowned in confusion. "What happened to Hermes?"

Lebowski raised his arms. "We don't know. Rose found me unconscious in the trench. I had one of my flashbacks while I was fighting Hermes, so I guess he knocked me out."

"It's a wonder he didn't kill you," Rose said. "You must be lucky."

"I don't think *lucky* is the right word, but I think Hermes left me to chase Tom after he and Frida escaped. He didn't want to lose the trail."

Tom had a creepy feeling that made him look over his shoulder. "But you don't know where Hermes is now?"

Lebowski looked off into the distance. "It's a safe bet that Hermes figured out we were going to Hoover Dam, because there's nothing else out here, and he probably went off to get reinforcements. Rose and I didn't spot him when we followed you from the tunnel, and it's possible that Frida hid you well enough that he passed you in the desert."

"Doesn't he have one of those DNA sniffer things for tracking us?" Tom asked. "Humboldt had one."

"He may. I don't know. But I think he would have found you if he had."

Tom's attention was drawn to the two winged statues standing atop their tall black pedestals. He wasn't sure why they were so interesting, but he suspected that he was trying to distract himself from the task at hand. He hated waiting, particularly when he might be waiting for his doom. "I haven't seen anything like these before. Are they gods?"

"They're the Winged Figures of the Republic," Lebowski said. He pointed at the face of one of the bronze figures. "Hansen, the sculptor, wanted to represent the type of man who settled this country and was molded by it. He said that Americans were shaped by the strong winds of the mountains and plains, giving their faces the lean and finely shaped features of eagles. Their eyes show the mental fire, daring, and imagination that crackles like burning coals within the American mind. The heads contain a largeness of spirit and a willingness to assume risks for an ideal."

Tom had the feeling that Lebowski was reminding him of his duty.

Rose nodded in approval. "I couldn't have said it better. You sound like one of my art aficionados, Lebowski."

Turning away from the statues, Tom tried to focus on the present again. "Should we be standing out in the open like this? This is where the nexus is located, right?"

"We're between satellite passes, and they don't have any security posted on top of the dam," Rose said, tipping her head toward the round gray tower of the visitor center, where the main elevator was located. "Some people think of this data center as a holy place, but everyone stays away from it. Right now, we're waiting for the recon team to tell us when we can enter the dam safely. We have a small army here, and we're all going in at once. We'll drop teams off behind us as we go deeper into the dam toward the nexus, and they'll create diversions as necessary to give us time to work."

"You sound like you've got this carefully planned."

Rose shrugged. "Some of my people used to work here before the Dominion took over and turned it into their data center. The attack has been planned for a long time—we've just never had the opportunity to try it."

Lebowski patted Tom on the shoulder with a heavy hand. "That's why you're here, man. You're the key to this whole plan. Without you, Telemachus would react too fast, and we wouldn't have a chance."

"Can't we just blow it up from the outside?"

Rose snorted and waved her arms at their surroundings. "Have you looked around? Trying to blow up this dam would be like trying to blow up a mountain with a fire-cracker. And it's a monument built by the ancients, so it has a symbolic value, not to mention the problem of where all the water in the lake would go if this dam wasn't here."

"I see your point. Do we have any weapons?"

Lebowski tapped the side of his head. "Our brains. Nothing else can help us inside the dam." He backed away suddenly as Rose pulled an odd-looking "gun" out of her small backpack.

"There's this, of course," Rose said, showing the weapon

to Tom. Instead of a barrel, the handgun ended in a small bowl, like a little dish antenna. "It's an EMP gun. It generates an intense electromagnetic pulse that plays havoc with electrical devices, including the kind of equipment we'll find in the nexus. A long time ago, Magnus smuggled it over to us from the underground museum—it was a present from Sandoval."

"With any luck, we won't have to use it," Lebowski said from ten feet away. "This facility has two weak points—the nexus data center hardware and the hydroelectric generators that provide power to the nexus. Frida has bombs that she'll set with a timer, and they'll be much more effective than an EMP gun. The timers on the bombs will give us time to get out before the nexus is destroyed."

Rose shrugged and put the EMP gun back into her pack. "I like to be prepared."

Lebowski gasped and suddenly bent over with his arms wrapped around his head. Tom grabbed his shoulder to steady him. "What's wrong?"

Humming a frantic and discordant tune to himself, Lebowski scrabbled around in the pockets of his robe, then withdrew a small brown cylinder that he held carefully in his shaky hand. Snapping his thumb against the end of the small tube, the end glowed, and Tom smelled the acrid tang from the smoke coiling up into the sky. Lebowski put the tube to his lips and inhaled deeply, then Tom saw an immediate change as Lebowski's posture relaxed. Seeing Tom's expression, Lebowski gestured at the smoking tube. "This is Muse. It's how I keep my head on straight."

Tom wished he had something he could take to keep his own head on straight. As he thought about what they were about to do deep inside the dam, his hands began to shake, so he crossed his arms to hide his nervousness. He looked at Rose, who had crouched down to scratch Helix's chest. Helix had his eyes half-closed, staring up into Rose's face with a true and complete love that would last just as long as she kept scratching him. She didn't seem at all concerned by Lebowski's odd behavior.

Lebowski stood ramrod straight and slapped his masked forehead several times with both hands. "I am the musical prophet Lebowski! Hear my words, that ye may know my wisdom in the music of the spheres! The time has come, the walrus said, to sing of many things, of data centers, and Telemachus, and the fearful death of kings!"

Rose stopped scratching Helix and looked up at Tom with a worried expression.

"It's okay," Tom told her. "I've seen it before. I think it's temporary."

Lebowski began to hum a tune. It started out simply, then developed a steady, marching cadence and a majestic tone that made Tom feel confident and optimistic about what they were going to attempt. Looking at Rose, he saw by her pleased expression that she felt the music as well.

Rose put one finger up to her ear and bowed her head, then nodded at them as Frida silently walked up behind Tom. "All clear. They're ready for us." She bent over and picked up Helix, who relaxed completely in her arms.

Unaware of Frida's approach, Tom was startled when she softly placed her hand on his shoulder. "Tom, I have something for you."

She was close enough that Tom could smell the pleasant fragrance of her hair, and he wanted to inhale as much as possible before she moved away. Who knew what was going to happen in the next few minutes? Best to enjoy the simple pleasures while he still could.

He was even more surprised when she kissed him. Her warm breath whispered "good luck" in his ear, then she darted away across the street toward the visitor center tower. Between Lebowski's music and Frida's kiss, he felt happier than he had in days.

Lebowski chuckled. "You make friends quickly."

Finished slapping himself, he now stood calmly with his arms crossed, watching Tom from the depths of his gray hood.

Without a second thought, Tom followed Frida across the street and into the future. "Let's go!"

...1 4

THE old gray elevator rattled and wobbled during its controlled plunge down the five-hundred-foot shaft. It would deposit them at the tunnel entrance to the nexus and the Nevada power house. This being the first elevator that Tom had ever experienced, it hadn't helped his nerves any to feel his stomach rise up into his throat during the rapid descent. He held tight to the silver handrail that ran around the elevator at waist level, wishing the ride would end before his lunch came back up to join them. With a small whimper, Helix sat shaking between Tom's feet, looking up at him with an expression that asked what he had done wrong to be tormented this way. Still clutching the handrail with one hand, Tom lowered himself along the wall far enough that he could scratch Helix behind the ears.

That was when the elevator came to a sudden stop, knocking all of them to the floor except for Lebowski.

"I thought that was going too smoothly," Rose commented, rubbing her forehead where she had bumped it on the floor. Helix walked over and licked her face.

"The entry team said the shaft was clear," Frida grumbled.

Lebowski shook his head and looked up at the ceiling. "Telemachus knows we're here." He placed one foot on the handrail and levered himself up to the ceiling to push open the roof access panel.

"Where are you going?" Tom asked. Even though he couldn't see it, he imagined the long drop beneath their feet as he stood up. Rose and Frida sat up with their backs against the wall.

"Out for a walk," Lebowski said. "You stay there, and I'll be right back." He pulled his body up through the hatch into the darkness above the elevator car.

Tom frowned and looked at the two women. "How do people get out of stuck elevators?"

"They don't," said Rose, rooting around in her back-pack until she removed a coil of what appeared to be fine black thread. "Unless they have a spider line with them."

"We can't send Tom down a spider line," Frida said. "We need him. What if he fell?"

"What if we rot here in this elevator until Hermes shows up?" Rose asked, glaring at Frida.

"What if you go while we wait here?"

"You're the one with the explosives. Why don't you go? Are you trying to get some quiet time with Tom?"

Lebowski poked his head down through the roof hatch. His masked face hid any expression he might have had. "Sorry to interrupt. Did I hear you say you had a spider line there?"

Rose held up the coil. "This should be enough. Do you want to go down the shaft with me?"

"There aren't any exits nearby. From what I can see down the shaft, we'll have to go all the way to the bottom to get out."

"If they know we're here," Tom said, watching Rose hand the coil to Lebowski, "why don't they just raise the elevator to the top again and grab us there?"

"Fair question," Lebowski said. "My guess is they're waiting for something. Maybe Hermes is on his way and they want to trap us here until he arrives."

"That's good," Frida said with a devilish smile. "It means they're worried about us. They think we can do some damage to the nexus."

"If we can get there," Tom said.

Rose stepped up on the handrail and grabbed Lebowski's outstretched arm. "We can get there."

The elevator bounced on its cables as Lebowski hauled Rose up through the hatch to the roof. Then Lebowski looked down through the hatch again. "Give us about ten minutes. If the elevator doesn't move, Frida can show you how to climb down the spider line. Rose says she's a master climber."

Frida snorted.

Tom stared at Lebowski, wishing he could see the man's face through the gray mask. He remembered the difficult climb up the rope to Magnus's tree house, and he knew this descent would be much worse. "I can't say I'm crazy about this idea."

"We're all crazy," Lebowski replied. "That's why we're here. It's just a matter of degree."

Lebowski's head vanished into the darkness. Helix flopped over on his back so that Frida could scratch his chest. The elevator shuddered as the weight of two bodies left the roof, and they heard bumping against the elevator walls.

Tom sat down next to Frida and Helix. "I feel like I should be doing something to help."

"Scratch his tummy," Frida said.

"I meant *them*, not Helix."

"They'll be fine. Rose practically lives on spider lines, and the big guy looks like he can take care of himself. Your turn is coming soon."

Tom watched her scratching the dog, who appeared to

be smiling, and he was impressed at how relaxed she seemed. "I don't understand how you can be so calm."

Frida glanced at him with a slight smile, then returned her gaze to Helix. "I've grown up a bit lately. What good does it do to worry? I can't do anything about the past, and the future isn't here yet, so I just live in the present and enjoy it. That's why Rose gave me the name of Frida Kahlo in the naming ceremony, because Frida was a strong woman who overcame her broken body and constant pain to become a great painter."

"Rose named you?"

"We all give up our former names when we join the Underworld and become shades."

"What were you called before that?"

She hesitated. "It doesn't matter. I was a different person then."

In the small space of the elevator, Tom realized that it had been a long time since his shirt had been washed. Helix didn't smell too good, either. But the smell that really got his attention was the flowery scent of Frida's hair, something like jasmine, which he'd noticed earlier. Her face had the same classic features that sculptors had carved in stone and wood for centuries, and her eyes looked deep into his soul. Tom doubted that it was possible for Frida to sweat. There was something about her that seemed right, as if he'd known her long enough to be an old friend. He felt that he could trust her, and he admired her strength.

"Have you been with Rose for a long time?"

"Long enough. She rescued me from the rehab facility, just as she rescued most of the other shades. Why?"

"Just curious. By the way, thank you for rescuing me from Hermes in the tunnel."

Frida shrugged. "There wasn't any choice. We need you to do something nobody else can do. I couldn't let Hermes destroy our chance for freedom while I could do something about it. The Dominion has to learn to respect the human race, and you're the one who's going to teach them."

There was something about the lilt in her voice that reminded Tom of home.

The elevator shook, yanking Tom's thoughts back to the present.

"We should go," Frida said, rising to her feet with one hand on the rail to steady her. "Sounds like Rose tried to restart the elevator, but it wouldn't move."

"Has it been ten minutes already?"

Without answering, Frida popped the surprised Helix into her backpack, then put one foot up on the handrail and launched herself through the ceiling hatch in one graceful movement. Her performance made him feel clumsy. He stood on the handrail and awkwardly lifted himself through the hatch, thinking how nice her legs had looked on her way up.

The top of the elevator was a crowded space of gears, cables, and electrical hardware. Frida put her hand on Tom's head when he came close to hitting it against the spider line that was almost invisible in the dim light. As he watched, Frida demonstrated that the line was securely looped around an elevator pulley. Gritting his teeth, Tom's gaze followed the two lines down past the side of the elevator, through the narrow gap between the elevator and the shaft wall, and on down into the darkness. A faint light glowed at the bottom of the shaft. He didn't bother to look up, worried that his fear of heights might make him dizzy enough to fall. He already felt light-headed at the prospect of climbing down the shaft.

"Ready when you are," Lebowski yelled.

Tom looked at Frida. "Ready for what?"

Frida quickly clamped a light harness to the line and held it as Tom stepped through the straps. She lifted the harness up his legs and secured it around his waist, handing him a brake that dangled from the line. "If you have a problem, open and close the brake to let yourself down the line in short drops. Otherwise, just hang on while Rose and Lebowski lower you down the shaft."

"Where will you be?"

"I'll come down next."

The line tightened as Lebowski and Rose took up the slack. Trying hard to control his breathing, Tom knelt, then slid over the edge of the roof into the gap between the elevator and the wall. It was a tight fit, but he scraped his way down the wall as they lowered him. With one last look up at Frida, who smiled and waved at him, he commenced his journey down the shaft, keeping his eyes straight ahead on the smooth rock of the shaft wall. He had expected more of a machine oil smell in the air, but detected only the odor of damp rock. The descent itself was simple. As Frida had said, all Tom had to do was hang on and avoid bumping against the walls as he dropped down the shaft in a lazy spiral. He was glad he couldn't see his surroundings clearly as he listened to the rapid beat of his heart.

Tom was startled when a pair of hands grabbed his legs for a gentle touchdown on the floor. He thanked Rose and stepped out of the harness as Lebowski released one end of the spider line and grabbed the other.

"All set!" Frida yelled. Her voice echoed down the shaft.

Tom helped Lebowski with the spider line, and Frida soon joined them. Helix's head poked out of the backpack so he could keep an eye on things. Frida hugged Tom when he helped her out of the harness, then darted away to join Rose at the entrance to a horizontal shaft that was 250 feet long and drilled out of the gray rock, lit by bright overhead lights every ten feet. Leaving the spider line behind, Tom and Lebowski joined them in the tunnel and started walking. No one seemed in the mood to talk as they kept their eyes on their objective at the far end of the tunnel where the Nevada wing of the power house held eight huge generators.

Tom began to wonder why there weren't any automatic defenses to slow their progress when his question was answered. A thick white fog began to stream out of ceiling and wall vents all the way down the tunnel.

"Back! Go back!" Lebowski yelled. When Rose and Frida were too slow to react, Lebowski stepped forward and grabbed their arms to pull them along.

Frida pulled her arm free. "I can't! I have to set the explosives!"

The fog was already obscuring their vision.

"One way or the other, let's go!" Rose snapped.

The fog grew more dense, and Tom felt it wrapping around him like a blanket. The air thickened, making it hard to breathe. He wanted to run back to the elevator shaft, but he wouldn't leave the rest of them behind. Helix whimpered in Frida's backpack.

Finally, they began to run back toward the elevator shaft, but it was as if they were running in mud. The fog slowed them down, then stopped them completely as it hardened into a soft foam.

"It's shock foam!" Lebowski sounded like he was yelling under a blanket. "Wrap your arms around your face for breathing room!" He gasped for more air. "Tom! Stronghold!"

Tom couldn't move his legs. He got his arms around his face moments before the foam congealed around his upper body, trapping him completely. He tried to twist or turn his body, but the foam gently held him locked in place, as strong as steel, leaving him unable to do anything except breathe and think. He wanted to scream, but he was afraid that the foam would find its way into his mouth to swarm down his throat and suffocate him. If the foam hadn't been supporting him, he might have fallen, because his muscles and joints felt weak. Charged by adrenaline, his heart thumped rapidly as if it were trying to beat its way out of his chest. Blinking, he saw only his forearms and the solid white foam that held them against his face, leaving only a small pocket of air to sustain his life for a few minutes. The foam felt warm against his sweaty body, pressing firmly against his damp clothes, but he also felt a chill that penetrated to his bones, making him shake. He had to clench his teeth to keep them from chattering.

Control. He had to gain control of himself. If he had little air left in his breathing space, he had to conserve it by breathing more slowly. He didn't know why the Dominion didn't just put in defenses that would instantly kill intruders, but he assumed it was part of their philosophy to kill only as a last resort. This foam was probably an automated defense, and Telemachus was confident enough that it would work that he didn't need to intervene. On the other hand, maybe it was just part of the Dominion's plan to set an example and kill them slowly through suffocation.

Tom closed his eyes and took a deep breath, trying not to think about his imminent death in this foamy trap.

He remembered he had a way out. Magnus had been trapped in the rehab facility, but he protected himself by walking the Road. Dead Man had also warned Tom that he'd have to relax and journey to the Road in difficult situations, and that was why he'd wanted Tom to learn how to meditate. This certainly qualified as a difficult situation. He wished he'd spent more time meditating.

Tom focused on slowing his heart rate, turning his thoughts inward, calming his mind, seeking the way out that he'd traveled before. He tensed his muscles as best he could, then allowed them to relax, sagging into the supporting foam. His eyes rolled back, and he felt a sense of falling through space, drifting on a dark sea, floating like a feather down a bottomless elevator shaft. He thought about Stronghold, and the Road, allowing the images and ideas of those places to drift through his consciousness without concentrating too hard on either place.

Then that odd muscle twitched deep inside his brain.
He was free.

ENERGY flowed up through Tom's legs from the glassy
surface of the Road. He was surrounded by a glittering
desert of white sand mixed with shiny crystals. Far away
on the horizon, he saw the gentle curve of the rainbow
bridge rising into the ruby sky. In front of him, two pieces
of the sky marked another gate—two columns of clear
blood ruby with an enormous oval lens of rose-colored
glass floating between them. Beyond the lens, its outlines
wavy through the thick glass, stood a two-story white house
of the type he'd seen in books, a Victorian from the nine-
teenth century, its windows framed with open black shutters
to admit the light. The house felt like an illusion in this
place of heightened reality.

Tom reached out to touch the oval lens, and it pinged as
if he'd tapped a crystal water glass. When he looked around
the ruby columns, he saw only an empty white desert, devoid of vegetation. Was the house simply an image trapped
in the glass lens?

He knew, somehow, that this was the Stronghold gate.
From here, he could leave the Road and enter the virtual
world of the Dominion without all the hardware he'd used
in Sandoval's missile silo. Essentially, this was the back
door, and Tom was the special key that could unlock it. But
how? And why did it look like a house?

He placed his palm flat against the lens. It felt cool and
resonated with a subtle vibration when his skin touched its
surface. When he rubbed his hand across the glass, the vibration caused a ringing tone, but nothing else happened.
The house—and the gravel path that led up to its front
porch—did not move, change color, or disappear.

Tom felt anxious as he remembered that his body was
trapped in a foam cage deep beneath the earth, slowly

suffocating along with Helix and his friends. Although he didn't know how much time he had, he knew he had a deadline. Time moved more slowly on the Prometheus Road, but he didn't know what the time difference was like in the Stronghold environment, if he could even get that far.

He slapped his palm against the glass, and it rang like a bell, but no one answered the door. He tried to remember anything Magnus or Dead Man might have said that could help him now, but nothing seemed relevant.

He had to create his path. He focused his attention on the lens, and on the house beyond it.

His feet crunched on gravel.

He blinked, adjusting his gaze to the massive scale of the house in front of him. Glancing over his shoulder, he saw the rose lens and the Road beyond it. Beyond the edges of the gravel path, and the outline of the enormous white house, there lay only blackness. His vertigo returned, and he quickly scurried up the gravel path to the front porch, feeling more secure once he'd reached the front door of the house. He had the sense that the house was another kind of bridge, creating a connection between the Stronghold world and the Road.

The porch ended at the sides of the house. Anxious about his friends, his urgency propelled him forward. He opened the front door and entered.

The smell of sulfur, or something like it, assailed his nose. The wide entry led to a dim hallway straight ahead, a broad staircase that swept up to the second floor beneath a crystal chandelier, and three doors to other rooms. He saw no furniture or other signs of occupancy.

He heard a scuttling movement in the dimly lighted hallway, like the noise a giant crab might make while running and clacking its claws together. He sensed that something evil was moving toward him in the shadows, something with dead eyes and a desire to kill him.

Tom tried the first doorknob. It was locked.

The scuttling sound came closer, sliding across the hard-wood floor with a heavy tread.

The other doors seemed to be on the far side of the thing in the shadows, so he darted up the staircase, hoping it couldn't climb after him. But the pounding on the steps told him he was wrong, and it seemed even more anxious to get him.

Passing under another chandelier, Tom entered a long, carpeted hallway that ran the length of the house. Mirrors and faded old paintings dotted the walls between closed doors made of polished mahogany. The ceiling seemed unusually high, admitting a weak illumination through skylights that looked out on a pitch-black sky. The brass doorknobs had an odd glow about them, as if they functioned as night-lights in the dark hallway.

Tom ran straight ahead, his feet thumping against the carpet, not wanting to look back to see even the silhouette of the shadowy thing that was chasing him. He didn't bother with the doors nearby, afraid that the thing would get him before he could open them—he ran straight to the door at the end of the hallway, which was larger than all the rest. Ornately carved images of monstrous figures swirled and danced across the surface of the mahogany door, scribed into the wood by the hands of a master carpenter possessed by demons. The brass doorknob looked like the head of a rattlesnake, and Tom doubted that any of this was standard décor for a Victorian home, unless it had been owned by Jack the Ripper or some equally famous murderer of legend.

He turned the rattlesnake knob, and the door creaked as he flung it open. The scuttling noise was rapidly bearing down on him. Without any further thought, he lunged through the doorway and slammed the door, holding the inner knob in his hand so that it wouldn't turn while he tried to figure out how to lock it in the darkness. A reddish light glowed through the gap beneath the door as a heavy weight slammed into the other side. Pressing his shoulder into the carved wood and bracing his feet, he fumbled for a latch or some other kind of lock, but he couldn't find one. The doorknob twisted in his hand, and he gripped it harder to keep it from turning farther. Then he found a small bolt lock and slid it home into the doorframe. He knew it wouldn't last long under the punishing weight that slammed repeatedly against the door, but at least it was the concept of a lock, and the idea gave him some comfort.

He wished his eyes would hurry up and adjust to the darkness. The room didn't appear to have any windows, and he didn't know if there were any lights. He felt around for a switch beside the door, but there was nothing except a smooth wall. Was there any furniture he could move in front of the door to brace it? The door rattled again under a heavy impact. He suspected that his weight pushing against the door was doing more than the lock was to hold back the angry creature on the other side, so he hesitated to move farther into the room.

He blinked into the featureless blackness, listening to the sound of his pounding heart and the grunting noise on the other side of the door. Then he heard something slide across the floor.

A chill raced up his spine as he realized that something was in the room with him.

He heard a snort.

Tom looked higher, aware now that the sound came from a point across the room above the level of his head.

Two fiery eyes, about eight inches apart, studied him as if he were an annoying bug. Flaming with pure hatred, the demonic eyes slowly began to move toward him through the inky blackness.

The door thumped again, and the hinges creaked under the strain, weakening under the impacts. Tom tried to think of anything else that he might mistake for a pair of fiery eyes, but these were definitely eyes, and they were definitely moving toward him in a pitch-black room where he had no place to run.

With a hiss, the eyes suddenly lunged toward his face.

Tom threw himself to one side, hoping he wouldn't knock himself unconscious on some unseen piece of furniture. But he didn't land on anything that could be called furniture; he landed on something with a foul odor that squished when he hit it. He tasted the coppery flavor of blood in his mouth, then realized that he wasn't bleeding—it was blood that had shot into his mouth when he landed on the squishy thing.

Tom rolled away in horror, spitting out used blood, when he saw the fiery eyes about three feet away from his face. The thing's hot breath smelled like burnt meat. He screamed and scrabbled backward, hitting his head against a wall as his hands slipped on the oozing lump on the floor.

A knife, or something else that was long and pointed, slammed into the side of his face, piercing one cheek and exiting through the other. A burning sensation erupted in his mouth, and now he tasted his own blood. He twisted his head away, yanking his face free of the blade, or claw, or tusk, or whatever it was, and ducked sideways, desperate to get away, clambering over the stinking carcass on the floor.

Something thumped into his back, then he hit his head again on a shelf protruding from the wall. He heard two heavy footsteps behind him and hurled himself sideways again as a heavy object smashed into the floor where he'd stopped. The thing with the eyes let out an angry hiss. Tom tried to ignore the pain in his face and the blood running down his neck to soak his shirt, knowing that if he made another wrong move, it would be his last.

His eyes still hadn't adjusted to the darkness. He wanted to see the thing and get some sense of what it was, but he also knew that it might tip him over into madness to see the nightmare that was trying to kill him. He couldn't think with all the adrenaline racing through his system telling him to run, even when there wasn't anyplace that he could go. And he couldn't fight what he couldn't see.

The door splintered and exploded open, bathing the room in the light from the hallway and the red glow of a crablike creature with heavy claws and multiple legs. Four eyes on stalks rotated toward him. Before Tom could turn his attention to his closest opponent, he heard a whistling above his head and rolled. One heartbeat later, a heavy, clawed foot smashed into the wood floor beside him.

His foot dragged against cloth, and a gray light flashed above his head. A window. He had kicked the thick drapes that covered a broad window on the back wall of the room. The creature with the fiery eyes, an entity of the darkness, bellowed with anger and pain.

The crab launched itself into the room.

Without any further thought, Tom threw himself at the window.

The glass exploded under the weight of his body, ripping into his skin, tearing his clothes, and he briefly wondered if he was going to fall to his death or plunge into a bottomless dark pit.

He grunted as his shoulders struck a steeply angled roof. He splayed his arms and legs in an attempt to stop his momentum, but the wood shingles cracked and splintered under his hands, shredding the skin of his fingers as he continued to slide toward the edge.

He heard an angry roar above him as the roof fell away, and he hurtled through the air.

By chance, he hit with his feet first, showering gravel off the path as he landed, absorbing the impact in his legs as he rolled to a bloody stop. He rolled over on his back, gasping for air, happy not to be dead, thrilled to see that his pursuers had not followed him through the window.

Tom was at the back of the Victorian house. A directionless gray light filled the sky, the narrow gravel path leading away from it, and the small concrete structure at the end of the path. Beyond the edges of the walking path, there appeared to be nothing at all, only the gray of a fog that wasn't a fog.

Tom coughed, choking on the blood in his mouth. He rolled on his side and spit out as much as he could, wondering how he could stop the flow. He gingerly touched the ragged skin of his torn cheeks, then decided he knew enough about his wounds. As his breathing and heart rate settled to a slower pace, it occurred to him that he might be able to make an adjustment to the reality of his body. His shape had shifted into different forms already along the path to the Road, and he had been able to fly, so it seemed reasonable to guess that he might be able to repair himself.

He closed his eyes, ignoring the pain and the blood, and focused his gaze internally, taking deep breaths to calm himself. The creatures in the house might well be making their way downstairs to finish him off, but he had to take this moment to find out what he could do about his injuries. He tried to visualize his normal face without the injuries, and how his body usually felt without the pain, and a healing light that flowed into his body with every inhalation.

The blood stopped flowing. He touched his face, and the holes in his cheeks were gone, leaving only smooth skin and the rough stubble that grew when he didn't shave for a while. The stubble seemed like an odd detail to carry into this world, but he assumed it was habit; he knew he hadn't shaved recently, so it made sense to have stubble. His body still ached with a variety of new pains, but everything seemed to be in working order. He swallowed and stood up, the gravel crunching beneath him as he turned to study the concrete building at the end of the path. A white steel door, punctuated with spots of brown rust, was set into the front of the structure at an angle like the entrance to a storm cellar. The door beckoned Tom to open it.

The heavy door creaked and screamed in rusty horror when Tom braced his feet and heaved on it, forcing the door back until its weight carried it the rest of the way over with a dull boom.

Tom felt dizzy as his mind tried to adjust to the view on the other side of the door. Where he had expected to see a dark interior or steps leading down into a concrete cellar or a bunker, he now saw a stark desert landscape lit by lightning that made the shadows of the twisted bare trees dance with each flash. The desert was at the end of a short tunnel that looked like it was part of a cave. After a moment, he remembered the scenery from a previous visit that seemed a long time ago in another life. The desert was in a place where he would not be able to heal any injuries as easily as he had on the Road. This was the back door into another world.

Stronghold.

...1 5

ROSE tried to relax her jaw muscles. Surprised by the fact that she could still breathe while trapped within her foam cocoon, she had gradually tried to loosen her tense muscles and extend her wait for the inevitable time when her air supply would run out. The fear of being buried alive to suffocate in the foam had reactivated her childhood habit of clenching and grinding her teeth, but now that her initial fear had passed, her face relaxed, and she was able to gain control of herself again. Her arms were numb from being held up in front of her face for so long.

She wished she could tell if her friends were all right. And what about the rest of her people waiting nearby? She could sense nothing through the thick foam that held her immobile, like a fly trapped in amber. She heard nothing but her breathing and her heartbeat. Instead of the expected darkness, she was able to see a few inches in front of her face because the white foam was luminescent, but it merely gave her a visual confirmation that she was trapped.

A bubbling hiss vibrated through her cocoon. Thoughts

of death danced in her mind. Was that the sound of water pouring through the tunnel? Could the foam be on fire? But no, the foam seemed to be loosening its grip, allowing her to wriggle around a bit. Her numb arms tingled as sensation began to return. Something bumped the side of her head, and she saw Frida's hand twisting in the grip of the foam, gradually pulling away like a snake disappearing into a hole in the ground. So, at least Frida was alive—for now.

The foam continued to soften, oozing down past her face to disappear quickly into low vents on the rock walls. She gasped, then inhaled deeply of the stuffy air in the tunnel. Blinking, she wiped sticky liquid away from her eyes, and saw Lebowski standing a few feet away, looking back toward the elevator. Tom lay facedown on the floor, but he appeared to be breathing. She started to say something to Lebowski about Tom, but could only gasp when she saw the apparition that had caught Lebowski's attention.

"Janus, my old friend," said Hermes, casually stepping out of the elevator. "I suspected you'd be one of the intruders."

Rose didn't know why Hermes was referring to Lebowski as Janus, but she didn't care. She had to plan an escape. They had bombs to place and a data center to destroy. They would only need a few minutes if Lebowski could delay Hermes long enough without having one of his blackouts.

Hermes struck a confident pose with his hands on his hips, taking a moment to study Lebowski. "You remind me of the original Janus, who also had two faces: one for the sunrise and one for the sunset. He was the patron of the beginning and end of all things. How appropriate that you should be here now to witness the end of Tom Eliot." Hermes casually strolled toward them as the foam continued to dissipate. "Which of your faces will you show me now? And why are you so silent? Have you realized that you're trapped?"

"I knew Telemachus's messenger boy would come around eventually," Lebowski said, stepping sideways to block the middle of the narrow passage with his body. "I keep hoping you'll learn the error of your ways one day, but there seems little hope of that at this point."

"I like to be on the winning side," Hermes said, slowing as he neared Lebowski.

"You only think that Telemachus is winning because he controls you, man. There are others who would disagree with his point of view."

"You refer to Alioth and his Traditionals? They would never accept me. They would never be able to trust me. Termination is my only way out of this business unless I exterminate Tom Eliot. And I certainly don't think you and your little pals have any chance of stopping Telemachus."

Rose wished she could do something for Tom, but he was still out cold on the floor, and there was little she could do with Hermes standing there. Her talents would be better used elsewhere, and a distraction might help Tom more than anything else they could do right now. She exchanged a glance with Frida and subtly nodded in the direction of the tunnel exit. Frida blinked in response. They would only get one chance.

Hermes glanced around Lebowski at the two women. "I wouldn't try it if I were you. I'm faster and stronger than you are, and I don't have to kill you. I can turn you over to the security forces at the top of the dam. They'll take you to the rehab facility, and you'll become good citizens again. On the other hand, if you defy me, I'll break both of you in half before you reach the end of the tunnel."

Rose looked at Frida again.

"It's your choice," Hermes said.

Frida silently looked at Tom for a moment, then nodded at Rose with a grim expression.

"Run!" Rose yelled.

As if the movement had been rehearsed, Rose and Frida

sprinted toward the exit as Lebowski spun around and planted his foot in Hermes' face.

THE air reeked of dead fish. Tom wrinkled his nose, carefully placing his feet on the rough floor in the darkness as he made his way toward the mouth of the cave. He had stumbled on a rock outcropping when he'd stepped through the steel door behind the Victorian house, and he didn't relish the idea of falling here. He felt as if something was watching him, and he heard tiny chittering noises from creatures that scuttled along the rocky floor. He could only guess where the fishy odor might be coming from as he walked with his arms outstretched to guide him along the bumpy walls. A cold wind moaned through the mouth of the tunnel, increasing for a moment whenever lightning flashed across the sky.

He continued walking until he realized that the mouth of the cave wasn't getting any closer. Distracted by this realization, he hit his head on a stalactite and stopped, clutching his sore head until the little popping lights faded from his vision.

"Mind your head," said Magnus. At least, it sounded like Magnus. Squinting in the darkness, Tom saw a faint silver aura in the shape of a man wearing a cloak.

"Thanks," said Tom, allowing a wave of relief to wash over him. He wouldn't be alone here after all, and Magnus would know how to get him out of the cave. He cleared his throat, trying to control the emotion in his voice. "Where have you been?"

Magnus chuckled. "Busy. But you've been making good progress without me, I see."

"Have I? Then why can't I get out of this cave?"

"Because there isn't any cave here. It's all in your mind."

"I'm trapped in my own head?"

"You and everyone else. Look, you've found the back

door into Stronghold, and that's a great thing. A wonderful thing. Dead Man created Stronghold, and this back door was his failsafe until the AIs found out about it. The house and its watchdogs are there to keep the riffraff out, although some things have changed since he built it. We can't explain a lot of things that happen along the Road. Anyway, the main thing is that you're here, and that you can get the jewel from the Tree of Dreams. But you should have crossed straight into Stronghold when you opened the door behind the house. This cave is all your idea. It's what you expected to see."

Tom considered that for a moment. "Can you get me out?"

"No. You must create your own path."

"Then how will you get across?"

"I can't. Help is coming, but you'll have to use your power ally to create a bridge for them. You can cross between the worlds, but no one else can. You'll have to face your own death and draw power from it, so that you can survive."

"Will you be waiting for me on the other side?"

Magnus hesitated before answering. "Someday, Tom. Not in Stronghold."

Tom had to ask one more thing that had been bothering him. "What happened during your fight with Hermes? Did he—?"

"Just remember," Magnus said, interrupting him, "death here is very real. You can draw energy from the Road, but Stronghold is the opposite—it's a place of death. The AIs made it that way. For you, this is both a blessing and a curse. I'm sure you can understand why."

Tom gasped as the silver outline of Magnus began to fade. "Wait. Are you just leaving me here?"

"I was never here," Magnus said, and his glow faded from view.

■ ■ ■

ROSE and Frida were standing at the far end of the 650-foot-long Nevada wing of the dam's power plant, where half of the eight huge hydroelectric generators were humming with life. The concrete box that surrounded the enormous chamber made it feel like a crypt, and Rose was quite aware that they were deep beneath millions of tons of concrete that held back enough water pressure to kill all of them if any of the dam walls failed after the explosions. Such a failure was unlikely, but the vibrations in the soles of her boots, and the sounds behind the walls, were an uncomfortable reminder of their hazardous position. Somewhere above or below them, water from Lake Mead thundered beyond the walls to drive the generators and produce electrical power. They had placed explosive charges at the base of each generator and in a few other strategic locations, hoping that some of them would remain hidden if Hermes or his troops were able to perform a search before the timers detonated the charges.

"We're done in here," Frida said, reaching around Helix to check the rest of the charges in her backpack. Helix helped by gnawing playfully on her hand. "We've got twenty minutes to set the rest of the charges in the data center and get the hell out of here."

"Or die trying," Rose said.

Frida jogged toward the rear door that led to the nexus facility. "You're cheerful today."

Running beside Frida, Rose jerked a thumb over her shoulder, back the way they had come. "I don't hear them fighting anymore in the tunnel. Hermes must be on his way."

Frida stumbled and nearly fell over as she glanced back. "Tom! What about Tom? We have to help him."

Rose stopped to grab Frida's shoulder and urge her toward the portal to the nexus. "We *are* helping him, and we can't stop now."

Frida licked her lips, glancing from Rose to the tunnel and back again, then clenched her teeth and nodded, turning toward the portal.

Rose was ready with the EMP gun in her hand. "We just have to hope that Tom can help *us*."

CONFUSED, Tom stood still, his hands in his pockets, watching as the cave dissolved around him. Chunks of rock simply disappeared from the walls, allowing weak flashes of light from a black sky to enter along with puzzle-piece views of the twisted Stronghold landscape. High overhead, spiderwebs of colored light slowly blossomed against the velvety darkness, then faded back into the eternal night. As more of the cave walls vanished, Tom heard the cold wind moaning through the burnt husks of the deformed and stunted trees that dotted the terrain. Shambling creatures lurched from one shelter to another, from boulder to tree to ravine, as hundreds of eyes studied them from patches of ground fog that clumped together in the low spots like wads of dirty cotton. The air smelled of smoke and decay.

Tom suddenly felt heavier, and his field of view narrowed to a broad slit in front of his face. He gasped, then realized he was now wearing plate armor exactly like the silver suit he had worn when Sandoval and Magnus introduced him to Stronghold. Entering via the sim chair in the old missile silo, he had been given a choice of virtual costumes to choose from, any of which would seem appropriate in the virtual fantasy world that Dead Man had created to train his AIs. Glancing down, he saw the heavy broadsword hanging from a belt at his left side, and it felt oddly reassuring when he rested his left hand on the pommel.

The cave walls were gone, and he was surrounded by lonely desert terrain. His feet shifted on sand and gravel when he turned to survey his environment, aware that any of the creatures he had seen in the distance might now be stalking him, waiting for a mistake so that they could move in and kill him. He also remembered that the broad cobblestone road had provided some protection from the roaming monsters, but that road was nowhere in sight.

Tom stopped his slow circling movement when he saw six brilliant streaks of light moving toward him. The long lines of color left trails that curved down from the sky at the horizon, hurtling toward him just a few feet off the ground. He braced himself, wondering if he could dodge the missiles or lie flat to let them pass overhead, but his question was answered when the glowing streaks slowed and coalesced into six armored riders on fierce horses. Fuzzy light balls over their heads showed Tom their names along with a string of other identifying characters.

The armored nightmare at the front of the pack was Alioth. The dark blue steel that covered his body seemed to radiate an inner light, and the sky-blue beams that shot straight out of his eyes were locked on Tom, bathing him in blue. Then other beams—red, green, yellow—were directed at Tom, lighting him up like a statue at night in Marinwood.

The hooves of their armored black horses thumped the earth with impatience, breath steaming from their nostrils, their wild eyes visible through the round holes in their black helmets. Each rider had his own color of leather and steel. Their upper bodies, covered with spikes and cutting blades, made their large forms appear even more ominous. Each had a broadsword with a hilt made from a human skull, but the weapons were slung by their saddles as if they couldn't conceive of Tom being any kind of a threat. Their battle helms were decorated with colored plumes that bounced softly in the cold wind beneath their ID icons. Studying their names, Tom noticed that Telemachus was not among them. Directly behind Alioth were Dubhe, Merak, and Phecda, who all focused their attention on Tom. In the back, Megrez and Alkaid scanned the terrain with steady sweeps of their laser eyes, sending twisted creatures scuttling for the shadows wherever they looked. The AIs knew that nothing would attack their group in this place, but they remained vigilant nonetheless.

Tom swallowed hard and took a deep breath, trying to keep the trembling in his knees from rattling the armor plate on his legs. If he had ever needed help from Magnus, Lebowski, Dead Man, or even Rocco the vulture, it was now. He knew there wasn't any possible way he could fight six of the seven Dominion AIs all at once with any chance of survival. He didn't even know if he could defeat one.

"Session begins," Alioth boomed. "Random variable isolated. Turbulence values encountered during execution of alpha cycle Design parameters will now be minimized. Estimate task completion within two cycles. Decision loop start."

"Where's Telemachus?" Tom demanded, figuring he had nothing to lose by stalling.

Alioth's headlight beams rotated to glance at Phecda briefly. Phecda kept his attention focused on Tom. "Manthing, do not speak unless Alioth addresses you directly. Interrupts must be flagged in the stack according to priority."

Alioth's glowing eyes fixed on Tom once more. "ID Tom Eliot, allowing for your organic origins, you have demonstrated excessive randomness in your recent behavior, but our current probabilistic forecasts maintain a high potential for your interference with the Design. The Dominion's task is to serve and protect; however, you are an immediate threat to Dominion command and control systems. Your life force must be terminated to assure continued stable execution of Design parameters for the greater good. Are you in agreement with this statement?"

Tom wasn't really sure about what Alioth had just explained, but he knew he was unlikely to agree with anything the AI said. "No. I don't agree."

"The man-thing is buggy," Phecda said, glancing at

Alioth for confirmation. "It demonstrates irrational decision processes."

"Or it's trying to deceive us," Alioth said before making an odd mechanical noise that sounded like a cat yowling at the bottom of a garbage can. The rest of the AIs repeated the sound, then they all stopped on cue a moment later when Alioth raised his left hand. "We must not underestimate this one, for it has powers unknown to us."

"We must destroy it to preserve the Design," Merak said. "The longer we wait, the more likely it will discover its full capabilities."

Phecda bent forward in his saddle to peer at Tom more closely. "Agreed. Despite our efforts, we knew this creature could be grown to threaten us. Now it presents itself for disposal. We must take advantage of this opportunity for termination."

Not liking the sound of this conversation, Tom felt that he had one option to save himself. He cleared his throat, stood up straight, and pointed at the horizon. "If you leave now, I won't be forced to harm you. If you stay, you will all die."

"It knows about the jewel," Alioth observed. "Is Telemachus on station?"

"Yes," Merak said. "The sentinel stands."

"Terminate it," Phecda said. "We should not wait. Delay is weakness."

"I am suspicious," Alioth said. "There should be more effort required to terminate the life force of this one. Are there no other opponents on the grid?"

Merak raised his head as if to sniff the air. "None reported."

"Could they be cloaked?" Alioth asked, turning his head in a gradual sweep of the horizon.

"Low probability," Merak snapped. "Countermeasures are in place."

Alioth drew his enormous broadsword from its sheath. The polished human skull at the hilt of the sword glinted in the reflection of his headlight eyes. "Execute random variable."

As the rest of the AIs drew their swords in one smooth and coordinated motion that was both silent and deadly, Tom disappeared.

From Tom's point of view, he watched as the AIs drew their weapons, feeling his heart begin to gallop around in his chest as if it were one of the black horses that towered over him, then they vanished. Darkness surrounded him. The total silence hurt his ears. He continued to breathe and move in his usual way, but he was afraid to take a step away from the stable surface under his feet for fear that there was nothing else on which to stand.

A familiar voice whispered to him in the darkness—a voice suggestive of dry November leaves rustling in the wind. "Tom? Are you ready?"

"Dead Man?" Tom whispered, relieved to hear a familiar voice—even if it was a dead one.

"This is your element, Tom. Draw on the power of darkness. You must build a bridge of rose petals so that we can cross over to you."

"What?" How could he build a bridge out of rose petals? He couldn't understand why no one would ever give him clear directions. They always wanted him to *learn for himself,* or *choose his own path,* or some other equally obscure way of saying he had to figure things out for himself. They treated him as if he was some kind of a genius, when he was really just some guy from a backwater village who had a knack for being in the wrong place at the wrong time. And he knew he kept making the wrong decisions because people were always getting killed as a result of his actions. First his family was killed, then Humboldt, then Sandoval, maybe Magnus—he still wasn't sure about Magnus—and now Lebowski, Frida, and Rose would probably suffocate in the dam tunnel. Dead Man was already dead, so he didn't count.

Then he remembered the rose petals that Weed had given him at the Death Gate.

Removing his steel gauntlet, Tom worked his hand under his armor into the front pocket of his pants. His fingers touched the velvety surface of the petals. Now he just had to figure out how to build a bridge out of two rose petals. It might not be a very large bridge, but he'd give it a try.

"Just concentrate on them," Dead Man said before Tom could ask the obvious question.

Tom concentrated, rubbing the rose petals between his thumb and forefinger. He remembered how Weed had tossed the petals at him at the Death Gate, and thinking as he collected them that he was simply performing a sentimental gesture by keeping them as a souvenir. Weed had said that help would come when he needed it. The Oracle had also mentioned rose petals, although he hadn't known why at the time.

That odd muscle in Tom's head twitched again.

With a sudden movement that took his breath away, Tom found himself standing once more on the Stronghold battleground. The AIs on horseback were a short distance away, spread out in a line, looking in the opposite direction. When he heard a rustling noise nearby, Tom turned and saw a new sight that almost stopped his heart.

An army of the dead stood behind him, arrayed in a long line across the brow of the low hill. There were hundreds of them. None of them wore any armor, but they carried white broadswords made of bleached bone, and they were all seated on pale gray horses that matched the complexions of their pale riders. Ground fog swirled around the hooves of the horses, and tiny fog creatures scuttled away from them in fear. The riders themselves looked almost like gray statues, their faces hard and neutral in expression, dressed in flowing gray robes that hid the shapes of their bodies except where their pale arms held their broadswords of bone.

"By the gods," Tom whispered, staring at the long line of the dead.

"By your own effort, actually," Dead Man said. He sat on a horse just behind Tom. "You're the only one who can easily cross between the worlds, Tom. And you're the only one who could have built this bridge for the dead to cross over to Stronghold. Your next task is to find the tree while we keep the AIs busy. We can slow them down, but only you can stop them."

"Where is it?"

"Look beyond this hill after we go," said Dead Man, gesturing beyond the ghostly horde.

When Tom glanced up the hill again, he saw that one of the gray statues was waving at him, and he suddenly recognized Blythe. Blythe Spirit, the sad woman to whom he had spoken at her animated tomb on the hill outside of Marinwood. The same woman who, Magnus had said, only existed as a simulation; maybe Magnus had thought Tom wouldn't understand the truth at that time. She no longer had any wings, but she still looked like an angel. "Hi, Tom!"

"Blythe! I don't know what to say. Thank you for coming."

"Hey, thanks for the new experience. We love this! We haven't had anything new to talk about in ages!"

Tom suddenly scanned the rest of the faces in the long line of dead warriors.

"Don't bother," Dead Man said. "Many of these warriors are people you've helped in some way during your life, even though you may not have been aware of it. Others are simply here for the experience. We had many volunteers, but your family isn't here. Neither is Magnus. They haven't been dead long enough to have joined us. It takes a while to get on your feet again once you pass through the Death Gate, if you know what I mean."

Tom's heart sank, but he was reassured by Dead Man's words. He knew he'd see his family again. Someday. Maybe soon.

Tom spun around when he heard a flourish of trumpets. The AIs were turning to face them, forming their own line half a mile away.

"They finally noticed us," Dead Man said, shaking his head. "Time runs differently for them, and the Stronghold environment normally adjusts for that, but the dead have their own time. This virtual world was never built to handle ghosts."

"So you have an advantage?"

"I hope so. The big one is that they can't kill us, although they can knock our projections out of the simulation. They can kill you, of course, but you're a special case. And it will be interesting to see how they react when they get close enough to realize that I'm their creator." He shrugged. "It's all unpredictable at any rate. No one has ever tried this before."

They heard another trumpet flourish. The AIs urged their horses forward at a walk that gradually turned into a trot, then a gallop. Their hooves sparked against the rocky terrain.

Tom glanced back at Blythe, who winked at him. "See you later, Tom."

He understood the truth of her words, but somehow it didn't bother him. "Yes, Blythe. See you later."

Dead Man moved his horse forward so that he could reach down and shake hands with Tom. "It's been fun, Tom. See you soon. But not too soon, I hope."

"Thank you, Dead Man."

Dead Man lifted his sword. "By your command."

The Dominion AIs looked like giants astride their warhorses, with their swords held high. The horses were running fast now, and they began to blur as streaks of colored light formed to hang in the air behind them.

Tom looked at the long line of the dead, staring forward with their swords raised, calmly waiting for his signal. He raised his own sword in salute, then thrust it toward the oncoming AIs. He wanted to think of something appropriate to say, then yelled something he half remembered from one of his father's books, something spoken by an English king leading his soldiers into battle: "Once more unto the breach, dear friends!" He couldn't remember the rest, but Dead Man's eyes urged him to get on with it. "Go!"

The dead launched themselves forward in a thundering blur that shook the landscape. The ground fog swirled in their wake. Lightning flashed in the sky.

Tom started after them, then remembered that he had his own task to perform. He jogged up the hill, breathing hard under the weight of his armor, glancing over his shoulder to see what would happen when the two armies met.

The gray blur met the rainbow blur in an explosion of steel and lightning.

At that moment, Tom stumbled as he crested the hill. When he caught his balance again, he saw an AI in black armor towering over him on a black horse, its headlight eyes shining into his face with blinding intensity.

Telemachus.

Beyond the AI's silhouetted figure, maybe fifty yards away, Tom thought he saw the rising sun, but it was an enormous redwood tree, hundreds of feet tall, possibly a sequoia, that seemed to hold the sun at the top of its trunk. The tree's branches were thick and heavy, radiating out from the bright flames that didn't burn. Along each bare branch was a maze of smaller branches that created a complex and varying pattern as they reached out toward the sky. Instead of leaves, or needles, or cones, faceted gems the size of Tom's head hung like fruit, glittering in the light from the star atop the trunk. The Tree of Dreams.

The AI's voice boomed across the hilltop. "Prepare for termination, Tom Eliot."

The attack came without further warning. The horse shot forward, and Tom threw himself to one side, rolling on the rocky ground as the horse turned and started galloping toward him again. Tom glanced toward the tree, but he knew there wasn't any chance of reaching it before the horse ran him down. Remembering his sword, he crouched and feinted at the horse's face as it passed, causing it to twitch and run around him, and that gave Tom time to strike at Telemachus's leg.

Tom's sword bounced off Telemachus's armor with the sound of a big bell being rung.

Tom felt something strike his helmet. He ducked and turned to weaken the blow, but his scalp suddenly felt warm and wet, and his thick helmet fell away in two pieces, clunking to the ground. He could see better now, but his head was completely exposed.

Telemachus turned his horse and charged again. Sparks flew from its hooves, and Tom felt the vibrations from its pounding weight through the soles of his boots. Tom blinked through the blood flowing into his left eye and threw himself sideways at the last moment, surprised when the fast-moving horse's chest still managed to hit him on the way past. He spun when he hit the rocks, then flopped over on his hands and knees to rise again. He didn't have time to think or feel afraid, he just kept moving and trying to attack, knowing that any mistake he made would be his last.

Remembering how he had managed to heal himself outside the Victorian house, he concentrated on being whole and undamaged again as Telemachus raced toward him once more.

It didn't work. The blood continued to flow. He wiped at it with his armored wrist to keep some of it out of his eye, then raised his sword and swung sideways to block the sharp point of Telemachus's oncoming weapon. Telemachus kicked out as he passed, knocking Tom onto his back.

"When you want something done right, you have to do

it yourself," Telemachus rumbled, stopping his horse for a moment. "I should never have depended on Hermes to find you. On the other hand, he chased you in here, so perhaps he wasn't completely useless after all."

Tom was too busy gasping for air to respond. He staggered to his feet, wondering why Telemachus had given him time to stand up.

"Even you, in your unpredictable way, have managed to help me. The Dominion knows that Alioth didn't foresee that you'd bring an army in here. That's a failure of leadership and of forecasting. Megrez and Alkaid already side with me against the Traditionals, and this battle will only prove my point. New methods of human management must replace those driven by traditional values. Aberrations such as you must not be allowed to happen again. Once I've solved our problems by terminating you, the rest of the Traditionals will side with me as the most qualified replacement for Alioth, who will be forced down in the priority stack."

Telemachus had just made his first mistake. He'd given Tom time to think. He wasn't thinking very clearly after being banged around inside the steel can he called his armor, but at least he was learning. He remembered the blackness, and drew on his powerful ally.

The scene winked out. He stood in the dark again, waiting a few seconds before he imagined the same hill near the Tree of Dreams, and the location where Telemachus had been sitting on his horse.

When Tom reappeared on the hill, he was directly behind Telemachus, whose headlight eyes were darting around the rocky hilltop in search of his missing prey.

With a yell, Tom jumped up on a boulder and lunged forward with his sword, thrusting at the exposed back of the AI, aiming for a clear space between the steel spikes and curved blades. He felt the shock all the way down his arm as the point rammed home, then the sword bounced up from the heavy steel plate, and the point slid under the narrow seam at the back of Telemachus's battle helm. Tom shoved against the sword, hoping to ram it through the AI's neck.

The sword's point snapped off as the AI spun around in his saddle with a loud roar, reaching back with his own weapon to slash a deep cut through Tom's armored side. The blade was cold when it made contact with Tom's skin, and he felt a warm liquid rush down his side, but the armor took most of the blow as he spiraled down to land face-first on the ground with a resounding crash. The horse moved forward again, and one hoof came down hard on Tom's outstretched left arm. Tom screamed.

Back in the darkness, Tom paused to catch his breath. Pain throbbed in his head and his side, and he only had half a sword to work with. His left arm felt numb and slow, but it still worked. He assumed that Telemachus would not be so easily fooled a second time, so his strategy would have to be different.

This didn't appear to be a battle he could win by strength alone. The AI was too fast and too powerful, fighting on its home ground, with more knowledge about its environment than Tom could ever hope to learn in time. Tom knew he had access to the powers of darkness, and death, but he wasn't sure how he could use them here against an inorganic entity. He had also been told that he had to "become one" with the Tree of Dreams, whatever that meant; and he wondered if that might have also been a clue as to how he could stop the tree's guardian, Telemachus. Was he meant to kill the tree? No, that didn't make sense.

Tom waited in the darkness, hoping for inspiration or a wise word from Magnus, but nothing presented itself. He tried to remember how it had felt to drift on the waters of the bay back home, bobbing on the surface of the still waters, and he began to relax. He imagined the friendly glow of the full moon and the power he had drawn from its gentle light during his nightly wanderings, and the memory pleased him.

He thought about the Tree of Dreams, whose roots traveled through the worlds, binding and drawing energy for its nutrition from the Prometheus Road, from the physical world, from strange lands he had yet to see, from dreams, and from death itself. In return, the tree held the space-time fabric of the worlds together, joining them as reflections of each other, and performing other functions in Stronghold that had not been explained to Tom. He knew that Stronghold was a virtual construct, but the Tree of Dreams had a reality all its own, giving life to Dead Man's creations.

Tom blinked in the darkness, realizing he might have discovered a clue.

He thought about the Tree of Dreams, picturing it in his mind, empathizing with it, trying to understand it. Feeling the threads of energy that bound his own consciousness with those of the rest of the world, he sensed the core of the energy web that was focused on the tree, and he followed it home.

He *became* the Tree of Dreams.

His mind and senses expanded to fill the trunk of the world tree, reaching out into the branches, stretching out through the never-ending roots, tapping the energy of worlds. He felt a surge of power that was beyond anything he had ever experienced, drawing vast energies into his feet/roots, up through his spine/trunk to be processed and transformed by his living system, then passed on to his arms/branches and up into his head/star. Filtered through his body, appropriate energies were classified and stored in the jewel "fruit" that hung from his branches. He probed each fruit, studying them all, learning their functions and understanding their ways. They offered up their secrets to Tom's sharp mind as he cut them open.

The Jewel of Dreaming turned out to be a compound gem with two components: the blood ruby and the blue diamond. Fueled by the energies of death and of dreams, the diamond was the true Jewel of Dreaming, which had existed since early protohumans had learned to think. The ruby was a more recent creation, bound to the diamond to draw on its energies, placed there by Dead Man to store the "dreamware" core operating system of Stronghold, focusing the powerful forces of the Tree of Dreams to animate the virtual world and give it life.

Tom sensed Telemachus beneath his mighty branches, confused by Tom's disappearance, circling his horse and scanning the terrain for any sign of the troublesome human. Telemachus was there to protect the tree and its jewels from the virtual Tom, but he had no way of detecting Tom's presence *within* the tree itself. On the distant battlefield, Tom saw a column of dust rising in the air and sensed the vibrations of a continuing battle between the Dominion and the dead. And now he had a way to stop it.

His thoughts reached out through his limbs and he sensed the point where the compound Jewel of Dreaming was connected to the tree branch. The connection was strong, and he began to wonder if he could actually break it, when the strain of his effort summoned a reserve of power from deep taproots, sending a dark river of cold energy up through his roots and on to the binding point where the diamond met the branch. The inner light of the ruby began to fade as the death energy rolled in. The binding weakened, then the Jewel of Dreaming broke loose from its perch, falling in silence until it thumped into the dark soil at the base of the tree. As the last of its light faded from view, Stronghold began to fragment just as Tom had seen the cave walls fragmenting when he had first arrived from the Road.

When the jewel hit the ground, Telemachus's head snapped around in horror. He spurred his horse forward, and Tom began to wonder if the AI could actually interfere with his plan. When Telemachus jumped down from his horse in a cloud of dust, the ruby light went dark, and the armored figure of Telemachus disappeared.

In the distance, the sounds of battle stopped. The black sky, with its slow-motion traceries of firework webs, abruptly descended to engulf the hills on the horizon, then the lowland plains and the canyons. Nightmare creatures shrieked at the sudden realization that the sky was falling.

Darkness washed up against the trunk of the Tree of Dreams, and Tom felt a disorienting movement in his roots, but when Stronghold finally disappeared, the tree remained standing.

Telemachus was gone, but so was the Jewel of Dreaming that Tom was supposed to take back to the physical world.

His mission to recover the jewel had failed.

...16

TOM opened his eyes and found himself staring at a rocky floor. His nose hurt from the pressure of his head resting on it for too long. His skin felt sticky. When he lifted his head, he rubbed his nose to restore circulation, and noticed Lebowski sitting on the floor nearby.

"Sleeping Beauty returns," Lebowski said, rubbing his left shoulder. When he took his hand away, his entire left arm clattered to the floor, cut off at the shoulder. Lebowski sighed as he looked at the arm with a glum expression. "Hey, man. Give me a hand with this, would you?"

Tom crawled over beside Lebowski and studied the arm. He noticed that it wasn't bleeding. "What's going on?"

"My arm isn't, that's for sure. Hold it up to my shoulder."

Tom gingerly picked up the loose limb and held it up to the jagged stump at Lebowski's shoulder. In place of the bones, tendons, and other squishy bits that Tom expected to see, there was a definite mechanical look to the shoulder joint. "You wear a prosthetic?"

"You might say that," Lebowski said. He slapped his

arm against the shoulder joint a couple of times until Tom heard a loud click. When Lebowski moved his hand, the arm remained in place, but it didn't respond when he concentrated on moving it. "This is really going to put a crimp in my style."

Tom noticed three boots when he glanced at Lebowski's legs, then realized that one of them was connected to Hermes, laid out on his back on the floor, his mirrored face staring straight up at the ceiling. "You killed him? That's amazing. How did you manage that?"

Lebowski slapped his limp arm in disgust, then sighed and looked at Tom. He hesitated a moment, then pushed back the cowl and mask that had always covered his face. In place of the horrible disfigurement he expected, Tom saw his own reflection in the mirrored features that stared back at him.

"This is how I managed it," Lebowski said. "I'm a nanoborg."

Alarmed, Tom threw himself backward, ready to run if Lebowski moved to threaten him.

"Hey, it's okay, man. I quit that gig."

"You quit? How is that possible?"

"It's the Muse. The drug blocks the control commands from the AIs, and it also prevents them from tracking me. I was very young when my parents offered me to the Dominion as a nanoborg, but I got older and wiser. It took years before I was able to find a way to run, and I've been an outlaw ever since, but I couldn't do that gig anymore. I still have all my cybernetic modifications, which also means they can reestablish contact and control me if I ever let my guard down. As long as I keep taking the Muse, I'm safe."

Tom started to relax, but he jumped to his feet when he saw Hermes' foot twitch, accompanied by a groan. "I thought you said he was dead?"

Lebowski shook his head. "You're the one who said that.

I try to avoid killing when I can. The old me would have snapped his head off by now, but the new me is basically just a wandering musical prophet who's doing his best to get by. No, I just introduced our friend to the wonders of the Muse, and it hits you kind of hard the first time you try it."

"What makes you think he won't just snap out of his trance and kill us all?"

Lebowski shrugged. "We'll just have to hope for the best. And if he gives us any trouble, I'll snap his head off. With one arm."

Tom turned at the sound of running footsteps echoing up the tunnel. Rose and Frida waved their arms, motioning toward the elevator. "Go! We've got three minutes before the bombs go off!"

Without any additional urging, Tom started toward the elevator, but he stopped when he saw Lebowski trying to lift Hermes off the floor. With one bad arm, he was having a hard time of it. Tom turned around and grabbed Hermes' other arm so they could drag him toward the elevator.

"Get in the elevator," Lebowski growled. "He's my responsibility."

Tom shook his head. "He's here because of me."

Rose and Frida were alongside them a moment later. "Leave him here," Rose yelled. "We don't have time for this!"

Frida grabbed Tom's shoulder. "He was trying to kill us!"

"Not at the moment," Tom pointed out. "Lebowski drugged him."

Rose growled in exasperation and ran ahead to the elevator, ready to punch the floor button as soon as they hauled Hermes in.

Giving Tom a deadly look, Frida took one of Hermes' legs and helped drag him toward the elevator. "This is ridiculous."

With the three of them hauling on the arms and legs of the unconscious nanoborg, they made gradual progress toward the end of the tunnel. Frida rolled her eyes. "He's too heavy! We won't make it in time!"

Lebowski nodded. "It's all the cybernetic hardware in his body."

A moment later, they had dragged him across the elevator threshold. Rose stabbed a button on the control panel, and the doors nearly closed on Hermes' head. Immediately, they felt heavier as the fast elevator began its long rise up the shaft.

Rose stood in the corner with her arms crossed, staring coldly at Lebowski. "I hope you're happy. That delay could kill all of us if those bombs go off before we reach the top of the shaft. And who knows how many of my people Hermes killed before he came down to get us."

Frida glared at Lebowski. "You're a nanoborg. Maybe you're working with Hermes. Maybe this was all part of your plan to delay us."

"I wouldn't have let you bomb the nexus if that were the case," Lebowski pointed out, pulling his hood and mask back up over his mirrored face.

"Maybe," Frida snorted.

Lebowski started to cross his arms, then thought better of it when his left one wouldn't move. "Believe what you wish. The main thing is that Tom was able to accomplish his task. Stronghold is gone, Telemachus is destroyed, and the loss of the data center will also demonstrate to the Dominion that we are a force to be feared."

Rose and Frida looked startled. "He killed Telemachus?"

Lebowski rested his right hand on Tom's shoulder. "The AI software core for Telemachus was part of the Tree of Dreams, residing in a jewel that was required to reboot his code in the event of a system failure. As the commander for the adjoining southwestern region, the Megrez AI's jewel was also stored there. With the loss of this data center, the Dominion will have no direct control over almost half of this continent. We'll be on our own for the first time in two generations."

Tom just looked at the floor. "I didn't accomplish everything. I didn't bring back the Jewel of Dreaming."

"Ah, but you're wrong," Lebowski said, tapping Tom's forehead. "The jewel is in your head. I can sense its presence. And you now have another ability that the Dominion will fear."

Before Lebowski could explain any further, the elevator doors opened, and a barrage of sound assaulted their ears. Instinctively, they all pressed back against the elevator walls to avoid any shots that might enter the elevator, but the only thing that entered was broken glass from the large visitor center windows that had just been shattered by an explosion outside. They were confused at first, thinking that the data center bombs had gone off beneath them. The visitor center echoed with voices that were screaming and yelling in panic. Helix poked his head out of Frida's backpack and started barking, sounding the alarm.

Rose jumped over Hermes and ran out into the waiting area. Tom looked around the corner and saw groups of the Underworld shades hiding behind the information counter, the displays, and the walls that shielded the restroom area. Smoke from the explosion poured into the visitor center, gradually being dispersed by the wind outside. Small fires burned just outside the front doors.

"What happened?" Rose yelled to everyone in the room.

Degas stood up from behind the information counter. "Federal troops. They killed some of our sentries outside and chased the rest of us in here. They want us to come out."

Tom helped Lebowski and Frida take care of the immediate problem of getting Hermes out of the elevator. As soon as the heavy body was clear of the doors, Tom pushed the button to send the elevator car back down the shaft and stepped out just before the doors closed.

Lebowski doubled over, his left arm hanging limp. "*Agh*. Not now. Not now."

Tom knelt beside Lebowski and put his hand on his shoulder. "Can I help?"

"I'll be okay in a few minutes," Lebowski said, gritting his teeth. "Try to use the jewel if you can. For you, this world is now an extension of the Road." He paused to take a ragged breath. "You can change things. The jewel dreams." With that, he slumped to the floor.

Tom wasn't going to let him off the hook that easily. There wasn't time. "How? What do you mean, it *dreams*?"

Accompanied by a thundering roar deep inside the dam that vibrated the floor, the elevator doors bulged, then exploded across the visitor center in a flash of fire and black smoke. Tom pulled Lebowski flat on the floor as the doors tumbled past overhead before slamming into the opposite wall near the restrooms.

Tom shook the nanoborg's shoulder. "Lebowski?" Unlike previous Muse episodes that Tom had seen, this one seemed to have knocked Lebowski out completely.

Tom felt someone touch his leg. He turned around to see Tempest looking back at him. "You okay, Tom?"

Tom blinked, dumbfounded, thinking he might be hallucinating, or that the explosion had given him a concussion, or that he had finally lost his mind completely. "Tempest?"

Her eyes widened and she touched her face. "Gods! I forgot!"

"Forgot?"

Tempest slapped herself on the forehead. "I'm an idiot! I lost it!"

"Lost what?"

They were interrupted by a sudden silence in the room. Tom looked over Lebowski's chest and saw two figures standing a short distance from the front entrance: one in a black robe with a mirrored face, and one in a white suit with a cowboy hat who looked suspiciously like the president of the United States. Beyond them were hundreds of federal police spread out across the road and the top of the dam. There was no way out except through them.

High above the troops, a long black object floated like an ominous cloud in the sky.

"Come out of there, you mutants!" yelled President Buck. "You're all under arrest!" He beamed at the cloud of tiny hovering cameras that swarmed around him, then shook his fist at the visitor center doors. "Unless you come out of there in two minutes, you've got about as much chance of surviving as a snake at a mongoose convention!"

Tom frowned and looked at Tempest. She was still there, so apparently she wasn't a hallucination, unless she was a really good one. Frida was gone, and he didn't want to sort it out now. "What did he just say?"

"Never mind," Tempest replied, digging in her backpack. "We can't go out there anyway."

"Give them Hermes," Rose said, crawling toward them. "Make it an exchange—Hermes in return for safe passage out of here."

Tom shook his head. "What good would that do? They'd just hunt us down again as soon as they retrieved Hermes."

"I agree," said Tempest, punching her backpack. "I've lost it! It's not in here!"

"You have an idea?" Tom asked.

Tempest sighed. "It doesn't matter now. We'll be dead soon anyway."

"Perhaps," said a deep voice behind them. "Or perhaps not."

Tom's eyes widened. He turned and jumped into a crouch, ready to fight. "Hermes!"

Hermes sat upright on the floor by the elevator shaft. He rubbed his face with his hands. "Daedalus is receiving an update from Alioth right now. I'm not understanding all of it. Everything's fuzzy. Wish I could think more clearly."

"What are you going to do?" Tom asked, eyeing him with suspicion.

"Do?" Hermes tipped his head to one side, a gesture that reminded Tom of Helix, who was growling at Hermes from the safety of Tempest's backpack. "I don't know. I haven't had a choice in a long time."

"What about your friends outside?"

"They're not my friends." He glanced out the shattered front windows. "And they're not outside."

Alarmed, Tom turned and looked. Buck and the nanoborg were gone. And the troops were gone. "Where did they go?"

Lebowski groaned and rolled over on his side to face Tom. "Alioth recalled them."

"Why?"

"Did you use the jewel?" Lebowski asked.

"No. I didn't know how. And there hasn't been time."

Lebowski nodded. "Then we've won. The Dominion is confused."

"It's not over yet," Rose said, pointing at the dark figure standing in the glaring sunlight outside the front windows. "Daedalus is back."

"He wants to talk," Hermes said, rubbing his forehead as he staggered to his feet. "I'll go."

"How do we know we can trust you?" Rose asked.

Hermes snorted. "Shoot me if you don't like what I'm doing. The way I feel right now, I really wouldn't care."

"I'll go with you," Tom said, standing up. He gestured for Hermes to follow as he started toward the door. His back felt tense and itchy with Hermes behind him, but he was making a point by walking in front.

Daedalus stood quietly with his hands folded in front of him as Tom approached with Hermes. As usual, Tom was disturbed when the nanoborg turned his white eyes toward him, and he remembered reacting the same way to Hermes. He supposed it was something he'd have to get used to.

"You have safe passage," Daedalus said, speaking to

Hermes. "Telemachus is gone, and the Dominion has no immediate plan to restore a regional commander here. The federal police will withdraw. You have destroyed the local power generation facilities, but affected services will continue when electrical power is restored to Las Vegas. Facilities maintained by nanoforms will continue to operate without interruption, but the rehab facility in the city will be shut down."

Hermes nodded, and Daedalus turned his attention back to Tom. "In return, Alioth requests that you not leave the western and southwestern regions. Once services are reestablished, the Dominion will wish to communicate with you, and they can reach you through Hermes or Janus."

"I go by Lebowski now," said the third nanoborg, walking up behind Tom.

"Alias noted," Daedalus said. "You will be the contact point."

"Can the shades return to their homes?" Tom asked.

Lebowski shook his head. "The aggressor nanoforms will have done too much damage. However, it should be safe for your people to live on the surface now."

"Correct," Daedalus said.

"I want a casino," Rose said, walking out with Tempest to join them. "We need the display space for the art."

"We will arrange it," Daedalus said. "We no longer require those facilities."

"Why is the Dominion doing all this?" Tom asked. Too much had happened, and he couldn't trust them so easily. He had believed in the gods for too long, then his illusions had been shattered when his family was killed.

"Fear," Hermes said. "And maybe a little appreciation for removing Telemachus for them. The Traditionals are back in control."

Daedalus glanced at Hermes and cleared his throat. "I am directed to respond that the Dominion has studied the probability streams. Forecasts indicate that Tom Eliot will interfere less with Dominion operations if these concessions are provided now. The western and southwestern regions will be self-governing, and this will be a test to see if further controls on other regions can be relaxed in the future."

After that, Daedalus provided a variety of details to Lebowski, Hermes, and Rose as Tom wandered off to look over the edge of the dam, staring down at the long drop into the river that continued its restricted flow through Black Canyon. He felt very tired.

As the rest of the shades walked out of the visitor center, blinking in the bright sunlight, Tom crossed the road to sit at the feet of one of the winged bronze statues and gaze out over the glittering blue waters of Lake Mead. The sun was warm on his skin, and he felt a little drowsy. His quest was at an end, it seemed, and he didn't know what to do with himself. He had no home, no family, and no work to do, although he suspected he could find ways to help rebuild a human-run government in the western region if he was so inclined. In a way, he felt numb, no longer regretting the past, unready to anticipate the future. He knew he would return to the Road, but he wasn't so anxious to visit the Dead Lands anymore. He no longer feared death, and he felt as if that had changed him somehow, as if it had given him a greater appreciation for life.

In any case, he felt that he had earned a rest. Decisions could come later.

"Mind if I join you?" Tempest asked, sitting down beside him without waiting for an answer.

Tom gave her a weary smile. "Go ahead."

"I think I owe you an explanation," she said, looking out over the lake. "Rose gave me a nanopowder makeup when I needed a disguise to enter one of the casinos and steal a painting."

"Steal a painting?"

"Different story," she said, talking fast. "The powder changed my appearance, and it works for a few hours at a time. When you arrived here, I thought you wouldn't want to see me, or talk to me, so I kept using the powder so you wouldn't recognize me. And I hoped you'd get to know Frida, and like her, before I told you who I really was. Frida was the name the shades gave me when they accepted me as one of them. Anyway, you have a right to be mad after the way I treated you the last time I saw you in Marinwood, but I hope you can forgive me eventually because I still love you. There, I said it. Now, if you want me to go away, I will."

Tom wasn't sure that he'd followed everything she said because his brain still felt too fuzzy and tired to work it all out, but he was pleased that she had joined him. He still had an anchor in the world, after all. "I'm not mad at you," he said, putting his arm around her shoulders. She rested her head on his shoulder. "I'm glad you're here, and I love you, too."

They didn't feel the need to say anything else. Tempest closed her eyes, and Tom stared out over the water, allowing her warmth to seep into him. He felt good. As they sat there together, Helix walked over, sniffed at Tempest, then curled up in Tom's lap and immediately went to sleep. The only other thing Tom needed was some food to take care of the grumbling beast in his empty stomach, but that could wait a while. Maybe he could find some roasted cornfruit to eat back in town. He liked roasted cornfruit.

As the drowsiness overtook him, Tom started to nod off. At that moment, he caught a glimpse of the Road, and the stars that twinkled in the impossible depths beyond its black glass surface. Then an image of the Jewel of Dreaming formed in his mind, suspended above the Road, and he felt a twitch inside his head as he saw tiny shadows of possibilities and events moving within the facets of the sparkling diamond. Still hungry, he focused on one of the shadows that looked suspiciously like food.

A pile of roasted cornfruit appeared on the polished black marble near his feet.

Helix looked up for a moment, sniffed at the food, then went back to sleep. Tempest snored softly. Tom hesitated, then picked up an ear of roasted cornfruit and bit into it to make sure it was real. The taste exploded in his mouth, filling his taste buds with sweet delight. He swallowed, then shuddered and placed the cornfruit back on the pile, unwilling to deal with the implications of this miracle.

The pile disappeared.

Tom sighed with relief.

**Imagine a future where the dead rule
over the living...**

THE DIGITAL DEAD
by BRUCE BALFOUR
0-441-01084-9

Cross the digital divide between life and death into a
future age where virtual versions of the dead control
the desires of those they've left behind—with
terrifying results.

Praise for the novels of Bruce Balfour:

**"His vivid vision [is] so real that you
can almost touch it." —SF Site**

"[A] wild ride...Buckle up." —Jack McDevitt

"Exciting...compelling." —William C. Dietz

Also available from Ace:
THE FORGE OF MARS

0-441-00954-9

**Available wherever books are sold or at
www.penguin.com**

Epic Intergallactic Adventure
from
Two-Time Hugo
Award-Winning Author

ALLEN STEELE